here for you

PAT SIMMONS

sourcebooks
casablanca

Copyright © 2020 by Pat Simmons
Cover and internal design © 2020 by Sourcebooks
Cover design by Elsie Lyons
Cover image © Jeremy Samuelson/Getty Images; Nickilay Khoroshkov/
Shutterstock; Vibrant Image Studio/Shutterstock; YK/Shutterstock

Sourcebooks and the colophon are registered trademarks of Sourcebooks.

All rights reserved. No part of this book may be reproduced in any form or by
any electronic or mechanical means including information storage and retrieval
systems—except in the case of brief quotations embodied in critical articles or
reviews—without permission in writing from its publisher, Sourcebooks.

The characters and events portrayed in this book are fictitious or are used fictitiously. Any
similarity to real persons, living or dead, is purely coincidental and not intended by the author.

All brand names and product names used in this book are trademarks, registered trademarks, or trade names of their respective holders. Sourcebooks
is not associated with any product or vendor in this book.

Published by Sourcebooks Casablanca, an imprint of Sourcebooks
P.O. Box 4410, Naperville, Illinois 60567-4410
(630) 961-3900
sourcebooks.com

Library of Congress Cataloging-in-Publication Data
Names: Simmons, Pat, author.
Title: Here for you / Pat Simmons.
Identifiers: LCCN 2020006230 (trade paperback)
Subjects: LCSH: Domestic fiction. | GSAFD: Love stories.
Classification: LCC PS3619.I56125 H47 2020 | DDC 813/.6--dc23
LC record available at https://lccn.loc.gov/2020006230

Printed and bound in the United States of America.
VP 10 9 8 7 6 5 4 3 2 1

In loving memory of
Tanishia Pearson-Jones
"She walked by faith and not by sight."

Chapter 1

DYING? RACHEL KNICELY REFUSED TO ACCEPT THAT. ONLY THREE weeks ago, her great-aunt Priscilla "Aunt Tweet" Brownlee was the life of the party at the wedding reception. Her eyes had sparkled, her dance moves impressive for an eighty-five-year-old, and her childish giggles made the evening more festive, sometimes stealing the spotlight from the bride and groom. How could she be dying? *Nope, I won't accept that. I need her in my life.*

Closing her eyes, Rachel rubbed her face and tried to make sense of her aunt's rapid decline. The youngest of three daughters, Rachel had made an agreement with her two sisters to share Aunt Tweet's caregiving responsibilities six months at a time, first with the oldest, Kym, in Baltimore, next with Tabitha in St. Louis. Now it was Rachel's "tour of duty" to care for their beloved role model.

Life was suddenly becoming too short. *I'm not ready to lose my auntie yet.* Rachel yawned and stretched on the chaise longue. She had put the piece of furniture by the bed in the makeshift guest bedroom in the loft of her Nashville condo. She forced one eye open briefly to check on her aunt.

Rachel was drained and wasn't sure how she could be so tired. It was only 2:00 a.m., on a Saturday morning in a city known for its nightlife. Before Aunt Tweet's stay, Rachel would have been out on the town with her best friend, Jacqui Rice, at one of the many "must-attend" events around Music City after a long work week.

She had tweaked her social calendar until June 1, when Kym would begin her second rotation as Aunt Tweet's caregiver and would relocate their aunt to Baltimore again.

Over the past months, Rachel had learned being a caregiver wasn't a nine-to-five shift. She did what it took to make her aunt comfortable, and her late nights were now spent watching over her loved one, even more so since the dementia symptoms caused by Alzheimer's had her aunt acting out of character.

Rachel had had no concept of the term *sundown* until Aunt Tweet began to wake in the middle of the night and wander through her condo, trying to get out. Her loving aunt had been downright mean and combative toward Rachel for more than a month. Aunt Tweet's behavior had crushed Rachel to the core.

A trip to St. Louis last month for Tabitha and Marcus's wedding had seemed to give her aunt a second wind, then after a few days back in Nashville, her aunt had slipped into another personality again.

Aunt Tweet stopped eating for two days. *Two days!* Rachel had freaked out and called her sisters, who in turn had a conference call with the doctor—the third one since Aunt Tweet was initially diagnosed more than a year ago. After moving Aunt Tweet from her home in Philly, she had a specialist in Baltimore with Kym, one in St. Louis with Tabitha, and now Dr. Allison Watkins here in Nashville.

"The kind of symptoms you're describing become severe as the patient transitions into the last stages of Alzheimer's," Dr. Watkins had said, too casually in Rachel's opinion, as her heart shattered. Was it fair that her designated time with Aunt Tweet was marred with worry that, at any time, her aunt would slip away?

"Aunt Tweet's doctor in Philly said a patient with dementia can live up to twenty years," Rachel pointed out.

"Yes," the doctor confirmed, "with no other contributing factors, but the average life span is usually four to eight years after diagnosis. Changes in the brain begin before any signs manifest."

"That's the preclinical period of Alzheimer's," Tabitha, the second oldest and a pharmaceutical rep, whispered.

"Yes, also called the mild stage, which allows her to remain active socially. Stages can overlap, so I suspect Miss Brownlee might have moderate to advanced Alzheimer's. It is usually the longest stage and can last for many years."

"Living longer is good news, but not with her condition worsening. My aunt is the sweetest person on earth." All Rachel wanted was more bonding time with Aunt Tweet so she could tell her over and over again how much she loved her, admired her, and would live up to the expectations Aunt Tweet had for her three nieces.

"Based on these new symptoms, let me see her in my office to determine if she has progressed to the next stage."

"Which is?" Kym, the oldest, asked, but Rachel wasn't sure she wanted to know.

"The late stage," Dr. Watkins said matter-of-factly. "Unfortunately, the last stage of Alzheimer's is the most severe. Without warning, she can lose the ability to respond to her surroundings, control movements, or she may stop walking, sitting, and eventually swallowing."

When the call ended, Rachel had been numb. The conversation had both depressed her and upset her stomach. Dr. Watkins's speculation was one thing, but taking Aunt Tweet into the office to confirm the inevitable was disheartening. Had her aunt stopped eating because she couldn't swallow?

The next day, Aunt Tweet woke with a voracious appetite. Relieved, Rachel cried like a baby with a wet diaper. This was proof that Aunt Tweet had not progressed to another stage. She had bounced back. "Thank you, God," she whispered and considered canceling the doctor appointment.

Kym was the first one to veto the idea. "Go, Rach, or I'll fly down there and take her myself," she threatened.

"All right!" Rachel reluctantly agreed.

On second thought, Rachel wondered if all three of them going to the doctor with Aunt Tweet wasn't such a bad idea. Depending on what the doctor had to say, they may need to hold each other's hands.

Unfortunately, one week later, Rachel was on her own as she escorted Aunt Tweet to the appointment. She didn't care what it looked like to others in the waiting room, Rachel held her aunt's hand as if she were a little lost girl, not a twenty-nine-year-old engineer who was at the top of her game.

After the preliminaries, Dr. Watkins gave Rachel the heartbreaking news. "From my assessment and everything you shared on the phone, your aunt has indeed transitioned to the last stage." She was quick to add, "Don't give up hope yet. It's not over. This stage can last from several weeks to several years. It's not the quantity of time but the memories you have with her that will give you comfort."

Rachel nodded but didn't feel any comfort in her words. It was the memories of Aunt Tweet's laugh, unfiltered conversations about life, and her attention to a meticulous appearance that was fading too fast, being replaced by a shell of a woman whose independence had been stolen.

"It's important that you keep a sharp eye on her for signs of pain, since her level of communication may become more limited."

Oftentimes, that meant Rachel sitting at her bedside throughout the night, reminiscing about happy times as a child, unsure if Aunt Tweet remembered or understood, but it was therapy for Rachel.

The influence Aunt Tweet had on the Knicely sisters—especially Rachel's life—was astonishing. Their aunt was all about confidence and character building, plus detailed attention to a woman's personal appearance.

As the oldest sibling, Kym inherited Aunt Tweet's wisdom. Tabitha's features were almost identical to a younger Aunt Tweet, as if their parents, Thomas and Rita Knicely, had no say in their daughter's DNA. As the baby girl, Rachel had a special bond with her great-aunt.

Aunt Tweet seemed to infuse Rachel with more of her personality: a flair for fashion, which included showstopping hair, nails, and makeup at all times and a thirst to achieve a high level of intellect with education being the primary goal. Then there were the many life lessons, including on how to act like a lady, and the most important was philanthropy. There was nothing wrong with enjoying the finer things in life, but one had to remember others less fortunate and help them climb to success.

Rachel sighed. There were so many life lessons learned courtesy of Aunt Tweet. The only topic her aunt didn't bring up much was living happily ever after with the love of your life.

Wednesday morning, Nicholas Adams was on his way home from his overnight shift when he received a call from his church. He was a project manager at the Nissan plant in Smyrna, about half an hour from downtown Nashville. However, he was never off duty as a minister for God. His pastor assigned him and several other ministers to visit church members who were sick, homebound, or hospitalized.

"Hello, Minister Adams," Mrs. Eloise Emerson greeted him when he answered. "I know it's early, but we received a call over the weekend from a Tabitha Whittington with an urgent prayer request. She's a member at one of our sister churches in St. Louis."

"It's okay, Mrs. Emerson," he reassured the elderly church secretary.

"Good, I'll send you the information," she said in a quiet voice. "Miss Whittington would like someone to visit her great-aunt, Miss Priscilla Brownlee, who is staying here in Nashville. I'm sure she'd appreciate your visit—the sooner the better, the note says."

Nicholas nodded to himself. If someone needed healing or comfort, it was his job to pray with them. As soon as he said, "I'm on it," Nicholas glanced in his rearview mirror and groaned. He had planned to get to the barber before heading home. His hair demanded a cut that was a week delayed.

His phone chimed as he took off. At a stoplight, he stifled a yawn as he glanced at the address Mrs. Emerson had texted him for Miss Brownlee. It was in Midtown, not far from Vanderbilt University, but a good half-hour drive during morning rush hour. It was also a bit early for a house call. Going home wasn't an option either. If he closed his eyes, Nicholas would be down for the count for a good seven hours. Not good in this case.

He rubbed his hair again and made a decision: a pit stop at Hats Off Barbershop in Antioch, which was in the direction of downtown. Hopefully, he could get in and out.

When he arrived at the place, he counted seven heads before him, or maybe his eyes had crossed. Nicholas resolved that he would have to wait longer than he had hoped. Making himself comfortable in an empty folding chair, he mumbled a prayer for Priscilla Brownlee before he dozed off. A few times, someone nudged him to pull him into a conversation about sports or to give his opinion about a world event from a "preacher's viewpoint," because his barber always addressed him as preacher.

Two hours later, he walked out a tired man with a fade cut to his wavy hair, a trimmed mustache, and a five o'clock shadow outlining his jaw. At least he had gone into the restroom to rinse his face with cold water and pop a breath mint. He slipped on his shades after squinting at the sunlight that seemed to have brightened while he'd been inside. Now he felt presentable enough to perform his task.

Once in his car, he confirmed the address again. It was after ten, so surely someone would be awake by now. He tapped the address to activate the navigation app and headed westbound on I-24.

The West End Avenue area was a trendy part of Nashville that attracted grad students and young professionals drawn to the surrounding downtown nightlife, Lower Broadway, or East Nashville.

Rumor had it that Midtown was so pricey the rent there was comparable to the mortgage of a custom-built house. Personally, Nicholas enjoyed being a homeowner in a quiet Smyrna neighborhood with a spacious ranch house that was close to his job. To him, that was preferable to living in the midst of a constant bustle of people.

Since the traffic flowed, he arrived in less than half an hour and parked around the corner. He grabbed his Bible from the back seat and headed to the building's grand entrance with a maroon awning and street-level retail shops lining the front windows. He strolled inside. Whoever lived in this place had money with a capital *M*.

The interior resembled a hotel lobby with marble floors and expensive decor. Voices above him made him take notice of a mezzanine. *Wow* was the only way to describe the Westchester. A middle-aged gentleman stood from behind a sleek desk in an office with see-through walls and strolled around to greet him.

He asked for Nicholas's ID, which he looked at carefully. "Who are you here to see?"

"Miss Priscilla Brownlee who is staying with her niece Rachel Knicely in 1402."

"Of course." He returned Nicholas's license and pushed a button to open the elevator doors.

Nicholas nodded his thanks and walked inside, where spotless mirrors, brass trim, and accent lighting surrounded him as the doors closed. He had never visited a residence with this type of security, but it was close to a busy area, so maybe that justified it.

On the ride up to the fourteenth floor, soft music entertained Nicholas until the bell chimed and the doors opened. The decor screamed elegance from the floor to the overhead mini chandeliers that lit the path. Should he remove his shoes to walk on the plush carpet? He didn't and continued to 1402, where an artistically carved wood front door rivaled the one at his house.

After he pushed the doorbell, Nicholas dusted any stray hairs from his shoulders. When he made first-time house calls, he liked to portray an image of a respectable, serious, and clean-cut man.

Respect, at times, was based on perception—what people thought a minister should look like and how elegantly he spoke. Nicholas didn't think that should matter. His attire wasn't dress slacks and a collared shirt. Instead, it was his Nissan polo work shirt and jeans.

He was about to ring the bell again when a woman answered. They blinked at each other. It was a toss-up whether Nicholas had wakened her or she didn't care about her appearance. Either way, her beauty wasn't dimmed, even with messy hair, wrinkled clothes, and one missing big hoop earring. Nicholas had seen worse. He offered a smile.

She looked at him as if she was in a daze. "Yes?"

"I'm Minister Nicholas Adams, from Believers Temple Church. I'm here to see Miss Brownlee."

The woman's eyes widened with fear, and she slammed the door in his face.

What? I don't have time for this. Nicholas was sleep deprived and hungry. Maybe his eyes were bloodshot and she thought he was drunk or high on drugs or something. Unfortunately, there were instances when he was met with hostility from families who weren't Christians and resented his presence.

Nicholas tried not to take their rudeness personally. This was his godly calling, and he was going in to see Miss Brownlee. He gritted his teeth and was about to knock again when the woman slowly opened the door with a sheepish expression. "Sorry. I wasn't expecting you."

Clearly. He kept that to himself, then relaxed. He smiled again to ease the tension, and she returned his smile, although hesitantly. "Your sister in St. Louis called our church office."

"Tabitha," she mumbled, then squeezed her lips together.

That somewhat explained her reaction. "Since I'm here, do you mind if I visit with Miss Brownlee?"

"She was alert a few days ago, but she's shut down again. I'm not sure if she'll know you're here." Rachel grunted. "I'm not even sure if she knows I'm here." The look of hurt didn't go unnoticed.

"I'm sure she feels your presence," he said, trying to console her. "You're Miss Knicely?"

"Yes, I'm Rachel Knicely," she confirmed.

"Nice to meet you. Again, I'm Nicholas Adams."

Before his eyes, Rachel's sluggish demeanor disappeared, replaced with alertness as she leaned on the doorjamb, crossing her arms. "First, may I see your ID?" As he reached into his back pocket for his wallet, she added, "I have a photographic memory."

Nicholas contained his amusement at her personality swing from fear to fierceness.

A Yorkie and a cocker spaniel appeared at her side, barking and wagging their tails, undecided if Nicholas was a friend or foe. He kept a straight face, trying not to show his amusement at their veiled threat as guard dogs.

Back to Rachel. He wasn't offended by her request. Despite the tight security to get to her door, a woman could never be too careful, whether a man was carrying a Bible or not. He only had a younger brother, Karl, but if he'd had any sisters, he would have taught them the same precautions.

He handed over his license. She glanced at it, squinted at him again, then handed it back, reciting his license number, height, weight, and eye color to prove she wasn't kidding. Did she say his weight? Seriously, hey, he had lost ten pounds since that was taken. He was lean and all muscle. She didn't need to know that, but he decided to tell her anyway. The woman had some serious skills. "Just so you know, I was ten pounds heavier then," he said in defense.

"And you had a bad haircut," she sassed back and stepped aside for him to enter. He couldn't tell if she was joking about his hair then or now. He refrained from asking and sized her up as well—about five feet four or five inches to his six feet two, messy dark brown hair—wig or weave—tired brown eyes, curly lashes, and a face that probably could use a morning wash. All in all, she was cute—very.

He stepped in and noticed the richness of her hardwood floors; they looked as if no one had ever walked across them, much less pets. He admired her living space, which was an open design with the dining room/eating area and kitchen on one side.

Nicholas followed her along a hallway that turned a corner as the dogs trailed behind them. They stepped down into a spacious living room with a nice decor and floor-to-ceiling windows. The sunlight was streaming through.

They climbed a few steps to a loft overlooking the living room, offering little privacy, except for a trifold room divider. Massive bedroom furniture held court. The dogs had beaten them and scrambled to a spot at the foot of the bed. "Nice place," Nicholas said, and he meant it.

"Thank you," she said without looking at him. Her attention was on the woman in the bed. "Aunt Tweet," she called softly. "Nicholas Adams is here to see you. He's a minister."

Her loved one didn't respond. The slight rise and fall of the cover was proof she was still alive. *Whew.* Nicholas had never witnessed someone taking their last few breaths. He didn't want to see it today.

Chapter 2

How embarrassing. Rachel couldn't believe she had slammed the door in a man's face—and a minister at that. The doorbell had rescued her from the vortex of a nightmare about a Death Angel trying to get inside her house.

She could thank her best friend, Jacqui, for putting that image in her subconscious. She had mentioned her family called a priest to administer the last rites to her grandfather, then minutes later, Mr. Rice died. Her mother said it was as if the priest had summoned the angel of death.

Still shaken from the dream, Rachel remained leery about whether the minister was there to give Aunt Tweet her last rites, despite not being a priest. She watched Nicholas from the doorway as he perched on the chaise that she had slept on for many nights. Leaning closer, he rested his hand on Aunt Tweet's forehead and softly called her name. "Miss Brownlee, I'm here to pray for you."

God, please let his prayer make a difference. The moment was tranquil, and she noted his gentle manner. Something she wouldn't expect from a man who had a handsome face with a fierce expression and the physique of a bodybuilder. His tenderness was endearing.

Aunt Tweet moved slightly but didn't open her eyes. Excitement, hope, and anticipation swirled in Rachel at her response. Next, Nicholas opened his worn leather-bound Bible. The pages seemed to part without a bookmark, as if they knew the passage he wanted.

As he began to read from Psalm 23, the softness of his voice deepened to a rich baritone. The sound was like a sweet melody. Rachel closed her eyes, drifting into serenity as she listened.

"'He makes me to lie down in green pastures: he leads me beside the still waters,'" Nicholas continued. "'He restores my soul…though I walk through the valley of the shadow of death, I will fear no evil…'"

Death. Wait a minute! Rachel's eyes opened in horror. Her aunt was very much alive, and she was hoping his prayer would keep it that way. Was the minister summoning death for Aunt Tweet? This was too much talk about death—the doctor, her sister, her friend, and now this minister.

The thought ignited a sob from somewhere deep within her, and Rachel couldn't stop the floodgate. She felt weak in the knees.

"Are you all right?" Nicholas looked at her and asked in a concerned tone.

She shook her head, unable to answer. He coaxed her to sit on the ottoman. She felt the seat shift as he sat next to her. When she inhaled, the faint scent of his cologne acted as smelling salts and revitalized her. It was a familiar brand that some of her colleagues and male acquaintances wore. The distraction was only temporary.

"Can I get you some water?"

"Yes," she choked out, as if he knew the layout of her kitchen. *Let him find his way.* She opened her eyes in a daze and glanced at Aunt Tweet. She was still alive, and Rachel exhaled in relief.

He returned quickly with ice water in a crystal glass. Her best dishes were reserved for entertaining, but she didn't care as she accepted the glass with trembling hands. Nicholas's hands steadied hers so she could drink. Rachel gulped down the water as if she'd been parched for days. "Thank you."

Nicholas took the seat next to her again. "Are you okay?"

"I don't know." She turned and stared into his eyes and noticed their unusual shade of brown. They weren't light or dark but almost sun-kissed, as if sunlight was drawn to them. "I lost it when I heard you say 'death.'"

Nicholas nodded his head, but she doubted he understood what a blow Aunt Tweet's passing would be, losing the last connection to her father's side of the family. "Death is part of life," he told her, then stood. "If you're all right, do you mind if I pray for both of you before I leave?"

"Sure."

Returning to the bedside, he smiled at Rachel, then at Aunt Tweet, who appeared to be resting quietly. Reaching inside his jacket, Nicholas pulled out a tiny bottle no bigger than a sample size of perfume or scented oil. Unscrewing the top, he placed a dab of oil on Aunt Tweet's forehead, then looked at Rachel inquiringly. "It's anointed oil."

She declined to take part in the anointing but joined him at the bedside. Closing her eyes, Rachel bowed her head and waited for the prayer.

"Lord Jesus, let this household feel Your presence and be at peace. All power is in Your hands, and nothing can be done without Your permission…" His short prayer was as soft as his reading voice, which had lulled even her cocker spaniel, Shelby, and Aunt Tweet's Yorkie, Sweet Pepper, to sleep, and finished with, "Amen."

"Amen," Rachel repeated, then exhaled.

Nicholas faced her. "If you'd like another ministerial visit, don't hesitate to call the church office."

You mean if my aunt is still alive, Rachel thought fearfully. Since that dream, she was having a hard time shaking this death thing.

"If you promise not to slam the door in my face," he added with mirth dancing in those brown eyes, breaking through her reverie. When he smiled, his dimples peeked out from his beard.

So he had a sense of humor. She returned his smile. "You spooked me." Rachel had only seen a woman slam the door in a man's face in the movies. That had been a first for her. She looked away in embarrassment before she tilted her head in a challenge. "You're not going to let me forget that, are you?"

"Consider it forgotten." He gathered his Bible and waited for her to show him to the door. He offered a slight wave, then walked down the hall to the elevator.

After closing the door, Rachel leaned against it and sighed. Of course, death was a part of life, but she didn't want it to happen on her watch. She needed more time with Aunt Tweet—just like her sisters had created recent memories with their great-aunt, Rachel had that right. She might not get her full six months with Aunt Tweet, but if God could give her a couple more weeks…

She sighed. "I'll be so thankful."

Yawning, she pushed off the door and headed back to Aunt Tweet's room. Passing by the hall mirror, she backtracked, then screamed at the haunting image staring back at her. Her curls were a matted mess, her face needed attention, and her lounge clothes were wrinkled. She'd taken unkempt to the next level.

If Aunt Tweet were alert, she would take Rachel to task about her appearance. "A woman should always get a man's attention, whether she wants to or not. Honey, take it as long as your beauty lasts" was Aunt Tweet's mantra.

Before Nicholas had arrived, Rachel had pushed all thoughts of men and the dating world aside to focus on caring for her auntie. How Nicholas Adams had broken through her resistance was a mystery.

Maybe it was because he was a man a woman could not easily dismiss, including Rachel. She had appreciated the eye candy for about thirty seconds—no, make that twenty-nine—but he was a minister. She doubted Nicholas had given her a second glance.

Back in the bedroom, Rachel checked on Aunt Tweet, who hadn't stirred. Neither had the two dogs. She had adopted her cocker spaniel from a shelter less than a week after she'd moved into her condo, and her pet had taken to Aunt Tweet the moment she'd arrived but not to Aunt Tweet's dog, Sweet Pepper. Then, oddly, a few weeks ago, the two made some sort of dog truce to live in harmony at her side.

Rachel bent and brushed a kiss against her aunt's cheek. For an eighty-five-year-old, Aunt Tweet retained her natural beauty. Flawless dark skin complemented her silver-and-white hair. She was a classy lady with a larger-than-life personality and the right of amount of sass to make a stranger crave to be counted among her circle of friends.

"I hope God answers this prayer. Love you, Aunt Tweet," Rachel whispered and descended the loft. She would shower, then prepare a light breakfast in case Aunt Tweet opened her eyes and was famished again.

Three times a week, Rachel employed a home health aide to assist with Aunt Tweet's care, so Rachel could go to the firm in the afternoons. The other two days, she worked from home to be close by.

Rachel had come to depend on Clara Rodgers on Mondays, Wednesdays, and Fridays, not only to do light housekeeping and patient assist but also to guide Rachel as a caregiver—even if that meant Clara had to endure Rachel venting her frustrations. Besides Clara, there was her best friend, Jacqui, who always had a listening ear, and her sisters were only a phone call or flight away.

Initially, it wasn't the Knicely sisters' plan to have outside help. They thought the three of them could handle Aunt Tweet's care on their own. Kym had sailed through her six months, but Tabitha's six months had been an eye-opener. No medical textbook could have prepared her for the practicum. Rachel expected a less mobile aunt but instead got living a nightmare with whispers of death. None of them were prepared for the dementia symptoms that plagued Aunt Tweet.

When Rachel's sister Tabitha had cried out for help, her friend and neighbor, Marcus Whittington, had answered. The two of them felt a home health aide would relieve some stress. At first, Rachel and Kym had been incensed about Tabitha leaving Aunt Tweet in the care of a stranger, but the woman turned out to be attentive and trustworthy, so Rachel hadn't thought twice about getting help when she'd brought Aunt Tweet to Nashville.

Since Rachel hadn't set her alarm, the minister's visit had been a life-saver. She pinched the bridge of her nose. That sounded too much like a pun, but she needed to prepare updates on a project that was almost complete. She couldn't ask for a better boss and company, both allowing her work flexibility during her brief tenure as caregiver.

It was after two when Rachel breezed through the doors of Gersham-Smith, one of the oldest and most successful engineering firms in Nashville. Rachel was respected among her peers and management.

She could probably credit Aunt Tweet for inspiring her to study math and science in high school and college before the STEM curriculum—science, technology, engineering, and mathematics—became popular. The subjects were so easy, and as a teenager, she had often been one of the few black girls in a class.

Aunt Tweet was Rachel's "shero", instilling her with confidence so she wouldn't be intimidated by men in the workplace. She preferred to impress with her brains, wit, and beauty—in that order—so she didn't believe in leaving the house without being polished from head to toe, not even to walk the dogs. She wanted her appearance to be as exquisite as her intellect. She was fashion-forward and could manage complex projects as though they were building blocks or simple puzzles.

Her boss, Harlan Goode, appeared as she stepped out of the elevator. "Afternoon, Rachel. How's your aunt?"

He was an older man with thinning hair on the crown of his head and a thick mustache. His father had started Gresham-Smith, and Harlan had expanded the firm to include offices in fourteen states and two overseas. The firm had drawn big-name clients to its roster with cutting-edge designs, including winning the bid to design a deep pump station project for the Metropolitan St. Louis Sewer District.

As a St. Louis native, Rachel took personal pride in handcrafting the design for the sump, dry wells, and other components for a structure that would be 180 feet belowground. It had been an honor to give back to her childhood city in the form of jobs and better living conditions.

The company stressed work-life balance, which Rachel had never fully appreciated until she became Aunt Tweet's caregiver. The past four months had been a roller-coaster ride, and it didn't look like the next few months would be any better, considering Aunt Tweet's deteriorating condition.

"About the same." She mustered a smile. Rachel believed in keeping a professional demeanor with her colleagues and tucked away the meltdowns until she was at home, behind closed doors. "My sister had a local minister come to pray with her."

"Good. They say prayer changes things," he said, then continued to his office for the afternoon briefing.

She believed prayer changed things—if only she could see a change with her aunt. Although Rachel was hopeful, she was realistic. The body required food and water to thrive, and Aunt Tweet needed to be alert in order to receive both.

Once in her office, Rachel had to force her mind to focus as she switched to job mode. Her team had been assigned to find solutions to ease Music City's congestion and reduce travel time for the ever-growing population and tourists. Millennials wanted no part of long commutes. They were attracted to communities where residents could work, live, and play, like she had been. One politician suggested adding more highway infrastructure. That would be a quick fix but wouldn't solve long-term problems.

Although Rachel was licensed as a civil engineer, her area of specialty was structural. While the client wanted to preserve some historical aspects in the area, Rachel wasn't convinced their request to build a tunnel for a walkway was sound. She and her team had a brainstorming session to determine whether the addition was possible and within budget.

After the meeting, Rachel delved into her RISA-3D program to ana-lyze the structures. It was impossible to cram eight-plus hours of work into a five-hour shift, but she had to get home to Aunt Tweet so Clara could go to hers. The aide was a nursing student and single mother of an eight-year-old girl.

With only a short commute, Rachel slipped behind the steering wheel in her car, and a craving hit. Although she practiced healthy eating, a serving of Monell's skillet fried chicken was her guilty pleasure. It wasn't far, but it would close in twenty minutes.

She called Clara. "I know you're off within an hour, but my senses got a tracker on some of Monell's skillet fried—"

"Chicken." Clara smacked her lips and laughed. "Bring me some and all is forgiven."

"Got it, and I'll get some extra in case Aunt Tweet ever gets an appe-tite again. Any change?"

"Sorry, no, there hasn't been, but her vitals are stable."

Rachel's reality was her aunt's failing health. Suddenly, her appetite dulled, but she'd practically promised Clara, so she turned north on Second Avenue for the short drive to Bransford Avenue.

She arrived ten minutes before they closed. While she waited for her order, Rachel's mind drifted to her loved one. "You've got to bounce back, Aunt Tweet," she mumbled. "You've got to."

With her order in hand, Rachel returned to her condo and gave Clara her sack of food plus a twenty-dollar tip, then she ate alone. She didn't make a habit of arriving late, mindful that Clara had a life too, and on the occasions when Rachel did, she always gave Clara something extra as a reminder that the woman's services were appreciated. Aunt Tweet wouldn't have wanted it any other way.

Her aunt had set up a monthly stipend of $5,000 for her care. She had stipulated that if the time came when she had to reside at a nursing facility, it had to be top tier.

Rachel had hoped the chicken's aroma would tease Aunt Tweet's senses, but the only thing that stirred in her aunt's bedroom was Shelby and Sweet Pepper, yet they didn't leave Aunt Tweet's side.

Rachel checked on Aunt Tweet again, then changed into her pajamas. Next, she grabbed her laptop and headed for her balcony. The nighttime view of the downtown skyline was worth the price she paid to live there. The antennas on top of the AT&T building resembled Batman, so she always pretended she lived in Gotham City and Batman was keeping her safe.

She loved Nashville, but not because it was the state capital. It boasted a large African American population. The city had a rich black history of struggle, determination, and empowerment that was seamless: before and after the Civil War and during the civil rights movement.

Her mind wandered as she booted up her laptop. There were so many unsung heroes during slavery besides Harriet Tubman. The Harding family was one of the largest enslavers in Tennessee, and they invested heavily in thoroughbred horses. Who would have guessed one of the most famous horse jockeys in the 1800s was an African American man named Isaac Murphy who was enslaved at the Belle Meade Plantation?

Fast-forward to post-Emancipation Proclamation and education was a priority for freedmen and women. Nashville fed the hunger of eager pupils with four historically black colleges and universities among the city's thirty-two.

Add other contributions to music and a thriving social scene, and it was a no-brainer why Rachel made the Athens of the South her home after her college graduation. There was never a weekend without an event to attend, and she and Jacqui hit the circuit.

Just like her hometown of St. Louis was more than the Gateway Arch, Nashville was more than the Grand Ole Opry, even though it was also nicknamed Music City and NashVegas.

Rachel caught herself from further drifting and took a deep breath. Reclining on her balcony was akin to a spa visit. Day or night, it was the perfect place to relax her mind and ease stress from her body. However, she hadn't been productive, so she stood, waved good night to Batman, and walked back inside. She padded across her living room floor and up the stairs to the loft-converted bedroom.

She settled in the chaise next to Aunt Tweet's bed with her laptop and prepared for a long evening of working and watching Aunt Tweet.

Rachel didn't realize she had dozed off until Aunt Tweet's mumbling woke her. Startled, she caught her laptop before it tumbled to the floor. Her aunt's aging brown eyes were watching her.

"Aunt Tweet!" She pushed everything aside and shooed the dogs out of the way and climbed into the bed. Rachel hugged Aunt Tweet as tight as she could without crushing her. "You've got to stop scaring me. Hungry? I got you some Monell's. But you're probably thirsty." She scrambled off the bed more than ready to do her aunt's bidding, then realized she hadn't yet thanked God for answering her prayers.

Shaking her head, Aunt Tweet pointed to the flat screen where Rachel had played countless movies for them to watch together, but her aunt had a fascination with one video. It was a keepsake of her niece's nuptials. The wedding video had captured raw emotion on Tabitha's and Marcus's faces that would make a skeptic believe in love.

Rachel had a bargaining chip. She rested her hands on her hips and shook her head. "Only if you drink and eat something—please." After a few rounds of stubbornness on both sides, Aunt Tweet consented in a weak voice to bottled water and toast.

She propped Aunt Tweet up so she was sitting in the bed and fed her. When her aunt became combative about the wedding tape, Rachel conceded. She had force-fed Aunt Tweet enough—half the bottled water and one of two pieces of toast.

If Aunt Tweet stayed awake, Rachel would give her a small snack in a little while. Rachel made herself comfortable, then started the video. Holding Aunt Tweet's hand, they watched in silence as if they had never before seen Marcus dabbing at one of Tabitha's tears in an emotional moment, or Marcus's brother, Demetrius, handing Marcus a hankie to wipe the sweat off his forehead, or Aunt Tweet yelling, "That's a whopper," in response to the bride and groom's passionate first kiss.

Somehow, the reruns of Tabitha's wedding sparked a happy place within Aunt Tweet that she had never shared with her nieces. They did know Aunt Tweet was briefly married, then divorced before the Knicely girls were born. Her aunt seemed content without a significant other in her life, but her love for watching the one-hour-and-twelve-minute video seemed to challenge that.

A mystery man's name always surfaced on her aunt's lips, Randolph, and sadness would wash over her face. The longing was unmistakable, and Rachel wondered if her aunt had missed out in love despite men's attraction to Aunt Tweet like flowers to the sun.

Not only did Rachel inherit Aunt Tweet's sass, fashion sense, and other mannerisms, she knew she had the physical assets to capture a man's eye too. To date, none had captured her heart, at least not the way her brother-in-law had her sister Tabitha's.

Despite the revolving door of men she allowed into her life, briefly including Demetrius, Marcus's older brother, Rachel never trusted a man to want her beyond her looks, so she had resolved herself not to expect it.

"Listen to me." Her aunt called her by name and pulled Rachel out of her reverie.

Some days, Aunt Tweet seemed unsure of Rachel's identity, but when she heard her name, her heart warmed. She gave Aunt Tweet her full attention.

"Make sure you don't let love pass you by, you hear?" She waggled her finger as if Rachel were a little girl again.

"Yes, ma'am." Rachel grinned. The nourishment, although very little, had given her aunt renewed energy.

"A good man isn't always the best looking. He's got to have a good heart too."

"Okay." Rachel agreed, but waking up to an ugly man every morning would be a test in any marriage.

Aunt Tweet seemed to become more sentimental after each viewing of the wedding video.

"Make sure he holds your hand...prays for you...feeds you...loves you." Her voice drifted off. Oh no, her aunt needed to eat some more, but right before her eyes, Aunt Tweet dozed off, and within seconds, Rachel heard a light snore. Not good at all.

The next morning, Rachel woke and stretched. From her place on the chaise, she glanced at Aunt Tweet, who seemed to be in the same position as yesterday. Had Rachel dreamed their conversation, or had it really taken place? She spied the remote on the bed and knew it hadn't been a dream.

Was there a subliminal message in that wedding tape? If her aunt was hinting that Rachel would be next, then Aunt Tweet would be disappointed. Rachel had no prospects, time, or desire to be anybody's wife. She was only twenty-nine. Maybe at thirty-five, she would look at her options. Until then, it was business as usual.

Chapter 3

FEAR. NICHOLAS HAD SENSED IT YESTERDAY FROM RACHEL. HE hoped that praying together on her aunt's behalf provided the niece comfort.

As he drove home Thursday morning from his overnight shift, Nicholas wondered if Rachel would request another prayer visit, which would be more for her own peace. Priscilla Brownlee was in God's hands whether Nicholas returned or not. He had never witnessed life leaving a person before, but from the looks of the woman in the bed, he doubted she could stay in that state much longer.

Why was that home visit still on Nicholas's mind twenty-four hours later? Maybe he had never seen a disheveled woman look so beautiful.

Attraction was far from Rachel's mind and for good reason. Her aunt was dying, and ironically, as a man who ministered to countless families, Nicholas had no personal experience with that within his own close-knit family. He was grateful the Adams family had been free of tragedy. *Thank you, Jesus.*

There was more to Miss Knicely than what he saw on the surface, because he couldn't stop thinking about the aunt and her niece during the short drive home from the Nissan Smyrna plant to his brick ranch house on Nautical Street. He pulled into the two-car garage where his other car, a Nissan Infiniti QX60, was parked.

The upside of living four miles away from his job was it was a great community, a good investment, and a time-saver when he worked overnight. The downside was he lived a good half hour from the Believers Temple Church in Brentwood and twenty minutes from his parents and his brother's family in Antioch.

He yawned as he strolled through the garage door to the kitchen and disarmed his alarm. He glanced around his humble dwelling—not bad for a bachelor. It wasn't pristine like Rachel's condo, but it was comfortable, with a spacious master bedroom, another one reserved for when his twin nephews visited, and a third bedroom that was part home gym/ storage room/computer room/whatever he needed it to be at the time.

He had done enough thinking for one morning, so he grabbed a bottled juice, then headed for his bedroom to get some rest. He prayed, then slid under the covers, sighed, and closed his eyes, ready to succumb to blissful sleep.

Nicholas felt a nudge that stirred him from his sleep. He strained to open his eyes as his body protested the interruption. Did someone touch him? Nicholas scooted up and glanced around the room before blinking at the clock to bring the time into focus: 11:00 a.m. What? His body demanded five more hours.

Pray for Rachel. The thought came unbidden. Nicholas blinked and immediately became alert. *She's going to need comfort. Be there for her.*

His heart sank. Was Rachel's Aunt Tweet passing so soon? There was no question the two had been on his mind. He swallowed his sorrow for them and slid to his knees to pray. Almost an hour later, Nicholas climbed back into bed, but this time, sleep didn't come so easily.

Rachel couldn't wait to tell her sisters the latest on Aunt Tweet's condition during a Skype call. "All this talk about death got in my head. My friend Jacqui had mentioned about a family priest giving the last rites for a relative, then my dear sister"—she squinted at Tabitha—"summoned a minister to my doorstep without giving me forewarning, not to mention Aunt Tweet's doctor discussing the symptoms of the latter stage of Alzheimer's. It was too much." She shivered.

"I know, Sis, I know," Kym said. "Anything encouraging going on?"

"Well, yeah." Rachel nodded. "Aunt Tweet woke last night wanting to see the wedding video again."

Tabitha rocked her head from side to side, blushing. "It was romantic. Did she eat?"

Rachel's shoulders slumped. "Not much. I fed her some water and toast. I feel so cheated."

"Why?" Tabitha and Kym asked in unison.

"My quality time with her isn't what I had hoped for or expected when we agreed to the caregivers pact."

"None of us knew what to expect," Kym explained.

"Well, I'm not trying to be a drama queen…"

"But you usually are." Kym lifted a brow and laughed, and so did Tabitha.

"Okay, you got me." Rachel chuckled, then sobered. "You experienced the Aunt Tweet we knew and loved during your six months as a caregiver. Tabitha, you shared Aunt Tweet with Marcus to create memories…" She patted her chest. "Me? Aunt Tweet has been either combative or withdrawn. It hurts. I had imagined us bonding during long walks and her sharing life lessons like she used to. Last night, she mumbled something about prayer and hand-holding. I want to do more for her," she admitted in frustration, "and with her. What's my purpose in her life now?"

"Maybe it's just to hold her hand," Kym said and shrugged.

"You know, she said something like that to me," Tabitha said. "'You never know whose hand will give you that last piece of bread.'" She shivered. "Whenever she talked like that, it scared me."

Rachel crossed her arms against her chest. "I don't want it to be *my* hand that feeds her her last meal or my eyes that watch her take her last breath. We agreed to take care of Aunt Tweet, not watch her die." She started tugging on her hair until she tangled it in a curl. "Even the doctor said she could live a long time in this stage. I just need to get her healthy."

"Sis, prayer strengthened her. Maybe that's what she wants now. Why don't you ask Minister Adams to add her to a rotation for prayer?" Tabitha suggested. "You need it too. Prayer brings about peace."

Rachel was silent. The fact that Aunt Tweet asked for prayer troubled her spirit. She couldn't get the priest and the last rites thing out of her head. "I don't have his number."

"Let me give you the number to the church," Tabitha said, then repeated it slowly, waiting as Rachel tapped the number into her phone.

"Okay, I'll call," she agreed hesitantly. "At least this time, I'll be expecting him and won't look a hot mess."

"You?" Tabitha screamed and laughed. "Since when are you a hot mess? Even going to bed, you dress up in pajamas and head wraps as if you're about to do a photo shoot for lingerie."

"Not as a caregiver. Flannel pj's and socks have been my sleepwear. My nightly beauty regimen is on hold. Thank you very much."

"And what would Aunt Tweet say about a disheveled appearance in front of a gentleman? I'm just trying to lighten up the mood here." Kym joked, but Rachel didn't laugh. "A gentleman like Minister Adams. Was he old, young, a big guy?"

Rachel didn't want to think about a man, not at the moment, but her mind had other plans. Nicholas Adams was very attractive. It had been a while since she had seen a man look that handsome. He reminded her of actor Daniel Sunjata, but she wasn't going to tell her sisters that. "My mood is tentative. It will change to upbeat if I can get Aunt Tweet to eat more."

"Hey, Marcus is making too much noise in the kitchen. Got to go. Remember to call the church!" Tabitha said and ended the call.

"I'll talk to you later too. Love you, Sis. Give Auntie a kiss for me," Kym said and was gone too.

Rachel's emotions remained unsettled. Was she ready for a repeat of yesterday? Aunt Tweet mumbled, "Prayer," so Rachel had no choice but to do her aunt's bidding. She would make the call, but first she had to take another look at a client's requested change so she could email her team. Whether she was at home or at the firm, it was still a workday.

While Aunt Tweet rested, Rachel powered up her work laptop and switched to work mode. She bounced back from her 3-D program, trying to create a visual and input math formulas in the STAAD.Pro program for analysis. She had been so focused on the project that she had forgotten to eat lunch. Going into the kitchen, Rachel made a veggie sandwich, checked on Aunt Tweet, then called the number Tabitha gave her.

"Good afternoon, Believers Temple Church. This is Mrs. Eloise Emerson."

Rachel cleared her throat and explained the reason for her call. "Hi, this is Rachel Whittington. Is it possible for Minister Adams to come and pray with my aunt, Miss Priscilla Brownlee, again? I know it's too late for today, but hopefully tomorrow, Friday morning. The sooner, the better."

"I'll get this message to him," the woman said.

"Thank you." At least this time when he arrived, she would be awake and presentable.

That night, Rachel played Tabitha's wedding video, hoping it would coax Aunt Tweet to awaken. It didn't, so after a few minutes, Rachel turned it off and opened her laptop. She was determined to give the client what they wanted, but as a structural engineer, her focus was on ensuring the design and construction of any walkway tunnel was sound and not subject to collapse. She had to review documents before she scheduled an early morning conference call.

She was starting to feel the pressure of being on top of her game at work and an attentive caregiver. *If only I could be cloned*, she thought as she drifted off to sleep.

Seven a.m. came too soon when Rachel was operating on five hours of sleep. She stood and studied Aunt Tweet. She moaned a little as if she was about to wake, but her eyes never opened.

Rachel didn't know if she could describe her current feelings: flustered, discouraged, scared. Every night, she prayed, but to be honest, she didn't have confidence in her prayers. At least she looked forward to Nicholas's visit to pray. She liked the sound of his soothing voice. His prayer had changed things. Rachel had no timeframe for when he would come, so she hurried to her bedroom to shower, noting the time for the conference call was within forty minutes. If he came during her conference call, at least she would be presentable.

After the shower, she dressed in slacks and a sweater, then combed her long hair into one braid and twisted it on the top of her head. Her beauty enhancement was pink lip gloss.

"Sorry, Aunt Tweet, this is the best I can do," Rachel whispered to her reflection. In the kitchen, she prepared a bowl of fruit and oatmeal, gave thanks, and nibbled. If she had time between the conference call and Nicholas's visit, she would freshen up Aunt Tweet and her bed, even though it was Friday and Clara would come to do those tasks.

With a few minutes to spare, Rachel set her laptop on the dining room table with her handwritten notes on one side. She had several windows open on her computer. By 8:00 a.m., she was patched into the conference call with her boss, two team members, and the client.

"Good morning, Mr. Thomas," Rachel began. "We've had a chance to review the addition you requested for the common ground play area. Although the tunnel might enhance the overall appearance, the area is prone to flooding, and that would compromise the physical integrity of any walkway tunnel."

She listened as her colleagues offered suggestions as they emailed design options. An hour and thirty minutes later, the call ended with a plan to review building codes and sewer locations. The easy way out was to tell the client no, he had agreed on the plans, but her company didn't do business by telling clients no.

Rachel tugged strands of hair out of the braid—a childhood habit she still did when she was baffled about a problem or situation. Her doorbell rang. Nicholas. She had momentarily forgotten he was coming.

She opened the door with a cordial smile, then blinked. The person standing before her wasn't Minister Nicholas Adams. The woman was as thick as the huge Bible she carried and was dressed in white from her bonnet to her stockings and shoes. Did Tabitha call for a hospice nurse? Did the agency send a different home health aide besides Clara? Who was this stranger?

"May I help you?"

The woman lifted her chin. "You called the church for a prayer warrior, and I'm here. Mother Jenkins, sugar. May I come in?"

Rachel frowned and stepped back. "I...I was expecting Minister Adams."

"Mm-hmm," she mumbled, "they all do." Then, with a no-nonsense expression, she asked, "Now, where is Mother Brownlee?"

What does that mean? Rachel wondered as she closed the door and led the way to the loft. Where Nicholas's tone was soft and smooth, this Mother Jenkins's voice boomed as if she were about to sing a song loud enough to raise the dead. Rachel cringed at the pun, but in this case, if it would prevent her aunt from dying, Rachel welcomed it. "She's my aunt, not a moth—"

"Oh, praise God," Mother Jenkins said when she saw Aunt Tweet, then she glanced over her shoulder and held her hand out to Rachel. "Aren't you going to join us for prayer?" The side-eye she gave Rachel conveyed that there would be no opting out.

She came to the bedside, and Mother Jenkins clutched her hand. The woman had such a strong grip that when she yelled, "Jesus," she practically crushed Rachel's fingers.

Rachel cringed and bit her lip to keep from crying out in pain.

"Lord, we come boldly to Your grace, where we may obtain mercy and favor for our dear sister here, Mother Brownlee…"

Rachel picked her battles. She wasn't about to attempt to correct her again that Priscilla Brownlee was an aunt and never a mother. However, the woman's body language took "hold your peace" to a whole new level.

"In Matthew 8, we know that if You speak Your word and we believe Your word, Mother Brownlee can be healed, according to Your will… This is all about You, Jesus!" Mother Jenkins prayed with such power, Rachel trembled as she whispered her requests. Soon, the prayer ceased, and silence filled the room.

Rachel opened her eyes to see Aunt Tweet smiling. Rachel sniffed. It wasn't as if she didn't believe in prayer, but to see instant results was amazing. Yes, Tabitha was right: adding Aunt Tweet to a prayer rotation schedule was much needed, whether it was Nicholas or Mother Jenkins. "Thank you," she whispered.

"Thank God." She patted Aunt Tweet's arm, then looked at Rachel. "My job here is done. Keep praying and praising God, and everything will be all right."

After walking the woman to the door, Rachel thanked her, then returned to see Aunt Tweet smacking her lips. "I can't remember the last time I ate."

"It's been a while." Rachel chuckled. "I'll get you something, then freshen you up."

The doorbell rang while Rachel was preparing soup. Why was she disappointed to see Clara? Rachel smiled at the home health aide while chastening her own thoughts. Did she really think it would be Nicholas after Mother Jenkins had already visited?

Whatever tug-of-war was going on inside her, Rachel had to stop it. Her sister's wedding tape was starting to play with her head.

"How's Miss Brownlee?" Clara asked, staring at her.

"Oh." Rachel jumped and closed the door. "She's having a good day. Go on back."

Clearly, Nicholas had moved on to the next sick church member. Rachel doubted she would see him again, which was fine. Mother Jenkins was a good replacement.

Chapter 4

DEAD. NICHOLAS DIDN'T REALIZE HIS PHONE'S BATTERY HAD DIED overnight at work, and he didn't have his charger. Once at home, he powered up right away. He didn't expect the first call he received would be from Mother Jenkins, who could be long-winded. He withheld his groan as he answered, craving sleep.

"I tell you, Minister Adams, you need backup when you visit these women. They're all jezebels."

"Now, Mother Jenkins—" Nicholas tried to interrupt politely. She was called Mother Jenkins instead of Minister Jenkins because of her no-nonsense manner that dared anyone to cross her. The older woman was not only a powerful prayer warrior, but she had also appointed herself Nicholas's protector from all women—church ladies didn't get a free pass either.

"You should have seen that woman in those skinny jeans and top— Mother Brownlee's niece. Showed too much curvature, then those lashes were too long to be real. She was disappointed when I showed up outside her door instead of you…"

Really? Nicholas no longer tried to interrupt. So Rachel had been expecting him? It was a toss-up whether that tidbit amused or flattered him. Placing his call with Mother Jenkins on speaker mode, he checked his phone log, and sure enough, he viewed three missed messages, two from Mrs. Emerson at the church. This explained Mother Jenkins's call.

His heart pounded. What was going on—not with Rachel but with her aunt? What happened to cause Rachel to call the church—or maybe it was her sister again. Nicholas needed to ask, but he had become too distracted with Mother Jenkins's description of Rachel's assets. He was glad she hadn't slammed the door in Mother Jenkins's face. That would not have been good.

"Excuse me, Mother Jenkins, how was Miss Brownlee?" He held his breath.

"The way God wanted her—alive and well," she stated as if he should know.

Nicholas exhaled. "I'm sure they were both glad you visited."

"Mm-hmm, but remember what I said, Minister Adams. That girl is too cute for her own good. I'm ready to go in with you, into the lion's den, when these women are trying to dig their claws into you."

He nodded as if she could see. "I'll take your offer under advisement." When Mother Jenkins paused to take a breath, Nicholas used that space to say goodbye. Besides the calls from Mrs. Emerson, the other one was from his brother. He listened to Karl's message first.

Just as Nicholas had suspected. His brother needed a babysitter for his five-year-old twins because he and his wife had been invited to speak at a church. Again? The two were a "spiritual power couple" who fed the hungry, ministered to the sick, taught seminars, and more.

Whenever Karl and Ava were out of town, Uncle Nick was the default.

Both Adams brothers were ministers. There wasn't much sibling rivalry between them, but how did his younger brother by four years beat him to the altar? It would be nice to have a special someone besides his family to share his life with.

If his chances were left up to Mother Jenkins, that wouldn't happen in his lifetime, but she did have a point. Many of the women were fascinated that he was a minister. What they didn't understand was that being a minister wasn't glamorous. Nicholas wanted a woman to love who could be a wife, a mother, and a helpmate, like Ava was to his brother. In essence, Nicholas craved a Proverbs 31 woman.

At thirty-six years old, he was still waiting for that woman. Ladies always said they were waiting on their husbands. Men were no different. "We're waiting too," he mumbled. Reining his thoughts in, he texted his brother that he was available to watch his nephews. Without a social life, of course he was available. He stifled a yawn.

Although his weekend began Friday morning, all Nicholas wanted was sleep. First, he slid to his knees to pray for Rachel and Miss Brownlee. Next, he petitioned the Lord Jesus for the well-being of the elderly everywhere, for the homeless, for fatherless children, and more until he realized an hour had passed.

In bed, his body was ready to succumb, but his thoughts were still on Rachel and her aunt; then their images faded as he turned over and fell asleep. He didn't wake up again until an hour or so before the twins were set to arrive and turn his house upside down.

He grudgingly climbed out of bed and headed for the bathroom. He showered, dressed, then padded across the house to the kitchen. As he munched on a bowl of cereal, his thoughts turned to Rachel—again— and he thought about whether he should personally check on her. He noted the time and wondered if the church secretary was still in her office on a Friday evening at five thirty.

Mother Jenkins's warning, which was warranted around single women, rang in his head, but he called the church office anyway. Surprisingly, the secretary answered cheerfully.

Yes! "Hello, Mrs. Emerson. I'm sorry I got your message late about seeing Priscilla Brownlee. Mother Jenkins said her visit went well."

"Good. The niece, Rachel Knicely, called and wanted you, but I left a message and never heard back, so Mother Jenkins was the next contact."

He nodded. Yes, protocol was to go down the list of ministers until one could be reached. "Did Miss Knicely leave a number?"

After a brief hold, she returned to the line. "Yes, she did." She proceeded to give it to him.

After thanking Mrs. Emerson, Nicholas immediately called Rachel. She sounded like she was on the same sleep schedule as him. "Did I wake you?" he asked.

"Who's calling?" Rachel's voice was soft.

"I'm sorry for not identifying myself. This is Minister Adams—Nicholas."

"Oh, hi." She cleared her throat. "Yes, you did, but I've learned to catch a nap whenever I can."

"I called to apologize that I didn't get your message in time. It wasn't Mrs. Emerson's fault. My phone died, and I didn't have my charger."

"And I thought you were standing me up."

Was that a tease, or was she serious? Either way, he was interested. "Never. I understand Mother Jenkins ministered to your aunt. How is she doing?"

When she was slow to answer, he braced for the worst.

"Why don't you come and see her for yourself?"

What? Nicholas wasn't expecting an invitation. Was his mind playing games with him, or was Mother Jenkins's warning ringing true? "Thanks, but I'm babysitting this evening. Can I visit tomorrow?" His heart stopped, waiting for her answer.

"A minister who babysits." She chuckled and he smiled, liking the sound of her laughter. He was honored to contribute to any of her happiness at this time in her life.

"They are my nephews, Kory and Rory, and I'm their favorite uncle."

"Let me guess, you're their only uncle, right?"

Nicholas grinned. "Yep." He enjoyed talking to her when she wasn't stressed out, but he had to go and prepare snacks for the twins. "Sorry to disturb you. If the Lord wills, I'll see you tomorrow. Is noon too early?"

"See you then, Uncle Nick." She laughed and ended the call.

Now, how did she know that's what they call me? He liked her.

Less than an hour later, Nicholas answered the door and was attacked by his pint-size nephews who adoringly were a reflection of him as a boy.

"Uncle Nick!" Both boys vied for his attention, and Nicholas lifted the lightweights in one scoop.

Almost four years apart, the best revenge a big brother could bestow on his little brother was Karl's sons being mini versions of Nicholas. It was payback for all the mischievous pranks Karl pulled as a child and for which Nicholas got the blame as the oldest.

As they grew older, the two became not just brothers but best friends. The Lord had called them into His ministry in the same year. Karl first, then Nicholas. Karl and Ava had been best friends in high school. Years after graduation, they started dating and married at twenty-seven. Ava always had Karl's back.

Nicholas desired a relationship like that. "God, please remember me," he whispered to the wind to carry to the Lord's ear. He wanted a woman who would look beyond his title and love him for being Nicholas Adams. Where was that woman? It would put a dent in being his brother's babysitter. He was creeping close to thirty-seven and still unmarried.

Suddenly, Nicholas's quiet house turned into a playground. Besides his nephews' favorite games, he made sure there was plenty of space to wrestle with them.

Ava shook her head and stood on her toes and kissed him on the cheek. "You really do need to get a life. It's Friday night, Brother-in-Law."

"You mean a wife," Karl said. "But if he does, there goes our free babysitter."

Nicholas set his nephews on the floor, and they took off for the bedroom where they slept whenever they spent the night. Within minutes, the two five- year-olds returned, dragging out comic books, LEGO Junior construction pieces, remote control cars, and other gadgets Nicholas had stockpiled for their visits. He snickered, loving their energy and enthusiasm.

Ava anchored her fists on her hips and lifted her trademark mother brow. "Boys, put back every piece before you leave."

"Yes, Mommy," Kory said with a wide grin, and Rory mimicked his older brother by two minutes.

"Will you two leave already? Playtime is in full force!" Nicholas rubbed his hands together as if he were cooking up a scheme.

His nephews bought into the possibilities and shouted, "Yeah!" while bouncing up and down.

"Who's ready for some fries and hot dogs?" Nicholas steered his nephews to the kitchen and waved good night to Karl and Ava. "Don't stay out too late, lovebirds."

"You need a lovebird. And I've been looking out for one for you." Ava nodded with a knowing gleam in her eyes.

Nicholas cringed. He was done with blind dates. After two, he declined anybody's else assistance. "Put on your dark sunglasses, Ava, and stop looking."

"Come on, Uncle Nick," Kory whined. "We're hungry."

"Boy, your mother fed you before we left home. Don't start," Karl warned, stepping into his daddy mode.

"You're going to be late," Nicholas reminded them.

The couple made their sons give them hugs and kisses, and they were out the door.

"I thought they would never leave." Nicholas grinned and rubbed the tops of his nephews' heads as they walked into the kitchen. *Game on!*

———

The next day, Nicholas stepped off the elevator and walked toward Rachel's condo. According to the portrait Mother Jenkins painted of her encounter with Rachel, Nicholas expected a vixen to open the door and greet him.

That didn't happen. He was relieved that Rachel was dressed in a blue sweatshirt with *Fisk Bulldogs* in gold letters. The pants matched and so did her blue socks. Mother Jenkins hadn't called it right this time.

But it might have been overkill that she was sipping from a Fisk University coffee mug. Rachel smiled, and her gorgeous dimples appeared. They were soft and delicate, not as deep and defined as his. "Good morning." Her eyes sparkled, but not in a seductive manner. She seemed genuinely happy. She stepped backed and allowed him to enter.

"Alumna, I assume?" He chuckled and admired the long lashes that Mother Jenkins had called fake. From his quick deduction, they were as natural as her beauty.

"You win a trivia point, and I'm proud to be."

"And you should be." He nodded. *U.S. News & World Report* had ranked Fisk University in the top ten of historically black colleges and universities.

"Jealous?" She jutted her chin and lifted a brow. "You?"

"TSU." He pumped his fist in the air, and they shared a laugh.

There were more than a hundred historically black colleges and universities across the country, and Nicholas and his brother were proud of their education that came from one of them. They each received a lucrative job offer upon graduation, with degrees in accounting for Karl and business administration with a double minor in information technology and industrial electronics for Nicholas. Nissan Smyrna had snatched him up as if he were a first-round draft pick, and he had been with them ever since.

As he trailed Rachel to her aunt's bedroom, he noticed her steps were lighter and her manner relaxed, a contrast to the frazzled woman who had slammed the door in his face earlier in the week. The only thing that hadn't changed was her hair was pulled back from her face and trapped in a messy ball. Did the woman ever comb her hair?

At the top of the loft stairs, she turned around and graced him with another amazing smile. "See, prayer does change things, but I guess you already know that." She turned back and walked to the bed. Her aunt was sitting up against a couple of pillows, asleep. "She's still dozing throughout the day but has been waking up for a couple of days now."

Rachel faced him, folded her hands, and her eyes misted. "I'm so grateful God was listening." Then she turned to her aunt. "Aunt Tweet, Minister Adams is here to see you," Rachel said softly, and the woman opened her eyes and looked around until she met his gaze. Rachel had her aunt's eyes. That was where the seduction came from—those eyes.

Nicholas swallowed and sat. He was in double trouble. He was a sucker for pretty eyes. *Stay focused*, he chided himself as he felt Rachel watching him at the same time as her aunt was staring at him too.

———

Rachel didn't want to interrupt Nicholas's ministry, so once again, she stayed in the doorway as a quiet observer. The other day, he'd looked tired and been dressed in his work clothes. Today, he appeared refreshed. Although he still was casually dressed, his choice of clothes was high quality.

If Rachel passed him on the street, he definitely would turn her head.

She had never met a minister who was that fine. She cleared her head of those thoughts. God sent him to minister, but he was a good distraction, because she was starting to battle bouts of depression associated with Aunt Tweet's condition.

She admired Nicholas's interaction with her aunt. She bit back a smile. If Aunt Tweet were half her age, she would have flirted with the man, but now, Aunt Tweet was subdued.

"How are you, Miss Brownlee?" Nicholas asked and waited patiently for her to respond as if he had all the time in the world just for her. "Do you mind if I read to you and pray with you?"

If she were to describe Nicholas, he would be the old cliché "a gentle giant." He had a larger-than-life presence, but his manner seemed personal and his voice soothing and comforting.

Whether it was the loud, commanding presence of Mother Jenkins or the humbleness of Minister Nicholas, they both knew how to invoke the "effectual fervent prayer," a phrase Rachel had heard Tabitha say that meant God listened when they prayed. Rachel hoped God was listening now.

Instead of opening his Bible to a designated passage, Nicholas flipped through the pages as if he knew what he was looking for.

Rachel perched on a nearby ottoman to listen. She anchored her elbows on her knees, then rested her chin in the palms of her hands.

"Our hope comes from First Thessalonians, chapter 4, beginning at verse 14…"

There was power behind Nicholas's reading. It wasn't as if Rachel didn't read her Bible, but it was inconsistent. She never seemed to incorporate it into her daily routine like her beauty regimen.

This time when he mentioned death, she didn't freak out. As long as folks prayed for her aunt, Rachel was happy for more time to be with her. There was another thing: Nicholas was making her crave more Scripture. Maybe this was what Tabitha meant when she said she could breathe in every word of the Bible as if it were food for her soul.

"'Comfort one another with these words,'" Nicholas said, finishing too soon.

Aunt Tweet nodded, then closed her eyes.

Rachel wanted to close her eyes too, but when Nicholas stood, she did as well, disappointed that his visit was so short. "Thank you," she whispered and led him out of the room.

"No need to thank me." He shrugged. "It's God who gives her breath every morning."

Rachel stared. How could a man be this humble? She wasn't ready for him to leave, but she had no reason for him to stay. "Ah, I'm sure you don't want a cup of coffee? It's Thrive Market organic breakfast blend?" She scrunched her nose playfully. "I know it's afternoon, but it's never too late for a good cup of java."

Nicholas released a low chuckle. "Organic?"

"Yep. I believe in eating healthy. Including my coffee blend." She paused and blushed. "Well, not all the time."

A hearty laugh escaped, and Rachel laughed too. It was the first real amusement she'd felt in a long time.

"Thanks for the invitation, but I have some errands to run."

"Of course." She nodded and walked him to the door. Nicholas Adams was proving to be a dedicated man of God—she couldn't remember the last time a man had turned down the opportunity to share a drink with her, even a cup of coffee.

Chapter 5

THERE WAS SOMETHING ABOUT RACHEL THAT MADE HER SPECIAL, and Nicholas didn't know what it was. He resisted the urge to invite her to call him if she wanted to talk or if she wanted him to return and visit with her aunt. Until Nicholas knew what it was about her, he wasn't about to ask for trouble.

In previous instances, he hadn't given the cordial gesture a second thought...until one family member started calling him under the guise of praying for her loved one, then counseling her one-on-one. It didn't take a blind man to sense her motives, and they weren't pure.

The woman, whose name he couldn't recall, had tried to seduce him with a dinner when no one else was home. Nicholas walked away and blocked her number. It had been a lesson well learned. His only mistake had been mentioning the incident to Mother Jenkins. He had never seen the older woman so hot! Her nostrils flared, her mouth twisted, and her eyes squinted as if she were aiming to fire. "What's her number?"

Never again would he tell Mother Jenkins another thing about a woman's behavior—good, bad, or indifferent. Countless times after that, Mother Jenkins planted bugs in many of the single male ministers' ears that Miss Such-and-Such wasn't sincere, and she appointed herself as the single men's motherly guardian, as if they didn't have mamas. Nicholas thought of his own mother. Vera Adams was well aware of the women who liked her son, always reminding him, "Your heart will know the one."

Mother Jenkins would be proud that Nicholas didn't cave in to a gorgeous face, natural allure, and assets that would have many men ogling. Yet he sensed Rachel wanted nothing more from him except a lifeline for her aunt.

He reined in his wandering thoughts. Rachel's aunt might have awakened, but she seemed lethargic. Nicholas expected there would be another call, sooner rather than later, and the next trip might not be the scenario Rachel desperately hoped for.

Hospice? Surely, Rachel hadn't heard the doctor right. Hospice was a precursor to death. That meant all hope was gone. She couldn't let that happen—not yet. There had to be more she could do for Aunt Tweet.

What had happened? For the past week, Aunt Tweet had seemed fine. With the home health aide's assistance, Rachel had been able to get her up to the rooftop pet garden to watch the dogs play and enjoy the warmth of a sunny spring day. Then in a blink of an eye, Aunt Tweet had stopped eating again. It had been going on for four days now.

"Her vitals aren't looking good, Miss Knicely. Her blood pressure, breathing, and heart rate are fluctuating," Clara said. "I think you need to call her doctor."

When the home health aide appeared concerned, Rachel was near hysterics. She frantically called the doctor, who somewhat calmed her down, then put Rachel in touch with an agency that provided hospice care.

Frazzled, Rachel was scheduled to go into the office that afternoon. She called her boss in tears and advised him that she wouldn't be in.

"Take care of your aunt. We are all in the loop on the project, so rest your mind and keep me posted," Mr. Goode said.

The next morning, hospice RN Linda Gentry arrived and assessed Aunt Tweet and listened to what Rachel had observed over the last couple of days. She was horrified to learn that Aunt Tweet's lack of appetite wasn't the culprit.

"Your aunt is struggling to swallow," Linda said, and the prognosis was bleak. "It sounds like your relative has been in the pre-active phase of dying for a couple of weeks." She paused. "I think the active phase has begun and could last anywhere from three to five days. I would contact your other family members."

Rachel wailed. "You don't know my aunt! She'll survive! Aunt Tweet is strong willed and not a quitter!"

When Rachel gave her sisters the heartbreaking news, they cried together before Marcus joined the Skype call and suggested they all pray. He led them until sniffs replaced their tears. Would God hear them? Would it matter?

Her sisters and brother-in-law made preparations to come. "And stay…" Tabitha's voice trembled.

"Until the end," Kym finished in a whisper.

That was a day ago. Rachel and the dogs had kept a steady vigil at Aunt Tweet's bedside, Rachel watching her aunt sleep her life away. She grabbed Aunt Tweet's Bible and opened it, then slowly closed it. She didn't have enough strength to force her mind to comprehend whatever she tried to read. "God, help my aunt, me, and my sisters."

If the hospice nurse's prediction was right, Aunt Tweet had two to four more days on this earth.

She opened her Bible again. Didn't God have a say about those calculations? The pages opened to Job 14. She scanned the passage, beginning at verse 1, but the words from verse 5 seemed magnified before her eyes: *Seeing his days are determined, the number of his months are with thee, thou hast appointed his bounds that he cannot pass.*

Could that mean that God had a different calculation? Rachel didn't know if she should be hopeful or not.

Later that night, a soft voice stirred Rachel from her sleep. "Good morning."

Opening her eyes, Rachel looked around, then met Aunt Tweet's stare. "You're awake!" She sighed in relief and couldn't contain her emotions as she cried with joy. Just as she had told the nurse, her aunt wasn't going down without a fight.

But Linda had advised that any sudden awareness could be a brief period of terminal lucidity. "Your relative may become fully aware and return to her normal personality," she'd said. "Call it God's blessing that you're getting some last glimpses of your loved one." Rachel pushed that warning aside and doted on Aunt Tweet, situating the pillows so she could be more comfortable, then turning on the television.

"Water…rivers of living water…"

Her aunt's mumbling continued as Rachel hurried to the kitchen for a bottle of water. When she returned minutes later, Aunt Tweet's voice had ceased, and so had her breathing.

Rachel dropped the bottle on the table as she screamed, "Aunt Tweet! Aunt Tweet!" She shook her—nothing. Her aunt wasn't cold, stiff, or rigid as many described death. Aunt Tweet was warm, soft, and relaxed. Rachel checked Aunt Tweet's pulse and listened for her heart—time stopped.

"No! I still have four more days." Her sisters and brother-in-law were scheduled to arrive midmorning so they could keep vigil over their aunt. She had thought her aunt wanted water. That had been the only reason why Rachel had left her side.

How could she be gone? Rachel bawled and threw herself on the bed. The dogs seemed to mourn through their whines. Only when her reservoir was empty, she looked up and strained her eyes at the clock. She had no idea how long Aunt Tweet had been gone. Time of death: 2:42 a.m.—or rather, that was the time when Rachel stopped crying. The pain that shot through her heart seemed to travel throughout her body. Her life had changed again—first her parents, now her beloved aunt was deceased; the Knicely sisters had only each other.

She reached for Aunt Tweet's hand and squeezed. "I love you, Auntie. I love you," she choked, then sobbed. The dogs tried to comfort her with their licks of love. Despite being a dog lover, she didn't welcome licks to her face. Tonight was an exception to the rule, because their affections were comforting. It took almost half an hour to contain her emotions, then she debated whether to wake her sisters now, hours before they had to get up, or wait until she met them at the airport.

The torment of suffering alone overruled her compassion. She called Tabitha first and gave her the devastating news. Once they were somewhat composed, Tabitha called Kym, who had already checked in at the Baltimore/Washington International Thurgood Marshall Airport.

When Rachel broke the news, Kym tried to stifle her emotions, to silently mourn in a public place. Finally, Kym's voice cracked as she advised Rachel to call the hospice nurse, then the mortician.

"I can't." Rachel shook her head vehemently as if she were a little girl again. "That...that makes it so final. As long as her body is here, a part of her is here with me."

Tabitha said softly, "Aunt Tweet isn't there. She's gone." She paused. "Call that minister too."

"Why? There's nothing more he can do." Rachel was angry, confused, and devastated.

"Because we all need prayer," Tabitha said before their tearful goodbyes.

Chapter 6

Why didn't Rachel call him directly? Nicholas's heart had sunk when the church secretary informed him of Priscilla Brownlee's passing early this morning. He should have called her to check on her aunt. Had he tried to protect his emotions and failed to show compassion?

"I happened to come in this morning to help with a project, and Mrs. Whittington, the niece from St. Louis, contacted us to see if her sister had been in touch. Miss Knicely hadn't, and I offered her our condolences. Mrs. Whittington didn't want her sister to be alone until they arrived."

His heart grieved for the woman he had only met twice. "I'll pay her a visit."

Nicholas tapped on Rachel's number from his contact list. It went straight to voicemail. "Rachel, I'm sorry to hear about your aunt's passing. If there is something I can do, please let me know."

Since he had finished his workout minutes before Mrs. Emerson called, Nicholas showered, then ate a light breakfast, all the while checking his phone. When Rachel hadn't returned his call within an hour, he made the drive to the West End.

As he rode the elevator to the fourteenth floor, he chided himself for not bringing something: flowers, food, a card. Hopefully, his presence would be enough.

He knocked, and a man opened the door. Rachel hadn't mentioned any brothers, so who was this guy? Could this be an on-and-off boyfriend who came to console her? "Hi, I'm Minister Adams. You have my deepest sympathy. I'm here to offer prayer and words of comfort."

The solemn expression on the man dissipated as he exhaled and opened the door wider. They were about the same height and probably around the same age. "Thank you for coming. I'm Marcus Whittington, Rachel's brother-in-law from St. Louis." He extended his hand. "My wife is the one who initially reached out to your church."

Nicholas nodded. At a loss for words, he asked the standard, "Is there anything I can do?"

"Pray for us, please." Marcus choked back his emotions. "Aunt Tweet was the sisters' rock after their parents died. If it wasn't for Aunt Tweet wandering through the neighborhood…"

"Excuse me? She what?" Nicholas blinked and leaned closer. Surely, he hadn't heard right.

That brought a smile to the brother-in-law's face. "Long story." Marcus placed an arm around his shoulder, then patted Nicholas's back before leading him through the house to where the ladies were gathered in the living room. He spied the loft and noted that the bed was made. As expected, Aunt Tweet's remains were gone. The sisters were sifting through photo albums.

From behind him, Marcus spoke in a low voice. "Aunt Tweet is the reason I met Tabitha. I have no regrets." He pointed to the ring on his hand. "We're newlyweds."

"Congratulations." He paused as the women looked up from the table and stared at him with blank expressions. Even Rachel looked right through him. Her aunt was gone, and she seemed to have taken a piece of Rachel with her. "Good morning, ladies. I'm Minister Nicholas Adams, and I'm so sorry to hear about your aunt's passing."

One sister, who had to be Marcus's wife judging by the rock on her finger, jumped up to meet him. "I'm Tabitha Whittington. Thank you so much, Minister, for visiting. We really appreciate your prayers." Her husband wrapped his arm around her shoulder and kissed her hair.

Their show of affection sparked a longing inside Nicholas, even at this solemn time. He refused to be envious of their love. God had someone special for him to love too. *Where is she?* he wondered for the umpteenth time.

"This is our sister Kym," Tabitha said, and the woman mustered a tentative smile.

Rachel didn't look at him or move, sitting as if she were in a deep trance. He wanted to sit next to her, touch her hand, and break the spirit of sadness that lingered on her.

Instead, he moved closer to the table and squatted before her. "I'm here for you. No matter what you need," he said softly. Slowly, her acknowledgment came in a nod as if a puppet master were pulling the string. Taking her hand in his, he squeezed her fingers to add warmth, then stood. "Do you mind if I pray now?"

"Please!" Tabitha's and Marcus's desperation was said in unison.

Bowing his head, Nicholas closed his eyes and petitioned God for comfort, also thanking the Lord for being a giver of life.

"Amen," they all mumbled at the end of the prayer.

Nicholas took a deep breath. He guessed his job was done. He had no reason to stay. Marcus escorted him to the door, then stepped outside in the hallway with him at the same time as a group stepped off the elevator, heading their way with boxes of food and flowers.

Marcus smiled and greeted them as they stopped at Rachel's condo door. Two identified themselves as her coworkers. The woman at the back of the group spoke to Marcus and gave Nicholas a quick appreciative glance.

"Hey, Jacqui. Go on in," Marcus told them and opened the door.

Once they were alone again, he turned back to Nicholas. "As you can see, Rachel is taking it hard. I can't imagine being the last one to see someone alive and then the first to see them dead."

"Me either," Nicholas admitted, rubbing the back of his neck.

"Although we knew it was coming," Marcus said, "it's hard for us to accept she's gone."

Nicholas could feel the sorrow and pain piercing Marcus's heart. The impact the woman had on her family was apparent, making him wish he had met her when she was vibrant.

"Knowing someone has prepared to see God makes the transition easier, believing God's promises," Nicholas reminded him. "Take my number and let me know about the funeral arrangements. I'd like to be there." Priscilla Brownlee's eulogy was sure to give him a glimpse of his missed opportunity at not having crossed paths with her earlier.

Marcus tapped in the numbers. "The wake and funeral will take place in St. Louis. The mortician here is preparing her body to be shipped, and our church in St. Louis is checking the dates to accommodate the family for the service."

"I'll make plans to be there," Nicholas said and waved goodbye.

When Nicholas made it back to his house, he couldn't shake Rachel's distraught image from his mind. As a matter of fact, when he closed his eyes, her sad expression haunted him in his sleep.

The next evening, Marcus texted him the arrangements; it would be held in a week. The next day at work, he planned to request Friday off. He booked his flight for St. Louis. He didn't want to get on the road tired after working the third shift, even for the short four-hour drive.

"What?" He looked up from his phone and stared at Karl and Ava, who had apparently asked him a question.

"Is something wrong?" Ava frowned. "You just zoned out on us."

His brother and sister-in-law had invited him to Sunday dinner as a way to thank him for watching his nephews. As a bachelor who was only a decent cook, Nicholas never turned down a free meal from his mother or sister-in-law. "Sorry, funeral arrangements." Nicholas set his phone aside and cut into his steak.

Karl frowned. "I don't recall hearing any announcements this morning about a church member passing or Mom and Dad mentioning anything."

"Miss Brownlee wasn't a member. She's from St. Louis, but she was added to our sick and homebound list when one of her nieces called the church," Nicholas explained.

"So you're going to St. Louis for the funeral of a woman who probably didn't know you were there to see her?" His sister-in-law looked bewildered.

To Nicholas's ears, Ava's recap didn't make sense. "I'm going to be there for the family."

"Are you speaking on the program?" His brother slipped green beans in his mouth and chewed while waiting for an answer. It wasn't unusual for visiting ministers to give remarks about the deceased.

"I'm going strictly as a friend for Rachel and the family."

"Rachel? Hold up." Karl rested his fork on the plate. "Why do I feel there is more to the story?"

"She must be special for you to fly across the country for her after knowing her for what?—A month?" His sister-in-law gave him a suspicious expression.

"No, a few weeks, like three," he corrected. "I don't consider an hour and a couple of minutes a flight across the country," Nicholas stated.

"Seriously, what makes this woman so endearing?" Karl wouldn't drop the subject.

"I'm a minister, and she has a wounded soul that needs healing."

"Mm-hmm," the couple said in harmony.

Nicholas ended the discussion when his nephews ran into the room, wanting him to play football.

When he returned home, Nicholas called to check on Rachel again. Her voicemail was full. Although disappointed, he was glad that she had an outpouring of support.

After getting home from work Thursday morning, Nicholas crashed. Good thing he had already packed for the short trip. That evening, while sitting in the terminal for his flight to St. Louis, his conversation with his brother and sister-in-law resurfaced. Why *was* he dropping his plans—although he had nothing urgent for the weekend anyway—to attend an out-of-state funeral where he barely knew the deceased or her family?

The flight was uneventful and ahead of schedule, and Marcus had insisted on being at Lambert Airport to greet him. "Glad you could come, man." They exchanged a fist bump and pat on the back. "It means a lot to us and to Rachel." The man treated him like an old friend and opened his home for lodging, but Nicholas declined.

"Thanks for allowing me to be a part of the family's healing process," Nicholas said, shifting his garment bag over his shoulder. "So how is Rachel coping?"

"I think it's gonna take a while for all of us, but especially for her, to move on. Aunt Tweet left a legacy." They chatted about the flight and nothing important as Nicholas followed Marcus to his car in the parking garage.

"Hungry? We have way too much food at the house." Marcus slid in behind the wheel.

"I'll eat something at the hotel, but thanks for offering." He didn't come to be a burden. This was their family time, and Nicholas didn't want to intrude, even though he wanted to see Rachel with his own eyes. He would have to wait until tomorrow.

The Hilton St. Louis Airport Hotel was really close. A six-lane highway separated it from the airport terminals. It only took a few minutes for Marcus to drive Nicholas to the hotel entrance.

"Sure you don't want someone to pick you up for the wake and funeral in the morning?" Marcus double-checked before Nicholas stepped out. "Bethesda Temple is minutes away. It's not a bother."

"I'd rather stay in the background. I'll take a Lyft, so I'm good. Thanks."

Nicholas checked in, and once he was in his room, he asked himself, "What am I doing here?"

No answers came to mind, so he relaxed, texted his family that he was safe, then ordered room service.

Before climbing in bed, Nicholas stayed on his knees longer, asking God to give the family and mourners comfort in their souls.

The next morning before leaving the hotel, Nicholas second-guessed his decision to fly to another city to support a woman who didn't know him beyond his first and last name and the church he attended. His mother had called this morning curious too. Nicholas was sure his big-mouthed brother had been more than happy to put a bug in his mother's ear.

"I know you have good instincts, Son. Try to keep your heart safe while you get to know this woman better," Vera Adams advised.

Who said his heart was vested? "Thanks, Mom. I'll keep you posted on any developments worth sharing." They spoke a few more minutes, then ended the call so he could make it to the funeral.

When the app alerted him that his Lyft driver was within one minute of him, he grabbed his things and left his hotel room, joining others waiting at the elevator.

He arrived at Bethesda Temple Church in no time, minutes down the interstate from his hotel. The parking lot was packed, so that gave him an indication of the number of mourners inside. Clearly, the woman was well loved. Thanking his driver, Nicholas gave him a cash tip in addition to the one given on the app, then stepped out with his overnight garment bag. He strolled inside and was amazed at the line to sign the condolence book. He took his place, too, if for no other reason than for Rachel to know he came and was among the many to pay their respects.

After his turn, Nicholas walked into the packed sanctuary. He craned his neck to peep out at the family in the front near the pearl-white casket. Marcus spied him and left Tabitha's side to come and shake his hand.

"Glad you could make it, man." Marcus glanced around and shook his head. "Aunt Tweet touched many lives."

Nicholas nodded as he glanced around. "I see. That's why I'm here."

Tabitha walked up next to her husband. Her eyes were watery, and her face was red. "Thanks for coming." Her voice was shaky.

"Of course. Again, you have my condolences."

"Rachel's over there, practically guarding Aunt Tweet's casket. I'm sure she'll be glad to see you."

Nicholas kept his eyes focused on Rachel as he trailed other well-wishers who had formed a line toward the front to view the body and offer their condolences. When Nicholas finally reached the casket, he stared at Priscilla Brownlee's remains. The morticians had done a wonderful job of leaving a lasting impression.

He looked up at Rachel, who seemed to stare past him. Her eyes were swollen. Grief draped her face. He had never seen her hair down—it was long—nor had he seen her dressed in anything but lounge clothes and socks.

"Whatever you need, I'm here for you." He reached out and cupped her hands. They were cold and trembling. He rubbed her fingers to give them warmth, then released them to step aside so others could offer their sympathies.

She nodded. "Thank you," she mumbled in a whisper.

Nicholas faded into the crowd and took his seat before the service began. The songs were upbeat, and a handful of people were on the program to give remarks that were cheerful. The mood shifted when the sisters shared their emotional memories of their aunt.

"As the oldest sibling," Kym said, "Aunt Tweet, along with my parents, instilled in me the importance of leading by example for my younger sisters. I'll never forget how Mom and Dad turned my failures into teaching moments, which inspired me to pay it forward in academia…"

Next, Marcus assisted his wife up the stairs to the pulpit, then helped Kym down them. Tabitha sniffed. "Simply put, Aunt Tweet was my shero." She smiled. "Growing up, I was often called mini Priscilla because I looked like her, but I want to think I received more than what was on the outside—a piece of her pure heart. Whenever I needed someone to talk to, Aunt Tweet was never too busy to listen…"

Finally, it was Rachel's turn, and she ascended the steps slowly. Marcus kept a grip on her arm but didn't rush her. *What a burden that must be, to be the sole brother-in-law to take on the responsibility of three sisters.*

Rachel swallowed and began, "As my sisters will agree, I'm the 'spoiled to a fault' baby of the family, but the confidence that was nurtured in me as a child allowed me to achieve amazing things as an adult. I loved my parents, and I especially enjoyed being a daddy's girl. My mother was always there when I needed her." She bowed her head, then looked up to the ceiling and sniffed.

"But it was Aunt Tweet who gave me an extra dose of her special type of love. I found myself wanting to copy my aunt's achievements. As her last caregiver—" She paused and patted the podium as if she were keeping time. Nicholas whispered a prayer for her strength. She took a deep breath and exhaled. "Whew. I'll hold her talks and words of wisdom close to my heart." She crossed her arms against her chest. "I'll always love you, Auntie." She touched her fingers to her lips and blew a kiss to the casket. Her shoulders slumped as if she had released a heavy load.

Marcus was there to help her down, then he released her into the arms of her sisters. Time stood still as they consoled Rachel, guiding her back to the front pew.

Priscilla "Aunt Tweet" Brownlee had had an impact on her nieces that would live on, Nicholas mused.

The musicians struck up a melody as Pastor Kevin Mann approached the podium. He sang a few choruses of "I'll Fly Away," which seemed to settle the spirit in the sanctuary. The pastor gave a short but heartfelt eulogy about how death isn't the end. "In Second Corinthians 5, verses 6 and 8, Paul says, 'We are always confident, knowing that, whilst we are at home in the body, we are absent from the Lord.'" He paused. "I don't know about you, but I want to be with the everlasting God. Verse 8 gives us that hope. Sister Brownlee had hope that she would be present with the Lord."

At the cemetery, Nicholas stood in the background, observing the three sisters huddled together in a somber moment, watching as two cemetery workers lowered the casket. Mourners seemed to move back in unison, giving the sisters space for their parting thoughts.

Surprisingly, Marcus left his wife's side and came to stand next to Nicholas with a man he introduced as his older brother, Demetrius. Nicholas shook his hand, then commented, "Rachel's grieving is so tangible. I can feel the heaviness of her heart from where I'm standing."

"Yeah." Marcus didn't look at him as he slipped his hands in his pockets. "Aunt Tweet passed away under her care. A couple of times, Tabitha and I thought Aunt Tweet might not make it when she lived with her, because she was getting worse. Aunt Tweet was in different stages with each sister, but with Rachel… Whew." He shook his head. "It was all downhill."

"I know, right?" Demetrius spoke up. "And that's why the timing wasn't right for us to be in a long-distance relationship just as she was about to become a caregiver too." He shook his head. "Sorry, Bro, I couldn't be there for her like you were for Tabitha."

How insensitive is this man? Nicholas thought. Demetrius and Rachel had been an item and the man deserted her when she needed him most?

With his sunglasses shielding his eyes, Nicholas studied him. Where Marcus was friendly, his brother seemed too serious and not well suited for Rachel's personality. She needed pampering, and Demetrius didn't seem like the type of man to appreciate her.

Wait a minute. Nicholas nipped his judgment call in the bud. He didn't even know her personality. One thing for sure was Rachel's commitment to her loved one. Couldn't that man see it?

Demetrius folded his arms. "Despite a little weight loss, she's still fine and has those nice legs. I'll give her some time, then I'll call to check on her."

"I thought you said ten years was too much of an age difference between you two?" Marcus asked.

Demetrius shrugged. "Maybe, maybe not."

Ten years older than Rachel, and the man still lacked wisdom. Nicholas noted that today was the first time he had seen her appearance polished, and her hair flowed down her back.

He was surrounded by beautiful women inside and outside the church, but he guarded his heart. He had already been burned—no, scorched—when he'd revealed God's calling him into the ministry and that it may require sacrifices on his time. The woman he'd had the longest relationship with had walked away without looking back. She didn't want to share him, not even with God.

"Tabitha thought I was a jerk when we first met, but you're a bigger one, Bro," Marcus said.

Score. Nicholas kept a straight face, but he wanted to smirk and give Marcus a fist bump. As Rachel started to cry and became unsteady on her feet, Nicholas motioned to go to her rescue, but Marcus's hand kept him rooted in place.

"This is their private moment. My brother and I have learned not to interrupt the Knicely sisters. As the oldest, Kym likes to handle situations with her sisters," Marcus said.

One day, Rachel wouldn't need her sisters but would rely on a man who loved her to be there to console her, love her, and cherish her. Nicholas frowned at his assessment, wondering how he thought he knew so much about a woman he barely knew. When the sisters turned to head back to the waiting limo, the crowd followed, including Nicholas, who hoped to find answers to his muddled thoughts.

Chapter 7

WHAT AN EMOTIONAL DAY—NO, AN EMOTIONAL WEEK—NO, HER LIFE as Aunt Tweet's caregiver had been a roller-coaster ride. While others were eating, chatting, harmlessly laughing to cheer up the family at the repast, Rachel slipped out of the fellowship hall to the parking lot to breathe. It had been a long day.

Despite the large turnout for Aunt Tweet's homegoing, Rachel felt alone. Jacqui would probably strangle her for saying that, as her best friend hadn't left her side since the day after Aunt Tweet's passing. Come to think of it, Rachel was surprised Jacqui wasn't hot on her trail now. She was aware that Nicholas had attended the funeral, and she would forever be grateful for his act of kindness.

Yet even with her best friend and sisters, Rachel felt empty. Aunt Tweet had always understood her moods before Alzheimer's set in. As the wind blew, she looked up and searched the clouds. Nicholas had mentioned a passage in Thessalonians about a trumpet announcing God's return through the clouds.

With Aunt Tweet gone, there would be no more ministerial visits. It was up to Rachel to do her own soul-searching, and she needed inspiration now more than ever to ease the hurt of her wounded spirit.

She continued her stroll down one aisle of the parking lot, inhaling the unseasonably warm April air and gaining strength from the sunshine. Although her mind was drifting as she recalled happy times with her aunt, she heard footsteps behind her.

"Rachel." The voice was unmistakable. Had she conjured him up? A breeze brought a whiff of a familiar cologne to confirm Nicholas was nearby.

She shaded her eyes from the sunlight with her hands until he stood within a few feet of her. She had never seen him dressed up before, and he was handsome beyond measure in a suit and tie. He looked serious until he caught her staring again, and he smiled.

"I saw you step out. I wanted to check on you. Are you okay?" He frowned.

"Will I ever be?" she said more to herself. "I was hoping no one saw me," she said, "especially Jacqui."

"Yes, you will, and I did." His voice was barely above a whisper. "I'm flying out in a few hours, but I would like to pray with you before I go."

Why did his words seem to lighten her burdens? "Thanks for coming here." Rachel's eyes watered, but she got a handle on her emotions. "I didn't realize ministers attended the funerals, especially those who are out of town."

"I wanted to be here for you. The location didn't matter."

"Thank you, Minister Adams."

"Always Nicholas to you. I don't need the title to do God's work." His words were kind and thoughtful.

"Okay." She studied him, really looked at him. *Was there a special lady in his life waiting for him to propose?* If so, the woman had a keeper, Rachel thought as he watched her.

Nicholas blinked first, then cleared his throat. "I called a couple of times to check up on you. Did you get my messages?"

Rachel shrugged. "Jacqui has been checking messages, answering emails, and stuff. I'm sorry." She bowed her head, embarrassed.

"Hey." That low voice of his gently commanded her to look at him. "I'm available to listen about anything whenever you want to talk."

He reached for her hands. His fingers were coarse but gentle. "Father, in the name of Jesus, let Rachel feel Your presence from this day forward. Comfort her when she's lonely, and when she's weak, give her strength. And let the memories of her aunt give her joy…"

His words were like a balm to her spirit. Rachel whispered, "Amen," with him when he finished. "Thank you."

"Anytime. Take time to heal emotionally and mentally. There's no expiration date for the process, and remember what I said—if you call me, I'll listen." He frowned, and his stare was intense. "I mean that, Rachel," he said and squeezed her hand.

Although the gesture was comforting, Rachel yearned for a hug, one of those cocoon-type embraces where she could close her eyes and sigh as she snuggled. But she had no one to offer her that.

When he released his hold, his eyes seemed to dance with amusement as he glanced down at her feet. "Oh, and I wouldn't walk too far in those heels. My feet hurt even thinking about it." He shivered, then chuckled before he swaggered away.

"A man with a sense of humor." Mirth stirred in her belly until a chuckle escaped her lips. He actually had made her laugh.

Later that night, back at Tabitha and Marcus's house in her old neighborhood, the sisters' heels, dresses, and makeup came off. They lounged in the family room in their flannel pj's, reminiscing about Aunt Tweet and the sizeable inheritance she had left them.

Marcus entered the room. "Came to check on you ladies and give my wife this." He leaned over the sofa and brushed a kiss against Tabitha's lips.

Rachel's heart fluttered; she longed for that type of deep-rooted affection. The couple was a perfect match for each other. He had been Tabitha's rock when she needed it. Aunt Tweet had been a handful while she stayed with Tabitha, but Marcus had somehow wormed his way into their lives and charmed her aunt and Tabitha too.

"Okay, I came for what I needed. Carry on." He grinned and ducked to escape the pillow Tabitha aimed at her new hubby's head.

When Tabitha faced her sisters, Rachel and Kym were smiling.

"You've definitely got you a winner, Sis," Kym said and sighed. "Honestly, I thought Rachel would beat us to the altar."

"Me too," Tabitha agreed, "but I have no regrets about being first. Aunt Tweet harped on having no regrets, and I have none being Mrs. Marcus Whittington."

"I don't know why you thought I would get hitched first." Rachel shook her head.

Kym gave her a surprised look. "Because you draw men like a car show—from your sultry voice to your calculated catwalk to your form-fitting fashions. You, dear baby sister, have men wrapped around your manicured finger."

"I think that was wishful thinking, but you don't see any standing in line with a ring, do you?" Rachel challenged them.

"Nicholas Adams might be a prospect. Marcus likes him, and he did make a special trip to be by your side during our sorrow." Tabitha nodded. "And that man is downright good-looking."

"Nope." Kym shook her head. "He's hot—sizzling," she teased.

"He's a minister. That's what he does—prays and is there for people."

"I think you need to rethink that, because I would give that darker version of actor Daniel Supta a second look."

"It's Sunjata who played on *Graceland*, and both men are unmistakably handsome. I figured ministers are attracted to women of God like missionaries or evangelists, and as my two sisters have pointed out, I may have other men wrapped tight, but Nicholas—I mean—Minister Adams's focus is on God's work."

"If you say so," Kym said and eyed Tabitha. "You may be part of his work in progress in a personal way."

Nicholas wasn't interested in her in that way. He hadn't asked for a date or dinner but offered her prayer, which, surprisingly, Rachel couldn't get enough of, as if she were dying of thirst and hearing it quenched it.

Chapter 8

NICHOLAS KNEW RACHEL WASN'T GOING TO REACH OUT TO HIM. Now that he was back home in Nashville, he would give her some time, then call to check up on her. She had dominated enough of his thoughts. He had to switch gears. It was six o'clock on a Saturday night, and it was date night—just not for him. Nicholas didn't get a chance to count to ten before his doorbell rang. He smirked in amusement as he answered his door.

"I was hoping you would be back in time for our date night," Karl said, his twin sons jumping between their parents, screaming, "Uncle Nick."

"You know, I think our parents need to retire so they can sit at home like old folks and wait for their grandkids to come visit."

Nicholas chuckled. That wasn't going to happen anytime soon. Vera and Thurman Adams still worked and had a large circle of friends who kept them entertained on the social calendar. Plus, his father was a deacon at the Believers Temple Church. Despite their busy schedules, their parents spent as much time with their grand twins as they could, and so did Nicholas.

Unlike their last visit, his nephews wanted to binge on children's programs. What kind of uncle would he be not to indulge them? Nicholas watched television with them until they became bored and begged him to read to them. By the time Nicholas finished the *Do Not Bring Your Dragon to the Library* thirty-plus-page book, the boys had dozed off. Smiling, he planted kisses on both of their heads. Whenever he had children, Nicholas hoped they would be like his nephews.

His mind drifted to Rachel. At her aunt's funeral, he could feel the heavy sorrow in her heart. How was she faring today? When would she return to Music City? He had so many questions and no right to the answers.

A week later, Nicholas got an unexpected call. It was from a St. Louis area code, and the only people he knew lived there were Rachel's family, so he answered.

"Man, thanks again for being there for us," Marcus said. "We're going to be in town next week to start packing up Aunt Tweet's things. She doesn't have much—bedroom furniture, clothes, and some knick-knacks. The sisters want to do it together. Why don't you stop by? I could use another male in the house."

Nicholas grinned. He liked Marcus's friendliness but gave the invitation a second thought. "I'm sure that will be an emotional moment. Are you sure you want an outsider there?" Nicholas believed in giving people their privacy.

"You're not an outsider. God sent you into our lives for a reason," Marcus assured him.

Nicholas wondered if Rachel felt the same way. "Thank you for saying that. Since it's Rachel's place, please understand that I would like to double-check with her." Marcus's call gave Nicholas a reason to reach out to Rachel. Minutes after ending their call, Nicholas's heart pounded as he dialed and waited for Rachel to answer.

"Hello."

Wow. Although he had only spoken to her on the phone once, he hadn't noticed then how sultry her voice sounded. It made his heart race. He refocused before he became tongue-tied. "Hi, this is Nicholas. How are you?"

"A little better than the last time you saw me. Each day sparks a new memory, but I'll get through it." Her answer sounded forced, as if she was trying to convince herself and him.

"I had hoped you would've called me." Nicholas watched his tone to mask his disappointment and not to come across as accusatory.

She sighed. "I thought about it, especially when I wake up and there's no one there to check on or sit with or to prepare a meal for." She paused and sighed. "I figured you were ministering to other families, so

I didn't want to bother you. I mean, I'm a big girl, so I'll have to handle my emotions by myself."

It hurt that Rachel thought she was merely a name on a list. "Despite what women believe, a man can multitask. I want to hear your voice, even if you think you're just rambling." It was a voice that could lure a man into a trance—maybe the phone wasn't a good thing. "I'm calling because Marcus asked that I stop by and help you pack up your aunt's things. I would like to if you're okay with that."

"I'd like that." She sounded like she might be smiling.

"Then I'll be there." He guessed she had nothing else to say. "Thanks for letting me into your life." He found himself blushing.

"No, thank you for coming into Aunt Tweet's life and mine."

When Nicholas ended the call, Rachel's words lingered in his head. Now he had a reason to see Rachel again. What was wrong with him? "The woman is still mourning, and you're attracted to her?" he scolded himself.

The next week, late Saturday morning, Nicholas arrived at Rachel's condo bearing pastries and coffee from Frothy Monkey, which roasted their beans locally. Their coffee was always fresh.

Rachel opened the door, and her eyes widened in delight. "Oooh." She snatched the box from his hands. "My favorite." She turned toward the kitchen, then looked over her shoulder as if remembering his presence. "Oh, thanks, Nicholas. Sorry. Come on in." Her eyes sparkled, and her sass was welcoming.

Yep, he liked this in-person encounter with Rachel much better. Nicholas gave her a quick perusal. Her hair was in a long braid, and she wore a T-shirt with #TeamTweetyBird, which he assumed was her favorite cartoon character.

"Put me to work." He smiled and closed the door to follow her into the kitchen, where a couple of boxes were set up.

"Not until we indulge in these goodies," Rachel said.

"Hey, we just took a break," Kym said, fussing as she came around the corner, then pausing when she saw him. "Hey, Nicholas, thanks for coming, because Marcus needs help."

As if the doorbell indicated a time-out, Rachel's best friend, Jacqui, jogged down the few steps from the loft, and her eyes widened. "Hi, Minister."

Shaking his head, he slipped his hands into his pockets. "Please just call me Nicholas."

"Okay." Jacqui grinned, then nudged Rachel as if there was a secret between the two ladies.

As the ladies decided on their selections, Marcus appeared, huffing as he dumped a heavy box on the floor. He stood and greeted Nicholas with a handshake and hearty pat on the back. "Good to see you, man."

Marcus put him to work right away, disassembling the bedroom furniture. The packing was slow going for the sisters. If it wasn't for Jacqui taking charge, Nicholas doubted anything would get done.

After a few hours, he and Marcus took a breather. "Are you sure you don't want us to take Sweet Pepper back home?" Marcus asked, rubbing behind the Yorkie's ears.

"Nope." Rachel shook her head. "Shelby needs someone to bark at. We agreed: I'll keep the dog; you and Tabitha get Aunt Tweet's furniture."

"Don't forget her scarves, especially the red one." Marcus grinned, then winked at his wife.

"Ah, yes. The infamous red scarf that was Aunt Tweet's calling card on Marcus's porch." Tabitha closed her eyes and sighed.

The sisters shared giggles but not the story that piqued Nicholas's curiosity. Maybe one day, he would hear about Priscilla Brownlee's antics.

"And we're still debating on the jewelry," Kym said. "Rachel and I might split that."

"Deal." Rachel nodded.

Nicholas watched the sisters' harmonious interaction, and it warmed his soul. So many times, he had witnessed downright bitterness and discord among families over the deceased's material goods.

"Speaking of pooches, I'll take them outside for exercise," Marcus volunteered. "Nicholas, walk with me."

It didn't sound like an invitation. Nicholas heard the underlying command, so he went along. Inside the elevator, the doors had barely closed when Marcus turned to him. "You like her, don't you? No need to deny it." He didn't give Nicholas a chance to confirm or deny. "Those Knicely sisters are hard to resist, man."

Once they were outside on the sidewalk, Marcus handed Shelby's leash to Nicholas and asked, "Which way?"

After giving it some thought, Nicholas made a suggestion. "Elmington Park is closer than Centennial Dog Park."

"Sounds good," Marcus said, and they started their trek as the dogs led the way. "So, back to Rachel. I can see you really care about her, and she needs that from a man."

"She didn't have that with your brother," Nicholas couldn't help but say. "I gathered from the conversation at the cemetery."

"My brother"—Marcus shook his head—"needs a relationship 101 class. He's not your competition."

"Noted." Nicholas tugged on the leash to keep from steering toward another dog. "Since we're having this heart-to-heart confidential chat: I'm struggling with my emotions. The attraction is there for me. But should it be? Is it too soon?" Nicholas didn't wait for an answer. "I'm not sure if she is attracted to me or she considers my sole purpose performing God's ministry and nothing more. Where do I stand with her?"

Marcus bobbed his head as Sweet Pepper stopped for a potty break. "You've got a lot of questions going on there. I suggest you get answers."

—

After the men left, Rachel knew it was only a matter of time before Jacqui would start meddling.

Jacqui fanned her face. "Whew. That minister is too good-looking to be single!"

"No doubt about that. He's pretty-boy fine," Rachel said casually as she folded up more of Aunt Tweet's things. "It's his eyes that got me the first time, but it's something about his touch—"

"Hold up." Kym stopped what she was doing, turned around, and squinted. "Touch? What kind of touch?"

"Get your mind out of the gutter. I've been a caregiver, remember?" Rachel shrugged. "Nothing close to being sexual. I'm talking about when he held my hand to pray." She refrained from shivering, remembering his strong hands and gentle voice.

"Then he's a keeper," Tabitha said with a wide grin. "Marcus was there for me every step of the way with Aunt Tweet. I love that man like crazy."

Kym laughed. "We know."

"Nicholas hopped on a plane to be at the funeral," Jacqui reminded her. "I'll give the preacher man a brownie for that."

"You did the same thing," Rachel pointed out.

"Yeah, but I'm your bestie, so I'm supposed to be there. Hmm."

"You're not attracted to him?" Kym asked and lifted her brow, then returned to sorting items to be given away to charity.

"Well, yes," Rachel slowly admitted, but she was quick to add, "I love to hear him read from the Bible. He's better than any narrator I've ever heard, and did I say I like the way he takes my hand and prays? Doesn't sound sexy, does it?"

"He sounds like a man I want," Jacqui added.

"Me too," Kym agreed.

"Got mine," Tabitha said smugly.

"Aunt Tweet is gone, so soon he'll return to his regular activities, which include church for him and not for me. Right now, I'm trying to adjust to a life without Aunt Tweet. I lost a part of me." Rachel patted her chest. "I need time to repurpose my life, and until I'm ready to reappear, I plan to stay hidden away in my cocoon," she admitted.

"I get that, and I'm definitely not rushing your healing process. Aunt Tweet was a special lady." Jacqui paused. "But come next Thursday, you've got to step out of that cocoon and come with me to the NFL Draft."

Rachel slapped her forehead. "I forgot about that." She sighed.

"Well, I just reminded you, because I got these pricey tickets, and I refuse to go with anybody else, so what time are we leaving for the NFL Experience?"

"Number one, *I* won the tickets in a sweepstakes, so you're not out any money."

"You weren't supposed to remember that." Jacqui grinned, and Rachel's sisters laughed.

Rachel was fine with the world moving on, but she couldn't right now. "Jac, I know they are nicknaming this event Draftville and there is a lot of hype, but I'm not sure if I'm ready to work the social scene again like I own it and act like I don't have a care in the world." She was becoming emotional, and they must have sensed it, because all three rushed to her side.

After a brief quiet moment, Kym spoke. "We all feel the pain, but I'm concerned that depression may creep if you shut out the world." She squeezed Rachel's hand and smiled. "Sis, we don't want that. I'm not saying resume your crazy social calendar when you're so busy we can't track you down."

"Yep." Tabitha nodded and folded her arms.

"I know if Baltimore were hosting the draft, my girlfriends and I would go," Kym said.

"See, keyword *girlfriends*." Jacqui lifted her chin.

Her big sisters' words carried a lot of weight, so Rachel gave it some serious thought. She had put her social life on hold to care for Aunt Tweet. Now that she was gone, Rachel did need to fill that void. If anyone had her back, besides her sisters, Jacqui did. Plus, she and her friend both had cleared their schedules after Nashville was picked as the host city. *Three days of music, entertainment, and sports*, she reasoned with herself. "Okay, maybe I can dig deep and turn on my charm for one night just for you." Rachel squinted. "But if I feel a meltdown coming…"

"We're out of there." Jacqui stood and lifted her arms in the air. "Touchdown."

Chapter 9

LIFE GOES ON. MORE THAN ONE PERSON HAD TOLD RACHEL THAT since Aunt Tweet's funeral three weeks ago—her sisters, friends, her colleagues when she had returned to work, even Mother Jenkins. But when did that happen?

Reclining on her balcony with the pooches under her feet, Rachel convinced herself she wasn't depressed. "I've just lost my creativity," she mumbled as the sounds of the city buzzed fourteen floors below her on West End Avenue.

She admitted she was lonely, which was odd. With a full social calendar, Rachel had never felt alone before. With Aunt Tweet gone, she longed for companionship, a family… *What is wrong with you?*

Rachel had too much down time on her hands. Maybe the NFL Draft Experience tomorrow would rejuvenate her. She caught sight of a plane taking off from the airport and suddenly wished she were on it, going somewhere far away from the emptiness of losing someone.

With her condo building loaded with amenities—library, game room, pool, shops, theater—there was no reason she should be bored. Rachel picked up her phone to call Kym. For some odd reason, Nicholas came to mind, and she thought about calling him. It wasn't the first time, but she stopped herself.

What did he care about her? He had done his ministry and had probably moved on to the next needy soul. Rachel really did like him as a person and enjoyed his presence, but they had two different lifestyles. "Exactly," she told herself and stood. She waved good night to Batman and went inside to get ready for bed. She would need her energy for Draftville.

The next day, Rachel left work early, pumping herself up with the excitement that surrounded her in Nashville. She had just walked into her condo when Jacqui called.

"Girl, it's going to be crazy fun. I'm spending the night with you—just saying—rather than trying to squeeze through traffic to drive home."

Rachel shrugged. It wasn't a big deal. They each had a set of the other's house keys for emergencies. "You got a spare key."

"The draft doesn't start until eight and goes until midnight, so we can hang out at the NFL Draft Experience near Nissan Stadium…"

Rachel couldn't drive past the stadium or watch a Nissan commercial without thinking of Nicholas. Then she always found herself smiling.

"There's this stage where we can get autographs from some of the Titans, so dress to work it," Jacqui reminded her. She was not one to have one strand of hair out of place or nail polish chipped.

Possessing the baby-sister syndrome, Rachel knew how to get her way, and she had learned how to get attention from the opposite sex. Dubbed the "accessory queen" by Tabitha and Kym, Rachel could sass up any attire, even in a hard hat and yellow construction vest. Rachel always looked her best. "I've got this."

Half an hour later after she showered and changed, Rachel scrutinized her makeup, then brushed her hair to the side. Next, she adjusted her big hoops earrings—her signature accessory. Finally, she slipped into her designer skinny jeans and half boots and donned her Tennessee Titans jersey. What little Rachel learned about football came from attending Super Bowl parties, so she knew when to cheer and when to yell at the referees.

Once Jacqui arrived, the two wasted no time in leaving for Lower Broadway and taking in every angle of the NFL Draft Experience. Local restaurants had set up food tents, so they grabbed snacks as they maneuvered through the crowds in search of the autograph stage.

Jacqui nudged her. "Glad you came?" She lifted a knowing brow.

Rachel playfully shoved her back as she munched on a veggie burrito. "You were right."

"See? Your best friend knows best."

"And this madhouse is going on until Saturday?" Rachel said as they strolled into the center to find their seats for the first picks. Families grinned in anticipation of team reps ready to make some athlete's dream come true.

"It's showtime," Jacqui said as she wiggled in her seat and craned her neck to watch the Arizona Cardinals make their first draft pick, then the picks were nonstop as each team announced their first-round choices.

While the Denver Broncos were announcing their choices, Rachel and Jacqui decided to take a quick potty break since the Titans' picks weren't until the nineteenth spot.

Near the concession stand, the two ran into familiar faces and chatted until someone caught Rachel's eye. She blinked as her heart danced at the same moment as his eyes connected with hers.

"Nicholas Adams," Rachel whispered. As he walked in her direction, she began to meet him halfway. "What are you doing here?"

"Rachel," he said in a low, deep voice that seemed to project above the other noise. "You look…stunning, and I happen to like football."

She blushed, something she rarely did when men complimented her. She usually owned it and responded with a saucy smile. "Thank you. You look amazing too."

He chuckled. "I doubt that. The only men staring me down are those who are wishing they had your attention."

They were quiet as they watched each other. "You haven't called me," he said in an accusatory tone that almost sounded like he was wounded.

He had no idea how many times she'd wanted to. Rachel glanced away, embarrassed, then exhaled. "I know."

"Why?" He gave her a penetrating stare, then folded his arms in a stance that indicated he would wait for her answer.

"I didn't want to bother you," she said honestly. "I figured you moved to the next person on the prayer list." She didn't mention Mother Jenkins *had* called her twice to check on her.

"Bother me." Unfolding his arms, Nicholas slipped his hands into his pockets. He smiled, and his dimples made an appearance.

She smiled too.

"I like those dimples," he said, complimenting her.

"I like yours too." Suddenly, a deafening roar erupted around them, and Rachel jumped, but Nicholas didn't take his eyes off her to investigate.

An excited fan walked by, shouting to anyone who would listen, "The Titans picked Xavier Nelson!"

Nicholas gave the guy a high five. "That linebacker from Alabama is a good choice." Then he turned his attention back to Rachel. His eyes sparkled. "See, I can multitask."

He had a magnetism Rachel found hard to pull away from, but she didn't want him to miss another highlight. "I guess I'd better let you go so you can enjoy the draft," Rachel said, but she really didn't want him to go. Until this moment, she hadn't known how much she had missed seeing him and hearing his voice.

"I am enjoying myself just fine." He reached out and took her hand. His touch left her fingers tingling.

Another guy approached Nicholas and cleared his throat. Although they resembled each other, Rachel thought Nicholas didn't seem happy with the man's presence.

"This is my brother, Karl Adams," Nicholas said in an annoyed manner, never taking his eyes off Rachel.

"Nice to meet you," Karl said with a sly grin. "I've heard so much about you."

Rachel raised her eyebrows in curiosity, and Nicholas gave his brother side-eye, his nostrils flaring.

"You have my deepest sympathies about your aunt," his brother added.

Of course, her aunt's passing. Why was she disappointed that Nicholas hadn't mentioned anything flattering about her? She exhaled. "It was nice meeting you, Karl, and good seeing you again, Nicholas." She turned to leave, but he touched her arm. Rachel stopped herself from shivering, but that didn't stop goose bumps from popping up.

"Call me, Rachel." His tone was gentle with a hint of a plea.

"O-okay." She was the first to walk away, and she could feel his eyes on her. She glanced over her shoulder and saw she was wrong. It was different admirers who watched and winked at her, but she was only attracted to Nicholas Adams. How had the women at his church let him stay single this long? Rachel was curious to find out.

Chapter 10

NICHOLAS HAD DONE EXACTLY WHAT HE HEARD GOD TELL HIM to do—pray for Rachel and be there for her because she would need comfort. But in the process, he had developed an attraction. She may be coping and ready to move on, but Nicholas couldn't go forward. Seeing her again at the NFL Draft had recharged his fascination.

Rachel Knicely was unforgettable. In less than sixty seconds, he had catalogued her every nuance—hair brushed to the side, flawless skin, seductive lashes, and delicate dimples. She had made the Titans' sportswear look fashionable.

Yet nothing moved Nicholas more than staring into Rachel's eyes and seeing a glimpse of light among the lingering darkness.

"Hello, hello?" His brother's voice pulled him back into the present, in Karl's living room. "You've got to stop zoning out on me like that, man!" He seemed annoyed.

Nicholas frowned. "What do you mean?"

"Help me to understand why you're moping around. You're the one who said women who chase you are a turnoff and you'd rather do the chasing, so…" Karl threw his arms up in the air. "I guess you'd better put on your best pair of running shoes, Bro, and chase."

Nicholas squinted and stroked the hairs on his chin.

"I stopped counting the number of times I commented on a play in this baseball game and your reply was 'Why hasn't she called?'"

Had he been thinking out loud? Nicholas sighed and shook his head. "I really don't know what to do."

"Yes, you do. Call her."

"And say what?" Nicholas stood and stuffed his hands in his pants pockets. Frustrated, he glanced out the window.

"Do I have to send you verbiage via text? Didn't look like you needed help when I saw you talking to her. On second thought, I think you two basically stared at each other. And you weren't the only one. There were gawkers."

"I know. She's beautiful and probably considers me just another admirer."

"Would you stop pacing my floor? You're hurting my neck. Sit down! Get a grip." Karl waited as Nicholas complied. "Remember when I was on the softball team?"

"Yep." Nicholas nodded. "You busted your knee trying to steal home. The rep told you to stay at second base, but no, not my hard-headed brother. I cringed when I saw the play. I could tell you were hurt bad, but you were holding it in." He laughed.

"Hey, I wasn't afraid to admit I was in pain. It did hurt, and if I had been a little boy, I'd have cried out for our mother to kiss it and make it better. Ava and I were dating then, and I couldn't hide my pain. I told her I needed her to hold my hand, and knowing she was there made me feel better." He paused.

"You know you're grinning, right?" Nicholas said and nudged his brother. "Now who is zoning out? What does your physical pain have to do with my mental suffering?"

Karl grunted. "I confessed to her that when I was weak, her strength made me stronger. It was the beginning of me seeing her as more than a good friend, more of a helpmate. After I proposed, she told me my honesty and vulnerability had swayed her to say yes."

Now, Nicholas grunted. "My little brother trying to give me a lesson on love."

"You better take note, Bro. I've got a wife and you don't. Rachel has only seen the minister side of you, which is so overrated by women." Karl shook his head. "Show her you. Call Rachel and be honest about your feelings. If she has no interest in a relationship beyond prayer, at least you'll know."

"I'm afraid to know," Nicholas confessed.

"Minister Adams, you of all people know God can't use no scary people. You know what God told Gideon when they were going into battle."

"And you know that has nothing to do with God fighting my sorry little internal conflict." That passage in the seventh chapter in the Book of Judges was deep.

"Well, judging from the torture on your face, you're deep in the trenches of a major battle. You better man up!" Karl said.

Later that night, back at home, Nicholas gave more thought to what his brother had said. What real man would show a woman his weakness? It hadn't worked for Samson. Karl's pep talk faded every time Nicholas spied his phone. Nah, he wasn't about to show his hand.

The following week, Nicholas had lost count of the church members who were admitted to the hospital. It seemed like dozens of them were ill.

Add the new ones to the numbers of those who had been home-bound for a while, such as Lila Dickerson. She hadn't been at church in more than a year due to her ailments. She had a sweet spirit and an encouraging word for everyone. Yet Nicholas always dreaded the visit, and today, he was weary and not in the mood to overlook her family's rudeness—not this evening. He hiked up the wooden stairs to the porch and rang the doorbell.

As he waited, Nicholas scanned the neighborhood. This house and the others on the block lacked curb appeal. When the locks clicked and the door cracked open, Nicholas turned around. As expected, Herbert, the woman's oldest son, who lived with her, stood there with a sneer.

"So you're back again, huh? I told you my mama don't need your prayers unless it's going to make her walk again." He motioned to slam the door in Nicholas's face, but not today.

Nicholas wedged his shoe in the opening to prevent it. "You may not appreciate my visit, but I'm sure your mother does. Her health is in God's hands."

"Then why are you here?" He smirked and twisted the toothpick in his mouth.

Nicholas kept eye contact with the man who had him by a couple of inches and fifty pounds and who seemed untrustworthy. While Nicholas calculated what moves would be necessary for him to be declared the winner going up against this man, his mind recited Scriptures about humility, peace, holiness, and turning the other cheek.

"To remind your mother that her church family loves her as well as the Lord," he argued and then silently prayed, *God, You got me here. Help me to do Your work.*

They stared each other down until Herbert took a step back. "I'll let you see her *this* time." It was a game he played *every* time. "Don't make too much noise praying and singing back up in there."

Herbert humphed, then led the way to a back bedroom where Lila Dickerson greeted Nicholas with twinkling eyes. The atmosphere changed immediately once he stepped into the room.

After they greeted each other, Nicholas took his seat and opened his Bible.

"You going to sing me my favorite song?" she asked with an expectant expression.

"Of course." Nicholas began the old Douglas Miller favorite "My Soul Is Anchored," and Lila Dickerson joined in off-key. At one time, no one could carry a note like her, but a stroke had taken its toll on her body.

"Now…Minister Adams, I sure would like to hear about my new body." Eager anticipation glowed on her face.

Nicholas smiled, knowing some things never changed whenever he visited Sister Dickerson. She requested the same song and Scripture. Nicholas recited the passage from 1 Corinthians 15, beginning at verse 53: "'For this corruptible must put on incorruption, and this mortal must put on immortality…'"

"That's right," she said and bobbed her head as best she could from her position in bed when he finished. "Now, please pray for me, and my knucklehead son…"

"I heard that!" Herbert barked from the other side of the closed door.

"Good. You should be in here with us," she said, fussing back.

You tell him, Nicholas thought and smiled at the elderly woman before bowing his head. They prayed until they felt the presence of God filling the room.

Soon after a short period of worship, Nicholas left on a good note. Whenever he had victorious moments, he liked to share them with his brother or dad. This time, Rachel came to mind. He wanted to talk to her—not about Sister Brownlee or her mourning but him and her. Patience had no peace where Rachel Knicely was concerned. It was time for him to take the first step.

Chapter 11

SUNDAY EVENING, RACHEL LOUNGED ON HER BALCONY, HAVING RUN out of tasks to occupy her mind. With the NFL Draft Experience over, many tourists had left Nashville, and there was room to breathe again. She had spoken to her sisters via Skype—a weekly routine they had started as Aunt Tweet's caregivers to keep one another updated on her condition. Now, it had become ingrained in them, so the sisters continued the tradition.

Attending the draft had been a one-of-a-kind experience, but the highlight had been seeing Nicholas. She always saw him in a spiritual role, not as a man doing everyday things, out with his brother instead of a girlfriend. Had she subconsciously put him on a pedestal? Not only had his presence surprised her, but he had encouraged her to reenter social life post-Aunt Tweet.

What was Nicholas Adams's story, and why did she care? His interest in her was strictly from a ministering point, right? When she told Jacqui and her sisters that, they all told her to open her eyes. Did she want to keep Nicholas tucked away in a box for when she had an emotional breakdown, or did she want to open the box wider and get to know more about the man with the mesmerizing eyes, sexy smile, and kind heart?

Nicholas had inspired her to pick up her Bible, and she brought it outside onto the balcony with her. She read a couple of random passages, but the meaning seemed to escape her. Everything had seemed to make sense when Nicholas read them to Aunt Tweet. Nicholas. She smiled.

Closing her eyes, Rachel welcomed the light breeze. She had just started to doze when her phone rang. Grabbing it, she blinked at the caller ID. Had she dreamed the man up? "Hello."

"Did I wake you?" Was it her imagination or was his voice always this deep of a baritone?

"Yep, from boredom." Rachel chuckled and he did too as she snuggled under her throw blanket.

"I need honesty from you."

"Have I been dishonest?" She frowned.

"I don't know." He paused as she waited for him to explain. "Help me here. Why won't you call me?"

"I—I—I," she stuttered.

"I can understand the lady waiting for the guy to call and show interest, but I need a sign from you that you're interested."

Rachel's heart skipped a couple of beats. "I know there are probably plenty of women who attend your church who are attracted to you."

"There is a difference between being attracted and feeling a connection. What about you? You have no shortage of male attention, and I was reminded of that at the NFL Draft."

Was she attracted to Nicholas? Yes, and it wasn't only the physical. She did feel a connection. "I'm not a bad person. I'm just not a church person. You are, and I'd think your compatibility would be among the church pool."

"Miss Knicely, I'm thirty-six years old and single for a reason. There is a difference between a woman who loves God and a woman who loves church—people change, rules change, leadership changes. If a person loves Jesus, really loves Him, his or her love will never change. That is the kind of woman my heart longs for."

There was so much passion behind his words. "*I do love Jesus,*" she said aloud, but it was meant for her ears only. Was she trying to convince him or herself?

"I'll let you read between the lines. The only way you can see me as more than a minister is to get to know me right now, at this moment."

So he was challenging her. "You're a minister, and I don't want you to step out of that role to be with me. I really respect you, Nicholas."

"That's good to know. I wish everyone did," he murmured, and that piqued her interest.

Rachel frowned and scooted up in her chair. She had a feeling there was a story behind that statement. "What do you mean? If it's confidential, then I understand."

There was silence on the other end. She wondered if it was the case.

"Only names and certain situations are confidential, but every family I minister to isn't appreciative."

"I hope no one slammed the door in your face," she joked.

"Well…the son would have if I hadn't jammed my foot in the door to keep him from doing it."

"Oh no," she gasped. Rachel hadn't expected others to be hostile to ministers. She thought it was just her, because of her own anxiety.

He grunted, then explained what happened. "Her son tries to come off as tough, but his soul is hungry."

"Maybe my soul is hungry too. I've begun to read my Bible again." She eyed the Bible beside her. "You seem to make the Scriptures come alive. I can listen to you for hours."

"I can listen to you for hours too. I don't want my attraction to be one-sided, so does this mean you will call?"

Persistent. "Whew." Coming from another man, it would be annoying. Hearing Nicholas utter it, she was flattered.

"Is that a good 'whew' or bad?" he pressed her.

"It's not bad, but…" Snoring from the dogs gave Rachel a distraction and time to form her thoughts and words carefully. "The day of Aunt Tweet's funeral, you followed me outside from the repast, and you were so kind. I wasn't sure if you were attracted to me. My curiosity kept building every time I saw you, but it was at the NFL Draft that I thought maybe…maybe you were interested. Of course, my sisters and Jacqui thought so."

"I'm very much interested."

Rachel smiled. "But this is where I'm struggling. My aunt just died. How can I think about a relationship when I just lost Aunt Tweet?" She gnawed on her lips, waiting for him to make sense of her confusion.

"To be honest, I had the same hesitation about approaching you when I flew to St. Louis for the funeral, but I knew I had to be there…

for you. I put my feelings on hold because I didn't want to come across as disrespectful while you were mourning. And there is no expiration date on grieving." He paused, and Rachel exhaled, relieved that he understood how she felt. He continued. "I didn't have the pleasure of getting to know your aunt, but I do know that without her, I never would have met you and felt the connection I have."

"Aw, that's sweet." Rachel patted her chest, touched.

"Are you making fun of me, Miss Knicely?"

"I would never do that!" she said too harshly, then apologized. She'd never mock him.

"You're forgiven."

Rachel exhaled when she could hear a smile behind his words, but it was the way he said "forgiven" that made her wonder if he was talking about himself or God forgiving her. "Again, Nicholas, I'm not opposed to becoming more than friends, but I don't know how this will work between us. My Sunday routine doesn't include going to church. I'm being honest."

Rachel stood, and the dogs scrambled to their feet. Before opening the door that led into the living room, she gave the Nashville skyline one more appreciative glance.

"Honesty is a good start. I like talking to you over the phone, but I'd rather look at you. Maybe next time, I can take you out."

"I would like that." She sensed that Nicholas was about to end the call, so Rachel said, "Before you hang up, do you mind explaining a passage in the Bible for me?" She was hopeful, like a child about to unwrap a birthday gift.

"You know I don't mind—ever. Bible study can be a date. Just sayin'." He chuckled.

"That's thinking outside the box." She lifted her brow. If he was flirting, she was soaking it in.

"I'm serious, so what passage?"

"Acts 8." Rachel gritted her teeth. "Do you mind reading the whole chapter?" She rushed on. "I know it's like thirtysomething verses, but if you can't, the verse about the eunuch."

"The Bible is like reading poetry."

Rachel followed along and asked a few questions, and like Philip in the chapter, Nicholas answered each one. *I guess the Bible really is a love story*, she thought, because all she felt was love and perfect peace.

Chapter 12

Nicholas wasn't complaining as one call turned into many. Every morning, Rachel called him as she enjoyed her cup of organic coffee while he drove home from his overnight shift at the plant. They clicked, as he'd suspected they would.

"Thanks," Rachel said out of the blue one morning.

"For?"

"Making the call."

His heart soared. "Thank you for taking it." Nicholas couldn't help but grin like a toddler. He didn't feel the same pressure from Rachel as he had from some women at church whom he had taken out to dinner a few times. Their conversation had always included statements about how they can cook, how they loved the Lord, and how they would make a good minister's wife.

Rachel wasn't making those claims, although Nicholas had a suspicion she could fill those shoes. She was indeed a breath of fresh air. All she wanted was to get to know him, and Nicholas wanted more, so on Thursday, he sent flowers to her office at Gersham-Smith with an invitation. Then he fell asleep on the sofa.

Will you join me for a date-night concert at Schermerhorn Center, Friday night? Send me a text. Type Y for Yes, N for Not now, 2 for Too soon. Nicholas

When the phone rang and he saw Rachel's number, Nicholas did his best to clear the sleep out of his voice before answering.

"Why do I need to text instead of calling?" She giggled, and the sound thrilled him.

"Because I didn't know if they would arrive while you were in a meeting or otherwise busy."

"Perfect timing," she said sweetly. "Oh! Did I wake you? I'm sorry. I'll let you sleep," she said.

"What's your answer, so I can sleep like a baby?"

"Y for yes and N for never too soon."

"I like how you spun that, Miss Knicely. I'll get tickets for this Friday's performance of Under the Streetlamp with the Nashville Symphony."

"Can't wait. Now, get your rest so you can wake me up when you're driving to work." The caring nature of her voice did indeed help him sleep like a baby.

On Friday evening, Nicholas arrived at her condo as excited as if he were going to senior prom—which he had skipped.

The symphony featured more than fifty date-night concert packages a season, which included two glasses of wine and a box of Goo Goo Chocolates. He wouldn't use the tickets for the wine, but he was sure Rachel would enjoy the candy, which was a hometown favorite.

Although he had sent her flowers earlier in the week, he didn't want to show up empty-handed. While online, Nicholas had stumbled on a website that sold personalized paperweights with a twenty-four-hour turnaround.

Nicholas knocked on her door and didn't have to wait long for her to answer. When she opened the door, his jaw dropped. Rachel's hair was brushed to one side again. The beige, or maybe it was cream or ivory—Nicholas never mastered the color chart—dress was form-fitting but modest, and the heels brought her almost eye to eye with him.

"Wow," slipped from his mouth as he handed her his gift.

"Ah. Thank you." She accepted it and invited him to come inside.

"If you're not ready, I don't mind waiting out here." He pointed to the sitting area down the hall near the elevators. Seeing the confusion on her face, Nicholas explained, "Rachel, there's no buffer between us—no Aunt Tweet or public setting. I have a good name, and so do you. I want to keep both unblemished. There's too much temptation for a couple when they are alone. Please say you understand."

She tilted her head as if she was processing it, then smiled. "I trust you, Nicholas, and though I don't fully understand the big deal, I won't give you a hard time."

"Thank you." Once she retrieved her wrap, she stepped out and locked the door. Together, they strolled to the elevator.

A true Nashvillian appreciated any genre of music—gospel, country, soul, jazz—and the symphony played it all. The concert serenaded them for hours. Although their words were few, Nicholas was aware of her every movement and the rhythm of her breathing. At the end of the night, his first date with Rachel had not disappointed his heart. It was as if they were a perfect match with the things they had in common—entertainment, food, and movies. Although there was more to explore, his heart sent signals to his brains that Rachel Knicely could be the one.

A few weeks later, while Rachel ate lunch at her desk, she confided in Jacqui on the telephone. "I don't know about the whole 'meeting the family' thing. I'm not sure where this is going."

"Ah, from what you told me, it's a casual dinner with his brother and sister-in-law. That is totally *different* from meeting his parents."

Rachel humphed. "Family is family. I don't care if it's a grandmother or godmother," she said before reaching for a bottle of water.

Jacqui laughed. "Hmm, sounds like Nicholas has you discombobulated."

Rachel rolled her eyes. "I know, right? But there's something about him that I don't want to disappoint, if that makes sense." She kept her voice low to avoid prying ears in the office.

"Yeah, it makes a lot of sense." Jacqui paused. "I believe you have finally met your equal."

Rachel spewed water and quickly grabbed napkins from her desk drawer to dab at the mess. "Girl, you are so off base. My equal. He's a minister, and I'm no saint." She rubbed her forehead. "Can't figure him out. I asked him why he hasn't invited me to church. I mean that's what you would expect from a minister, right?"

"Hmm. You've got a point. So what did he say?"

Nicholas's answer had been so matter-of-fact. "He told me Aunt Tweet had planted the seed in me, and he's here to water it, but God will shower me with whatever I need to grow."

"He's so deep, but I like that." Jacqui giggled. "No pressure, girl."

Actually, he was an open book, and Rachel's mind drifted to a conversation with him about transparency. She hadn't expected such honesty, which made him even more attractive.

"So, what are some flaws of ministers?" Rachel had asked in a teasing manner, putting aside work she had brought home.

Nicholas didn't seem offended. "You don't need me to answer that. There's breaking news whenever one of them acts contrary to how he should. I can only answer for Nicholas Adams."

She nodded. "Fair enough, so what's your vice?"

"Patience. I find myself lacking it at times," he admitted.

"I would never have guessed that. I've never met a more patient man than you, and I admire that."

He grunted. "My patience was running thin waiting for you to call, and you see how that turned out." They chuckled together, then he prompted her. "Your turn, Miss Knicely."

"You probably won't believe me."

"Test me," he urged.

"I'm not as confident as I appear to be," Rachel confessed, and surprisingly, he didn't respond as she had expected he would, saying he didn't believe her. He accepted that she had been honest with him.

That conversation had stayed with her, and by the time she had ended the call with her best friend, Rachel had made up her mind to accept Nicholas's invitation. She felt she could take him at face value.

Saturday afternoon, she was in a fashion dilemma and had her sisters on Skype, asking them what she should wear.

"This is definitely a first if you need advice from us." Kym laughed. "Let me mark this on my calendar."

Tabitha snickered too but brainstormed with her. "Sis, you got this. You've always dressed the way you feel, so what mood are you in?"

"Fun, carefree..."

"Ah, no," her sisters said in unison, shaking their heads.

"Leave the stilettoes and thigh-high dress at home," Tabitha advised. "Tone it down a little to jeans, blouse, and your hoop earrings. You'll be fine."

"O-okay." Rachel took their advice. "Got to go. Love you." She sent air kisses and signed off.

A few hours later, when Nicholas arrived, his eyes sparkled, then he smiled. "You're absolutely beautiful." He handed her a bouquet. "Fresh flowers."

She accepted, sniffed them, and walked toward the kitchen for a vase. She glanced over her shoulder. Nicholas stayed rooted at the door of the condo. "Right. I'll hurry." She would definitely have to get used to his resistance to being alone with her without a chaperone.

During the twenty-minute drive to Antioch on I-24 westbound, they chatted about family as they passed the airport and other familiar sights.

"As the youngest, I was always the spoiled brat, so tell me about your younger brother. I saw the resemblance at the NFL Draft Experience. You're a couple shades lighter." She leaned over and whispered, "For the record, you're cuter."

He released a hearty laugh, and Rachel giggled. She liked the sound of him being happy, so she angled her body to admire him and wasn't disheartened at what she saw. She doubted Nicholas could look ugly on a bad day.

His eyes twinkled when he glanced at her. "You are good for a man's ego."

Rachel blushed at his compliment. "Humph. Like you need it." Her heart warmed that he felt that way.

"Sometimes, a man doesn't know what he needs," he murmured, then cleared his throat. "I can see you being a spoiled brat." He winked. "But as the oldest, I was the example, so I had to show restraint in front of my brother. But when he wasn't around, I was as mischievous as the next boy."

"Not Minister Adams," she teased. "Let me get this straight. You and your brother are ministers, but your parents aren't involved in the ministry."

"They support the ministry, but they're in other positions at the church."

In no time, they arrived in Antioch, a mixture of old neighborhoods and new developments of big homes, town houses, and condos. Turning off Waterford Way onto a private street with ranch and two-story homes, Rachel immediately felt the charm of a close-knit community where she imagined the residents knew their neighbors and their children.

Nicholas parked in front of a two-story home that was brick on the lower level, including the steps that led to the porch. The dark window shutters matched the color of the door. The property was well kept. Nicholas came around to her side and helped her out. Together, they walked up the driveway, and before they could knock, the door opened.

"Rachel, it's nice to see you again," Karl greeted her. "This is my wife, Ava"—he pulled her to his side while two boys nudged an opening between them—"and our twins, Kory and Rory." Appearing shy, Nicholas's nephews disappeared from view, but not before she noticed how much they looked like younger versions of Nicholas. *Aw*, she thought.

Ava's eyes seemed to smile as she invited Rachel inside. The all-white decor reminded Rachel of her own condo. The only difference was Rachel's light hardwood floors, as Ava's were blackish gray. The Adamses' house was clean and neat, as if two rambunctious boys didn't reside there.

"Is she your girlfriend?" one of the twins asked their uncle.

"Maybe." Nicholas looked at Rachel and wiggled his brows. Was he challenging her to confirm or deny his answer? *Ha!* She wasn't saying anything on the matter. Their relationship was still too new for her to define.

The boy tilted his head to the side as if to decipher what "maybe" meant.

"Stop asking questions, Rory." Ava rubbed her son's curly hair. "The food is hot, so let's eat."

Nicholas took Rachel's wrap and rested it on the back of the sofa until Ava cleared her throat. "Closet, Uncle Nick."

Rachel snickered. That woman ran a tight ship and was a fellow neat freak. She loved it. Rule number one was always there is a place for everything. No wonder her home was spotless. After doing his sister-in-law's bidding, Nicholas led Rachel into a room across the foyer.

"Shall we?"

"We shall."

Rachel played along as the other twin whispered loudly, "I told you that's his girlfriend. He's holding her hand."

Not really, Rachel mused. It was a slight brush against her hand, because her skin tingled. Now she was disappointed that he *didn't* take her hand. Surprisingly, Nicholas didn't defend himself.

"Hey," Karl protested. "I hold your mother's hand," and he quickly grabbed Ava's.

"But she's Mommy, not your girlfriend," the other twin explained.

They all laughed, then Rachel offered to help Ava bring dishes to the table.

"No, you're our guest." She walked toward an open-plan kitchen with dark granite countertops and big glass balls that hung from the ceiling with bright light.

"I love your black-and-white color scheme," Rachel said as Nicholas slid in the chair behind her.

Karl grunted. "It may be my wife's color scheme, but she made me do all the work a few years ago when we gave our house a facelift."

Ava blew kisses. Soon the table was set, and Karl gave thanks and asked for blessings over their food. Although his words were sincere, she liked the way Nicholas prayed better. Boy, she was becoming biased. While enjoying an Italian meal, Rachel was amused by the lively discussion about family stories. Even the twins wanted to share a story.

The adults listened with patience, then laughed as the boys giggled. Careers were the next topic. Ava worked at Vanderbilt University Medical Center in the billing department, not far from Rachel's West End condo. Karl held down a senior accountant position at a downtown accounting firm, and she already knew where Nicholas worked, but she was impressed when he shared his accomplishments at Nissan. Finally, it was Rachel's turn.

"You build things?" Rory asked. His eyes widened. "I make stuff with my LEGOs. Wanna see?" He raced off without waiting for her answer, his twin trailing him.

"We're in trouble now," Ava said as their sons returned, dragging a box loaded down with colorful pieces of various shapes.

Karl was about to order them back in the room, but Rachel waved them off. "It's okay with me. You never know how young minds work."

That earned her cheers from the boys. She smiled at Nicholas's surprised expression when she got down on the floor and began to assist them. Yes, jeans had been a good choice. As she helped assemble the pieces, Rachel explained the importance of creating a structure that was friendly with the environment. In her element, she had not only the boys but the adults captivated too.

—

While Rachel used the bathroom, Ava dragged Nicholas into her kitchen, grinned, and danced in place. "I like her!"

Her excitement was contagious. "Me too." He blushed like a schoolboy.

"And she's gorgeous with all that beautiful hair. I'm so jealous." She frowned. "Not really." She beamed, then squinted. "Okay, maybe a little." Ava ran her fingers through her hair that she chopped off a couple of years after the twins were born. Even his brother liked Ava's new look. Loading the dishwasher, she continued her rambling in a hushed tone. "What are you going to do about her?"

"Hmm…I was thinking about keeping her." He chuckled.

She swatted him with a towel. "She's not a pet. You know what I mean." She lowered her voice and peeped over Nicholas's shoulder. "What about her commitment to God?"

"I believe it's coming. I'm watering God's harvest, and He'll cause the seed to grow."

"Good answer but watch your chemistry. Don't let your hormones get you in trouble."

"Ye of little faith. We're both taking it slow and respecting each other." But Ava was giving him a word to the wise. Rachel was extremely beautiful, and it was hard not to take notice. They were going to have to deal with resisting temptation.

"Oh, I've got faith. But Rachel has yet to receive that keeping power, so remind yourself often of yours," Ava said as if she were the big sister instead of the little sister-in-law.

"She's becoming more important to me each day." Nicholas smiled as Rachel strutted back into the living room. "Now, I better go and rescue her from your sons before they think she's their girlfriend."

Ava laughed, but Nicholas frowned. "Seriously."

Chapter 13

NICHOLAS HAD NEVER SEEN RACHEL BLUSH SO MUCH. NEITHER had he seen his mother give out so many compliments. That was what happened when he and Rachel stopped by his parents' house after leaving Karl and his family.

Vera Adams had opened the door and clicked immediately with Rachel as if they had been friends forever. His father didn't say much but gave him a nod of approval. Later that night, they shared with Nicholas that their reaction had little to do with Rachel's outer beauty but something about her warm spirit that drew them to her. That convinced him nourishing a relationship with Rachel was worth it. Now, all they needed was to be in accord spiritually.

Since the date night with the Nashville Symphony, Nicholas and Rachel had been inseparable on the weekends. They attended a pre-Memorial Day barbecue given by one of her sorority sisters, then a movie that Nicholas fought not to sleep through.

For this upcoming weekend, they'd made plans to listen to a jazz band, but because of a computer glitch that affected production, Nicholas had to work overtime.

"I'm sorry to disappoint you," he said when he called Rachel. "I was looking forward to our weekend."

"Me too." Her voice was filled with regret. "Jacqui accused me of neglecting her, so I'll hang out with her."

Nicholas had mixed emotions about single women going out on the town, even if Rachel and Jacqui were veterans of the nightlife. Yet he had no voice in what she did. He didn't expect his unofficial or maybe girlfriend to stay homebound because they couldn't do things together. He trusted Rachel but not the men whose eyes lingered on her. Nicholas had witnessed firsthand the damage those two ladies could do together to a man's hormones at the NFL Draft.

In order to spend more time with Rachel, Nicholas put in a request for a shift change from third to first. Finally, after three weeks of waiting, his request was granted. Nicholas called Rachel with the good news as soon as he received the email. "Getting off at four-thirty instead of waking up is going to take some getting used to, but I look forward to spending more time together."

"Yes! I'm doing a happy dance."

"How about we celebrate this weekend? We can do whatever you like." Nicholas was hyped. He had been on the overnight shift since he'd started. At the time, it had been no big deal. Now, he felt like he was being released into the world, and he wanted to explore it with Rachel.

"Uh-oh," Rachel began, then paused. "Jacqui and I already have plans. We've always attended the biggest All White Party in the South. Black ladies and gents never looked so good dressed in all white. Fun, food, and three DJs. Plus, the fashion show is worth the price of admission," then she paused, "but I know that's not your crowd."

No, it didn't sound appealing at all, but Nicholas wanted to be with her while he waited on God to nudge her toward the church doors. "If you invite me, I'll go."

There was dead air until Rachel said in a low voice, "I didn't think it would interest you."

"But you do. Ask me and I'll tell you," he challenged her.

"Okay." He could hear the teasing in her voice. "Will you go with me to the All White Party?" she asked sweetly, then giggled.

Stepping outside his comfort zone, Nicholas agreed. "Tell me what time to pick you up."

On Saturday evening, Nicholas arrived at Rachel's place to chauffeur her and Jacqui to Nashville Sounds Stadium.

"You look very handsome," Rachel said, flirting when she opened the door.

"And you're stunning, as expected." As she blushed, Nicholas reached for her hand and squeezed her soft fingers. He knew compliments were probably commonplace to her, but knowing his words affected Rachel made him want to stand taller than his six-two height.

"What about me?" Jacqui appeared in the doorway. "I'm feeling like the third wheel already."

"You look nice too," Nicholas said without giving Rachel's best friend any perusal.

"Rachel gets stunning, and I get nice?" Jacqui shook her head. "I've been robbed. That's all right. I'll find some guy tonight who will find me stunning."

Nicholas didn't doubt that. It wasn't that Nicholas didn't like crowds. Music City swelled with them for conventions and other attractions. Churches were filled with hundreds or thousands of them on Sunday morning. But he was on full alert around a large number of people, and the amount of alcohol being served didn't mix.

At the event, he kept Rachel by his side with their hands intertwined as they mingled and chatted with people they both recognized. Jacqui strutted off solo, garnering attention from gawkers looking for a good time.

When the disc jockey played popular songs, folks stormed the dance floor.

"Are you going to dance with me?" Rachel tugged on both his hands and gave him an alluring smile.

Nicholas resisted the temptation to succumb to her bidding and shook his head. "I'll watch from afar."

"Watch?" The surprise on her face was amusing. Clearly, Rachel wasn't used to a man telling her no. She lifted a brow. "Are you sure?"

"Definitely." He slipped his hands into his pockets. Was this a test for him or her? Nicholas wasn't sure, but this would be an interesting night.

⟶

Bummer. Rachel and Jacqui had attended the white parties since they graduated from Fisk University years ago and never missed a beat. It was one function where Rachel danced the night away. The problem was leaving Nicholas's side, and although he said he was okay with her dancing with other guys, she couldn't disrespect him like that. There wouldn't be a lot of dancing tonight. Returning to his side, they watched, laughed, and commented on some dance moves as Nicholas possessively held her hand in his.

At the end of the night, Nicholas asked if she was hungry. "How about Monell's?" he suggested.

Rachel countered with breakfast at Sun Diner in Lower Broadway, next to the Johnny Cash Museum. Tourists who wanted to relish the glory days of the Sun Records label flocked to the hot spot. The record company was where icons like Elvis Presley, Charlie Rich, and Johnny Cash got their break.

Jacqui had run into a mutual friend who'd offered to give her a ride home. Rachel and Jacqui had an arrangement whenever they went out on the town: come together, leave together, and never depart with the opposite sex. But since it was another sorority sister, Rachel didn't feel like she had broken their agreement.

At the diner, Rachel and Nicholas talked about the event and some of the outrageous outfits they saw over their meals. They laughed like silly teenagers, and it felt liberating that she didn't have to play the part of a sophisticated diva all the time.

Soon, they both decided reluctantly to call it a night. Sighing in contentment, Rachel relaxed in Nicholas's Maxima as he drove the scenic route back to her condo.

Finally, Nicholas parked in front of the Westchester. He rounded the car and assisted her. When she stepped out, he twirled her under his arm. She giggled at their silliness.

"For the record," he whispered close to her ear, "here's your last dance."

"Ah, I think it's my only one, and the best." They held hands past the reception desk, up the elevator, and to her door. She was already experiencing separation issues.

"I have a confession," she said, reaching for her keys.

"Okay. I'm listening." He frowned, not hiding his apprehension about what she was about to say.

"The next time you ask me out, I'll cancel other plans to be with you. I've always enjoyed the All White parties, but tonight"—she paused to form the words she wanted to convey—"it lost its luster compared to you. You were my highlight. Thank you for coming."

Her heartfelt words must have touched his heart, because Nicholas's breathing deepened as he searched her eyes. "Then I'll look forward to our next time." For the first time, he brushed his lips against her cheek, and she closed her eyes to savor it. When she opened them, Nicholas stepped away to leave, but she stopped him.

"Why haven't you invited me to church?"

He pivoted on his heel and stared into her eyes. "It's all about God's timing. I want you to come to God of your own free will."

"Good answer." She nodded, then challenged him in a game of tit-for-tat. "Invite me to church."

He took the bait and grinned. "Would you like to attend Sunday morning worship with me?"

"Yes!" She beamed, then slowly came down from the momentary high and pouted. It dawned on her that this Sunday, she was to serve as the mistress of ceremony in the morning at a fashion show fund-raiser. If he was disappointed with her when she told him, his face gave nothing away. "I guess you wouldn't like to come with me, would you?"

Nicholas shook his head. "Not on a Sunday. Good night." He smiled and strolled away, leaving Rachel feeling torn between honoring her commitment and wanting to spend more time with him. Entering her apartment, she resolved they would be on one accord next weekend, by any means necessary.

Chapter 14

"YOU WHAT?" KARL GAVE NICHOLAS AN INCREDULOUS LOOK THE next day after church at his brother's house. "Let me make sure I heard right. You don't like those big social events, yet you invited yourself." He shook his head and squinted. "Who are you? This is so not the MO of my minister big brother."

Even his sister-in-law gave him side-eye. "I like her, but where's the compromise? She doesn't have a desire to come to church? A couple needs God in their relationship." Ava looked disappointed.

Nicholas wasn't going to allow them to pale Rachel's image. "Oh, she's willing, but she was waiting for an invite from me." Nicholas glanced away. "Which I didn't know, or I'd have asked her day one."

"Why didn't you?" Karl frowned.

"Because God has to draw her. How many people have you and I seen who are in the church one Sunday and gone before the next service, not fully believing in the redeeming power of the Lord's salvation?"

"True." His brother nodded. "The parable of the seeds falling on all types of ground."

"Exactly." Nicholas shoved his hands in his pants pockets. "I want a woman on solid ground with deep roots. That said, I did ask her about this Sunday."

"And?" Karl and Ava asked in sync. His wife wore an eager expression.

"She has to MC at the For the Love Fashion Show fund-raiser."

"Oh yeah. They raise a lot of money for college scholarships," Ava explained. "Like you said, she's got to make her own commitment."

"Exactly. We have to meet people where they are. And she's not there yet."

"Brother-in-Law, please don't take this the wrong way. What if she turns out not to be worth the wait? I don't want to see you get hurt, because she's not ready today, tomorrow, or even next month," she said softly, concern etched on her face.

"I have time to wait."

———

Rachel never gave much thought to her social calendar except to keep it full. As a single woman, she had the right, but with her budding relationship with Nicholas, she was content with his presence. Now that he worked the day shift, they were more in sync as far as their free time.

With an open calendar, depending on Rachel's work schedule, Nicholas made the half-hour drive from his house in Smyrna a couple of times a week after work so they could enjoy walks through the park with the dogs, bike rides, or grabbing dinner at one of the neighborhood hangouts. He never called them official dates, but every moment she spent with him was special.

One Wednesday evening, Rachel left work late but decided to make a stop before heading home when she had car problems. She pulled over, got out, and immediately saw the culprit—a flat. She gritted her teeth in frustration and glanced at the traffic zooming by her. She carefully got back in her car and called AAA for assistance.

"Your estimated wait time is forty-five minutes, but it could be sooner," the dispatcher advised.

Great. She checked the time. No doubt Nicholas was on his way to Bible class, so she was at the mercy of waiting for help. Rachel sent him a text.

On the side of the road on I-24 WB. Flat tire.

Seconds later, he called. "Where?" She told him the mile marker, and he said, "I'm on my way."

"Whoa, aren't you going to Bible class?"

"Yes, but I also can't have you stranded. Once I know you're okay, I can get to church with a clear head to hear what the pastor is teaching."

Rachel's heart fluttered. The man never seemed to miss a beat with her or the Lord. Sooner than she expected, Nicholas pulled up behind her Ford and went to work removing her flat and putting on the spare, despite her protests that AAA was close.

"You think I'm going to wait for another man to take care of my lady?"

His declaration slipped off his tongue as if it was a given, and Rachel's heart fluttered. She smiled to herself and tucked the endearment away. By the time the motorist assist driver rolled up behind them, Nicholas was finished and went to speak to the man, who apologized for the delay.

Once she had exited off the highway, Nicholas followed her home, then he took off for church, leaving a lasting impression in her heart: Nicholas Adams was a keeper.

Later that night while preparing for bed, he texted her. You really should get a Nissan.

She laughed. Although the car plant was there in greater Nashville, the model never crossed her mind. She called him. For the next hour, they talked about cars and silly stuff, then she grew serious and asked about the lesson taught at Bible class. "Hold on." She grabbed Aunt Tweet's Bible and flipped through to the passage Nicholas indicated, 3 John 1. Rachel felt like a kindergartener whenever she asked him to read from the Bible.

Somehow, he seemed to breathe life into the Scripture, so for the next ten minutes, Nicholas read all fourteen verses. "The focus was on verse 2. 'Beloved, I wish above all things that thou mayest prosper and be in health, even as thy soul prospers.' The pastor was reminding us that God doesn't want to withhold blessings from us, but in order to live life to the fullest, it has to be balanced: physical, mental, and spiritual."

"Interesting," Rachel said. "Thank you for the insight. Without reading this verse, I was somehow convinced that God didn't want us to have materialistic treasures."

"To the contrary," he explained. "From Genesis on, God has always provided for His people. And the rich and poor offered a portion of their substance to the Lord."

"I don't know why I always looked at church as a straitjacket of a place full of 'can't dos.'"

"Woman, you have so much to learn," Nicholas said with mirth in his voice.

"I couldn't ask for a better teacher." She beamed.

"I'm honored, Rachel, that you have so much confidence in me, and I give God the praise for that, so maybe you'll accept my invitation to hear me preach on Sunday."

"Preach! When were you going to tell me?" Rachel screamed in excitement. "Of course, I'll be there. I'm not sure about the sitting-in-front-row thing, like my parents used to do to show support, but I want to be there."

"Although it's my invitation, I'm praying that God has a special message for you. Maybe Jacqui can come with you."

"Can't make a promise on that one, but I'll try." After they said their goodbyes, Rachel was grinning. "Aunt Tweet, did you know this was going to happen?" She chuckled to herself as she said her prayers, then climbed into bed.

A few days later, Rachel and Jacqui met for lunch downtown. "Hey, I know you're going out tonight."

"Yeah, and without you," Jacqui said in an accusatory tone, then pouted before she perked up again. "I'm not mad at you, but I never suspected you would fall for a church guy."

Rachel glanced out the window by their table, then turned back to her friend and shrugged. "Me either, but I don't have any regrets." She tapped a manicured nail on their table. "I was planning to call you, but since we're having lunch… Nicholas is preaching this weekend, and I'm hoping you will come with me."

Jacqui groaned and dabbed at her lips. Ladies never wiped their mouths, she always said. "Sundays are meant as a day of rest."

"Yes, they are, and I'm sure you're going to need it after staying out all night, but I don't want to go alone."

"The things I do to prove my friendship," Jacqui huffed. "You'll owe me."

Rachel beamed. "You know I've got you covered. Whatever it is."

On Sunday morning, Nicholas sent a text as Rachel stepped out of the shower.

I hope to see you soon.

You will, she texted back with a smile.

She slipped on a mustard-colored, short-sleeved dress that was fitted to her waist, then flared past her knees. It complemented her figure while keeping it modest. She wore minimal makeup and jewelry to offset her attire, then sent a selfie to Tabitha with the caption: Church flow. Her sister would be proud.

Her sister called immediately. "Yes, you won't regret it. I went to appease Aunt Tweet. If it wasn't for her, I don't think I would've surrendered to Jesus. That goes for Marcus too. I needed the inspiration. I'm glad Nicholas is leading you in that direction," her sister said.

"I don't know what I have to surrender. I treat folks the way they treat me."

"Ah, you have that twisted." Tabitha laughed. "Get ready and go. I'll quiz you later."

"Right. If I don't beat Jacqui to church, I'll never hear the end of it. Bye."

Believers Temple Church was twenty minutes away in Brentwood, and the drive there was smooth. Seconds after arriving, Jacqui texted her. Here. Where are you?

Parking. Meet you in the lobby. Rachel hurried across the lot to the entrance, where she saw Jacqui craning her neck to search for her.

"You look cute." Her friend greeted her with a hug.

"And you look tired."

"Humph. Somebody woke me up. All I've got to say is Nicholas better not put me back to sleep."

Rachel hushed her. "Lower your voice. I think we're supposed to call him 'Minister' here."

"Oh...okay." Jacqui looked around. "I guess we need to find somewhere to sit."

An usher appeared as if summoned and led them into a sanctuary that could accommodate a thousand plus easily. He directed them to seats midway between the front and back.

"You see Nicholas?" Rachel leaned over and whispered.

"Yep. He's looking right at you." Jacqui pointed toward the group of chairs on either side of the pulpit.

How could he find her in a crowd of folks? Rachel waved. Nicholas responded with a slight nod as the praise singers had most of the congregation on their feet, singing along with gusto.

But she was eager to hear from the soft-spoken man with a gentle spirit and easy smile. Soon enough, the pastor made his way to the podium. "As you know, our church has many capable ministers, and during the summer, one Sunday each month, I want us to hear from one of them." He glanced over his shoulder and motioned for Nicholas to join him. "Minister Nicholas Adams is this morning's speaker."

Applause and "amens" circulated within the sanctuary. Rachel clapped enthusiastically as if Nicholas could hear her.

"Praise the Lord." Nicholas didn't waste any time with preliminaries and directed them to Lamentations 3:22–23. "God's compassion and faithfulness are unmatched."

Rachel sat in astonishment as his voice seemed to roar like a lion.

Nicholas cited another Scripture. "Jeremiah 31 says, 'I have loved thee with an everlasting love: therefore with loving-kindness have I drawn thee.' What's keeping you from coming to Him? *Shh.*" He placed a finger on his lips. "God is calling you. Do you hear Him? Listen to His voice…"

For the next half hour, Nicholas preached with authority, and Rachel soaked up every word, wondering if he was talking to her or the audience in general. Nicholas was so compelling that she was losing the argument she had been telling herself over the years that God wasn't concerned with the nuances of her life.

The music was soul stirring, and the energy of worship was electrifying. All the years that she thought a tall guy with broad shoulders or a handsome face and stable income was sexy, she had been so wrong. It was a man of God who could take command of the Scriptures like she had never heard before. No wonder the women within her sight were hanging on Nicholas's every word.

Let God draw you, not man. Rachel shivered. Was God speaking to her? She patted her chest and looked around, but no one was paying any attention to her.

"What do you think?" Rachel whispered to Jacqui.

"About what?" Jacqui seemed clueless.

"Committing to the salvation walk with God," Rachel explained.

"You're thinking about making a lifestyle change?" Jacqui's eyes widened in surprise.

"I don't see how I can say no after hearing that message." Rachel gnawed on her lips. What was really stopping her from making a commitment? She felt almost persuaded—almost. She was teetering. The message was powerful.

After the benediction, Rachel wanted to share her thoughts with Nicholas. However, there was a steady stream of folks flocking to speak with him.

Jacqui whispered, "Girl, if we don't jump that line, we'll be waiting a long time."

"You're right," Rachel said but continued at a snail's pace behind the others. When she came face-to-face with the powerhouse preacher who seemed larger than life on the pulpit, Rachel froze, trying to reconcile him with the sweet soul who drew her.

Nicholas took her hand as she had seen him do with the others, but she doubted he gave them a gentle squeeze that caused their hearts to flutter. The energy exchange between them made her want to pull away, but his grip tightened. They stared at each other until Jacqui cleared her throat.

"Did God speak to you this morning?" Nicholas asked.

"Yes." Rachel nodded, then she blurted out, "I'm ready."

"For?" He lifted a brow, and a smile tugged at the corners of his lips.

"You're serious?" Jacqui echoed behind her.

Rachel swallowed. "I can't tell God no. I want what you have with the Lord."

The look in Nicholas's eyes seemed to connect with her soul.

"Everything is about to change in your life, including things between us," he said.

Rachel felt that too. The anticipation made her heart leap. She was ready for a new chapter in her life.

Chapter 15

"You win the lottery or something?" Jackson Clark, one of Rachel's teammates, commented as they discussed the next phase of the park project.

Before she could answer, Patti popped her head into the conference room, grinning. "Hey, these just arrived for you." She lifted flowers sealed with white paper from a local florist.

"Whoa." Rachel jumped up. "I'll take them." Then she looked back at her coworker. "Be right back." She hurried to her office and quickly peeled away the wrapping. The arrangement was a colorful mixture of flowers in a thick, square glass vase. She reached for the envelope and slipped out the card. *Celebrating your new life in Jesus, 2 Corinthians 5:17.*

Closing her eyes, Rachel grinned and held the card close to her chest. She'd wait to look up that Scripture. She positioned the arrangement at the preferred angle on her desk, then slipped the card into her purse before returning to the conference room, where Jackson was twirling in his chair with mischief in his eyes.

"Hmm. Someone had a great weekend. No wonder you're shining bright as the sun."

Rachel shrugged and sat at the table again in front of her laptop. "My whole life changed yesterday at church. I surrendered my will to the Lord."

Jackson stopped twirling and frowned. "Why? Are you dying or something?"

"Nope," she said matter-of-factly. "I'm very much alive, but I realized that I need Team Jesus in my life. I think I made a good choice."

"Interesting. Church." Jackson grunted and shook his head in amusement. "My life is fine the way it is. No reason for me to make any changes. If you start having prayer meetings and stuff up in here, I'm moving my office."

Rachel chuckled. Jackson didn't, so they got back to business.

Throughout the morning, Rachel's thoughts drifted to what her colleague had said. It seemed odd that her life change wouldn't be well received, but then again, she could relate. Church was never a necessity in her life, but after Nicholas's sermon, Rachel felt she didn't have anything to lose. Actually, her mindset toward God had started changing before the morning message. When? She didn't know.

Finally, she took a late lunch. Having a taste for veggies, she headed to Gino's for a harvest salad. While walking down Second Avenue, she texted Nicholas. Can you talk?

His response was an immediate phone call. "Hi."

Rachel slowed her steps to enjoy the sound of his voice. "Thank you for the flowers this morning...and the Scripture! Do you know it by heart to recite it?"

Nicholas chuckled. "'Therefore if any man be in Christ, he is a new creature: old things are passed away; behold, all things are become new.'"

"I like knowing that. Jacqui is still confused that I wanted a change. One of my coworkers thought I was dying, but when I called my sister, Tabitha and Marcus were ecstatic. Talk about a mixed bag of responses... So when is the next church service?"

"Wednesday Bible class."

"I'll be there." She was eager to extract whatever she could from the Scriptures. "It's amazing—I've been around a Bible all my life but never took the time to study what's in it. I've basically done surface reads, so I'm looking forward to Bible class."

Two days later, Rachel made sure she left work on time to change out of her business suit into something casual for Bible study. Ever since the past Sunday, she'd had a spiritual thirst that could drain a lake. Just as she used to stay up all night to read a good novel, she had the same fascination with passages in the Bible that she'd barely thought about before.

"Was it like this for you too?" she asked Tabitha as she was about to walk out her door.

"I guess so. God drew me with the message about rest—and I needed it mentally and physically. Jesus said to cast my burdens on Him, and I uploaded them. Whew."

"I see the Lord knows how to customize His messages." Rachel liked that. They chatted a few more minutes before she had to end the call so she could drive to church, a twenty-plus-minute drive on a good day.

She rolled with the flow of traffic and turned into the church parking lot, arriving on time. As Rachel searched for an empty space, she spied Nicholas stepping out of his Maxima. Waving, her heart fluttered, and she grinned, pulling into a space a few cars away. He seemed to stand at attention as he waited for her to park, then he swaggered to her driver's side and helped her out.

"Hi," he greeted her with warmth and awe. "You're trying to beat me to church now?" he teased.

She giggled. "Can I help it if I don't want to be late?" They strolled leisurely across the parking lot to the front entrance. "Nicholas, are you sitting in the pulpit?"

"Nope, it's Bible class, so I'm a student in the audience. Come on. I'll show you where I sit." He lowered his voice. "It doesn't matter to me, but remember to call me 'Minister' at church. Otherwise, folks might think you're not respecting my position. Silly, huh?"

"You'll always have my respect, Minister Adams." She smiled and followed him to his seat.

Nicholas felt almost—and it was a good almost—as if he was competing with the Lord for Rachel's attention. The feelings he had developed for her only deepened as he watched her highlight passages in 2 Timothy 3 on her tablet. Occasionally, she would tilt her head to ponder what the pastor had said.

She could probably tell him all that he was missing from the lesson because he was distracted watching her. He chuckled to himself. That night, the two had an hour-long post-Bible class discussion over the phone. Rachel was truly the desire of his heart.

Friday evening, Karl and Ava invited them to a game night to play Sequence—a family-friendly board game that the twins enjoyed. It didn't go unnoticed that his nephews vied for Rachel's attention when Nicholas wanted her all to himself. Rachel didn't disappoint the boys as she smothered them with hugs. Jealous or not, Nicholas could see Miss Knicely fit easily into his life.

Saturday was a comfortable June day, with temperatures in the low eighties. Perfect. The couple had some one-on-one time as they strolled through the Gulch with her dogs and admired the street art on the buildings.

"I'm in awe of this artist's mural," Rachel said as they noticed tourists pose between a pair of twenty-foot-high angel wings on Eleventh Avenue South.

Nicholas admired the artwork. "I think I read somewhere that Kelsey Montague flew into Nashville and used a boom lift to work on the masterpiece, using sixty paint pens. Incredible."

"Come on." Rachel's eyes sparkled, and she grabbed his arm. "Let's play tourist, too, and take a selfie in front of it."

Grinning at her silliness, he agreed. After a couple of poses, someone offered to take their picture. When he looked at the photo, he saved it as his wallpaper, and Nicholas imagined them actually sharing wings.

As they resumed their stroll, Rachel continued to rave about Kelsey's craft, so Nicholas turned the tables on her. "You know what I think is more impressive?"

She frowned and shook her head.

"You, a smart, talented, and creative engineer. You talk to my nephews about building stuff. Let me play tourist in your world."

"Awww. That's sweet. Thank you." They walked back to her apartment and put the pooches up, then took off in his car. As they cruised through the city, Rachel pointed out buildings that had historic black significance that either Nicholas didn't know or had forgotten about.

"Pull over," Rachel said, so he did and parked in front of the former Pearl High School. "This was the 'for-blacks-only'"—she made air quotations with her fingers—"school during the Jim Crow era. Nashville is steep in black history from my superb education that Fisk U and other HBCU schools imparted on their students in the Music City to legends. Take, for example, the McKissack brothers, who founded an architectural firm and built several impressive structures throughout Nashville. They definitely left a legacy."

"For someone who didn't grow up here, you sure know a lot about our history."

"There's a reason for that." She angled herself in the car. "Have you ever felt like things that happen in your life are a series of dots where one event connects you to another?"

Nicholas shrugged. "I never really thought of it that way, but I do know that God orders our steps."

She nodded. "I think about Aunt Tweet and how she carved out a path for me and my sisters to follow. She attended a historically black college in West Virginia and drilled into my head and my sisters' that education was key. She was my idol growing up, and I wanted to be just like her—smart."

"Which you are." He squeezed her hand.

"Thank you." She blushed, lowering her long lashes.

"Plus, you're beautiful, which I know you hear all the time." Nicholas brought her hand to his lips. "You're all of that, Miss Knicely."

"Coming from you…" She paused, looked him in the eyes, and placed her right hand over her heart. "I feel it's more than empty words."

Touched, Nicholas was choked with emotions that he made her feel that way.

"You're distracting me," she said, "you know that? I'm supposed to be *your* tour guide." She smiled. "What I don't have to tell you is Nashville played a major part in the civil rights struggle."

"That much my parents ingrained into Karl's and my heads before we started school. They participated in the Nashville sit-ins in the sixties at the Woolworth counters reserved for whites only."

"My inspiration for pursuing engineering came from the McKissack brothers: Moses and Calvin. Calvin attended Fisk and later built a dorm there, then designed libraries on other college campuses. When I came to

Nashville for college, I wasn't sure of my major. After learning about how the brothers were refused entry into college and were forced to receive their architecture degrees through correspondence courses, I made my decision. They were among the first registered architects, even though the state didn't want to issue them a license." She sighed. "After hearing their story, I wanted to leave my stamp on buildings and parks and…"

"And me." Nicholas waved his hand in the air and looked up. "Lord, thank You for this incredible woman You placed in my life."

She laughed. "You're the man." She waggled a finger at him. "I got some side-eyes from women at Bible class who wanted your attention."

"I choose you." He winked. "And I feel like God is sharing you with me, and I want to treat you with the utmost care." She was speechless. Surely, others had treated her the same. He didn't want to ask about her past, so he continued, "Since you have a passion for history, how about dinner at Woolworth on Fifth?"

"I'm learning more about my passion every day," Rachel said and glanced out the window as he drove off for their impromptu dinner date.

Chapter 16

"DON'T TAKE THIS THE WRONG WAY, BUT NICHOLAS IS RUINING our friendship," Jacqui teased over the phone.

Rachel laughed. She had spoken with him not long ago. "Jealous," she teased back.

"Yes. I want one of them, minus the minister part."

"He's a package deal," Rachel said, staring out her office window overlooking Broadway. This part of downtown was the pulse of the city. "So how is Nicholas ruining our friendship?"

"Girl, please. You cancelled the yearly Fourth of July bash you always throw from your condo."

"Yeah. Since this year is supposed to be the biggest celebration, Nicholas is taking me on a cruise to watch the fireworks between the Shelby and Woodland Bridges."

"See! That is why I need me a Nicholas clone. How romantic. You two have been dating for two months now."

"Actually, two months and a week." Rachel giggled. "I want to spend as much time with Nicholas as I can. I really, really like him."

"I knew you would as soon as you opened your eyes."

"You were right, Jac, so thanks for understanding that I want to spend the holiday with him." She felt a bit guilty for ruining their routine. "Somebody must be throwing a pool party or a party to watch the fireworks."

"I know of a couple, but it's not the same without my girl." She paused. "But I'm happy for you. He really cares about you."

"He does," Rachel agreed softly, then checked the time. "Ooh. I have a meeting in twenty minutes. Got to go. Love you. Bye."

Late that afternoon, when Rachel opened her door for Nicholas, she sucked in her breath. Whether in a suit and tie or polo and jeans, he was always handsome. He looked patriotic in a red, white, and blue polo. "Ready? The General Jackson Showboat boards at five, and we don't want them to sail off without us."

After grabbing her shawl and purse, they were off and, within minutes, maneuvering through the crowds to get to the riverfront.

Rachel was glad Nicholas suggested a cruise to admire the fireworks instead of watching from the Shelby Street Pedestrian Bridge. Renamed the John Seigenthaler Pedestrian Bridge, it spanned the Cumberland River from East Nashville to downtown and was one of the longest pedestrian bridges in the world.

She respected the architectural and aesthetic design of the truss. It was no wonder it had been listed on the National Register of Historic Places. The structure had been set for demolition because it was no longer safe for cars, but there had been an uproar about erasing history because of its significance in the civil rights movement.

Years before she'd even thought about her current occupation, Gersham-Smith had lost the bid to restore the structure. Still, the winning company's architectural restoration was magnificent, with an impressive lighting system that made it perfect for a romantic evening stroll with the downtown skyline as a backdrop. Maybe after all the Fourth of July mad rush, she and Nicholas would take a stroll there on the weekend with her dogs.

"It was a good thing we left early," Rachel said, frazzled, but once the showboat set sail, all the hassle was forgotten as they enjoyed a sumptuous meal on the second floor of the Victorian Theater. Perfectly timed, the live performance on the boat ended at the first sound of the firework explosion.

Standing on the outside deck with Nicholas beside her, a happiness that she had never felt before in her life filled Rachel's being. *It is the perfect night to fall in love*, she thought with every explosion of color. Was she falling?

"Hey," Nicholas whispered in her ear and caused her to turn and stare into his eyes.

"If you're ready, I want us to become an official couple." He didn't blink.

Rachel smiled and lowered her lashes before looking at him again. "I thought we already were."

"Me too, but I didn't want to assume." Nicholas gave her a lopsided grin. "Then in that case, carry on." He turned back to the fireworks as they shared a laugh.

———

"Congratulations" read the subject line in an office email a few weeks later. "Gersham-Smith has been awarded a multimillion-dollar contract by the county government in Lexington, Kentucky…"

By the time Rachel finished reading the lengthy memo, her boss was standing outside her door. "Good news, huh?" He grinned, tilting his head toward her monitor.

"Excellent."

"You're a more than superb structural engineer. When it comes to public spaces, your think-outside-the-box innovation helps to bring our clients' visions to life. I'd like you to use your expertise to assist the team in Lexington on the Town Branch Greenway in a consultation capacity only. I have confidence in the team leader there, but the design the client chose is similar to our Lentz Public Health Center project that we completed, so you can save them from some missteps. As you know, it's going to require traveling for the next year, but this could mean a regional director position for you, depending how you assist the team."

A regional director position was not only more money but a coveted spot for a person of color. Rachel didn't have to think twice. "When do I need to leave?"

"Next Monday. Plan for a week to get your bearings. Lexington is going to be your second home during the start of this project."

"Got it." This was her opportunity to shine in everything she did. Like the McKissack brothers, Rachel wanted to leave her mark in the history books. While in her reverie, Nicholas texted her.

Busy? Want you to know I'm thinking about you, miss you,
and praying for you.

Rachel paused and reflected on his words. She loved everything
about this man. She blinked, then reality set in. How would she bear
being away from him? Thank you for all! I got news about my job. Why
don't you take your girlfriend out to dinner tonight and I'll tell you?

Then it's a Tuesday night date.

Hours later, Rachel had showered, dressed in jeans and a girly top,
then slipped into her high heels to accent her look. When Nicholas
knocked at the door, she greeted him with a smile when she wanted a
hug. She understood his reason for minimizing public affection to hand
holding. She did get a kiss on the cheek. Rachel respected the restraint,
but it didn't mean she liked it; however, she didn't want to taint his name
with scandal. Besides, who would see them steal a kiss or two?

"You are gorgeous, you know that, woman?" His nostrils flared in
appreciation. Nicholas took a deep breath and turned away, exhaling.

Her heart always fluttered when Nicholas said it. She'd told him the
truth, that she had heard the compliments the moment she hit puberty,
and she learned to sway her hips just to make the guys freeze midsentence. *Natural beauty*, Aunt Tweet used to say. None of that mattered
anymore. She had captured Nicholas's heart without trying. His praise
always included her intelligence and passion. He made her feel beautiful
inside and out, like her inner beauty was visible only to him.

Nicholas chose a more upscale restaurant than she would have
thought of for a midweek dinner. They slid into a booth facing each
other. After placing their orders, he reached across the table for her
hands. She welcomed his touch.

"So, Miss Knicely, what's this news?"

She wiggled in her seat at his intense stare. He always gave her his
undivided attention whenever they were together. "I've been picked to
work on an impressive project."

He grinned. "Congratulations!"

Bowing her head, she fumbled with her fingers. How could she be excited and bummed at the same time? "It's in Lexington." Rachel looked up to gauge his reaction.

Stunned, his jaw dropped. "As in Kentucky?" His words came out slowly.

"Yes." She nodded, then gave him the details. "For the next year, I'll be traveling a lot. I'll be gone for days, weeks, or even a month at a time."

Disappointment flashed across his face, and her heart cracked when she saw his shoulders slump.

"I leave on Monday, and I'll be gone for a week at first, but as we get into the details, my colleagues and I could work long days and a lot of weeks."

Huffing, Nicholas glanced around the restaurant and didn't say anything, making Rachel wonder about his thoughts. Finally, he gazed into her eyes again, then exhaled. "I finally fall in love, and my lady is testing me with a long-distance relationship…" He rambled on as if he hadn't said anything earth-shattering.

"Rewind." Rachel tilted her head as he gave her a lopsided smile. "I'm going out of town, and you, Nicholas Adams, now profess that you love me?" She cherished the moment. Yes, their feelings were strong and they were headed in that direction, but for Nicholas to declare it first made her surrender her heart too.

"I love you back," she heard herself whisper in awe. Rachel never imagined she would say that to a man who was a minister.

His stunned expression was almost amusing—maybe he thought she would never have uttered it too. Time seemed to slow so they could revel in their emotions.

"You love me," he repeated in awe as their server placed their salads before them. He held his breath until the man left their table. "I had acknowledged my feelings for a while and again when we were on that cruise. Although it felt natural to say, I struggled with maybe it was too soon, then as my heart beat stronger whenever you were near, I knew I couldn't keep it locked in." He looked away sheepishly, like a bashful little boy, before he seemed to regain his resolve. "I'd planned to tell you the next time we went to dinner."

She leaned forward. "Well, this is our *next time*, so tell me again, then bless our meal."

He met her halfway. "Woman, you are everything I want and more. I love you, Rachel Knicely." Nicholas bowed his head and clasped her hands. "Father God, in the name of Jesus, thank You for this woman and this moment. I ask that You bless us to grow in You and our meal. Give us the resources to bless others who might be hungry. In Jesus's name. Amen."

"Amen," she whispered and began to fork up her lettuce. "You're the only man I've met who makes me feel like you care about me beyond what you see," she choked out and patted her chest.

"Make no mistake, Miss Rachel, you are hot! But you're so much more than those dainty dimples, sultry voice, long lashes, clear brown eyes, pleasing proportions, silky long hair, and confident personality. Should I go on?" He winked.

Rachel shook her head. He had said more than enough.

———

Nicholas was blown away by Rachel's declaration. His heart was still trying to regulate its rhythm. "All the men you've met in the past have looked at you and seen only what their eyes could behold, but I have a vantage point," Nicholas said in a deep, serious voice.

She squinted and squeezed her lips together until a dimple appeared. Her eyes sparkled. "And that is?"

"The source of your beauty—your heart. After your heart captured me, then your free spirit did, and that opened my eyes to see the beauty the Lord gave you."

Rachel was silent. "You, Nicholas, are deep. I've never let a man see me when I'm not at my best physically. My aunt drilled into me that it's unattractive. You saw me at my worst—physically, mentally, and spiritually…" Her words trailed off.

"Babe." Her words humbled Nicholas. "You've always been beautiful to me, but as Christians, we are charged by God to do double duty. We're supposed to be aware as we walk in this world but have spiritual eyes to discern."

"I thought you were coming to minister to my aunt…"

"And you. You were the one who needed healing and comfort. Your aunt was already confident in her faith and where she was going." He was quiet. "I said all that to say this. I love you, and I'm interested in building a relationship that includes everything you need in a mate—a friend, confidant, and…more." He never wanted this night to end, but it did, three hours later.

Chapter 17

WHEW. WHEN NICHOLAS ESCORTED RACHEL TO HER DOOR, SHE was a ball of crazy emotions. From the look on his face, he seemed as flustered as she was. Good, they were in this together. She wanted a long hug and kiss.

"I love you so much. Trust me, after tonight, our attraction will grow stronger, so we have to rein in our hormones to honor our Christian walk." He paused to glance down at their intertwined hands. "Intimacy between married people is worth the wait." Staring into her eyes, he brought her hands to his mouth and brushed his lips against them. She shivered and exhaled.

"Good night." Stepping back, Nicholas waited for her to go inside.

When she closed her door, Rachel broke out in a sweat. *Whew.* What was her blood pressure? She had a machine around here somewhere from when Aunt Tweet was with her, but she realized she had packed it up.

Sweet Pepper and Shelby came galloping from around the corner. She squatted to scratch their ears. "He loves me." Rachel was about to cry. Men had told her they loved her before, and it sounded good, but this was like a trumpet vibrating her core. She had never felt like this— never. "Thank you!" Rachel lifted her eyes toward heaven.

Minutes later, she put the leashes on her pooches' collars for a quick trip to the rooftop doggie park. As she sat on the bench watching her pets frolic with other hounds, reality set in again, and she called Jacqui. "Nicholas is in love with me!"

Jacqui screamed in Rachel's ear. "My favorite color is coral. I prefer a June wedding. Definitely white roses, and please make sure his grooms-men are bachelors."

Was her best friend planning her wedding? Rachel laughed, and it seemed to unravel her pent-up energy. "We are so not there yet, but I don't know what to do."

"Back up. When did you ever need my advice concerning men?" Her friend chuckled.

"I mean, this is crazy," Rachel said without responding to her friend's query. She shut her eyes tight and wanted to scream but restrained herself. "I've never felt this way ever! I'm scared but happy. I feel like I'm going to faint or explode like fireworks." Rachel couldn't stop rambling. "This is a life-changing moment."

"Yep." Jacqui giggled. "Have you told your sisters?"

"Oh." Rachel patted her cheek as if to wake herself from a dream. "I haven't! I've got to go and call them." Her heart pounded with excitement.

"Okay, but make sure you let them know I knew first. Bye."

—

Nicholas counted down the days before Rachel's departure to Kentucky. How could he go from being full of bliss because he'd found the love of his life to being sorrowful in a matter of days?

Rachel explained she would only be gone one week—at first. As the project progressed, she could be away weeks at a time, even more than a month.

He understood her work commitment—she'd worked hard to achieve her goals. Nicholas got that, but his heart would long for her. Until she left, he wanted to spend as much time together as their schedules would allow, which explained why he drove past his church to pick up Rachel for Bible class Wednesday evening, then doubled back to Believers Temple Church. Every moment counted.

Nicholas had everything planned out. On Thursday, they would go to the movies. Friday would be fun night at Donelson Plaza Strike and Spare Bowl, then on Saturday morning, Nicholas would slip into his role as Minister Adams to visit and pray with those on the sick list.

Since three church members were in St. Thomas Midtown Hospital, Nicholas could make those rounds easier. One was an elderly mother with a fractured hip. The next was a young man who had been in a car accident.

The last stop was to Jason Kimbro's room. Doctors had given the fifty-year-old father of three teenage boys months to live. His health was deteriorating fast with stomach cancer. The end-stage-of-life visits were always bittersweet. Nicholas thought this particular man was too young to leave his family. Mr. Kimbro mustered a smile when Nicholas entered the room.

"Minister Adams." He extended his hand weakly to shake. Nicholas took it, then sat in a nearby chair. "I'm waiting to take my flight. Can't go until Jesus calls me."

Nicholas nodded in agreement.

"It's going to be a great day, Minister Adams!" He closed his eyes with a slight smile on his face. "Tired now."

Nicholas opened his Bible and read from 1 Thessalonians 4:16–18, then he prayed softly. When he stood to leave, he looked back, wondering how much longer the man would linger.

On his way to the car, he took a series of deep breaths in order to revive himself from the dire moments, then filled his mind with inspiring Scriptures and happy thoughts. He texted Rachel. Still out shopping?

Yep. If you're finished with God's work, come join Jacqui and me.

He called her. Upon hearing her voice, happiness instantly filled his being. "I'll feel like a third wheel."

"Jacqui knows I'm going to miss you like crazy."

Nicholas sighed. "Me too."

"How about I ditch my best friend, and we'll grab something to eat?"

"Hey, I heard that," Jacqui said nearby and giggled. "Hi, Nicholas."

All three laughed before he declined her offer and decided to drive by his brother's house. Hopefully, his sister-in-law had cooked something good, and he could let his twin nephews wear him out. If not, his mother always had a pot warming on the stove.

Ava opened the door and teased, looking over his shoulder, "Hmm. Where's your Rachel?"

"Hanging out with her girlfriend." He walked in and kissed her cheek.

After a couple of hours of visiting, he did stop by his parents' house but with a full belly. Surprisingly, they were at home and not away at a church-related function.

His mother had the same question as Ava. "Rachel's not with you?"

"Nope." He gave her a hug and entered.

"And you look like a lost puppy." His dad chuckled and stood from his spot in the recliner to shake Nicholas's hand.

Nicholas took a seat and stretched out his legs. "I know we just met in the spring, but it seems like she's always been a part of me."

His mother's eyes twinkled. "That's called your other half. You two look so cute together at Bible class, and she seems like she really loves the Lord…and you."

"I'm going to marry her," Nicholas said matter-of-factly.

"We both knew that, Son," his dad said. "But give her time to grow in the Lord and have her own testimonies about His goodness."

Reading between the lines, Nicholas got his father's message: Don't rush it.

Sunday morning, Nicholas picked Rachel up for church. The sermon, Worship Will Take You Places, taken from Matthew 8, stirred the congregation. After service, they headed to a buffet. With their plates overflowing, they dug in after Nicholas gave thanks and asked for blessings over their meal. Their conversation bounced from message to work to her upcoming trip and the funny things their families did. Discussing the sermon and Bible class highlights had become commonplace after church.

"Pastor's message was so deep," Rachel said. "When I reflect on my past, it seems like I was always begging God for something—most recently, Aunt Tweet's health."

"We're all guilty of that." Nicholas nodded. "That leper in the sermon was smart enough to know that if it wasn't in God's will, no healing was coming his way."

Night came too soon, and Nicholas finally took Rachel home. As he escorted her to the door, he whispered, "I'm going to miss you, lady, but I'll be here by 7:00 a.m. to take you to the airport."

"Really?" Rachel didn't hide the surprise in her beautiful brown eyes. "I was going to get an Uber. Plus, you have to work."

"I am *your* Uber, so I'll go in late."

Rachel reached up and rubbed his thin beard, then exhaled and stepped back. "Pray for me before you leave."

"Of course." Taking her hands, he bowed his head. After he whispered, "Amen," he reluctantly walked away. Once inside the elevator, Nicholas exhaled. Maybe a little distance between them would tame his hormones. Telling a woman he loved her had him thinking about being a husband and father. But his father had reminded him to let Rachel walk with the Lord and give her own testimonies before moving to another phase in their relationship.

The next morning, Nicholas held in his emotions as he walked into the airport with Rachel and checked her luggage. "Call me when you get there, be safe, and I'll text you Scriptures."

He couldn't refrain from engulfing her in a hug, so he indulged ever so briefly, then released her. This work assignment was going to be either torture or a blessing for both of them.

Chapter 18

ONCE RACHEL ARRIVED AT THE LEXINGTON LOCATION OF Gersham-Smith & Partners, there was no time to breathe. The $1.7 million project would take a village to pull off on deadline. Her firm was selected to design and implement a multifunction complex that would promote a "share the road" campaign with a downtown greenway where pedestrians, cyclists, and motorists could all travel, creating a business epicenter.

She was only acting in a consulting capacity with the senior transportation engineer, who would lead the project. The first thing she did was review the proposal, which included sketches, then compared it with the related project in Nashville and other projects they had developed in other cities. There were some similarities, but the differences were tricky.

The dilemma was how to incorporate green space that wouldn't interfere with traffic flow while promoting foot traffic downtown. It turned out to be a day of tweaks.

When she got back to the hotel, she ordered room service and checked in with Jacqui, her sisters, and then Nicholas, who was at the top of her list mentally.

"Hey." His deep voice seemed to flow smoothly in her ears. "How was your day?"

"Exhausting." She proceeded to tell him about the project and the challenges the company faced. "Personally, I think the budget is too thin and the timeframe too tight for dealing with antiquated infrastructures." When she finished, he asked questions to show her he was listening.

"Even though you're not here physically, your presence is felt everywhere. I saw your company's name posted at a job site near our Nissan plant at Topre Corporation about an expansion."

"Yep. We're everywhere, which is why I love to work here. I consider myself blessed with a capital *B*."

"Amen. So I know you just got there, but when are you coming home?"

Rachel smiled and imagined he had a pout that mimicked his nephews'. It felt good to be missed and not only by family. "Sometime Friday, maybe late evening."

"I'll check your flight and be there to pick you up."

Before ending the call, they read some Bible passages and prayed. Everything was all right in her world. She had the right job, man, and God.

———

True to his word, Nicholas was waiting with balloons, flowers, and a sign that read: *Welcome home*. Once his eyes tracked her leaving the terminal, he quickened his steps to meet her.

Rachel's response was exactly what Nicholas had hoped: happy and seemingly embarrassed from the attention she was getting.

"What a homecoming," she whispered and giggled as she accepted Nicholas's brief welcome-home hug and his gifts. "You are seriously making Jacqui look bad. I get a curbside pickup with her and a drop-off in front of the Westchester, and a wave as an afterthought."

They shared a laugh, then Nicholas told her to tell Jacqui she had been officially relieved of her duties. "I'll take it from here."

"I think she'll be happy to hear that," Rachel said as a stranger approached them.

"Would you like me to take your picture?" The woman was elderly, but she had a warm sparkle in her eyes.

"Yes," Nicholas said and showed the woman how to use the camera app on his phone.

"You two make a cute couple," the impromptu photographer said. "Where are you coming from?"

"Lexington, Kentucky, for work. I've only been gone a week," Rachel said, blushing and shaking her head.

"Don't complain, honey." Another woman, not as old, joined them. "Let that young man love on you." She gave him and Rachel a knowing nod.

"Exactly." Nicholas agreed and took his phone, and together all four of them admired the photo. "I'm so glad you're back." Linking his fingers through hers, they rode the escalator down to the baggage area.

"Hungry?" he asked.

"Yes and tired. It's been an intense week, but those nightly Scripture readings lulled me to sleep."

When Rachel spotted her luggage, Nicholas retrieved it, thinking, *Lord, I asked You for a woman who loves You more than the notion of going to church. I think I've found her.* He glanced over his shoulder, and Rachel smiled at him as his reward.

Chapter 19

Nicholas Adams was going to propose to Rachel Knicely. She was the perfect woman for him. He would never be complete without her. Of course, the many women at church had tried to convince him otherwise.

There was no denying Rachel was gorgeous. Her hair alone was a showstopper. Add her curves and facial features, and she was perfect to complement any man.

But all that was secondary to him. One thing he learned when he first met Rachel was that she loved hard. He wanted to be on the receiving end of her love and to give that type of love back.

He decided that a proposal on Rachel's birthday at the end of September would be memorable. If the world could celebrate the twelve days of Christmas, who could deny him thirty days to show Rachel his love, even if she was out of town?

On the first of September, he called Rachel instead of sending her a text.

"You're late, Mister," she fussed jokingly when she answered.

He poured his heart into singing verses from Psalm 103 as if it were a love ballad.

"Wow, that was worth the wait. I thought you had a sexy voice before, but your singing abilities could melt chocolate."

Somehow, this woman knew how to make him blush with her compliments. "Thank you. I love you, and I wanted you to know."

"I know," she said softly. "I know, and I love you more."

"I doubt that," he said in a strong voice, chuckling before he said goodbye and disconnected, not giving her a chance to counter his declaration.

Distance didn't deter Nicholas from doing something every day to remind Rachel how special she was to him. Since he had the hotel's address in Lexington, he had dinner delivered one evening, a care package another, and an inspirational musical snow globe one morning.

The day of Rachel's return, Nicholas once again waited at the airport with flowers for her, tracking each passenger until her familiar face came into view. His heart raced, and his palms became sweaty. Everyone around them blurred as they locked eyes. It seemed to take forever until Rachel was within arm's reach. They shared an ever-so-brief hug. "Welcome home," he whispered.

She stared into his eyes, and he could see all the love she possessed for him. "Home is where the heart is," she replied.

A week before her birthday, he presented her with a small gift while they were dining at STK Nashville.

"You're taking this 'showering me with gifts' thing to a whole new level."

"Is that a complaint, Miss Knicely?" He wiggled his brows, then reached across the table to play with her fingers and complimented her manicure.

"Absolutely not!" She flirted, batting her eyelashes.

"I didn't think so." He snickered. "Now, open it."

She did and tilted her head, studying the narrow box that contained pieces of a puzzle. "What's this?" Rachel gave him a bewildered look.

"Remember the first time you returned from Lexington?" She nodded. "My heart did somersaults when I saw you. A nearby woman took our picture." That photo had captured their feelings, and he looked at it constantly, especially when she was away. "I had it made into a puzzle that we can put together," he explained, offering a slight hint that he wanted to put the pieces of their lives together. He had already picked out her engagement ring, and in one week, he hoped to have it on her finger, where it would sparkle like her eyes when she looked at him.

As September 30 quickly approached, the proposal consumed Nicholas's thoughts—soon enough, Rachel would be his wife. "And to think my brother will no longer have a default babysitter." He grinned to himself as he carefully trimmed his beard.

In a few short days, he would propose over a romantic dinner, and come Thanksgiving, Nicholas would be thankful for his fiancée. Maybe by the end of the year, he would have a wife, he mused. Who would have thought back in April responding to a prayer request would have led to love? Then in July, Rachel turned herself over to God, and Nicholas was humbled to be a part of the process.

———

"Happy birthday!" Rachel's sisters shouted on a telephone conference call before they sang a few verses of "Happy Birthday."

"Finally, we're all of us in our thirties. 'Bout time you caught up," Kym teased, six years older than her baby sister.

"Do you and Nicholas have any big plans for today?" Tabitha asked.

"The man has outdone himself the entire month. What more can he do except propose?" Kym joked.

Rachel reflected on all the trinkets and love gifts she had received throughout September; she cherished them all. "I don't know what he has planned, but I doubt it's marriage. We've only been dating five months—" Her phone chimed. Nicholas's name came up on the caller ID, and she grinned. "Sorry, Sisters, your time is up. My love is calling me. Bye."

Before she said hello, he began to sing a melodious "Happy Birthday."

She closed her eyes and listened. "Thank you. That was beautiful."

"You're welcome. Tonight, it's me and you and dinner to celebrate your big day."

She tugged on a strand of her hair. "I can't wait."

Nicholas blew her a kiss over the phone before rushing off to drive to work.

———

At the firm, Rachel received more birthday wishes and shared a cake with other colleagues with September birthdays. Since she would fly back to Lexington next week, she looked forward to enjoying her birthday celebration with the man she loved. The workday sped by, and Rachel left early to get ready.

At her condo, she disrobed and jumped in the shower. She was humming a song she heard from the praise team at church when she froze, then frowned. Something wasn't right. *Uh-oh.* Rachel hadn't felt that before. She performed her routine breast exam again, and sure enough, something was hard like a pebble. She hurried and rinsed off to get out of the shower as her heart raced.

Rachel wiped the steam off the mirror and took a deep breath. She stared at her reflection. "Okay, clear your head and take your time." She counted to three, lifted her left arm, and performed the same routine self-check she did every month.

Something was definitely there that hadn't been last month, or was it the month before? She swallowed as her heart raced. "Oh God." She leaned over the sink. "All right. Probably changes in my body after my period."

Fear kicked in. "What if it's cancer? I'm too young to die." Time seemed to stop. No woman in her family had breast cancer. She grabbed her towel as she started to perspire, then ran cold water over it before applying it to her face. Her hands trembled.

She walked into her bedroom on autopilot, her body shivering from the cool air. Only after she spied the outfit on her bed did she remember her date with Nicholas. Suddenly, she felt faint and nauseous; a headache was creeping up her neck. How could she go out and eat as if she hadn't discovered anything? Wait a minute. This was Nicholas. He always helped her find her peace.

She tried to regulate her breathing to pray. "Yes, Lord, please help my mind right now not to worry—please. *You* are my peace."

After taking a series of deep breaths, Rachel slipped into her dress and ankle boots. It was Friday night, and Nicholas had planned something special for her birthday. Her birthday. Thirty was too young to be diagnosed with cancer, wasn't it?

"I'm not going to ruin my birthday with fear," she resolved and walked back into her bathroom. She dutifully applied makeup that she wasn't feeling at the moment, a twenty-minute regimen on a given day. "It's just a bump, not a tumor. Cancer doesn't run in my family.

Probably a little old benign cyst." Rachel gave herself a pep talk. No need to worry or say anything—just yet.

When her doorbell rang, Rachel ceased her prepping. Opening her door, she saw all the love Nicholas had for her, and her problems drifted away, and she refused to let negative thoughts resurface without visiting her doctor's office.

Rachel survived dinner as best she could, not wanting to spoil the mood Nicholas had created, doting on her. Tonight's gift was a spa certificate. She thanked him as she accepted with trembling hands. All his gifts were thoughtful, but the best gifts were Nicholas being a part of her life and God being in her life to comfort her.

As the sun was setting, they were sitting on a bench outside the restaurant. Nicholas turned to her and gathered both her hands in his. "I love you. My soul beats for you each day. I want our lives—"

"I might have cancer," Rachel blurted out.

"Wh…what did you say?"

The dam broke, and Rachel couldn't contain it. In her professional world, she and her company would have designed and constructed a structure that would have been foolproof, so water wouldn't break through. Right now, in her personal world, nothing was strong enough to hold back her storm of tears.

"I found a lump…"

Nicholas didn't let her finish. He broke protocol and wrapped his strong arms around her. The more Rachel cried against his chest, the tighter he held her. When she was able to inhale without releasing more tears, Nicholas gently released her. Concern was etched across his forehead as he dabbed at the remaining moisture on her face.

"Now, very slowly, tell me what's going on. You were okay when we talked this morning and afternoon. What changed within four hours?"

"I was taking a shower…I felt a knot—no, it was a bump, lump…" she rambled, trying to untangle her jumbled thoughts. "Something was there."

"Baby, I'm confused. A bump doesn't mean cancer. I want you to make a doctor appointment ASAP." She shook her head, and he sighed. "Have you spoken with your sisters or Jacqui about this?"

"No," she barely heard herself say. Rachel hadn't planned to mention anything to him either. It just spilled out.

"I won't want you worrying. Let's make a doctor appointment, and we'll take it from there."

She liked the sound of "let's," but it wasn't enough. She sniffed. "I'm scared to go to the doctor. What if I *do* have cancer? It'll kill me." She pulled one hand from his hold.

"It's going to be okay." Nicholas took her hand back and rubbed it softly, coaxing her to look at him. "Don't work yourself into a frenzy. Trust in God. Whatever it is, we'll handle it."

"Okay." She nodded. The rest of the night was a blur. Rachel felt like a zombie. This couldn't be her real world.

Later that night or maybe it was early in the morning, Rachel stretched across her bed, still in her clothes. She stared at the ceiling with her arms folded against her forehead. "Lord, please help me. I'm scared."

She finally dozed off thinking about God's help.

Chapter 20

NICHOLAS'S WORLD CRASHED—NO, EXPLODED—WHEN RACHEL broke down before his eyes. In his opinion, she had held up better as her aunt transitioned from life to death. Her birthday celebration was over.

Taking her home was the best decision, but it left him in a dilemma. She was in no mindset to be alone, but she didn't want to tell Jacqui or her sisters in case it was a false alarm. Currently, he was as emotionally discombobulated as she was.

"You need to call your best friend."

She nodded mindlessly.

"If you don't call Jacqui…" He paused to consider their options. "I'll have to call Marcus. Because I love you. Please, baby. I can't leave you by yourself in this state." He prayed she heard and saw his desperation.

When Rachel consented, he exhaled, and they waited in the lounge area by the elevator until Jacqui arrived, but he was still hesitant to leave her.

"Go, Nicholas. I'll take care of her. I'm spending the night. Go." Jacqui wrapped her arms around Rachel's shoulders.

Nicholas was rooted in place as he watched the love of his life and her friend walk slowly down the hall. He waited until they were inside before he summoned the elevator. *Whew.*

"Jesus, we need you," he whispered over and over on his drive home. This night was supposed to be memorable, as their first night as an engaged couple; instead, their lives could be shattered. He gripped the ring box in his pocket. This wasn't how he'd expected to spend her thirtieth birthday—tortured.

He pulled the ring box out of his pants and clutched it as his heart sank. The more he prayed, the more he didn't know what to pray. More than anything, he wanted Rachel to be his wife. But right now, she needed a prayer partner, and he needed to be that man.

Before climbing into bed, he called Rachel, but it went straight to voicemail. At least she wasn't alone. He huffed, then closed his eyes. It would be a long night.

The next morning, he called Rachel. Jacqui answered and said Rachel was resting. Saturday evening, Nicholas couldn't stay away any longer. He didn't call but showed up with flowers.

Rachel's appearance reminded him of her anguish when he'd visited her aunt. "Have you been praying?"

She nodded. "I've tried, but I can't seem to focus. So many thoughts keep running through my head."

He didn't stay long because she looked as if a nap would help, and Jacqui agreed. Before he left, he read her a passage from Psalms.

"Want me to pick you up for church in the morning?" Nicholas stood. He did his best to encourage her.

She shook her head. "No. I think I'll stay home and read. You saw how I collapsed last night after I told myself to hold it in. Right now, I need solitude, not crowds." Her eyes pleaded with him to understand.

"Okay," he said softly, although he didn't like her suffering in silence. He waved to Jacqui, then tugged on Rachel's hand for her to stand and walk him to the door. "Remember I love you. Don't shut me or God out."

"I'll remember." Rachel's voice cracked.

Sunday morning, Nicholas did his best to act like everything was okay without Rachel by his side. Most of the time, Rachel didn't miss a church service unless she was out of town. It was turmoil to withhold her suspicions from his family and the few church members who asked about her absence.

When Monday arrived, Nicholas was distracted at work during meetings and interacting with his employees. His question was when could Rachel's doctor see her? The sooner the better to calm Rachel's fear, and his too, or to escalate the agony.

It was one fifteen when she texted him: Dr. Brooks can see me this afternoon as her last patient at 4:15, or first thing in the morning at 8:30. What should I do?

She was asking him? Rachel wasn't thinking clearly. Give me your doctor's address, and I'll meet you there at 4:10. There was no way he wanted her to go through another night without consulting a medical professional.

OK. Love you sooo much, she texted back and included the location.

I love you sooo much more.

Nicholas left work at three thirty and made a pit stop at the florist. His woman needed sunshine, and he hoped the bouquet he purchased would boost her spirits. When he turned into the parking lot of the medical building, he looked for Rachel's car but didn't see it. He parked and drummed his fingers on the steering wheel while glancing in his rearview mirror. When he spotted her vehicle pulling in, he got out and waited for her to park, then took long strides to her car.

She stepped out and collapsed in his arms.

"*Shh.* Baby, I'm right here." Nicholas did his best to restrain himself from displaying too much public affection, but at the moment, she needed the physical comfort, and he needed to give it to her.

Once she was somewhat composed, he laced his fingers through hers and handed her the flowers. "For you, just because. How are you doing?"

Unshed tears filled her eyes. "Scared and nervous." She swallowed. "I'll be okay," she said, either trying to convince herself or both of them.

They entered the waiting room, and Nicholas was thankful that only one patient was there, and she was very pregnant. This was his first time inside a female doctor's office. Even if the room had been packed with pregnant ladies, Nicholas might have felt like a fish out of water, but he still wouldn't abandon Rachel.

She signed in, then joined him at a cluster of seats near the back. Exhaling, Rachel glanced at him. "If this isn't good news, then this is going to change everything between us."

"Not for me. I plan to keep loving you." He patted her soft hands.

"Please stop worrying. Since last week, I've been on the internet, trying to find out as much information as I could. On WebMD, I read an article that said eight out of ten breast lumps aren't cancerous and may be cysts that can go away by themselves. Let's have faith in God that this is simply one of those cases, okay?"

She took a deep breath, then exhaled. "Oka—" Rachel jumped when Dr. Brooks's nurse called her name.

Nicholas stood with her, giving her a genuine smile of encouragement until she disappeared down a hall and a door closed behind her, shutting him out. He flopped in the chair, closed his eyes as he tilted his head back against the wall, and prayed to be strong for Rachel and to let God be in control.

Since he had forgotten his phone charger again, Nicholas grabbed a random magazine about women's health from a stack and began to fumble through it. He could only read so many articles about babies and well-woman exams, so he found another magazine about home decorating.

After an hour, Rachel still hadn't returned, so Nicholas stood, stretched, and began to pace the empty room. The waiting was driving him crazy, so he walked down the hall to the men's restroom.

When he returned to the office and opened the door, he almost collided with another woman. "Excuse—"

"Minister Adams?" Leah Clemens frowned. "You're the last person I expected to see at an OB/GYN office. What are you doing here?"

He wasn't at liberty to tell her, but just then, an inner door opened, and Rachel reappeared, giving him an exit from the conversation. Rachel's angst didn't look as if it had subsided. Without thought, Nicholas sidestepped Leah and opened his arms for Rachel. She accepted his hug, sniffing.

"I'm so scared."

Looking over Rachel's head, he realized Leah hadn't moved from her spot. The church member seemed to study their embrace. It was a rare sight; Nicholas prayed hard to not get himself into compromising situations that could be misunderstood. Judging from her curious expression, Leah did misunderstand.

Leah and Nicholas had been a brief—very brief—item. He had taken her out to dinner a couple of times. That was when he realized there was a difference between a woman who loved being part of a congregation and a woman who truly loved God. He liked Leah, but for that reason and others, they weren't a good match.

He led Rachel to a seat. "Talk to me," he whispered, peering into her eyes but watching Leah in his peripheral vision. He turned to her, and she jumped.

Embarrassed that she had been caught trying to eavesdrop, Leah hurried out the door while Rachel covered her face.

"I really need you to talk to me," he said, prying her hands away from her tormented face.

"She…" Her lips trembled. "Dr. Brooks is concerned about the size of the lump and wants to have a breast ultrasound done as soon as possible." She inhaled and swallowed her tears.

Nicholas tightened his hold on her. When the staff turned off the lights and stepped into the waiting room with the doctor, Nicholas stood and helped Rachel to her feet. Gathering her purse, Nicholas guided her to the door as Dr. Brooks approached them.

"Miss Knicely, try to get some rest. There is no need for you to upset yourself with something that may not be." She paused and eyed Nicholas, then Rachel.

"All right," Rachel said, then stepped into the hallway in a daze.

Outside, Nicholas slid behind the wheel of her car and drove to her condo. He would take an Uber back to his car. On the drive there, Nicholas asked repeatedly if she was okay.

"Yes," she stated. Her eyes glazed over as she looked out the window. They pulled up to the condo and parked, and he walked her to the door.

Nicholas didn't believe her. "Are you okay alone? Do you want me to call Jacqui? Give me her number, and I will."

"I'm still processing the unknown, but I'm much better than I was on Friday. Plus, Jacqui has an after-work function."

"Okay, but I'm trusting you to call me for *anything*," he emphasized and handed over her car keys. "Try to get some rest. I'll call and check on you later."

When her door closed, Nicholas turned and walked toward the elevators, debating whether he should call in reinforcements. By the time he stepped off the elevator into the lobby, he had made an executive decision. Nicholas requested an Uber driver first, then he placed another call.

"Hey, man," Marcus answered jovially.

Nicholas measured his words so as not to cause more unnecessary alarm. "It's about Rach—"

"Babe!" Marcus shouted for his wife. "Something about Rachel," he mumbled.

So much for not scaring anyone, Nicholas thought.

"What's wrong with my sister?" Tabitha's panicked voice screamed in the background.

"We hope nothing. Rachel felt a lump in her breast—"

"I'll be there in the morning," she said, cutting him off. "Why didn't she call me or Kym herself?" Tabitha fumed.

"She hasn't been herself since I took her out for her birthday," Nicholas explained.

"Her birthday? Kym and I both talked to her and wished her happy birthday and emailed her gift cards. She sounded okay to me and didn't mention anything as serious as this," Tabitha said with an edge to her voice, as if she was challenging him.

"Rachel discovered a lump while she was showering before our date." He paused. "I don't think she planned to tell me, but it was eating her up inside, and it just came out. Her doctor wants to ultrasound the lump within the next day or so."

"Kym and I will be there in the morning, and I'll call Rachel tonight. I know she must be a mess."

"To put it mildly." Nicholas couldn't shake the horror of uncertainty on her face. "I don't have Jacqui's number. Will you call her too?"

"I'm on it. We'll see you tomorrow." Without a goodbye, the call ended as his driver pulled to the curb.

Chapter 21

NOT MUCH SCARED RACHEL. SHE CONSIDERED HERSELF FEARLESS, but hearing herself confess her fears to Nicholas made her feel like a little girl again. The what-ifs had been plaguing her. Would she die before her next birthday?

"Just prepping myself for bad news," she whispered in the darkness of her bedroom as the phone rang. She wasn't a drama queen, she told herself, despite Tabitha's and Kym's unprofessional diagnosis that Rachel suffered from the baby-sister syndrome—sulking until she got the attention she wanted. Most of her life, she got it. But somehow, none of that mattered at the moment. What she was feeling was real.

She reached for it and read the caller ID: *Tabitha.* Rachel groaned. She wasn't in the mood for conversation. Getting herself into character, she answered. "Hey, Sis." She capped it off with a smile she didn't feel, hoping it would come across over the phone.

"Don't 'hey, Sis,' me," Tabitha scolded. "Kym's on the line too. Why do we have to hear from Nicholas what's going on with our sister?" she screamed.

"Nicholas has a big mouth," Rachel griped.

"I'd call it a big heart," Kym said, chiming in. "Now, what's going on, and why are we the last to know?"

Rachel twisted a thick lock of her hair, a stall tactic she hadn't outgrown. "Because why should I get you two upset when it may not be anything? Depending on the results, I was going to say something. It's no biggie," she added with a shaky voice. *I hope.*

"We'll be there in the morning—"

"I have meetings all day tomorrow...but your presence would give me some distraction." Although Rachel didn't know if there were enough distractions to keep her mind from playing the what-if scenarios.

Her sisters were silent, contemplating her request. Finally, Tabitha spoke up. "Kym already booked her flight."

"I can change it," their oldest sister said.

"Marcus and I'll drive down and be there late tomorrow. I know you think this could be nothing, but if Nicholas is concerned, then that's telling us you're not all right."

The more Rachel tried to hurry them off the phone, the chattier they became until Rachel begged them to end the call so she could get ready for work the next day. She was scheduled to fly out to Lexington early the following week, so the briefings were crucial. How could she in this frenzy?

"Let's pray first," Tabitha said. She led the prayer while Rachel listened until they all said, "Amen."

Before climbing into bed that night, Rachel wondered why it seemed so hard for her to pray and receive peace. "Lord, I don't understand what's going on or why this is happening to me. Help me to trust You. In Jesus's name, amen."

Pastor Mann had preached that God answered prayers. With all the people praying for her, surely one of them would be answered. Climbing into bed, she closed her eyes and fought her way to slumber land.

———

Two days later, on Wednesday morning, at 7:12 a.m., Nicholas met Rachel's family at the outpatient center at Vanderbilt University. It seemed every time he saw them, it was over a sad occasion—their aunt's death, the sisters packing their aunt's belongings, now this.

Nicholas got a glimpse of Rachel as she was disappearing behind a door and called for her to wait. Reaching her with long strides, he took her hand and prayed for her peace. *I love you*, he mouthed.

Stepping back, he released her, dropping his shoulders from the helplessness that overwhelmed him, then faced her family huddled in a cluster of chairs. Their heads were bowed and hands joined. They were praying silently.

Nicholas hoped that Rachel living a long life was God's will. He stared out the window and watched Nashvillians cluelessly go about their lives as usual while his and Rachel's were waiting in limbo.

If the lump was cancerous... He squeezed his eyes shut to block out the thought before opening them again. No. He had to encourage himself. A grip on his shoulder made Nicholas turn around.

"You okay?" Marcus cringed. "Sorry, man. Wrong question." He squeezed his lips. "Honestly, I'm at a loss for what to say." He shrugged. "We're all scared."

"I'm worried." Nicholas slipped his hands in his pants pockets. "Every Scripture about faith, trust, belief, hope, and prayer without ceasing is coming to my mind like flashcards." He huffed. "If Rachel has cancer, then I'll know what to pray for, although I'm hoping this is a big scare and nothing else."

"Come on. Let's walk to the courtyard café and get the ladies something to eat and drink." Marcus nudged him.

"Yeah." Nicholas trailed Marcus to the elevators. Once inside, he turned to Marcus. "Nobody knows this, but the night she told me about the lump, I had planned to propose."

"Planned?" Marcus frowned. "Have you changed your mind?" He didn't look pleased.

Nicholas didn't like the insinuation. If he had gone ahead, he doubted Rachel would have remembered. "From what I've heard you all say, you and Tabitha didn't start off as friends. Did you walk away from your wife when things got crazy with Miss Brownlee?"

"Of course not!" Marcus seemed mad that Nicholas would assume such a thing.

"I'm glad we have a common understanding. One thing I have learned from her is how to love hard." He smiled. "For the record, I haven't changed my mind. When I propose, I don't want anything else on her mind but to say yes."

Nicholas thought about a portion of the wedding vows: until death do us part. *Lord, I don't like that option.*

When the outpatient procedure was over, all of them left the medical center the same way they'd entered: not knowing. Until the pathology report came back, the waiting continued. It had been a long, stressful day.

Rachel was back in her condo, sitting in the living room with her sisters by her sides while the men talked. Finally, Nicholas announced he had to leave for Bible class. He squatted before Rachel. "You know I love you, right?"

As she stared into his eyes and whispered, "Yes," he noticed the light in her eyes was dimmed.

"Remember, I'm praying. Okay?" He waited until she nodded, then he stood, and Marcus walked him to the door. "I'll check on Rachel later," Nicholas told him.

Nicholas yawned as he slipped behind the wheel of his Maxima and headed on I-65 South toward Brentwood. He rubbed his neck a couple of times as he drove on autopilot, his mind lingering on Rachel. He was beat after getting up early to be with Rachel and had barely slept the night before.

His heart would be heavy tonight, knowing the reason why she wasn't attending the Bible class with him. He prayed that the test would come back negative.

Nicholas was ten minutes away from church when his brother called. Nicholas grunted.

"Hey, Bro. Is everything okay?" Karl asked.

If only you knew. Nicholas tried to sound upbeat. "Yeah, I'm almost there, my dear brother's keeper. What's up?"

"Well, brace yourself for rumors when you get here." Karl didn't sound happy.

Suddenly, Nicholas was alert and frowned. "Rumors? What kind of rumors?"

Karl spoke to a couple of church folks in the background before rejoining the conversation in a low voice. "It's about you and Rachel. Someone said they spotted you and Rachel leaving an OB/GYN's office and she might be pregnant."

"What?" he roared and had to jam on his brakes to keep from running a red light. "You can stop right there." Nicholas didn't have to guess the culprit. How dare Leah try to smear Rachel's name with lies?

"First off, Rachel is not pregnant by me or any man. Second, she needs prayer badly right now. She's facing some unknowns, and it would crush her to hear those nasty things. I'm not at liberty to share what's going on with her, so please pray that this trial will pass from her. When I get to church, I know who I need to confront."

Karl exhaled. "Thanks for clearing that up." He paused. "Although I know you, I also know how much you love Rachel. The temptation is real for singles."

"Yes, the struggle is real," Nicholas agreed. "God is helping us."

"Glad to hear you say that, because...I know you're mad, but remember God is calling us to a higher standard when it comes to conflict resolution. We're still charged with ministering to the troublemakers with the love of God."

Nicholas knew the passage in Luke 17 well. "Thanks for the reminder. I'll calm down and think before I speak. I'm turning into the parking lot now." He thanked God for his baby brother's wise counsel, because he knew exactly where Leah Clemens sat in Bible class.

By the time he parked and walked through the church doors, Nicholas had cleared his head. Stepping into the pew that he and Rachel often claimed, he bowed his head and asked forgiveness for his attitude. He glanced at the monitor for the lesson reference and ignored any curious stares directed at him.

Pastor Mann taught from Ephesians 6:1–5: *Brothers, if anyone is caught in any transgression, you who are spiritual should restore him in a spirit of gentleness. Keep watch on yourself, lest you too be tempted. Bear one another's burdens...*

How timely, Nicholas thought.

The pastor emphasized, "We should never rejoice to see someone suffer. That is not God's will." He cited examples of how people could be cruel to one another. "As a companion text, read 1 Corinthians 6:11."

I hear You, Lord, Nicholas thought. *Please let Leah hear You too, or whoever was the offender, if I'm wrong.* Although he grasped everything that was being taught, he kept his fellow church member in view. He wouldn't let her leave without confronting her.

Finally, after the closing prayer, he made a beeline to where Leah was chatting with some other women. They seemed to part like the Red Sea when they saw him coming.

He greeted them with a smile. "Sorry to interrupt, but do you mind if I have a word with you, Leah?"

They scattered but not before casting a suspicious look her way.

Leah leaned against the wall, clutching her Bible to her chest. Lifting an eyebrow, she smirked. "Why, Minister Adams, what can I help you with?"

Taking a deep breath, Nicholas coaxed himself to remain calm. "My brother heard rumors around the church about me and Rachel Knicely that were not complimentary. Do you have any idea how those rumors were started?"

She shrugged. "I mentioned how shocked I was to see you and Rachel in a doctor's office hugging."

"You're letting your imagination stir up things that aren't there," he stated and glanced around, double-checking they had privacy.

"I know what I saw." She raised her voice in a challenge. Then she looked hurt. "Why did you put on this big front while we were dating that we couldn't do this and that and not touch? I saw a lot of touching going on. You're a hypocrite." She pointed her finger at him.

"Will you lower your voice?" He glanced around.

Folding her arms, she twisted her lips. "Why, Nicholas? What makes her so special? I get it that men are attracted to women with long hair, but what about spiritual maturity? Does she have that?"

After this trial she's about to face, God will have taken her to a new level of maturity. "Leah, we're all in different places in our relationship with God. The Lord was the matchmaker. It wasn't her hair that captured me. It was her heart, and I love her." He paused to let that sink in. "You have wronged both of us. I forgive you—and it's not easy—for tarnishing a good name. When the truth comes out—and it will—I hope you'll see what you've done."

A frightened look crossed her face before she humphed at him and stormed off.

Chapter 22

THE NEWS WASN'T GOOD FOR RACHEL. THE BIOPSY REVEALED SHE had cancerous cells. Rachel had stage one breast cancer.

A gut-wrenching moan escaped from deep within her. "No." She would have collapsed if she hadn't already been sitting with her sisters by her side in the doctor's office.

"We caught it early. That's the good news," Dr. Brooks said. "Now let's discuss our game plan to attack this head-on. You will be a cancer survivor."

Will I? She guarded her thoughts so as not to say them aloud. How could Dr. Brooks put *good news* and *cancer* in the same breath? Rachel felt sick to her stomach, and there wasn't much in her stomach. Despite not having an appetite, her sisters had forced her to eat some breakfast.

"You have invasive ductal carcinoma or IDC, which is stage one. It's the most common type of breast cancer, and it starts in your milk ducts and spreads as it invades the fatty tissue surrounding it. Your tissues are being tested to rule out if certain proteins may have been feeding your cancer. It's important to know whether your estrogen or progesterone receptors are the culprits. After that, we'll discuss the best treatment plan."

"Which is?" Kym asked cautiously.

"Could be a combination of surgery, radiation or hormone therapy, and chemotherapy."

It was so much information. Rachel wanted to know one thing. "What are the chances of my survival—really?"

"Your prognosis is good." The doctor smiled. It was genuine. "Your self-examination was the key to early detection. You'll be a survivor."

If only those words would come from the Lord, Rachel would

have been more encouraged. Even with all the petitions going up on her behalf, she hadn't heard a whisper from the Lord. Did the life of a survivor include a husband, a family, good health?

Kym asked, "Dr. Brooks, although my sister and I aren't your patients, would you recommend we get mammograms now?"

"Yes."

That one word sent chills through Rachel. What if her sisters had cancer too? Her lips trembled with fear.

"As a precaution," Dr. Brooks added.

Rachel sat quietly, as if she were a little girl again on the sidelines while her big sisters fought her battles. As adults, all three were a force to be reckoned with.

Tabitha faced the doctor. "I'm in pharmaceutical sales, and I know most of those chemo drugs contain morphine and have terrible side effects."

Rachel sighed and spoke up. "I'm thirty years old, single, and have no children. If my cancer was caught 'in time'"—she made air quotes with her fingers—"what are the chances of me having children one day?"

Tabitha and Kym nodded their heads in agreement.

"Most oncologists recommend waiting from six months to two years before trying to have a baby. That allows the drug to completely work its way out of the body," Dr. Brooks said. "The longer you wait, the more the risk decreases of your baby being born with birth defects from eggs damaged by chemotherapy. Also, the risk of your cancer recurring is usually the highest within the first two years."

Lord, I'm turning to You for survival, because I'm just not convinced of my odds here, Rachel thought once they left the office.

It was almost two thirty, and Nicholas hadn't heard from Rachel. He tried to give her space since her sisters were in town, but he needed to know what the doctor said.

Hey, baby. What's going on?

He stared at the phone, waiting for her reply. Finally, she typed back.

My doctor is about to declare a WAR ON CANCER.

Nicholas's heart dropped. He had hoped beyond hope for better news. He swallowed and texted back. When do you start treatment?

Next week or two. Soon as some more tests come back.

No, God, please don't let me lose her. I'll stop by after work. You want any of your favorites?

No appetite.

Not good. Nicholas would bring some of her favorites anyway, including Goo Goo clusters and a Chai's Mystique, an all-natural ingredients Rush bowl. Rachel would eat, even if he had to force-feed her. It was time for Nicholas to call in reinforcements—the prayer warriors.

That evening, he arrived with chicken from Hattie B's. Tabitha greeted him at the door. "How is she?"

"Down. We all are. I can't wrap my head around the fact that my baby sister has cancer." Tabitha frowned. "I can't comprehend that." She sniffed and stepped back for him to enter. "That smells delicious."

"There's plenty."

"Aunt Tweet told me never pass up a free meal, so I won't." She mustered a smile, but it didn't reach her eyes.

"Rach, your knight is here," Tabitha called out in a tease, then lowered her voice. "I hope you can cheer her up."

"So do I." He set the bags on the table and began to arrange the assortment of food.

Nicholas sensed Rachel's presence before he sniffed her perfume. Turning around, his heart dropped at the sadness draped over her face. He opened his arms, and she walked into them. He trapped her in his embrace.

Nicholas rubbed his jaw against her hair and whispered, "I love you very much." Stepping back, she looked up into his eyes. He hoped she saw his sincerity. "I mean that. Come on. Eat with me." He tugged on her hand.

Rachel shook her head. "Not hungry," she said.

While Nicholas wanted to be gentle with her, her sisters wouldn't take no for an answer. Kym's big-sister mode kicked in, and she ordered Rachel to start slow. "Chew whether it tastes good or not."

While at the table, Nicholas kept an eye on Rachel as she nibbled. He was losing his appetite too, but he had to lead by example. If he pushed the food away, so would she.

Kym joined them at the table and answered some of Nicholas's questions. "She's having a lumpectomy on Monday. We'll call Jacqui to see if we can coordinate a schedule to be here with her."

"Don't count me out," Nicholas said.

After they left the table, Kym and Tabitha tidied up the kitchen while Rachel cuddled next to Nicholas on the sofa facing the double french doors that opened to an amazing view of downtown's skyline. He stretched out his legs on the ottoman, and Rachel chuckled.

"What?" He smiled at her.

"What's with the socks?" She smiled back.

Nicholas looked at his ankles. "Hey, my nephews gave their unc these Predators socks. They're fascinated with hockey, so I'm representing the home team." He grinned as Rachel rested her head on his shoulder again.

"This is so much for me to take in. It's surreal. Two weeks ago, my life was normal. This week, I feel like I'm fighting for my life. I keep asking God why me. What did I do wrong to deserve this? I've been reading my Bible, praying, and going to church, then this happens."

Nicholas had heard this statement more times than he could count from new converts. They thought all their trouble in the world would be over, but sometimes it was just beginning.

"Being a practicing Christian doesn't exempt us from life's troubles." Nicholas turned her chin toward him to look into her eyes. "Please don't feel God is deserting you. He's not."

"I'm so scared, Nicholas." Her voice trembled. "I'm too young to have cancer." Closing her eyes, Rachel rubbed her hair. Her torment was tangible.

Doing what he did best, Nicholas pulled his phone from his belt. "Remember, God will always be our comforter." He tapped the Bible app on his phone and scanned for Psalm 27. He began to read until he heard a light snore.

Nicholas smirked and fingered one of her long strands until he had twisted it around his finger as he watched her. "Lord, give her peace through this storm and remind her she is never alone. I ask this with thanksgiving for all Your blessings, in Jesus's name, amen," he whispered, then gently lowered her onto the sofa and tucked her in with a soft throw.

He peeked his head around the corner and motioned for Tabitha, who was working on her laptop in the loft that once held Miss Brownlee's bedroom. "I'm heading home. She's resting."

Tabitha stood and sighed. "Good. She's been a wreck. How do you prepare for something like this?"

"You pray," Nicholas answered. He had to take his own counsel, because this was hard for him too.

"Right." She bobbed her head. "I think I'm going to let her sleep out here until she wakes up." She paused. "Nicholas, thank you for coming into my sister's life. She's changed in a good way since meeting you." She smiled. "Please don't go anywhere."

Nicholas smiled too. "I'm here to stay."

Chapter 23

PAIN FROM THE LUMPECTOMY CAUSED RACHEL'S PRAYERS TO BE mixed with tears. The nerves in her left breast throbbed and radiated throughout her body. How could removing something so small have such a strong hold on her body? She was three days into her recovery, and the doctors had told her to expect leakage and other side effects.

Although Tabitha warned her about possible side effects of hydrocodone, Rachel would risk it if it would stop the pain. After her sisters returned to their homes, Kym thought it was a good idea for Rachel to have a home health aide come during the day while Jacqui and Nicholas were at work.

Rachel felt some kind of way when Clara Rodgers, the same woman who had cared for Aunt Tweet, reported for duty. Rachel had burst into tears. "I guess I'm dying now," she mumbled.

Clara consoled her. "You're recovering, Miss Knicely, and I'm here to help you."

"Don't you think it's strange that you cared for my aunt and now you're caring for me?"

Shaking her head, Clara smiled. "I care for the old and the young. That's what I'm called to do. Now, are you hungry?"

"No. I hurt too bad to eat."

"I'll need a list of meds you're taking and how often. It may be time for another dose, so your pain level won't become so intense. I also received a text that your sister forwarded from Minister Adams. I have been instructed to hand feed you if I have to." She gave Rachel a pleading look.

Taking pity on the caregiver, Rachel resolved herself to eat something. "Maybe a small bowl of Cream of Wheat. I'll try to force that down. And please, call me Rachel. I'm not as old as my aunt."

"All right. Have you taken any medicine this morning?"

Rachel nodded. "Early this morning when I woke to use the bathroom, and it's done absolutely nothing."

"The food will help it circulate through your system quicker."

While Clara prepared the light meal, Rachel texted Nicholas. I'm eating. She added an emoji of a face with a tongue sticking out. Afterward, she stared out her balcony window, desperately wanting to be among the masses, collaborating with colleagues on projects that would make life easier for people to navigate the world. Looking for a distraction so as not to focus on the pain, Rachel called the office for an update and to offer her assistance from home.

"Rachel, I want you to concentrate on getting better. I sent Jackson to Lexington as your backup. Take advantage of the Family Medical Leave Act. It's supposed to be three months of unpaid leave, but the firm will compensate you for half your salary during that time."

It wasn't about the money. Aunt Tweet made sure her great-nieces would never want for anything if they used wisdom in managing their money. But Rachel earned a good salary, almost six figures, so his generosity was humbling. She thanked God for the blessing, then her boss as tears sprang up in her eyes.

"You're a valuable part of our team," Harlan said. "We want you healthy when you rejoin us."

"The contract we won requires a dedicated team, so maybe I can Skype in on conference meetings," she pleaded. Rachel wasn't a homebody by nature, so boredom would only make her wallow in depression. "I'll go crazy sitting at home for three months."

Harlan huffed. "Didn't you start going to church a while back?" He waited for her answer before continuing. "Read your Bible. Did you get the basket Jenny sent from the office?"

"Yes, and it will take days to find all the goodies stuffed in there." She spied the ridiculously huge, round picnic-size basket on her kitchen counter. On the surface, she saw toiletries, snacks, even a white teddy bear she had taken out and used for something soft to hug since her surgery. Someone had put in a box of fake eyelashes, along with a couple of surgical masks—some were plain, others had lips drawn on with a marker that were colored bright red, like lipstick. These had to be for laughs, and they did make her smile. There was an adult coloring book and other small boxes and bags she hadn't yet investigated.

"Keep us posted, young lady," her boss said, then signed off as Clara set food on the table before Rachel.

Surprisingly, the warm substance felt good in her stomach, but it did nothing for the pain. After eating about half and taking another pain pill, she braced for the nausea that tagged along with hydrocodone. When it hit not long after that, Rachel hurried to the bathroom.

Exhausted afterward, Clara helped her into the bed. Hours later, Rachel stirred from her nap when the doorbell sounded. Getting her bearings, she scooted up when she heard voices that grew louder coming to her bedroom. The door slowly opened, and Mother Jenkins with her booming voice stood in the doorway. Her presence made Rachel smile. "Mother Jenkins!"

"Why, praise the Lord, sweet Sister Rachel."

True to her persona, the woman stood larger than life in her white blouse, black skirt that matched her cape, and white stockings and shoes. She clutched the same worn, big, heavy Bible. Although Rachel would rather see Nicholas, Mother Jenkins was a welcome sight.

Rachel tried to scoot up more, and a wave of nausea hit her. Clara and Mother Jenkins were at her side immediately and helped her into the bathroom, where she barely made it to the toilet before she spilled her guts. She moaned. "I'm so sorry."

"It's okay, Miss Knicely—I mean Rachel." Clara dabbed to clean Rachel's mouth and chin.

"Come on, sugar. I'll help you back to your bed." Mother Jenkins guided her gently into her bedroom, then pulled back the covers and exposed her white teddy bear to her company.

"I still sleep with one of those." Mother Jenkins pointed and chuckled to herself. Once the woman took her seat, she seemed just as winded as Rachel.

"Now, how you feelin'?" Mother Jenkins asked.

"Not a good day." Rachel shook her head. "And I haven't even started chemotherapy. I know God doesn't want me to be fearful, but in the back of my mind, I'm wondering if I'm going to make it through this."

"It's all according to the will of God that we live, die, and have our being. Is anything too hard for God?" Her voice boomed.

Rachel shook her head. But was it God's will for her to suffer? Then she remembered God suffered for her.

"Jesus is in charge of our lives," Mother Jenkins said, breaking into her reverie. "I'm a survivor of two cancers."

Rachel perked up. "Really?"

"Yeah, chile. You've got to go through something to have a testimony about God's goodness."

"That sounds good until it's your turn." Rachel paused to let the pain pass. "Then you'll want to skip your turn."

Mother Jenkins humphed. "I didn't skip my turn. Cancer hit me twice, and I fought back with the strength the Lord gave me. After that battle, God gave me ten children."

Rachel blinked. She was looking at a survivor. "Children," she repeated. "I hope I have one or two."

"Why stop there when God can give you eight more?" Mother Jenkins said with such a serious expression that Rachel dared not laugh. It hurt, but the woman's statement was amusing.

To keep a straight face, Rachel changed the subject. "Now I understand what it means to be on the sick list. I'm the person who is waiting for someone to take time out of their busy schedule to come and bring me some cheer and encouragement." And to think she balked at the idea of a minister showing up to pray for Aunt Tweet as if he were the Death Angel. Now it was Rachel's turn.

She looked away and blinked back tears before facing the older woman. "I can't recall the last person I visited who was convalescing at home, or in the hospital, for that matter."

"Life keeps us busy until it slows us down." Mother Jenkins leaned closer. "The Bible tells us to visit the sick and those in prison. Some ministers preach, others evangelize, but the ministers who petition God on behalf of the sick folks and homebound count it a privilege to be faithful to strengthen someone with hope."

Opening her Bible, Mother Jenkins fumbled through some pages before she read a passage. Her voice wasn't soothing like Nicholas's, but it was powerfully clear that Mother Jenkins believed what she read there.

Rachel closed her eyes and found herself drifting. She was getting tired. She had almost dozed off when she felt Mother Jenkins dab oil on her forehead and, as if she were summoning every angel and saint of God, she shouted "Jesus!" Rachel shivered and imagined every creature bowing to God's presence. After Mother Jenkins finished her prayer, Rachel drifted off into a peaceful rest. No nausea or pain, just peace as she mumbled, "Jesus, please let my healing be of Your will. Amen."

Chapter 24

SATURDAY MORNING, NICHOLAS WALKED INTO VANDERBILT University Medical Center to visit one of two church members who were recovering after surgery. Then he had one more stop before going to see Rachel. She had suffered the death of her aunt, and now she was dealing with her own life-threatening illness.

He cleared his mind and said a prayer before strolling into Deacon Cates's room. He could feel the heaviness of sorrow from the handful of the Cates family who were cramped in the small private room. Sullen faces brightened when some recognized Nicholas.

"Minister Adams! Thanks for coming," the deacon's wife greeted him softly. Tears moistened her eyes, and worry lines marred her forehead.

Nicholas smiled, then turned to her husband. "How you doing, Deacon Cates?"

"The stroke has left my husband partially paralyzed, so he can't respond except for a few blinks," she explained.

The man's twisted features verified that. Nicholas nodded. "So how are you and your family holding up, Mrs. Cates?" He listened intently. The ministry was always more than just for the patient. "Deacon, we're praying for your recovery," Nicholas said and grasped his hand, which seemed lifeless as a brick.

Mrs. Cates shared the prognosis the doctors had given them. "The next twenty-four hours are critical, so we're holding a prayer vigil."

"I see." Nicholas nodded and faced the deacon. "The stroke might have robbed you of your voice for now, but your mind and spirit are still strong, so here are some encouraging words for you and the family from John 14: 'Let not your heart be troubled…'"

He read the entire chapter, ending at verse 31, then closed his Bible and offered a prayer of comfort.

A few family members sniffed and reached for nearby tissues.

Saying his goodbyes, Nicholas headed toward the elevators. He texted Rachel. Miss you.

Seconds later, she replied with Love you. You okay?

Am I okay? He chuckled and shook his head. I should be asking you. See you soon. Nicholas pushed the elevator button and stepped inside and hit the next floor. After sharing that one incident with the disrespectful son during a sick visit, Rachel always asked if everything was all right when he was making calls. Knowing she was concerned about him, even in her state, was heartwarming.

Nicholas knocked softly on the room assigned to Mrs. Anders, who was recovering from a knee replacement.

"Come in." He slowly opened the wide door. In contrast to the deacon's room, she was alone. "Well, look who the Lord sent: Minister Adams. How you doin' today?"

Her warm personality and sweet spirit endeared her to everyone. She slowly shifted in her bed.

"Do you need any help?" Nicholas rushed to assist, but she waved him off.

"What's it doin' outside?" She craned her neck to peek out her window, where the blinds were partially opened. "Doctors say I have to go to rehab before going home…"

Nicholas didn't interrupt. Sometimes, people wanted someone to listen as part of their healing process, but Mrs. Anders seemed more interested in Nicholas's affairs.

"What are you waiting on to get married, Minister Adams?" Her aging eyes twinkled. "Every good man needs an even better woman. There are plenty at the church."

He smirked. The woman knew he was dating. "I've settled on Rachel Knicely."

"Hmm. That's the one with all that long hair, ain't it?"

"Yes, ma'am."

Mrs. Anders bobbed her head as if she approved, then motioned for Nicholas to help her stand. "The doctors want me to get up and move around. Can you believe that? Well, thanks for visiting."

"Wouldn't you like me to read a Bible passage?" he asked as they made their way into the hall.

She shook her head. "God said He would put His Word in our hearts and minds, so pull something out of your mind and recite it."

Amused, Nicholas started with the first verse in Romans 12.

"That's right." She nodded as they inched along. When he reached verse 3, Mrs. Anders stopped him. "I know the rest, Minister Adams. Give me a word of prayer, and you can be on your way."

Nicholas laughed as he steered her to a nearby lounge that was empty of visitors and prayed for healing and blessings over her life. "Do you want me to walk you back to your room?"

"Oh, no, I'll be fine. Go on and finish doing God's business." She shooed him away.

His last stop was with a terminally ill member of the church. That morning, Nicholas had received word that Mr. Larson's condition had deteriorated, and he had been placed in hospice. The near-death visits were always spiritually draining and sorrowful, especially as Nicholas thought about the loved ones who would be left behind.

The tiny house was well kept. Four cars occupied the driveway. Nicholas parked and walked up to the porch. He heard voices before he knocked.

Mrs. Larson opened the door and bid him inside. He greeted everyone he knew from church and introduced himself to others and, after a few minutes, took a seat by the bed. Mr. Larson was breathing, but his eyes were closed. Whether he was conscious or not, Nicholas spoke to his spirit. He quoted John 3:16, then prayed. Mrs. Larson asked him to sing a song with them. Nicholas did, then twenty minutes or so later, he left.

⁓

Prayer was a struggle, but Rachel prayed to Jesus about her fears of the unknown. Was He listening? Sunday morning, the Knicely sisters attended church, and Pastor Mann's message hit home with Proverbs 3:5–6: *Trust in the Lord with all thy heart…*

He explained, "That means we have to trust God when things don't make sense. Trust Him just as much when things are going wrong as when things are going right."

Kym nudged her. "Trust, Sis, that everything is going to be all right." They joined hands.

I'm trying! she wanted to scream. "Right now, I need the faith," she said, feeling hopeless, "so I can trust."

Chapter 25

"Now for the fun stuff—chemo," Rachel said, trying her hand at humor as she braced herself for her first chemo session.

"None of us are laughing." Kym squinted at her.

Rachel exhaled and sighed. "Me either. I wish this were a dream." There was no turning back if she wanted to live. When she woke early this morning and grabbed her Bible, the pages opened to Jesus praying in the Garden of Gethsemane before his arrest and trial. He asked God, if it was His will, to let the cup pass from him. She had prayed and asked the Lord to let her bitter cup pass from her. She was beginning to struggle with her faith.

"I know, Sis. Me too," Tabitha said.

"I can't wait for this to be over," Rachel said and took another glance at her reflection in the mirror. She had planned to put on an old sweater and sweatpants, but her sisters wouldn't hear of it.

"That is not the Rachel Knicely I know. If you're going to fight this, dress to fight. Not only spiritually but physically. Put on a pair of your stylish jeans, a nice top, and comfortable heels. Jazz it up!"

Kym crossed her arms and snickered. "One day, we'll talk about the time someone had to give you fashion advice." She wagged her finger at Rachel.

"Right." Rachel found herself chuckling. Half an hour later, she was glad she took her sister's advice—upgrading her attire did help her attitude. Once at the Vanderbilt-Ingram Cancer Center, Rachel signed in and marveled at the inviting decor and seating arrangements for family privacy. There was no hint that anyone was sick or a death sentence was looming. Folks were chatting and smiling while they waited for their loved ones on the other side of the door.

Rachel was surrounded by love. Jacqui had taken off work, and her sisters had flown back into Nashville, racking up frequent flier points. Nicholas would be there shortly, after his managers meeting at the plant. She couldn't ask for a better support system.

"It really means so much to me that you're all here." Rachel exhaled as Tabitha and Kym wrapped their arms around her. "I'm nervous but glad I'm not alone." But after a ten-minute wait, Rachel became anxious. She wanted to get it over with. As if the staff read her thoughts, a nurse opened the door and called her name.

Rachel stood and wiped her sweaty palms against her jeans. She glanced back at the trio and nodded with a smile, then turned toward the nurse with dread. *I can do this, right?*

She remembered the words *Be not afraid for I am with you, even until the end of time*, and they seemed to tickle her ears. The calming effect seemed to flow through her body.

"Hi, I'm Amanda Ford, your oncology nurse who will administer your treatment." She scanned Rachel's attire. "Cute, but for your next treatment, wear something more comfortable and put those heels back in your closet for now. You might be unsteady after the treatments. Now, I'm going to take care of you, and if you have any questions, let me know. First, let me get your vitals."

The nurse closed the door to the lounge area, separating Rachel from the world that had seemed normal until a month ago. This new world as a cancer patient was still hard to accept.

In an examination room, Amanda recorded her blood pressure, temperature, pulse rate, and respiration rate. "I'll need your height and weight so I can calculate the right doses of medicine to give you."

"I want to double-check the names of the drugs you're administering again." Having a drug rep as a sister, Tabitha had drilled into her sisters to ask about the medicine.

"You're getting methotrexate and 5-fluorouracil as an infusion through an IV. The other medicine is Cytoxan in a pill," Amanda said.

Nothing had changed since her initial consultation. Tabitha said those drugs could cause some thinning but weren't linked to hair loss.

There were more drugs that Rachel couldn't remember, but Tabitha was keeping a list of them.

"Did you take your pre-chemo meds: dexamethasone and ranitidine?"

"Yes," Rachel answered dutifully while questioning why this fate had fallen on her.

"That should reduce your nausea and your chance of having an allergic reaction to the chemo. I'm also going to give you some fluids to help all your chemo meds work more efficiently."

Rachel scrunched her nose as Amanda set the supplies on the table. "I hate needles."

"You didn't want a port or catheter? That would have been a one-time prick."

After the lumpectomy, Rachel had an in-depth discussion with Dr. Brooks and an oncology team about treatment options and the entire process. Rachel didn't want to be cut again so soon, so surgically implanting a port to receive the chemo wasn't a favorable option for her. Plus, she had read horror stories about infections, blood clots, and the port not working properly.

Rachel shivered. "Just seems creepy." She frowned. "I mean I don't feel sick—at least not until I have this chemo treatment. To have those surgically inserted would be a daily reminder that I'm not well."

"But you will be. My job as an oncology nurse is to fight to rid your body of cancer." Amanda smiled and patted Rachel's shoulder. "I'm going to get a blood sample so we can keep track of the number of your red and white blood cells." After that collection, Amanda inserted the IV into Rachel's hand to start the infusion process.

Rachel took slow, deep breaths and braced herself for an invasion of medicine that could be just as deadly as the cancer in her body. The drug dripped from the bag, then seemed to race to her veins. She cringed at the slight burn upon contact. The sensation continued as the drugs climbed her arm.

"The treatment takes a while—hours—so next time, you might want to bring a headset to listen to music, or you can have one of your family members come back."

As nervous as Rachel was about the therapy, she didn't want anyone to see her endure the treatment—not yet. At the moment, it was "me and Jesus" time. She declined the offer.

"Whatever makes you comfortable," the nurse said. "However, you're going to need the distraction, because Dr. Brooks chose the dose-dense chemo over the traditional chemotherapy regimen."

"I hope my body can handle this intense attack every two weeks instead of the usual three weeks."

Dr. Brooks had explained that research found the dose-dense method, as they called it, would be more concentrated, improve survival rate, and decrease the risk of her breast cancer returning. At the time, the plan of attack seemed to be in her favor. Rachel would know for sure if the right choice was made after this dose.

"That's why it's important you take care of yourself while you're in treatment. I can't emphasize enough the importance of rest, because this treatment compromises your immune system and red blood cells."

"My sister, who is a pharmaceutical rep, says the Neulasta the oncologist prescribed has side effects." She gazed at her long, thick single braid, another gift from God Rachel had taken for granted all her life. "Including losing my hair."

"Sounds like you've done your research." Amanda patted her thigh. "But it'll grow back."

"With a sister like Tabitha, information overload can't be helped, but some things I don't want to know."

Left alone, Rachel napped, watched a couple of shows on TV, listened to the overhead music, and flipped through some magazines—anything that would keep her from watching the drips from the bag.

By the time Rachel completed her first round of chemo, half the day was gone. Amanda gave her another injection, then repeated the task of recording her vitals.

"Before you leave, it's important that you stay away from people who are sick. If you develop side effects…" Amanda thoroughly reviewed a series of dos, like drink plenty of water to push the medicine through her body and flushing the toilet twice after use, because the drugs were toxic, to maintaining good oral care to prevent mouth sores, to reporting skin rashes and using unscented lotions to combat dry skin. The list was lengthy.

She handed Rachel some pamphlets. "If you develop any of the symptoms I've outlined, call the number listed right away."

"I hope the chemo did some good." Rachel prayed for immediate results.

"With every treatment, you'll be closely monitored. We'll examine you, review your blood tests, and order X-rays."

Rachel stood slowly to get steady on her feet. She felt like the chemo had sucked all the life out of her. As a matter of fact, she felt drained. What did this medicine do to her? Getting her bearings, she walked through the door to the lounge. There was a handful of other folks waiting besides her support team; even Nicholas had arrived and stood to greet her. She began to wobble, and Nicholas rushed to her side in two long strides. She looked into his eyes. "Hi."

"Hey, beautiful," he whispered and angled his body so he could bear her weight.

"I survived." She chuckled.

"And you will survive," all of them said in unison before Rachel felt faint and Nicholas scooped her up in his arms.

"So tired," she murmured, then everything went dark.

Chapter 26

"ONCE WE GOT HOME AFTER RACHEL'S FIRST TREATMENT..." Tabitha told Nicholas over the phone. "She was so sick, it was heart-wrenching. Kym and I felt helpless, watching our baby sister suffer from nausea, then the vomiting. It wasn't a pretty picture. You know, chemo is considered a hazmat, so Kym and I had to use precautions for cleanup. This is hard for us as well as Rachel. I don't think any of us have come to terms with this."

That had been day one. Yesterday, Tabitha advised him that she'd had to wake Rachel to make her drink water so she wouldn't get dehydrated. She had slept eleven hours. Nicholas's heart sank as he listened to the despair in Tabitha's voice. If everyone lost hope, they still expected him to be steadfast, so he had fervently prayed for Rachel's healing and peace.

Now, three days later, Nicholas had to still rely on Tabitha for updates on Rachel's condition because she refused to see him. Or rather, Rachel's excuse was she didn't want him to see her. He had to resort to Tabitha as his go-between to find out how Rachel was faring.

Nicholas had to believe prayer was enough. Then why couldn't he sleep at night? *Because my heart is heavy*, he answered while searching for a file on his computer at his desk. He had to focus. He was the shift manager, and he had to manage his team, but he couldn't even manage his emotions.

"Nick, Nick. Where's your head, man?" a manager from another department asked, snapping his fingers in front of Nicholas's face.

Whoa. Nicholas blinked. He must have really been out of it. "Sorry." He hadn't heard anyone step into his office.

Warren May frowned. "Are you okay, man?" He took the liberty of leaning on the corner of Nicholas's desk. "What's up?"

"My girlfriend is sick—going through chemo—and it's rough on all of us." Nicholas couldn't believe he said so much to someone who wasn't much more than a coworker.

Yet Nicholas's mind was so saturated with concern, his mouth opened and words spilled out to relieve some of the pressure. "Sorry, didn't mean to unload that on you." Right now, he needed words of encouragement, and he didn't care who God used to give them.

Folding his arms, Warren shook his head. "Nick, I get that you're a good guy and a minister and all, but what I don't get is…" He shrugged. "She's not your wife. Why are you investing so much time in a woman who may not be part of your future? I'm not talking about her dying," he was quick to add and held up his hands to soften the blow, but the hit was felt anyway. "I had a cousin who was in a similar situation and was devastated when Beth passed away. I'm just trying to save you some heartache."

He gave Warren an incredulous stare. *Did he just utter those words to me?* "My heart is invested. I love her, and that's what people—family, friends, neighbors—do when they care about a person. They stick by them."

Warren bobbed his head. "What if she—"

"Really? A woman is fighting to live, and you're talking about her dying? Don't test me." He fumed, then had to regulate his breathing to tame his temper. What kind of godly witness would he be if he couldn't hold his peace? "Now, what can I help you with?"

Warren pointed out some flaws in a program, and Nicholas zoomed in on them right away and gave the man suggestions on how to correct them. Accepting Nicholas's expertise, Warren nodded and mumbled, "Thanks."

Once Nicholas was alone again, he took a deep breath and tried to free his mind of all thoughts of death before he bowed his head and prayed. *Lord, please let Rachel live.*

⸻

Rachel opened her eyes and scanned her bedroom. It seemed as if she had been sleeping forever, but she was still sleepy. What day was it? What time was it? And why was Tabitha stretched out on a chaise on the other side of Rachel's master bedroom instead of in the guest room?

Then Rachel remembered her big sister playing mother hen, fussing over her after the first chemo. They'd stared at each other and smiled. Rachel had been the first to speak. Her voice had cracked. "Like Aunt Tweet thanked me during her stay here in Nashville, I want to tell you I appreciate you coming to take care of me now that I'm sick."

"You're welcome." Tabitha had smiled. "But no thanks is needed when you belong to us. Age has nothing to do with it. You're our sister, so we'll always be here for you."

Rachel had sniffed and given a weak smile, then rolled over. She felt so helpless. "I've gone from being a caregiver—and maybe not a good one—to someone who needs care."

"The best caregiver is one who never stops loving, and you loved our aunt to the end," Kym had said softly. "I am not at the same place in my relationship with God that you and Tabitha are, but I have to ask, where's your faith in God?"

That her sister had called her out meant Rachel wasn't leading by example. "Honestly, my faith seems so far away most of the time that I can't grab it."

Rachel blinked now as her eyes adjusted to darkness. How was she supposed to survive months of treatment when she could barely get her body out of bed for the bathroom?

God, why me? She wondered if the Lord heard her. Her eyes misted. She remembered she wasn't alone. She thought of Jesus's words of reassurance and hope in Luke 12. *If God's eye is on the sparrow, why should I be afraid?* Reading the Bible always comforted her. If only Nicholas were there to give her insight. She reached for the phone.

"Baby, what's wrong?" Nicholas didn't mask the panic in his sleepy voice when he answered on the second ring.

It was one thirty in the morning. She felt foolish to have woken him. When she didn't answer, he asked again.

"Nothing, really," she said softly.

"I got the nothing part. What is the 'really' you're not telling me? Talk to me." His deep voice pleaded with her.

"I know it's selfish of me, but will you read Luke 12 with me?"

Nicholas's chuckle made even Rachel smile. "Woman, your request is such a small thing to ask of me. Hold on. Let me get my Bible."

She listened as he got his Bible, and the next thing she heard was him reading the chapter. When he finished, he asked, "Are you going to sleep on me?"

"Hmm." With her eyes closed, she felt at peace. "I love you."

"And I love you too, very much."

"Good night," she whispered and ended the call. "Thank You, God," she whispered again and drifted off.

Chapter 27

RACHEL PLASTERED ON A BRAVE FACE AS SHE ENDURED ANOTHER bout of chemo drugs. She wanted to show her sisters that she was independent, and they didn't have to put their worlds on hold to babysit her.

Reluctantly, Kym and Tabitha agreed to step back and give her some space—as long as there were no setbacks—and return to their lives while Nicholas and Jacqui had settled back into their work schedules. Plus, Rachel reminded them of Clara, who was at Rachel's beck and call.

Dogs really were man's best friends. Although Jacqui cared for her pets after each one of Rachel's treatments until she regained her strength, the pooches were Rachel's constant companions.

After preparing a small plate of eggs and toast with apple juice, Rachel stepped outside on the balcony to eat where she could overlook the bustle of the city dwellers below. She gave thanks for her breakfast—or brunch, now—and forced it into her mouth. It was tasteless, even with the added salt and pepper. If nothing else, her jaws got a workout.

Maybe the scenery would help her enjoy it. Despite being dressed in a thick sweater, sweats, and thick socks, she felt cold. It was an unseasonably chilly late November morning.

The sun shined bright, warming the city to sixty-five degrees. Fashion-wise, she loved this time of year when her wardrobe popped with the latest colors, so she could strut to work or play in updated outfits. Once, she had never left home without a cap or coordinating scarf. None of that vanity mattered now.

As she watched planes appear and disappear into the clouds, the thoughts of death returned. In her quiet time, she couldn't help but wonder about her mortality. How would her sisters craft her "Life Reflections" that mourners would be instructed to read in silence during her funeral?

Rachel Celia Knicely, 30, was the last daughter born to Thomas and Rita Knicely (née Gibson). Both parents preceded her in death… She leaves us to mourn her memories…

"Whew." Writing her own obit was too overwhelming. She would leave that task to her sisters. Rachel could imagine how they would endure.

When a breeze stirred, she shivered and reached for the throw she had brought outside as her phone rang. She smiled, recognizing Nicholas's ringtone.

"Hey, baby." His smile came through his words.

Rachel closed her eyes to cherish the moment. At one time, she thought they had a future. Now, she didn't know if *she* had a future on this earth.

"I'm checking in on you before my next meeting with corporate. How do you feel? Did you eat?"

She shook her head at his checklist. The man could be worse than her sisters. "Everything is good." She shrugged. "Just having a moment."

"Well, hold your moment until I see you later. I'm bringing you quiche. I hope you've got a taste for it."

"Me too," she said in an upbeat tone that she wasn't feeling.

"Love you and see you soon." Before ending the call, Nicholas gave her a Scripture. "Meditate on Jeremiah 29:11."

That was the irony of reading her Bible. Rachel couldn't understand how she could meditate on passages and feel comforted, then a moment hit, and she felt defeated. "Okay, I will. Love you too." She ended the call and closed her eyes as the sun brightened and warmed her skin.

A few hours later, Rachel was stirred from her nap when her door to the balcony opened and Clara stepped out. "I used the code you gave me to let myself in when you didn't answer the door." She shivered. "How long have you been out here?"

The pass code had been Tabitha's idea to give Clara access to the condo for well-being checks, and Rachel had agreed, since the home health aide had been loyal and trustworthy when Aunt Tweet was in her care.

"Not sure how long I've been dozing, but it is rather brisk." Rachel shivered and hurried inside the living room with Clara trailing her with dirty dishes. Although she could tolerate cool temperatures from growing up in St. Louis, Rachel didn't want to risk getting sick while the chemo compromised her resistance.

Her aide turned on the gas fireplace to warm Rachel, then tidied the kitchen, bedroom, and bath. The rest of Rachel's spacious twelve-hundred-square-foot loft remained untouched. She had purchased the pricey condo because she could afford it and considered it a showpiece when she had friends over. Now, it seemed like wasted space. She didn't know when she would feel sociable again.

Thanking Clara, Rachel walked into the bedroom for her Bible to read the Scripture Nicholas suggested. She flipped through the pages until she found Jeremiah 29:11. *For I know the thoughts that I think toward you, says the Lord, thoughts of peace, and not of evil, to give you an expected end.*

"God, what are Your thoughts about me?" Rachel mumbled. "Lord, please give me faith as I go through these treatments. I know doctors practice medicine, but You are the master physician." She closed her eyes for a moment.

Rachel opened her eyes and continued reading. She didn't realize she had read a couple of chapters until Clara reappeared.

"Would you like me to prepare a snack or something for you?"

"Oh, no, Nicholas is stopping by and bribing me with some quiche." The foods she craved before the start of chemo seemed to have lost their flavor. Her tongue had been affected, and her taste buds seemed dormant. Not only had the chemo robbed her of her lifestyle, but it had robbed her of her appetite too. Would her hair be next? The chemo was killing more than her cancer cells.

Nicholas arrived two hours earlier than expected. Clara opened the door for him, and he entered with a smile, a sack from Marché, and a bouquet of flowers.

"Hi, beautiful." He kissed her cheek and proceeded to the kitchen.

Although Rachel didn't feel close to beautiful, Nicholas could make her believe anything with his sparkling eyes and engaging smile, including convincing her that somehow beauty was still left inside her, so she smiled and accepted his compliment without any argument.

Clara had already set the table for two with Rachel's china and stemware, which Nicholas preferred when he brought her food, saying, "You deserve the best."

"Clara, I brought extra for you." He handed her a bag.

"Thank you, Minister Adams." Clara said, then disappeared into Rachel's spare bedroom to study for her exams to become a registered nurse.

"Let's say grace," Nicholas said softly and reached for Rachel's hands and rubbed her fingers. "Hmm. Still soft as ever."

He had no idea the effort it took to keep her skin moisturized with unscented lotions for sensitive skin. Rachel was accustomed to fragrances and colognes. Still, she blushed and listened to him give thanks for their meal. Before he concluded, Rachel whispered a silent prayer for God to give her an appetite to eat it.

"Now, Miss Rachel Knicely—my lady, the love of my life, I need you to eat. I don't care how long it takes," he said sternly, pointing to the quiche, "and as much of the vegetable medley as you can, or I'll feed you myself." It didn't sound like a threat, but his deadpan expression hinted he was serious. "We'll share the fruit salad," he added with a smile.

"I'll try," she said softly.

He nodded. Along with dinner came his sense of humor about his nephews. They laughed together, and before Rachel realized it, she had eaten most of her food, even if it did take her twice as long as it took him to eat. He rewarded her with a soft kiss against her forehead before he stood to clear the table.

"I love you," she whispered as he rinsed and placed their plates and glasses in the dishwasher. Glancing over his shoulder, he caught her watching him.

"What are you thinking about, Miss Knicely?"

"Thank you for leading me to Christ."

"You're welcome, babe." He frowned. "But I can't take credit for that. Your aunt planted the seed in your heart. I came along to water it, but it was all God's doing."

Rachel nodded and rested her chin on top of her linked hands. "I meditated on the Scripture you gave me earlier."

"And?" He turned around and continued his task.

"Verse 11 saddened me, but even there, God sent an encouraging word. I keep waiting to hear from the Lord about whether I'll survive this."

Nicholas turned back around and was about to open his mouth, but Rachel held up her hand to stop him.

"At least my soul is in order in case I die."

"You might live too," he said with hopefulness lingering in his eyes. "I'm praying that you'll join the ranks of cancer survivors. God can put it into remission, never to resurface again." He joined her at the table.

She reached for his hands and rested her small ones on top of his. "Nicholas, I love you." She swallowed. "But I don't know how much time I have left. I never imagined I would be facing death just after my thirtieth birthday."

"You're facing an illness, babe. There's a difference," he countered, making her wonder if he was trying to convince her or himself.

"Cancer is known as a death sentence," she said quietly. "Aunt Tweet once told Tabitha she hoped people would miss her when she was gone."

"And, baby"—he shook his head—"you do. Your grieving tore at my heart," Nicholas admitted, patting his chest.

"Please talk to me like you would any other church member about death," she pleaded softly and squeezed his hands. As they stared at each other, Rachel imagined she could hear his heart beat.

Nicholas seemed to be made uncomfortable by her request, so he didn't address it right away. The man ministered to the sick, so how could he be speechless?

"Death is part of life…" Nicholas began.

Rachel listened intently as he talked about all things spiritual that made her heart leap for joy. She needed to hear this, wanted to hear this, but her sisters wanted to shy away from any mention of death in the beginning, so she'd kept her fears inside. She didn't realize she was crying until Nicholas leaned closer and wiped at her tears. "I didn't mean to upset you, baby. I'm sorry."

"You didn't. Thank you for not ignoring me." Closing her eyes, she rested her forehead against his. "I guess I'm okay either way."

"Yes." He leaned back, causing her to open her eyes and watch him dig inside his jacket pocket. Nicholas pulled out a blue velvet box.

Tilting her head, she squinted before asking, "What's this?"

"Your reason to live." He inched it across the table toward her. "To be my wife."

Sucking in her breath, Rachel rested her hand on her chest to calm her heart. "You're proposing to me now?" In her condition, she didn't know how she felt about that. Was he asking out of pity or faith? A proposal was supposed to be romantic, during happy times. This moment was not one of those times.

"I don't know what you're thinking, but whatever it is, stop and listen to me very carefully." Nicholas seemed to tug at her thoughts until he had her full attention.

She still hadn't touched the box but eyed it suspiciously as if it would explode or something.

"I'm beyond ready to ask. You don't have to be cancer free for me to bend one knee and ask you to be my wife. Fight for our love and life. Fight for me, baby. I'll be fighting alongside you. If you can take me as I am, I want you as you are. Now, open it," he said softly.

Rachel swallowed, then bit her bottom lip as she contemplated her next move. Shaking her head, she pushed the box away. There, she touched it. Nicholas's crestfallen expression wounded her. "Nicholas Adams, I will not look at my engagement ring without a romantic dinner, *you* on that one knee, and my health restored." Thinking about it made her smile. "I will fight."

Nicholas leaped out of his chair as if she had said yes without realizing it. He lifted her effortlessly in the air until she giggled.

With no more discussion about the big C, they watched a movie. Nicholas left a couple of hours later. Clara said good night not long after that. Alone, Rachel Skyped her sisters and gave them a recap about the unopened ring box.

"See, that's why I like that man," Kym said. "He's one of a kind and perfect for my baby sister. You two make me so jealous," she said and capped it with a pout.

"I believe God has someone special for you too. Without Aunt Tweet, you won't have to worry about meeting him at a stressful time in your life," Tabitha told their big sister. "But our auntie also steered us to find God in our lives."

Rachel sighed. "Yeah. I thought I had done everything right with God, and whoa, without warning, I get cancer from out of the blue. I told Nicholas that I would fight, but sometimes, I question what my purpose is."

"To be an aunt," Tabitha said quietly.

"You're, you're—" Rachel and Kym screamed at the same time.

"No, not yet, but it's on my to-do list in our marriage."

Nicholas didn't exhale until he had driven away from Rachel's condo. That woman had scared him silly talking about her demise. That had not been on his mind when he'd picked out the ring. He wanted to talk about life and their future and sidestep any mention of dying. He believed one day their hearts would beat as one in marriage.

He didn't avoid the topic when he visited the sick, but he'd rather not think in those terms when it came to Rachel. "Lord, if it is Your will, please speak Your Word to her soul and give her a measure of faith to believe in Your healing. In Jesus's name…" He was about to whisper *amen* when he added, "And, Lord, help me to trust in You for a miracle like never before. Amen." He couldn't allow this situation to shake his faith, but it was.

Back at home and in his bedroom, Nicholas removed the ring box from his pocket. Of all the men who vied for her attention, Rachel had fallen in love with him, and he loved her more than she could ever imagine, which was why her rejection—no, her hold off—stung a little.

The next morning, Nicholas still hadn't shaken their conversation.

After checking in with her to see how she had slept, he called the church, and the secretary greeted him warmly.

"Mrs. Emerson, I would like to make an appointment to see the pastor." He waited while she tapped on the computer to review his pastor's schedule.

"He has four forty-five available," she said.

"I'll see him then." Nicholas would use some comp time to leave early.

Hours later, Pastor Mann welcomed him into his office. After the handshake and pleasantries, Nicholas took his seat and immediately unloaded his burdens. "It's hard watching Rachel go through this, because I love her so much and want her better, not only for her, but me…"

The pastor didn't interrupt, and his expression gave nothing away. When Nicholas took a breather and leaned back in his chair, Pastor Mann spoke.

"Minister Adams, this sounds as if this is as much Rachel's test as yours. When you haven't experienced the death of a close loved one or close friend as you've indicated, this hits close to home. Not only do you have to work the ministry God called you to do, but you have to believe it no matter what you see or hear."

"Yes, sir." Nicholas listened to valued counsel. "She asked valid questions."

Pastor Mann linked his hands and nodded. "One of the worst injustices is when preachers tell those who are sick that God's going to heal them. Unless the preacher has sought God's will, then they are deceiving the sick." He paused. "Resist the temptation to speak this unless you're certain God tells you. Do you want me to have Mrs. Emerson remove you from the sick visit rotation during this season?"

"Oh no." Nicholas shook his head. "Although it's hard to see her like this and her name is on the sick and homebound list, I have to keep ministering to others. I need prayer. Help me to be strong."

By the time Nicholas left the church, he was encouraged and reenergized, despite not knowing whether Rachel would recover. He had to accept the fact that the Lord wasn't going to tell him either way.

Chapter 28

ALONE AND DYING. THAT WAS WHAT RACHEL HAD BEEN FEELING LIKE since she woke up. Bouts of depression were slowly creeping in, uninvited. "God, only You know how this is going to end."

Each day, she tried to rebuild her strength in preparation for the next round of chemo, which would knock her down again. So far, she had been able to tolerate the IV. "God, why me?" Her eyes teared and she sniffed. The more she tried not to play the victim, the more of a victim she felt.

Each week, well-wishers sent cards in the mail or e-cards to her inbox. Their acts of thoughtfulness always cheered her up, followed by sadness, reminding her of her battle. Rachel eyed the basket from her coworkers amid the balloons, flowers, and plants that filled her living room. The thing was so big and heavy, no wonder it took two of her colleagues to deliver it.

Every time Rachel rummaged through the basket, she seemed to find something new. It was like a bottomless pit of goodies. She pulled out what appeared to be a scroll and unrolled it. It turned out to be a poster made out of gold foil from an Australian company, Peppa Penny Prints, with the wording, "You Were Given This Life Because You Are Strong Enough to Live It."

"Am I, Lord? Are my mind and body strong enough to go through this?" She prayed desperately to know God's will.

Next, she picked up a white tissue-paper-wrapped gift to reveal a beautiful journal that was covered with faux jewels and rhinestones: *Let Your Thoughts Be Your Inspiration.* The more she tried to meditate on her faith, the more fear seemed to sneak in. "God, please help me."

Something within Nicholas stirred him to pray, so while he was out in the plant observing production, he quietly sent up intercessory prayers—for whom, he didn't know. Twice when Nicholas called Rachel, he sensed she wasn't having a good day. The treatments were wreaking havoc on her mind and robbing her of joy. She was even losing her desire to go out to shop, eat, or relax at the nearby park. He had to get her out of that condo.

Nicholas sent a text. When is the last time you used your building's amenities? Up to hanging out in the common lounge? He was relieved when she texted back that it was a date.

That evening, the first thing Nicholas noticed when Rachel opened her door was the sadness that engulfed her spirit and seemed to weigh her down like a thick, dark cloud. It crushed him.

She was slowly losing her glow, and he wasn't referring to her beauty regimen. Nicholas hoped the small bag of goodies he'd brought would cheer her up.

He immediately wrapped his arms around her to give Rachel strength, then loosened his hold. Rachel had her head bowed, so he lifted her chin with his finger. "Hey." He searched her eyes. "I think you needed that." He brushed a kiss on her forehead. "And that too."

"I did." She smiled.

Her pets wagged their tails, waiting for attention. He squatted, scratched behind their ears, then stood again. "Ready?" He reached for her hand, then spied chaos behind her in the background. Rachel was a bit of a neat freak, so the sight was unlike her. He frowned as she was about to close the door. "What's all that on your dining room table?"

She glanced back and shrugged. "Every time I get bored, I raid the gift basket from my job and discover something new."

"Find anything good?" His interest was piqued.

Rachel walked back into her condo, shuffled through the items strewn across the table, and lifted a book and brought it with her. "This—a journal."

It was covered in jewels and rhinestones, very feminine.

"I'm supposed to chronicle my cancer journey," she said nonchalantly.

They made it to the elevator, and Nicholas pushed the button. How had he forgotten the bag in his hand? "I went to the Goo Goo Shop in SoBro and got you some clusters."

She faced him. "Thank you. I'll try to enjoy them. If not, you can eat them."

Nicholas tried to hide his frustration; he wanted her to feel his compassion. "I know you're trying to eat to live, and God knows I'm doing my part to help. I don't want to threaten to always force-feed you. All I ask is that you sample whatever I bring. You never know what food, snack, or treat may rejuvenate those taste buds."

"Okay." She reached inside the bag and retrieved a treat, then popped it in her mouth.

Nicholas rewarded her with a smile.

Looping her arm through his, Rachel rested her head on his shoulder as they strolled down the hall to the elevators with her dogs at their sides. The doors opened in seconds, and the two stepped in, greeting another couple inside.

He pushed up to take the dogs to the roof to the doggie park. After their potty break, they rode the elevator down to the mezzanine that overlooked the lobby area.

With their hands intertwined, they walked into one of the lounges where a few residents were focused on a basketball game. He guided her to an overstuffed sofa for two with a large ottoman where they stretched out with Rachel snuggled close, resting the bag and journal beside them.

"All things considered, how are you feeling inside?"

Rachel sighed and shook her head as more residents strolled in for complimentary snacks of fruit, nuts, bite-size cookies, and drinks. "It changes from day to day."

"Babe, keeping a journal might free you to verbalize what you're feeling."

"How am I supposed to write out my thoughts when I can't even pour out my heart in prayer? I mean, I'm praying..." She closed her eyes and leaned her head back. "I'm depressed, angry, sad, confused, and all this could be in the span of a day. Would you want to write about that?"

"Honestly, no." He squeezed her hands. "It may be good therapy to read what you write down that you can't express to others."

She grunted and opened her eyes to look at him. "That's too much soul-searching."

They were silent, so Nicholas observed her as she became lost in her thoughts. Maybe whatever was on her mind, a journal would be a good way for her to release doubts and fear and take them to the Lord, but he wasn't going to pressure her.

"I'll write in the journal if you do." She turned to him and jutted her chin in a challenge.

"Me?" He pointed to his chest and stuttered, "I don't think men keep journals."

"Ooh." She shrugged and looked away.

Nicholas sensed disappointment. How were they going to fight cancer together if he couldn't do this small, mundane task? He backtracked. "I'll have to get a notebook. It won't be anything fancy like what you have."

For the first time that evening, a glow appeared on her face and spread to her lips, which curled into a smile. It was then that her eyes finally gave a glimmer of light. Without knowing it, he apparently had made her day. Then she bowed her head as if she was unsure of something. "This might be best. I think about death—sometimes a lot."

He would never forget this moment of fear, when it sounded like she was giving up. If he hadn't been reminded of Revelation 21:8—"But the fearful…"—Nicholas might have lost his faith.

"I know everyone expects me to be positive in my sickness, but I'm not there yet. I can't be open about my insecurities, because no one wants me to mention my cancer." Rachel glanced up and looked into his eyes as if she was searching for something. "Will you be honest with me and open up about how my cancer is affecting you? Promise?"

"Yes," he said softly, responding to the pleading that filled her eyes. This was going to be a hard process.

"And I want to read it."

Nicholas blinked. "Huh? Isn't a journal supposed to be personal?"

This was going to be a nightmare. What had he committed to? Yet Nicholas planned to follow through. "Sure, babe, only if you share yours with me." Could he stomach knowing the raw emotions Rachel was experiencing? "As a matter of fact—"

"Okay." She agreed fast, not giving him time to change his mind.

Nicholas expected her to put up a fuss. She had called his bluff. The real question was could he have a heart-to-heart on paper?

Hours later on the drive home, Nicholas chided himself. "What have I done?" Feeling that he had backed himself into a corner, he fussed as he stopped at a light. It was a good thing Bluetooth was commonplace, so the driver next to him wouldn't know he was arguing with himself. "Note to self: never suggest anything to Rachel that may backfire on me ever again!"

Chapter 29

RACHEL HAD CONSUMED FIVE GOO GOO CLUSTERS—THEY WERE that good—with Nicholas, then washed them down with complimentary bottles of water from the open market bar. It felt good to change her surroundings, even if she was still in her building.

Hours later, she curled up in her bed, her pillow against her back, with the journal. She grabbed a pen and let her mind roam. She seemed to be in a trancelike state, reviewing snippets of her life before and after the cancer diagnosis.

Dear Nicholas,

I know this isn't supposed to be a letter, but since you're going to read it, why not?

First, I love you so much.

Second, why are you sticking around? I want to push you away at the same time as I want you to stay forever. When no one is around and I'm alone, I wonder if God is going to allow me to live or let me die. Cancer makes me think this. Would He let me go sooner rather than later to minimize my torture and my family's? I don't like being alone—I grew up around sisters and a loving family. I've made lifelong friends. I've enjoyed life—my career, my social circle. Just when I get a taste to fully know and love God, this happens.

I thought my life would change for the good when I surrendered my will to Christ, but it's the opposite. I want God to rescue me! In my condition, I feel ugly and unclean. I'm used to the girly stuff—perfumes and scented lotions, which I can't use now. I'm wondering if my hair will fall out...

———

Nicholas was scared. Not spiritually fearful but emotionally. A couple of days had passed, and he had yet to purchase a journal—a notebook for him so he and Rachel could exchange thoughts.

How was he going to do this? Nicholas was supposed to be her rock. To disclose his insecurities about her illness would crush her. Nicholas knew he could write anything, but she had asked for a heart-to-heart.

The next day at work, he realized he didn't have to buy a notebook; there were plenty in the bottom of a file cabinet that was recently cleaned out in a vacant office. Nicholas picked one from the stack, swallowed, and stared at it as if he had never seen or used one before.

Hours later, he took the notebook home with him where it remained untouched. He secretly hoped Rachel had forgotten about it, because she hadn't mentioned it again. "Now who is the hypocrite?" he asked himself. Nicholas huffed as he worked out on his treadmill in the spare room. He realized it was fear that was keeping him from being honest with himself.

There was that word again—*fear*. Where was his faith? After checking on Rachel for the night, he clicked off ESPN and sat at his kitchen table. Nicholas was surprised that once he picked up the pen, his thoughts flowed from his heart.

Dear Lady Rachel,

He smiled, liking the sound of that. He didn't care that they weren't royalty, or she wasn't a pastor's wife; it was the pedestal he gently placed her on.

I selfishly want you to live, but I'm scared that it may not be God's will, and that shakes my faith. I understand your fear, because I'm experiencing it too. I think I have a good relationship with Jesus, and He has revealed many things to me over the years. As a matter of fact, I felt I was there to minister to you while your aunt was alive, that you were going to need it. At the time, I didn't know it would involve your own sickness and not your aunt's.

I'm not angry at God, but I feel cheated that you were cheated.
And honestly, if your life ends, my life will cease without you in it...

Nicholas stared at the words through the tears built up in his eyes. It was a confession that he hadn't planned to make, but she wanted to know what was in his heart. Maybe now she would see that he did feel her pain. He hoped this exercise would be a part of her healing—and his own too.

———

Days before Rachel was scheduled for another treatment, she wanted to read Nicholas's journal. "Sure, babe," he had told her earlier, so later that evening, he stopped to visit before Clara left for home.

Rachel eagerly met him at the door with a smile. His heart warmed seeing her spirits lifted. "Thank you for suggesting this and doing this with me." Her eyes sparkled as she stepped back and allowed him entry.

"Hi, Minister Adams," Clara said as she straightened the kitchen. "I made a pot of coffee. I know it's late, but Rachel had a craving, so I didn't hesitate."

"You did right. Thank you." *So what if a cup would keep both of them up all night?* He chuckled to himself. Maybe her taste buds were adjusting.

He kissed her head and asked how she felt and what else she'd eaten as he sat on the sofa and waited for her to join him. Rachel kept eyeing his notebook as if she were about to steal it.

"Enough stalling, Nicholas. I'm ready to read your thoughts," she said in an antsy manner as Clara placed cups of coffee in front of both of them.

Nicholas laughed and handed over his notebook as she placed her journal in his open hand. Side by side, they made themselves comfortable. Rachel counted to three, and they opened to the first pages in unison.

She had three long entries to his two short ones. Nicholas could feel her emotions lift off the pages. He was sipping coffee when it turned bitter and his heart dropped. He had to keep his composure.

Nicholas, knowing that you have immeasurable faith in God comforts me while my faith is leaving me. Thankfully, you're a call or text away for me to extract some of your strength and to increase my faith, to believe like you believe that God is going to heal me...

Uh-oh. He swallowed. Surely, she had read by now that wasn't the case. When Rachel sniffed, he had to look at her, and the hurt in her eyes seemed to burn a hole in his heart.

"So you do think I'm going to die?" Her lips trembled, and her eyes watered. "You don't have enough faith either?" Then the dam broke, and she became inconsolable.

He tried to wrap his arms around her shoulders as her hands covered her face to hide her tears.

"I'm sorry." His participation had been a bad idea. His honesty had hurt her. He silently prayed, *God, grant me Your wisdom. Help me to fix this.*

Clara hurried into the living room. "Is everything all right?"

Nicholas nodded as Rachel shook her head and said, "No!"

"I got this," he assured the aide and waved her off.

"No, Nicholas, I want you to leave!" She uncovered her face. The agony was tangible. "Now, please."

"Babe, let's try and work through—"

"Why?" She jumped to her feet. "What's the point if you don't believe I'm going to live either?"

"I'm sorry, Minister Adams," Clara said, coming to Rachel's side. "Maybe, it would be best to leave so I can get Rachel settled down for the night."

Nicholas looked from Rachel to Clara before pressing his lips together in frustration. He wanted to tell Clara he wasn't going anywhere until they could resolve this, but it wasn't his call. Rachel had spoken.

"All right. Good night. Please call me if you need me." He snatched the notebook from the sofa so as not to leave any evidence behind.

Grabbing his jacket, he headed toward the door, opened it, and kept walking without looking back. The only thing he wanted to write in his journal was *You're going in the trash.*

Chapter 30

WHAT HAPPENED? NICHOLAS WOKE THE NEXT MORNING STILL TRYING to process last night at Rachel's. He had hoped with the dawning of a new day, she would wake with a clear head and a forgiving heart.

Nicholas was losing hope of that as the morning turned into the afternoon at work and Rachel hadn't responded to the Scripture he'd texted her as he did every morning. His heart sank in guilt. She had to know he wasn't trying to hurt her. Maybe she thought he was a hypocrite. That would hurt him.

Four thirty couldn't come fast enough. He felt as if he had worked a twelve-hour shift instead of eight. He was tormented all day. Instead of heading home, he showed up at his brother's house.

As soon as his sister-in-law opened the door, she knew something was wrong. "Oh no. Is Rachel okay?" She covered her mouth with her trembling hand. Why did tears moisten her eyes before he could even answer?

"Rachel? What happened?" Karl asked, coming to his wife's side. He was next in line to work himself into a frenzy.

Nicholas slumped his shoulders and twisted his lips in defeat before he answered. "She's mad at me and put me out."

Ava exhaled, relieved, then gave him side-eye. "What did *you* do?"

"Why does it always mean the man did something?" Nicholas frowned.

She folded her arms. "Nicholas Adams?"

Buying himself some time, he broke through their barricade, leaving them standing in the foyer while he wandered through the house, looking for his nephews. Their squeals and excitement replenished the love he felt he'd lost with Rachel.

After the family ate with a lot of tension at the dinner table, Karl sent his sons to their room to play.

Once the coast was clear, Ava put on her game face. "I've fed you without charge, so spill it," she ordered.

Nicholas rubbed the back of his neck. "What happened was…"

Although they didn't interrupt him, Karl's and Ava's stiff body language revealed whose side they were on.

Karl spoke first when Nicholas finished. "Man, you never," he said, shaking his head for emphasis, "ever tell a woman something that raw. It's a trap."

Ava elbowed her husband and frowned at Nicholas. "It wasn't a trap! She asked for honesty and you gave it to her, but…" He leaned closer as she lowered her voice. "You really don't believe God's going to heal her, so worried that it's shaken your faith? That is scary."

Nicholas threw up his arms in frustration. "I never said that. Listen, am I scared? Yes. Am I praying? Absolutely. Do I want God's favor because I love her?" He paused in his self-defense. "More than anything." *Lord, please help my unbelief.*

"Brother-in-law, Rachel is going through something we have never experienced in our families. She's probably having some overwhelming mood swings going on right now. Me?" She patted her chest. "I'd be hysterical. One thing for sure, I would want Karl right there beside me, and we would be afraid together until the Lord strengthens our faith to cast out the fear." His brother leaned over and kissed his wife's lips, and she rewarded him with a grin. "This is Rachel's fear and frustration talking, so don't take it personally."

"Too late. When a woman puts a man out of her house, it's very personal. I can't believe we had a fight." Maybe it wasn't a fight. Nicholas frowned, still stunned and wounded.

"First time for everything, because I'm about to put you out of my house so I can spend time with my wife." Karl wiggled his brows. "We'll keep praying that God will give Rachel mental strength and you too. Now, bye, Bro." He stood up, which was Nicholas's cue to head toward the door.

—

"He said what?" Jacqui practically roared through the phone the next day as Rachel left nothing out about what was in Nicholas's notebook.

Rachel's mind had seemed to take a snapshot: *"But I'm scared that it may not be God's will, and that shakes my faith."*

If the man who loved her, the man who was a minister, and the man who prayed for the sick didn't have faith, then Rachel could be as good as dead. "It hurt me so bad, Jac," she choked out as tears reappeared for the countless time of the day.

"Hey, it's going to be okay. Read your Bible, take a nap or something, just calm down. I'll leave work early and spend the night."

"Okay," Rachel whispered and opted for the nap as the something.

That evening, Jacqui used her key to let herself into Rachel's condo. She waltzed in with the flair and confidence they'd shared at one time. Her friend's smile turned to horror as she looked at Rachel. Even Sweet Pepper and Shelby, who had stayed with her friend after Rachel's most recent treatment, seemed to stop wagging their tails.

"Oh no." She rushed to Rachel's side and gathered the clump of hair she was holding.

Rachel stared ahead. She couldn't bear to look at her hair, which was at least twenty inches in length. She felt numb. "It happened," she whispered, still in disbelief. Since her hair hadn't fallen out right away, Rachel had hoped it wouldn't. The delay was yet another false sense of security, and this came right after the insecurity from Nicholas's thoughts.

"I used the bathroom. After I washed my hands, I ran my fingers through my hair… If you touch it, the rest will probably come out." Rachel flopped in a nearby chair. "My oncologist said my body was responding to the chemo, and it seems to be working. Hooray, I thought, then he dropped the bombshell that he was adding radiation treatment to be sure." He had also advised the radiation could cause some disfiguration to the affected breast.

She didn't know how long she rambled, but Jacqui listened as she walked into Rachel's bathroom and retrieved a comb. In slow, steady strokes, she combed Rachel's hair until she could feel the teeth scraping her scalp. There was very little left, so her friend took a pair of scissors and clipped the remaining stubborn strands.

"It'll grow back." Jacqui leaned over and kissed Rachel's cheek. "But this…" She glanced at Rachel's long, loose hair that was now gathered into a ponytail. "I'll see if we can donate it to Locks of Love."

She no longer looked like a human being but a skinned cat, a creature from a sci-fi movie, or worse. "Why am I beginning to hate myself? Am I crazy?"

"No, you're scared, angry, and confused." Jacqui sat and faced her. "Listen to me. I know this is scary. Hopefully, this nightmare will be over soon, and something good will come out of this."

"What?" She begged her friend to tell her something.

"Don't know, but I believe." She shook her head with a sad expression. "I don't know what God's plan is, but He knows your suffering."

Rachel hugged her friend, wishing Nicholas had said those exact words.

"Have you eaten?" Jacqui asked as she wrapped Rachel's loose hair in a rubber band.

"I was thinking about eating until *this* happened." She rubbed her bald head. She always thought bald men had smooth heads. Now that she was bald, her scalp felt uneven.

Jacqui squatted so she was eye level with Rachel. "I'll cook you something light, then we're going to talk about your Nicholas, because he is yours."

Within twenty minutes, Jacqui set a small portion of grilled chicken strips with stir-fry veggies and rice in front of Rachel with a tall glass of apple juice. Next, Jacqui retrieved Rachel's bottles of medicine from the bathroom.

"Is Clara staying on top of making sure you take your drugs?"

"Yep."

Taking a seat across from Rachel, Jacqui tapped on the table. "Now, ask for the blessing so we both can eat."

After giving thanks for her food, Rachel sampled a few bites, then reached for her glass to wash it down.

Jacqui didn't waste time to speak her mind. "Now, you're mad at Nicholas for telling you the truth? If you were to ask me the truth, you'd learn how scared I am that my best friend could be taken away from me, and your sisters would probably say the same thing." Her eyes filled with tears. "But we're all praying for you, and we have to believe. So are you mad at me now and want to put me out like you did Nicholas? Put me out and I'm taking the dogs with me."

Rachel laughed at her friend's silliness and mumbled, "No," as she picked at her food until Jacqui grabbed her fork out of Rachel's hand, clearly annoyed.

"Open," Jacqui ordered, then scooped up some vegetables and gently fed them to Rachel, mindful of any mouth sores. "Chew." She gave her side-eye. "If you lose any more weight, then I'll look fat."

"Fat?" Rachel chuckled. "Size fourteen isn't fat—please. Plus, full-figured women have no shortage of getting a man's attention." She paused and looked at her own body. Rachel's size ten clothes were starting to hang so loosely on her, she was becoming self-conscious about her weight.

"I still don't understand why you came down so hard on Nicholas." Jacqui coaxed Rachel to accept another mouthful.

"How do you expect…" She paused and swallowed. "How do you expect me to talk after you shoved all this food in my mouth?"

"Multitask." Jacqui shrugged and swapped Rachel's fork for hers so she could eat her own cooking. A couple more times, she threatened to take the fork again, so Rachel kept a steady grip on her utensil.

"It hurt me so bad when I read that he was scared. He's supposed to have faith big enough for both of us. What hope do I have if he doesn't have any?" She rubbed her face, then reached for her hair to twist a strand around her finger—gone.

Jacqui said, "You have to have your own faith, Rachel. You once told me that Nicholas told you that our faith impresses God."

Rachel had embraced faith in God wholeheartedly, so how could this cancer have happened to her? She was feeling like a victim.

Her shoulders slumped. "I'm losing everything. My mind could be next," she said sadly, then pushed away her plate. She had eaten half of her portion. "I'm tired now. I think I'm going to lie down and read my Bible."

"Good idea," Jacqui said, standing to gather the dishes.

In the middle of the night, Rachel woke to relieve herself. She didn't know what time it was, only that she'd fallen asleep while reading her Bible. She turned on the light in the bathroom and muffled a scream at her reflection. She had lost weight, and her skin looked dry despite the lotion she constantly applied, but it was the hairless woman who stared back that startled Rachel. She had never looked so horrible.

But you are alive, she thought.

It took a moment for her to contemplate all she had to be grateful for. "Yes, I am." Rachel nodded and turned away from the mirror. She returned to her bed and didn't wake again until her phone rang when the sun was shining through her blinds. "Hello."

"Hey, Little Sister. Kym is on too," Tabitha said. "Sorry to call early, but we both have crazy busy days, and we wanted to check on you."

Rachel scooted up in bed. "Well, it happened."

"What?" the two said in unison.

"My hair." Rachel rubbed her scalp. "It's gone. Came out in clumps. Jacqui spent the night and combed the rest out." She sniffed. "I had hoped I would be spared that, but no."

"You know it will grow back after your treatments," Kym said, trying to console her.

"The women on both sides of our family have always had long, thick hair," Tabitha added.

"Yeah, but none of them ever had the big C." Rachel couldn't shake her negative thoughts.

As they were ending the call, Jacqui strutted into Rachel's bedroom. "Good morning!" she called out in her singsong voice. "Feeling better?"

"I guess so for a bald-headed woman," Rachel said, trying to jest.

"And a bald woman never looked so good." Jacqui humphed. "If you can joke, then you're in better spirits than when I arrived last night." She rested her fists on her hips. Her friend was stunning in her black suit with gold buttons and a soft yellow top, but the expression on Jacqui's face meant trouble for Rachel. "So what's going to be our beauty regimen for you the next couple of months?"

"It will be longer than that until I have hair again." Rachel shrugged.

"Whatever." Her friend dismissed her comments. "Wigs or hats?"

"Neither." Rachel rested her arms on her knees.

Jacqui shrieked. "You are not going to let Nicholas see you like this?" She shook her head in disbelief. "You are breaking every code in the beauty rule book."

"I don't plan on Nicholas seeing me for a while."

"Now I know that cancer has eaten your brain cells. Oops." Jacqui slapped her hand over her mouth. "Sorry, I wasn't thinking."

"It's okay. The chemo is taking no prisoners." Rachel rubbed her bald head. "Men are attracted to women with hair—the longer the better."

"But that's not what drew Nicholas to you. He's the exception."

"Yeah." Rachel gnawed on her bottom lip. "I think I'm too much drama for Nicholas and me. I'm so frustrated with myself. I need to get control over my emotions. I'm going to apologize, but I need some time to meditate and pray. Nicholas will only distract me."

"He's a good-looking distraction." Jacqui dropped her arms to her sides. "We'll talk about your crowning glory later. I've got to get to work, then home afterward. I'll check on you throughout the day, but I think you need to talk to Nicholas."

Jacqui walked closer and pressed a kiss on Rachel's head, then stepped back, leaving a dark orange lipstick imprint on her scalp. "Nah, not a good shade on you."

Rachel laughed. "Bye, silly. Have a good day, and thanks for coming. I love you like a sister."

"Girl, I am your sister. Kym and Tabitha just don't know it. Bye."

Chapter 31

Nicholas's spirits lifted when Rachel responded to his morning Scripture text.

> Thank you for the inspiration, and I'm so sorry about how I treated you the other day. This is hard. I'm still trying to adjust. Forgive me?

"Of course," Nicholas whispered with a grin and texted back. Always. Can I come by and see you before I head out to Bible class? This time, her response was slower.

> I don't have any hair, Nicholas. Can you give me a couple more days? I need some quiet time.

The first thought that came into Nicholas's head was, *No.* He wanted to be there with her. But he had to be okay with giving her space, so he texted back: I'm here when you need me. Praying for and loving you.

Memories of their happy times were constant companions as he drove and then as he strolled inside the church. Rachel's text had brightened his day and dimmed it. Were her mood swings part of the chemo side effects? If so, until this nightmare was over, Nicholas mused, he would have to accept the reality.

Distracted when he stepped into the foyer, he looked up in time not to run into Mother Jenkins. "Sorry, I didn't see you."

"I figured as much, since you weren't watching where you were going." She scolded him mildly, then gave him a concerned look. "How's

Sister Rachel coming along? I've been praying for her. That's a hard thing she's going through. Hard thing." She shook her head.

"I don't know. Her hair fell out, and she doesn't want me to see her bald. The woman's going to be hairless for months. What am I supposed to do?" He rubbed the back of his neck, frustrated.

"God's in control of the situation, especially when everything seems out of control. Although I'm not assigned to visit her this week, I'll see if Sister Rachel is up for some extra company."

Nicholas perked up, relieved. "Thank you, Mother Jenkins. Maybe you can get her to see me." He hoped his puppy-dog expression looked authentic, because he was feeling it in his heart.

She chuckled and patted his shoulder. "No need for the face. It might have worked with your parents, but I'm not fooled."

He struggled through class to follow the lesson, his mind drifting to Rachel. He wasn't aware of Leah's presence until she tapped him on the shoulder to get his attention.

"Hi, Minister Adams," she whispered. "I'm so sorry about the misunderstanding I had about you and Rachel. I saw her name on the prayer list. Is there anything I can do?"

Nicholas nodded. "Pray without ceasing."

"Okay, ah, if you need to talk or want someone to help you shop for a gift for her, I'm available to go with you to pick out something a woman would like."

He turned around in his pew and gave Leah his full attention. She seemed hopeful. "You know, that's a good idea."

Leah's eyes widened as her shoulders relaxed. "I'm available tomorrow after work, and—"

Nicholas had to stop her. "No need to interrupt your plans."

"I don't mind," she was quick to say. "You know I'm a caring person." She smiled.

"I appreciate your thoughtfulness, and you gave me a good idea. I'll take my sister-in-law with me. Thanks, Leah." Nicholas's spirit was lighter as he turned his attention back to the lesson.

Rachel was miserable not seeing Nicholas. It wasn't that she didn't want to see him, hold his hand, or smell his cologne, depending on how her olfactory senses were functioning. It was just that she had been experiencing some type of chemo PMS or something hormonal. Her phone rang as she came out of her bathroom. She frowned at the unknown number. "Hello?"

"Praise the Lorddd, Sister Rachel," the familiar voice seemed to roar over the phone. "This is Mother Jenkins. How you feeling?"

Rachel released a dry chuckle. "Not like myself. Nor do I look like myself either." She pouted.

"I would like to come by and visit whenever you feel up to it."

"Do you have the time today?" She had enjoyed their last visit.

"I'll be there in an hour." She ended the call without giving Rachel a chance to counter with a better time.

Initially, the woman's no-nonsense personality was intimidating, but her visits made Rachel feel like a daughter or special friend, not a name on a list. As fast as she could without moving too fast, Rachel freshened her appearance.

She spied the time and scooped up some fresh fruit and made a slice of toast. Neither sounded appealing, but the nurse stressed that Rachel needed to eat more to keep healthy, especially since she had lost weight after her last treatment.

Rachel made the mistake of relaying that update to Clara, who would prepare snacks and sit at the table while Rachel ate as if she were a four-year-old. If she ate an amount that was acceptable to Clara, then the home health aide would resume her other tasks.

Giving thanks, Rachel bit into the toast. Sometimes, she could taste a hint of seasoning or sugar, but this meal was tasteless. She tried the fruit, and it tasted bitter, even though it was fresh. She forced as much down as possible on the brink of nausea.

When her doorbell sounded, Rachel was relieved for an excuse to stop torturing herself. She opened the door and greeted the larger-than-life prayer warrior.

Mother Jenkins stepped in and opened her arms. Rachel cringed, bracing for a tight hug, but the woman surprised her with a gentle hug around her shoulders. "It's good to see you."

"It's good to be seen," Rachel responded with a smile. "Can I get you coffee, tea…"

"Not a thing." Mother Jenkins walked in and took a seat, then patted the sofa. "I came to minister to you and be a blessing. Have a seat and tell me how you are coming along." She scanned Rachel's face and head. "I see you're at that stage."

"Yeah." Rachel rubbed her scalp, feeling some hair nubs.

Her guest rocked on the sofa as if it were a chair. "Beauty isn't in your hair. It's in the eye of the beholder. You know, you're breaking Minister Adams's heart." She gave her a pointed stare.

Rachel bowed her head, then fumbled with her fingers. The woman pulled no punches. Her heart began to shatter. "I…I don't want him to see me like this. When I look in the mirror, I scare myself. I feel ugly."

"Hmm." Mother Jenkins bobbed her head. "Never shut out a person—a man—who loves you through thick and thin. He's the marrying kind."

"I know." *I saw the ring box to prove it*, she thought but kept to herself.

Mother Jenkins gave a sermonette about love, opened her Bible, then flipped through the pages. "Get your Bible. I want you to memorize and meditate on this passage throughout your treatments."

Rachel did as she instructed and read along all the verses in Psalm 46.

Mother Jenkins repeated the first line in verse 10, "'Be still and know that I am God.'" She closed her Bible and looked at Rachel. "Be still and listen for God's voice. Be still…and let Minister Adams hold your hand through this journey. Be still, be still, be still."

Who could tell this missionary no? Rachel couldn't. "Okay."

Next, Mother Jenkins reached inside her bag and pulled out a sample-size perfume bottle, like the one containing the oil Nicholas had used for Aunt Tweet. She dabbed Rachel's forehead with the oil and prayed, calling on the name of Jesus in a voice that surely had the demons trembling. Rachel could feel the power and presence of the Lord.

Too soon, Mother Jenkins uttered, "Amen. Now." She took a breath, then wagged her finger and headed for the door. "You call that young minister."

Mother Jenkins probably hadn't stepped on the elevator when Rachel decided to take the woman's advice and text Nicholas: Call me when you get home. Love you.

Seconds later, her phone rang. "Not at home. Does that disqualify me from calling now?"

Rachel giggled. It felt good to smile.

"I've missed us," he said lowly. "How was your time with Mother Jenkins?"

His love, concern, and longing were endearing. "She reminds me that God is helping me." She shook her head. "And I need His help. I read the passage about casting all my cares on Him, because Jesus cares for me. Instead of writing in the journal, I've been praying more."

"Amen. Let me get to my office." He paused, then she heard a door close out the background voices. "I want to pray with you."

"Please." She frowned. "You would think I would have this big faith and be positive and no doubt, but instead, I struggle to believe."

"Don't beat yourself up," Nicholas told her. "As long as we are in this flesh, there are going to be trials." He paused and closed his eyes. "Lord, Your word says that You desire that we prosper and be in good health even as our souls prosper." He prayed and ended with, "Please continue to minister to my beloved, because I love her…"

Rachel's heart fluttered at hearing him call her *his beloved.*

"And restore her body and soul, according to Your promises—"

"Including my hair," she said as her emotions slipped.

"But you're still here," he reminded her. "Your hair has never ever defined your beauty," he said convincingly, and she believed him. "Rachel, hearing your voice has made my day. I wish I could see you tonight, but I have a meeting at church. How about tomorrow after work?"

"I have another treatment tomorrow. I decided to drive myself. I've seen other cancer patients come and go by themselves. I have to move forward."

"Ah, what if you're feeling ill after the treatment? I don't think you should be alone or try to drive home." He didn't sound happy about her decision.

"If that is the case, I'll call an Uber and have Clara come to stay until Jacqui can come."

Nicholas sighed. "O-okay. Well, maybe you'll be up to doing something this weekend."

"Without any hair, not even eyelashes or brows, I'd rather stick to going to the doctor and coming back home. I'm not comfortable going out on a date. One step at a time," she explained.

"Not seeing you isn't an option. How about I bring game night to your place with Karl and Ava and snacks in tow? All you have to do is tolerate our company for an hour or so or until you get tired."

"I'd like that. Love you sooo much." She blew kisses over the phone.

"Hey, that's my line. Love you sooo much too. Bye."

After she ended the call, she texted Jacqui. Scarf. Nicholas and I kissed and made up over the phone. You have three days to show me how to tie an Ankara scarf.

Jacqui texted back with smiley faces, hand claps, and emojis of different colored hair. Now that's the diva I know. I'm on it.

Rachel rubbed her face, void of eyebrows and lashes. In the bathroom, she stared at her reflection in the mirror. Remembering the box of eyelashes from her company's gift basket, she hurried to her dining room table. She had to get the victory over these hide-and-seek bouts of depression. She scrutinized the box.

She and her sisters had played dress-up with their dolls, using all kinds of stuff they found around the house. Time for dress-up with those lashes. Rachel headed to the bathroom, where her makeup lay untouched since her first chemo treatment.

The next morning, Rachel raided her closet for a head covering. Why did she own only one baseball cap, and it was stretched out of shape, a clear giveaway that she was bald? Without Jacqui, she had no idea how to tie a scarf to stay on a slick scalp and didn't have time for a video tutorial.

She spied the classy hats she had worn to teas and fashion shows, and she could hear Aunt Tweet. *A lady should always look as if she's about to step on a runway*, she had drilled into her nieces' heads, but only Rachel had taken it to heart. However, at the moment, a runway was the furthest thing from her mind.

Gnawing her lips, Rachel could still hear Aunt Tweet's encouraging words to go for it. Rachel exhaled and mumbled, "Okay, sisters," to herself. "Y'all call me the accessories queen, and I could turn heads in a T-shirt and jeans. Let's see how I can work jeans, tennis shoes, and one of these hats." It didn't take her long to get ready.

It had been more than a month—almost six weeks—since she had been behind the wheel of her car. A few times, Clara had been her chauffeur. Other times, it was Jacqui. Kym had come for a weekend visit to take her for the treatment. Grabbing the car keys, Rachel was a little nervous. She needed independence to regain her confidence, even if after her chemo she felt too sick to drive back home. The drive was liberating.

"Going somewhere after your treatment?" her oncology nurse, Amanda, asked with a slight curve of her lips when Rachel arrived.

"Yeah. There's no place like home." Rachel removed her sunglasses and hat to reveal her bald head.

———

Nicholas walked into the church sanctuary looking for his brother, who was in the same ministers' meeting. Spotting Karl, Nicholas turned in that direction, but Mother Jenkins cut him off and didn't move. "Has my girl—I mean Rachel—called you?"

"Yes, she did. Thank you for whatever you said to encourage her."

"She needs a lot of love and patience right now. As you know, some folks think when they surrender to the Lord, all their troubles are over. They have no idea some trials continue, and new ones pop up, but God is faithful to keep us through all of them."

"Amen." Nicholas bobbed his head in agreement.

With a slight wave, Mother Jenkins walked in the direction of where other elderly ladies sat while Nicholas slid into the pew next to Karl. Nicholas shook hands with his brother.

"What's up?" He squinted at Nicholas. "Really, what's up?"

Nicholas grinned. "Rachel is speaking to me again, and you and Ava have plans for Saturday evening."

Karl frowned. "No, we don't."

"Yes, you do, at Rachel's. Oh, and bring snacks. Light refreshments will be fine," Nicholas said smugly and directed his attention toward the front.

"It's a good thing you're my brother and my wife likes Rachel, or I'd have said no." Karl nudged his shoulder for good measure as Pastor Mann walked into the sanctuary where dozens of ministers were assembled and waiting for the meeting to get started.

"Thank you all for being here. Our church has several ministries: prison, sick and homebound, couples, and more." He paused and glanced at his tablet, then at the group again.

"I feel that we need to add more ministers to further our community involvement," the pastor explained. "The needs are great, so I'm going to redirect some of you to that group while adjusting other numbers. Also, I would like to introduce three new ministers who transferred from our sister church, Faith Temple: Evangelist Darci Union, Missionary Jocelyn Gates, and Elder Thomas Fields." He asked them to stand. "Please take some time to introduce yourselves to them when we're done."

Pastor Mann gave a PowerPoint presentation, focusing on strengthening the ministry. He concluded the meeting two hours later. While some stayed for fellowship, Karl said his goodbyes, eager to get back home.

"Praise the Lord, Ministers Adams and Adams." Evangelist Darci Union came over to talk to Nicholas and Karl. "I'm assigned to the sick and homebound team."

"Welcome to our congregation." Karl greeted her. "You'll be working with my brother Nicholas here. Sorry, I can't stay to talk. I have a wife and twins waiting for me." He nodded and left.

Evangelist Union turned to him. "Do you have a family waiting too?"

"Not yet," Nicholas said and smiled, "but I do have to check on my lady. Good night."

Chapter 32

"I'M NERVOUS," RACHEL CONFESSED AS SHE SAT AT HER VANITY table in her master bath, staring at her hairless reflection while Shelby and Sweet Pepper fought for space on her lap. The four-pound Yorkie won out. She glanced at the mirror again. It was hard to look at herself. Rachel felt she didn't look human.

"Why?" Jacqui asked as she sorted through a bunch of scarfs she'd purchased as gifts. "You said you and Nicholas made up, right?" She squinted at Rachel's reflection. "And you've met his brother and sister-in-law, so why are you nervous? You feel all right, don't you?" Panic flashed on her face.

"I'm feeling good, and I'm up for company for a few hours." Her breast was still sore from this week's radiation treatment. She would be glad when everything was over, but it was only a few weeks before Thanksgiving, and the oncologist expected her treatment to last into the New Year. She didn't want to think about her cancer, her ailments, her treatments. Nicholas was coming, and Rachel was hyped.

"Aha. This will work!" She held up a scarf that had Rachel's favorite shade of blue with yellow and purple accents.

"Nicholas has never seen me hairless." She pouted. "If it weren't for my eyes, nose, and mouth, no one would be able to tell my back from my front."

Jacqui rocked her head to one side and frowned, giving it some thought. "You've got a point, but we're going to fix that after we do your makeup." She laid the scarf aside and picked up Rachel's massive makeup holder and went to work while Rachel scratched behind Sweet Pepper's ears.

Her friend didn't miss a beat as she applied each layer of the makeup regimen: moisturizer, primer, eye shadow and highlights, the fake lashes from the gift basket, foundation and blush, contour, lipstick, and on and on. Rachel closed her eyes as her friend sprayed her face with a matte finish.

"I look"—Rachel leaned forward and touched her face in awe—"real again...beautiful."

"If you cry," Jacqui said, warning her and squinting, "and mess up my masterpiece, I will smear orange eye shadow on your forehead, cheeks, neck. I'll leave no spot untouched." She softened her voice. "You are beautiful. Watch and see if your Nicholas won't tell you the same thing. Whew," Jacqui huffed. "Time for your headdress. I'll show you how to wrap an African Ankara scarf." Step by step, her friend demonstrated how to place the fabric on Rachel's head, where to tie and fold it.

"Sister-girl, you've got skills," Rachel said in awe. "I hope I can remember everything."

"You will." Jacqui patted her shoulder. "Let's see what you should wear."

For the next hour, Rachel modeled different garments until they settled on a round-neck gold crocheted sweater with long sleeves and ruffles at the ends.

"Nice." Jacqui nodded from her perch on Rachel's bed, rocking one leg she had crossed over a knee. "Now, I must be going, darlin'. The night awaits my presence."

It had been a tagline they used when they went out on the town. Jacqui slipped on her jacket, then took the pets upstairs to the rooftop dog park for Rachel before she headed out.

Her home was spotless. Clara had made sure of that the day before. Even her meds were concealed in a small floral box. With nothing to do but wait for her guests' arrival, Rachel picked up her Bible and read a chapter in Proverbs.

Promptly at four o'clock, her doorbell rang. Shelby and Sweet Pepper yapped until Rachel opened the door. Three bright smiles greeted her: Nicholas, Karl, and Ava. But the only smile that mattered was from Nicholas. When their eyes connected, Rachel couldn't pull away. Ava complimented her head wrap and condo as she walked in. Karl nodded, then Nicholas stepped inside and closed the door.

Before she knew what was happening, he guided her into his arms. The strength in his embrace was gentle but still caused her pain.

"Ugh." She screamed and jumped back as her affected breast throbbed. She turned away. Closing her eyes, Rachel rubbed her chest, coaxing the burning to subside.

"Baby, I'm sorry. I'm so sorry," he said close behind her, but he didn't touch her.

She faced him. "It's okay. I'm still tender from the radiation. The slightest touch can cause me some sharp pains."

"I'll be more careful." He ignored the pooches' wagging tails vying for his attention as he led her to the couch. "Sure you're okay?"

"Yes."

"You rest. We'll set up everything." He changed his mind and decided not to leave her side.

After a series of deep breaths, Rachel's pain was manageable. Taking Nicholas's hand, Rachel felt content as she watched Ava scrutinize a gallon jug of punch she'd brought. Karl pulled out snacks from Publix bags: crackers, pretzels, bagels, dips, finger sandwiches, and more. Rachel prayed her taste buds would allow her to enjoy every bite.

"Dear Brother-in-Law, are you going to help with the food or game setup?" Ava asked, watching them.

"Nope." Nicholas grinned. "I'm going to sit right here next to my lady love."

"Good answer, Minister Adams. Don't let my wife get you in trouble," Karl said.

Rachel watched their interaction and admired them. *Will that be me one day?* Rachel hoped. *Married with two children? Lord, I'm humbly putting my request in.*

"Sorry to take over your kitchen, Rachel. Do I have permission to rummage through your cabinets for paper plates?" Ava asked.

"Trust me, people have taken over my kitchen these last few months." Rachel waved.

"I prefer china for my queen." Nicholas stood and walked into the kitchen and retrieved the china and stemware as if he lived there, then set the table while Ava folded her arms, wearing an impressed expression. She got Rachel's attention and winked as she gave her a thumbs-up.

"And what did you bring to the potluck, Minister Adams?" Rachel asked.

"Tacos." He pointed to the bag on the counter that she hadn't noticed before. He claimed his seat next to her again and leaned closer. "You okay?"

"I'm getting stronger every day." Rubbing the silky hairs on his jaw, Rachel smiled.

"I've missed you," he whispered as his eyes roamed her head before settling on her lips.

She was giddy that the man wanted to kiss her. She didn't know how she felt about Karl and Ava being a detriment from that happening. She blushed.

"I never want us to push each other into something we both aren't prepared for," Nicholas said as he toyed with her hooped earrings.

"Me either." She bowed her head and looked at her unpolished nails. Rachel was surprised Jacqui hadn't fussed at her about needing a manicure.

"Now that that's out of the way." He lifted her chin with his thumb and turned her from side to side. "You're as pretty as ever."

Once he held her stare, he gathered her hands, then brushed his lips again her knuckles. Despite feeling like a Sphynx cat, his gestures made her feel beautiful.

Rachel's heart danced with his praise. "It's not too much makeup, considering I'm not going out?" She touched the head wrap. "Do you like my scarf?"

"I do. There is nothing about you I don't love." He bit his lip as he studied her headpiece. "But you didn't have to go through all the trouble for us."

"I didn't want you to see me with my bald head. Plus I wanted—no, *needed*—to feel beautiful."

"And you are perfect for me—"

Ava cut him off. "As soon as I heat up the dip, we can eat."

"How's your appetite?" Nicholas asked, squeezing her hands and assisting her to her feet.

She moved her head from side to side. "Better with certain foods."

Gathered around her dining room table, they joined hands and gave thanks for their snacks. As she slowly indulged in the food, she could feel Nicholas's eyes on her. Was he making sure she ate, or did she look odd with the fake lashes and the Ankara scarf around her head? Feeling self-conscious, she faced him. "What's wrong?"

"Absolutely nothing. I missed you. You're the best part of me, and you're stunning."

She lowered her fake lashes and blushed.

"Plus, I have to make sure you eat."

He also made her happy. She leaned within an inch of his lips and scrunched her nose playfully. "Just for you."

"Thank you."

Karl cleared his throat. "Hey, there are children in the room." He pointed to himself and his wife.

They all laughed, then Karl and Ava cleared the table to play the board game Sequence.

"I had so much fun playing this at your house," Rachel said.

"We know," Ava and Karl said, amused.

"Rachel and me on one team," Nicholas said and lifted her arm in the air, careful not to hurt her.

"Let's make it more interesting and play the men against women," Ava said, trying to reason with him.

"Nope." Nicholas shook his head like a stubborn child. He was adorable and comical at the same time, but he wouldn't budge. They may lose, but he was determined they be on the same team.

She and Nicholas were on the verge of forming the correct number of sequences on the board with their chips when he cleared his throat to signal to Rachel not to make a move.

"That's against the rules, man. You can't help a teammate. You have to pull a card and put it in the discard pile," Karl said with no leniency. "We played this at my house not long ago, so how did you forget that?"

Nicholas didn't bother to answer, and the game ended hours later. The husband-and-wife team beat them.

"This was so much fun. Thank you for coming and 'babysitting' us." Rachel made air quotes with her fingers before Nicholas grabbed her hand and squeezed. They shared a laugh. Were they both thinking about the kiss they were resisting?

"It's called accountability," Karl said.

"Yep," his wife chimed in with a smile. "We are our brother's keeper. When you love someone, the magnetism is powerful, and it was thick in here tonight." Her eyes danced. "So is the temptation. We love you both, and we want to help your relationship."

"I know it ain't easy, but it's doable." Karl nodded.

"Amen. Pastor Mann preached on that last Sunday." Nicholas rested his elbows on his knees and seemed to be in serious thought.

"I miss being in church." Rachel sighed. "It's not the same watching the service at home."

Ava frowned. "If you're feeling up to it, why not go tomorrow? I'll come and get you," she offered eagerly.

Until Rachel drove herself to the center for treatment, she hadn't realized that she had given up too much of her independence. "I can drive myself." She patted her head wrap. "But will I stand out with my Ankara scarf?" That sounded so ironic. She and Jacqui had thrived on being the center of attention. Funny how cancer makes a person want to shy away from public scrutiny—well, some folks.

Nicholas took her hand. "They will stare at your beauty," he said softly.

"You're saying that because you love me."

"He's right, Rachel," Ava said with a smile. "You know how to rock anything you put on. You've lost some weight, but you're still radiant."

"Thanks for the confidence booster. I've been struggling with that among other things, but I'm learning to be still and listen for God to lead me."

"Amen," her guests said in unison.

"Okay." Rachel came to a decision. "If I can get a good night's rest, fix my face, and tie my head wrap without too much trouble, I'll be there as close to on time as possible."

"Yes!" Nicholas lifted a fist in the air. "I guess I'd better help them clean up so we can be on our way. I want you well rested." She had never seen him move so fast. Rachel doubled over laughing until a few tears escaped.

At her door, Nicholas seemed to study her. "Baby, if in the morning, you're up to it but don't want to drive, I'll get you."

"Thank you," she whispered, admiring his handsome features. It seemed like forever since she'd seen him last instead of days. "I'm determined to come, and it will do me good to drive more." She shook her head. "If I'm going to fight and beat this cancer, I want to be surrounded by prayers."

Judging from the twinkle in his eyes, her statement pleased him. "Woman, don't make me drop to one knee and ask you one question that has only one right answer."

"I look forward to that one day, but not today," Rachel said softly as her heart fluttered.

"Fight, Rachel. Fight for you. Fight for us," Nicholas said in a low voice as she closed the door.

Chapter 33

RACHEL DIDN'T CARE HOW LONG IT TOOK, BUT SHE WAS DETERMINED to get dressed for church and drive herself. The previous night, she read the joy of the Lord was her strength from Nehemiah, chapter 8. She needed that strength this morning. After she prayed and showered, she forced food down in order to take her meds. Surprisingly, she could taste the sweetness of the grapes in the fruit salad Ava had left.

Next, she selected something as colorful as one of the scarves Jacqui had bought for her. She had a closet full of clothes that once flattered her figure.

After about fifteen minutes, she decided on a red and gold dress that had a lot of ruffles that would camouflage her breast ailments.

After the surgery, the oncologist had suggested she wear a soft breast prosthesis that could be attached to a camisole to give the affected breast a balanced appearance with her other one. The breast form had become as commonplace as slipping into pantyhose—uncomfortable at times because of the tenderness. Jacqui had mentioned some of their friends who wore this to appear more voluptuous. It was definitely a confidence booster for Rachel.

Finally, standing in her bathroom, scrutinizing her reflection in the mirror, she saw that cancer had its own look, even from a distance. Rachel applied her makeup and artistically sketched her eyebrows. She thought about the women who weren't makeup gurus. Rachel was glad Walgreens had a service for cancer patients.

Next, she tackled tying her scarf. This labor seemed to be payback for her refusing to wear a wig, even a donated one. She wasn't as adept as Jacqui, but the YouTube tutorials were amazing. She didn't know how much she appreciated African attire until now.

Nicholas had texted her twice before she could walk out the door. This was in addition to the initial morning text with a Scripture. Are you still coming?

Yes, she replied. She shook her head in amusement.

Half an hour later, he texted again: Are you on your way?

Walking out the door. As she drove to church, Nicholas's words kept vibrating through her head: *Fight, Rachel. Fight for you. Fight for us.*

"Lord, help me to fight the months ahead of chemo and radiation therapies when I'm so sick and weak. Help me," she prayed. "Feed me Your joy for strength."

———

Nicholas was hyped that Rachel had a desire to return to church, because he missed her presence. Yet he was concerned about whether she had the strength to drive the twenty minutes from her condo to Brentwood.

"Ava and the boys are holding Rachel a seat," Karl said after he came and stood next to Nicholas. "Is she still coming?" he asked with a concerned expression.

"Yeah." Nicholas checked the time on his phone. "She should have been here by now."

Karl nodded. "Morning worship is about to start. I guess we need to pray her all the way to her destination, Bro."

"Amen." He liked the sound of that.

While some members remained in the fellowship hall, finishing up the snacks served between services, Nicholas and Karl headed toward the foyer and glanced out into the parking lot, searching for Rachel's car.

"I'll meet you on the pulpit," Karl said after a few minutes.

When Nicholas had no time left to keep watching and waiting, he headed to the sanctuary where the praise team was singing a rendition of "I'm Available to You."

He took his post along with the other ministers on the side of the pulpit. The singers were finishing their second selection when it seemed as if God tapped him on the shoulder and pointed his head in the exact direction where he saw Rachel taking a seat next to Ava. She looked regal in her colorful attire. His nephews were bouncing in place, vying for her attention. Nicholas only hoped they wouldn't hurt her with their excitement.

He whispered his thanks to the Lord for her safe arrival and exhaled. Rachel had a magnetic pull on him, so he couldn't look away. He saw her send him a slight wave, then there was a second wave and a third before Ava told her sons to stop. Nicholas chuckled. All was right in his world.

Karl, who was two rows in front of Nicholas, glanced back and mouthed, *See her?*

Nicholas nodded and would have grinned, but the service was streaming live. If the cameras were on him, a viewer might misinterpret his behavior as disrespect.

Pastor Mann stepped to the podium and greeted visitors and members. He sang a few choruses of "How Excellent," then directed everyone's attention to Isaiah 26:3.

"My question this morning is how's your attention span? Will you remember today's sermon or Scripture reading? Can you focus on God's voice when you pray?" He paused and looked around the sanctuary while tapping his foot. Was he actually waiting for someone to answer?

For the next half hour, he preached hard on the formula for perfect peace. "Seek God in bad times and even when things are good at the moment."

The sermon inspired a heavy dose of praise and worship.

After the offering and benediction, Nicholas made a beeline to where Rachel was chatting with Ava. Mother Jenkins was coming from another direction as if they were racing to see who could get to Rachel first.

Somehow, Mother Jenkins shifted to third gear and beat Nicholas by four steps. "Well, well, well." Her face glowed with happiness. She was about to wrap her arms around Rachel when Nicholas linked his hands through Rachel's and moved her out of harm's way.

She squinted. "Minister Adams, please step aside so I can give her a hug."

Rachel leaned close to Mother Jenkins and whispered, "I'm still sore from my radiation treatment."

"Oh, of course." Mother Jenkins nodded. "You're always on my personal prayer list. I'll call and come visit one day this week."

Rachel's eyes lit up. "I'd like that. I always look forward to our talks."

"Hello."

Nicholas recognized Evangelist Union's voice before she approached.

"I caught a glimpse of your Ankara scarf in service." She scanned the headwrap as if she was cataloging the twists and folds to duplicate it. "It's beautiful."

"Thank you," Rachel answered in a shaky voice. She still appeared a bit self-conscious.

"Oh, I'm sorry. I'm Evangelist Union." She extended her hand for a shake, and Rachel loosened her fingers from Nicholas to accept it. "I'm also assigned to the sick and homebound list. If it's okay, maybe I can tag along when Mother Jenkins visits. My sister had breast cancer and recovered fully."

Rachel's eyes brightened. "That would be nice."

Mother Jenkins cleared her voice. "Too many visitors will wear Rachel out."

Nicholas blinked. Did Mother Jenkins ever let her guard down toward women? What unfounded suspicions did she have now? Didn't matter as Nicholas held his tongue. It appeared Mother Jenkins's overprotectiveness now extended to Rachel. And Nicholas liked that.

Chapter 34

"THE GOOD NEWS IS YOU'RE CLEAR TO TRAVEL THANKSGIVING, since you're taking a short flight to St. Louis. Your vitals look good, and your body continues to respond to the chemo," Dr. Rush, her primary oncologist, said after the nurse submitted Rachel's chart for review. "However, you should be aware of the risks and take precautions."

"What type of precautions?" The holiday was ten days away. She had just finished her radiation treatment, and Rachel looked forward to meeting Kym in St. Louis to spend the holiday with Tabitha and Marcus. She had already started to eat more to build her strength so her family wouldn't make a fuss over her at the dinner table.

"Cancer can increase your risk of deep vein thrombosis—or a blood clot—when flying." He cited more precautions. "I'll have Amanda give you some pamphlets on the dos and don'ts for cancer patients."

It was bittersweet news. Once Rachel returned home and read over the travel tips, she debated whether it was worth the four-day visit. Would fatigue get the best of her amid the expected crowds? If she had a medical emergency, her oncology team was hundreds of miles away. Should she go home, or should she stay in Nashville?

After a couple of days, Nicholas sensed her distraction. When she explained her dilemma, he suggested an impromptu field trip. "Just the two of us. We can go to the Country Music Hall of Fame and Museum, then we'll see how you feel navigating crowds."

Rachel wasn't sure if that was a good idea but gave his suggestion some thought. Neither of them had been inside the museum since the expansion was completed. The project had doubled the square footage and included interactive sections.

"We'll go at your pace and leave when you feel yourself getting tired." The compassion in his words and eyes melted her heart.

"Okay."

On Saturday afternoon, Nicholas showed up in jeans and white sweater, matching her choice of attire—a white sweater and jean skirt and leggings. "You look pretty."

He had no idea how much his words touched her. "Thank you."

Grabbing her hand, he brought it up to his lips. "And you look like you belong to me." He winked.

Surprisingly, Rachel tapped into her energy reserves and threw caution to the wind, ignoring the stares from people who might have suspected she was a cancer patient. Hand in hand, they viewed some historic video clips and admired only a sampling of the stockpile of costumes and music instruments the museum housed, dating back a hundred years.

The old music recordings and impressive photo collection alone were reasons why Nashville attracted so many tourists each year. Plus, there was an addition of the Taylor Swift Education Center. Kudos for Nashvillians.

Nicholas asked if she was ready to move to another display, but an odd sensation seemed to drape over her, and she couldn't move. He faced her. The worry in his eyes showed his concern. "What's wrong? Babe, talk to me."

Rachel was hesitant to say. "It will seem as if I'm complaining." She lowered her head in shame. "I keep having these mood swings." She thought she had overcome these pity parties, but they popped up without warning. She hated seeming spiritually as weak as her body, especially when she was reading her Bible more.

"Hey." Nicholas released her hand to lift her chin. "I'm here. You're going through major obstacles. Talk to me so I can understand."

She smiled despite her troubled spirit and debated if she should vent after his soothing words. "My life seemed so simple before my diagnosis—I worked hard and enjoyed what I did, my sisters and I traveled at will, I was active in my community… Being a cancer patient changed what was once commonplace."

"I know." He held her hand again and massaged her fingers. His warm smile encouraged her to continue.

"As a cancer patient, I have a risk of developing a blood clot if I choose to fly. During the holidays, I could be more susceptible to a pat down at the airport because of my head covering, and I might be asked to reveal…my prosthesis."

She shivered at the thought of someone seeing the effects the radiation had on her skin. "There are risks of an infection around large crowds. Like now, I'm becoming paranoid, wondering if someone is sick. This is crazy." She sighed, then faced the glass again as an old black-and-white film clip played.

Rachel rested her head on his shoulder.

He kissed her forehead. "Tired?"

"A little overwhelmed. This place was already big, but with the expansion, it is huge. You know I like skylines, so I really wanted to see the view over the city from the event halls."

"Another day, maybe." He looked at the time on his phone. "We've already been here for a couple of hours. Let's go to the café so you can rest."

She nodded and let him lead her. While she sat, Nicholas took off to get her something to drink.

He returned with bottled waters for both of them and a snack to share. "I'm taking you home for the holiday," Nicholas said out of the blue, his jaw set. "You haven't seen your sisters in weeks."

Rachel smiled and rested her hand on top of his. He was everything she never knew she wanted in a man.

"Aw. That's sweet, but I don't think I'm up for a four-hour road trip."

"You're not." Nicholas bobbed his head. For the next few minutes, he was focused on something on his phone, then he looked up and gave her a brilliant grin. "Booked. I'm escorting you home on the plane."

Speechless at first, Rachel could only stare at this man. "What about *your* family?" she finally asked, beyond surprised.

"Since it's a short flight, I won't miss a beat. After I get you to your family, I'll turn around and board my return trip back home. Airport parking should be cheap." He grinned.

Talk about sacrifice. The things he was willing to do for her. "You think of everything, and I couldn't love you more."

"Remember that when I ask you to marry me." He winked.

Huh? Marriage. A future. She still worried about her survival, and she still worried about the ups and downs in her faith. But for Nicholas's sake, she mustered a smile and replied, "Noted."

———

The day before Thanksgiving, the media reported an increase in the spread of flu cases across the Midwest. "Great." Rachel twisted her lips in disappointment. Would there always be some sort of emotional setback? Before she could text Nicholas about possibly backing out, he called.

"As soon as I saw the health alert about the flu, I thought of you and said a prayer that no harm, disease, or illness would come near you. Wear your surgical mask and pack your hand sanitizer. You'll be fine. God is a keeper."

"Yes, thanks for the constant reminder." Rachel ended the call and finished packing while she reflected on her past. It was sad that she and Jacqui had used their looks and sass to turn heads from the opposite sex, but now her physical beauty was in remission while her cancer took center stage. Nicholas never backed down from his feelings.

Her bald head, hairless face, and weak stature drew unwanted scrutiny, but she was working hard to change her image and attitude. Fake lashes, a brow pencil, and lipstick could do so much, even without the head wrap and full makeup application: primer, highlights, contour. Then, the perfect accessory was spiritual strength.

At three o'clock, Rachel gave her reflection one final check. Bright shades of blue had always enhanced her skin tone. She smiled at the sapphire sweater and same color cape that accented her off-white pants and cowboy boots—after all, she was from Nashville.

"You can pull this off," she told herself as the doorbell rang. Grabbing her surgical mask, she covered her nose and mouth, then looped the thick strings behind her ears. Nicholas had only seen her wear it a few times, usually after her treatments. Smiling behind the mask, Rachel opened the door and stepped back so he could enter. "I know it's going to draw attention—"

Nicholas held up his hand to protest and shook his head. "All that matters to me is you stay healthy." He grabbed her hand and squeezed. "I'll be right there beside you. Where's your luggage?"

She pointed to the hall. "I notified TSA Cares. Amanda, my oncology nurse, gave me a pamphlet. I advised them that I'm a cancer patient. A TSA lead officer will be there to assist me. They also gave me a preboarding pass. I might not have to remove my head wrap or reveal…you know. That would be sooooo embarrassing." She pointed to her designer luggage. One carry-on and one to check.

"You got your medicine?" he asked.

Rachel patted her handbag. After doing one final sweep of her condo to make sure she didn't leave anything, she walked out with her hand in Nicholas's.

At the airport, Rachel did her best to brace herself against the stares and whispers of "I hope she doesn't make us sick" or "I wonder what's wrong with her." To be honest, prior to becoming a cancer patient, she would have had the same thoughts.

Her heart raced as they inched closer to the security checkpoint. After Nicholas put her luggage and his overnight bag—just in case he missed his turnaround flight—on the conveyor belt to be screened, she held her breath.

Besides the compliments on her head wrap and a pat down from the awaiting TSA lead agent, her experience was stress free to her relief. Her preboarding ticket allowed her to board the plane with other passengers who needed assistance before the A-section travelers.

She claimed the window seat while Nicholas stored their luggage in the overhead bin, then they strapped their seat belts for the one-hour flight to St. Louis. Although Rachel tried to avoid eye contact, she could feel eyes lingering on her and her mask as passengers made their way down the aisle to find seats.

It didn't go unnoticed by her that a couple of women's eyes lingered on Nicholas longer than necessary. When one woman whose perfume permeated through Rachel's mask took the aisle seat next to Nicholas, Rachel rested her head on his shoulder. When he wrapped his arm around her, she closed her eyes. She would be glad when her treatments were over. She may not have all her hair and the same body again, but at least she was loved.

Soon, she and Nicholas landed at Lambert Airport in St. Louis. As the two of them exited the terminal, Rachel's eyes watered at the sight of her welcoming party. Her sisters and Marcus held balloons, flowers, even a stuffed toy. Rachel laughed as Nicholas squeezed her hand.

"You are loved, sweetheart."

"I know." She gazed at him.

The sisters took turns hugging and kissing Rachel. The mask didn't deter their affections. "Nicholas, thanks for bringing our sister home," Kym said with tear-filled eyes.

"You're welcome, but remember you have to give her back to me," he said, and emotions choked in Rachel's throat.

On the return flight to Nashville, Nicholas snagged a window seat and glanced out. Although he missed Rachel beside him, he knew he'd made the right choice in accompanying her home. The visit would be good for her as long as she stayed healthy. He saw the looks cast in their direction, and he hated that she had to be subjected to people's pity. He hoped, in the midst of pity, someone added her to a prayer list.

"Thanksgiving is all about family, and you brought me home to mine." Rachel had hugged him tight. He had limited his embraces for fear of hurting her. "Go and enjoy your folks," she said.

"I'll be back Sunday afternoon. Remember I love you and I'll be praying."

That was when her eyes sparkled. "Love you more and thank you."

With that, he had shaken hands with her family, given her one final hug, and made his way into the line for the security checkpoint. Despite his urging for Rachel to go, she didn't budge as he continued walking toward his gate.

"God, I love her."

"That's a bummer," his seatmate, a pretty woman with rich dark skin and stylish short curls, said. "I was hoping you weren't seeing anyone." Her lips curved upward. "You're not wearing a ring."

Nicholas didn't realize he had spoken his thoughts out loud. Slightly embarrassed, he chuckled. "Trust me, my woman has me wrapped around her finger." He waited for his flight to take off. The sooner he could get home and enjoy Thanksgiving, the sooner he could return to St. Louis for Rachel.

Chapter 35

THANKSGIVING MORNING, NICHOLAS SENT RACHEL A TEXT BEFORE he left for the annual church service. She would attend Bethesda Temple in St. Louis with her family.

She called him. Before he could say hello, she blurted out, "I love you, and I miss you!"

Her declaration breathed life into him, and he closed his eyes to savor the moment. Nicholas had never thought those three words had that much power. Hours later, he was still smiling when he showed up at his parents' house for dinner.

"Hey, Son," his dad said as Nicholas walked through his childhood home. While Karl favored their father, Nicholas had inherited his mother's facial features. His nephews barreled toward him when they heard his voice. He and Karl entertained the boys until his mother and sister-in-law set the table.

After his father gave thanks and asked for God's blessings, everyone ate. The conversation was lively, covering everything from the morning message to hanging Christmas decorations, which prompted the boys to shout out their gift lists, to his favorite topic—Rachel.

"Uncle Nick, is Miss Rachel going to die?" Kory asked the bombshell, silencing everyone.

Nicholas snarled at his brother. Number one: Where had his nephew heard that from? Number two: Karl, also a minister, should have had this talk with his son.

Nicholas selfishly hoped not anytime soon, but only God had that answer. To say no and then have Rachel succumb to cancer could affect his nephew's relationship with God in the long term. To say yes or maybe would be too much for even Nicholas to bear. "If we want to be with

Jesus, we have to have a new body, so the old one has to go away." That was the best Nicholas could do without encouraging more questions.

"I want to see Jesus too, but I don't want to die." Kory shook his head. "And I don't want Miss Rachel to die either." His bottom lip trembled.

"None of us do, Son." Karl spoke up for the first time and rubbed Kory's head. "Just keep praying for her, okay?"

Kory bobbed his head.

"I'll pray too!" Rory added.

———

Nothing like family love. Rachel felt more like herself surrounded by them. Since no one was sick, she didn't have to walk around the Whittington house talking through a surgical mask.

Rachel also appreciated not being bombarded with questions about her condition. Although she had to rest twice, she was able to work alongside Kym and Tabitha to help recreate Marcus's mother's secret pie recipe. If they missed the mark on the half sweet potato half pecan pie, would her taste buds know any different?

"You know, I'm glad you have Nicholas in your life," Kym said, then turned to Tabitha and patted her hand. "And Marcus is in yours. Although I'm the oldest, I didn't expect to be an old maid."

"You won't be for long." Tabitha playfully scrunched up her nose. "If you weren't so picky."

Kym lifted a shoulder and her chin. "It's called selective."

Rachel glanced at Marcus, who stood. "That's my cue. Sounds like a lively Knicely sisters discussion is about to start, so I'll take my leave." With that said, he hurried toward the hallway.

"Wait, babe," Tabitha called after him, and he pivoted around.

It was something about the twinkle in both their eyes that made Rachel suspicious of the glow on Tabitha's face. Rachel squinted. "Is my sister going to have a baby?"

Marcus had the nerve to grin. "Yes, we are."

Kym jumped up and did a happy dance.

Tears sprung from deep within Rachel, and she couldn't stop. She was happy and in awe before sadness seemed to close in on her. "What if I don't live to see her?"

"Him," Marcus corrected and came to her side as did Tabitha and Kym. "Rachel," he said with a serious expression, "let our baby be your inspiration to live."

"I'm trying." Rachel sniffed. "But some days are hard. I have bouts of self-pity creep up on me, and it's hard to shake."

"You've been happy since you arrived. Don't let the devil steal your joy. That is our ammunition," Tabitha said, then reminded Rachel of the Scripture in Nehemiah 8.

That night, lying in one of the guest bedrooms, Rachel couldn't sleep as the moon's light peeked through the blinds. "Lord, please help me to beat this cancer and live life to the fullest. I want to be an auntie, wife, and mother. In Jesus's name, amen."

The Sunday message after Thanksgiving inspired Rachel. Tabitha's pastor had cited Hebrews 12:2: *Don't be ashamed of your struggle…*

It made sense. Rachel meditated on Hebrews 12:2 most of the day. She needed a deep-rooted conviction that she could finish her course of treatment.

That evening, Rachel slipped on her surgical mask in preparation for the masses at the airport. *Lord, help me not to be ashamed of my circumstances*, she silently prayed as her sisters and Marcus drove her to Lambert International Airport, where Nicholas's flight had arrived from Nashville and he was waiting for her.

After hugging her family goodbye, she looked up and saw Nicholas clearing the double doors to retrieve her luggage and take her hand. "Enjoy yourself?"

"Yes. Thank you for making sure I got to see my family for the holiday."

His eyes sparkled. "No problem. Now, I'm taking you back home, and I don't think I'm going to let you out of my sight again for a very long time, Miss Knicely."

Rachel's heart swelled with his possessiveness. "That works for me, Mr. Adams."

"We didn't have enough time together," Tabitha whined.

"I'll try and get to Nashville during Christmas break at the university." Kym gave her a hug and whispered, "I love you. Remember, you're stronger than you think." She kissed Rachel's cheek, then Tabitha joined in the group hug as Marcus chatted with Nicholas.

After a few minutes, Nicholas broke up her goodbyes. "Come on, babe. We have to get you through security."

"Okay." She gave her sisters one more kiss, then took Nicholas's hand and headed to TSA preboarding.

While waiting for their flight back to Nashville, Rachel had more confidence than she had arrived with. She still drew stares, but instead of avoiding eye contact, she met them head-on and smiled with her eyes.

Nicholas left her side for the restroom while Rachel flipped through a beauty magazine.

"Look, Mommy. She's like me," a child said loudly nearby, pointing.

A little girl raced up to Rachel and patted her lap. The girl wore an identical surgical mask. She flopped in the seat Nicholas vacated. "I'm Emily. I'm seven, and I have acute lymphoblastic leukemia. What's your name?"

"Rachel."

"What type of cancer do you have?" the chatterbox asked, drawing curious eavesdroppers. The child's mother gave Rachel an apologetic look but did nothing to rein in her daughter's curiosity.

"Invasive ductal carcinoma."

"Oh." Emily folded her arms and scooted back as if she was ready for an in-depth conversation. Rachel peered through the crowd. Where was Nicholas? "What stage?"

Lord, please let her grow up to be a doctor, because she sure was a nosey little thing. Wait, Rachel needed to rephrase that. There was something about this child that seemed angelic. "One."

"Me too. One is good, because it's a small number." Emily's legs dangled from the chair. "Jesus told me not to be afraid because He loves little children. Do you have any kids?"

Rachel shook her head.

"When I grow up, I'm going to have kids." Emily reached up and fingered Rachel's head wrap. "Yours is pretty." She jumped off the seat, raced to her mother, then dragged a long scarf out of her mother's tote bag. She returned and handed Rachel the scarf. "Can you make mine like that?" Her eyes were wide with hope.

Rachel looked up and saw Nicholas to the side, smiling. His eyes sparkled with encouragement. Onlookers seemed curious too. Rachel had recently mastered it on herself; a pro, she wasn't. But she couldn't bring herself to say no, so she instructed the girl to turn around.

The child stood between Rachel's knees while Rachel tried to duplicate her handiwork. Of course, the slick head was a problem.

Lord, please let me make this little girl's day. Emily's mother squatted in front of them and put her fingers on Emily's scalp to hold the scarf in place. They had become the center of attention, with onlookers in the distance, and a few curious children drew closer.

"Can I help?" an elderly lady asked.

Rachel shrugged. "Sure." Accepting the help, Rachel worked tirelessly and finished minutes before the first boarding call. Applause spread around them.

Emily turned around and hugged Rachel with her bony arms, then kissed her cheek. "Thanks, Rachel." She waved and was about to skip off when Rachel stopped her.

"I have something for you." She reached inside her purse and pulled out one of two surgical masks her colleagues had drawn a pair of red lips on. She handed it to Emily. The girl's eyes widened in delight, earning Rachel another hug.

Nicholas rejoined her and grinned. "Yep." He nodded. "You'll be a good mother."

Tilting her head, she watched Emily holding her mother's hand and skipping away. "I think so too."

Chapter 36

"JUDGING FROM THE WAY YOU'RE DEVOURING OUR POPCORN, I would say your appetite has returned," Nicholas said, teasing Rachel. They were among a handful of residents on the mezzanine of Rachel's condo building watching a movie in the small community theater and munching on complimentary self-serve snacks.

"Not really." Rachel popped a couple more pieces in her mouth and chewed. "I have a game plan to feed my appetite until I'm eating everything on my plate."

"You've reached that this evening and then some with your second bag." He laughed and ducked as she balled up a napkin and threw it at him. Their sparring came to an apologetic end when others in the theater turned around and frowned at them.

Nicholas rested his arm on the back of her seat and pulled her closer for a brief hug, then curled his lips in amusement. "Happy?"

"Ecstatic." She closed her eyes and then opened them. "I believe God is going to restore more things in my life besides my appetite."

"Amen." He lifted his hand for a soft high five so they wouldn't disturb others. "Keep on that spiritual high."

"The Lord was already working on my behalf. I believe God sent Emily to open my eyes. Although I'm late to this war, I'm a fighter." She pumped her fist in the air.

"You're talking my language, woman." Nicholas grinned.

"I wish I had gotten Emily's number to stay in touch," Rachel mused. "I often wonder how she's doing and what she's doing." Rachel remained in awe of meeting the larger-than-life Emily, who didn't seem afraid of cancer or ashamed that she didn't have hair like everyone else. It was a lesson learned.

Nicholas chuckled. "I imagine the little spitfire is carrying out God's assignment to give hope to the hopeless and joy to the sorrowful."

"I believe that too." Rachel nodded. "No doubt. A few minutes in her presence and I felt as if months of burdens were lifted."

They fell into a comfortable silence as one of the superheroes appeared on screen to save the day while Rachel continued to munch on the popcorn.

"Hey, babe, I know you have another treatment on Friday, and you'll probably be recuperating on Saturday, but hopefully, you'll feel up to a carriage ride next week at the Gaylord Opryland so we can see the outdoor nativity display." Nicholas stood and walked to the bar for more bottled waters.

"I'd like that. I'll wear my faux fur hat, and none will be the wiser."

"You'll get another amen from me and a kiss," which he brushed against her forehead. "One day," he whispered, "I'm going to kiss you as if we're married—just saying." Nicholas began to whistle softly as he suddenly became interested in the movie they really weren't watching.

Rachel aimed a popcorn kernel at his head and fired, laughing. Soon, he laughed too. She looked forward to the day when she could say yes to marrying him.

———

"I've so missed you, lady," Nicholas said to Rachel's curious expression as she strapped on her seat belt so he could drive them to midweek Bible class.

"You've been right here with me, so how have you missed me?"

After checking the rearview mirror, he pulled out. "You're no longer tormented with fear of the unknown. You're truly free."

"I finally feel my freedom." She lifted her hand in the air in silent praise, then she said "Hallelujah." Nicholas joined in, and they sang and prayed until he drove into the parking lot.

Helping her out, they both smiled. "I guess we've already had church before we came."

"Definitely." Rachel laughed. "Another month or so of treatment, and I hope to be in remission. It will always be in the back of my mind that the cancer could resurface, but it's not going to haunt me. I'm going to own that possibility and keep stepping!"

"That sounds like my woman." Nicholas synchronized his steps with hers as they made their way to the church entrance and crossed paths with Mother Jenkins.

The woman stopped in her tracks. She eyed Rachel, then a slow grin spread across her face. "Well, well, you look different. The sadness that once lingered on you has lifted, and you're glowing. If you shine any brighter, I'll need sunglasses." She snickered. "I heard one of my grands say that. Continue to live one day at a time, and let God be your strength."

"Thank you. Amen."

On Friday, Rachel's joy remained unshakeable as she walked through the door of the clinic for her routine treatment. Sonya Green, a breast cancer patient, almost bumped into Rachel. "I'm cured."

"One day, that will be me!" Rachel gave her a high five. "I'll be praying that it will never come out of remission."

"Mm-hmm. Just in the nick of time too," Sonya said in a lower voice. "I think my husband's been seeing another woman."

Rachel gasped. "Oh no. I'm sorry." The two weren't friends exactly, but sometimes their treatments aligned. Beyond knowing the woman was an accountant and that she was married with two teenagers, they didn't share more than surface stuff. Rachel was surprised the woman revealed the heartbreaking tidbit to little more than a stranger.

The jubilance on Sonya's face moments earlier was wiped clean as she snarled. "Yeah. While I'm fighting for my life, Erik isn't fighting to hold our marriage together..." The woman stopped midsentence. If a patient didn't have a before-cancer photo, a person wouldn't know how much life and personality was lost. Sonya had shown Rachel a photo when she had competed in a cooking contest three years ago.

Rachel had not reciprocated. The transformation had been too painful.

"You're not married, right?" Sonya squinted.

"No." Rachel had told the woman as much. "But I have a special man who loves me." She wanted to shout that fact to the world with the same energy little Emily had, but Rachel didn't want to rub her happiness in this woman's face.

When she first was diagnosed with cancer, Rachel thought Nicholas would become scarce once he saw the effects of her treatment, but his smiles had never changed. He was truly a good man.

"Cheaters don't always wear a ring, honey. You never know if a man is faithful until he's tested."

Oh, Nicholas had definitely been tested. She was saved from more of the woman's tirade when the nurse opened the door and called for her.

The first thing Amanda said was Rachel was glowing. Good. She was determined not to let her light dim again. "It's getting close to when my treatments will end."

———

Emily. The girl had been on Nicholas's mind since Rachel had brought up her name. As he stood next to the child's mother at the airport, watching the interaction along with other curious travelers, Nicholas and the woman had spoken.

"You have an amazing little girl," Nicholas had complimented.

The mother nodded. "She has a mission in her short life, and that is to encourage those who are sick. Actually, she's adopted, and the agency didn't have a long history about her birth parents. I feel she's doing important work, so I don't intervene."

Rachel had done a 360 after her St. Louis trip and meeting Emily. She seemed to struggle less with depression and the embarrassment about her appearance, to which she was entitled. In essence, her faith in God had increased.

One day at work, Nicholas had a break and called to check on her. "What ya doing?"

She chuckled. "If it wasn't for Clara playing a board game with me, I'd be bored."

Nicholas chuckled. "Well, I hope you win. Anything else newsworthy?" He loved hearing her happy despite her circumstances.

"I can't wait to get back to work! I called my boss, just to inquire about the Lexington project, and asked him if there was anything I could help with at home."

"And?"

"He told me the construction is back on schedule after the client wanted to tweak a room size and add another doorway. That's one way to make an engineer frustrated." She chuckled. "But other than that, he asked how I was feeling and said not to worry about work."

"I agree." He blew her a kiss, told her he loved her, then ended the call to head to a meeting.

Later that evening when they talked, she was decorating her condo for Christmas. "I want to experience all the holiday festivities around Nashville."

Although Nicholas was more than willing to oblige, he felt he had to use wisdom and monitor Rachel so she wouldn't overdo it. Since she was tolerating food better, they started to visit some of her favorite healthy eating spots again in East Nashville. The two had started to do some holiday shopping while admiring millions of lights on display at the Delta Atrium.

One memorable holiday outing included an Adams family tradition. The twins had chosen the Cirque Dreams Holidaze at Grand Ole Opry. His family, Kym, who was in town, and even Rachel looked forward to seeing the show. Nicholas's concern was it was days after one of Rachel's treatments, but she seemed to be bouncing back faster, and she'd assured him she was too excited not to feel well enough to attend.

So at the appointed time, the two families were in awe as they watched the performers of Cirque do amazing stunts. He squeezed Rachel's hand. "Thank you for coming into my life."

She faced him with a smile. "I thank God for you every day."

His heart pounded with affection that earned her a kiss on the cheek and his nephews' *yuck*s and his parents' smiles.

Chapter 37

IT IS GOOD FOR ME THAT I HAVE BEEN AFFLICTED; THAT I MIGHT LEARN THY statutes. Psalm 119:71. Rachel connected with King David's testimony. It was mid-January, and today, Rachel, her family, Nicholas, and Jacqui were gathered in the family lounge at the cancer center. Doctors Rush and Brooks were meeting with her about the next phase of her treatment program after reviewing her test results. Whether she was cancer free or not, after enduring five months of chemo and radiation treatments, either way, Rachel was at peace. Finally.

With Nicholas holding her hand, her mind drifted. The treatments had sparked a roller coaster of emotions that eventually led Rachel to a deep self-reflection—not only one-on-one time talking to God and reading her Bible but also listening for His voice. From her close-knit family to Mother Jenkins to a chance encounter with little Emily to the prayer warriors on the church's ministry board, they had been her village.

"It's been a journey." Rachel looked into Nicholas's eyes as they held hands.

"Yes, for both of us." He nodded.

"No, for all of us," Tabitha said and pointed to Kym, Marcus, and Jacqui.

The door opened, and Amanda called Rachel's name. "Ready?"

Rachel swallowed, stood, and wiped her hands on her pants. "Can my family come back with me?" Before then, she had kept her family and friends outside the door so they would not be subject to what she endured as a cancer patient. Today, she welcomed everyone's involvement.

Amanda squinted at the group. "How many?"

"All of us," Kym answered, finger pointing to herself, Tabitha, Nicholas, and Jacqui. "That makes four."

The nurse nodded. "All right. I'll let the doctors know and grab some extra chairs."

"Nicholas, I know we've all been praying, but can you lead us in a short prayer before we go back?" Kym asked.

Without hesitation, he consent and grabbed Rachel's hand and began to give thanks first. He ended the prayer seconds before Amanda returned.

Rachel's heart pounded, and they followed the nurse to Dr. Rush's office, where Dr. Brooks was present too. The doctors took time to shake everyone's hands before taking their seats.

"Well, Miss Knicely." Dr. Rush folded his hands and leaned on the desk. "Let me be the first to congratulate you. The tests show both the radiation and chemotherapy have worked, and there is no sign of any cancer cells."

Praise and worship exploded from Rachel and the others. The doctors waited patiently until they had composed themselves. There wasn't a dry eye in the room.

Dr. Rush nodded. "This is worthy of a celebration, and we're glad our staff was part of your team through this difficult time. Although you'll still be considered a cancer patient, we hope your cancer stays in remission.

"Cancer has a greater chance of recurring within two years, so that is a critical time to maintain a healthy lifestyle, get plenty of exercise, reduce stress, and stay on top of your doctor visits. If the cancer doesn't return in five years, your chart will be marked as cured."

She prayed any potential cancer cells would remain dormant for the rest of her life. Nicholas squeezed her hand and leaned over and kissed her cheek. "I thank God for giving me you. Love you."

Nicholas's chest swelled with happiness as Rachel shared her praise report with the congregation and testified about God's goodness and grace. He even spied Mother Jenkins dabbing at her eyes.

"Thank you all for your prayers, cards, and visits. You helped give me strength in my spirit when my body was weak and my faith was tested."

To celebrate, Jacqui and Mother Jenkins had organized a reception in the fellowship hall in Rachel's honor for after the service, and Nicholas didn't leave her side. It was an emotional scene to witness the well-wishers form a line to give Rachel words of encouragement. Evangelist Darci Union shared with Rachel about her cousin who was a cancer survivor.

As the line thinned, Nicholas spied Leah heading in their direction. Since he had confronted her about the rumors months earlier, she had kept her distance, except for her failed attempt to help Nicholas shop for Rachel. Otherwise, when they crossed paths, they were cordial.

Leah made brief eye contact with Nicholas before speaking. "Hi, Rachel. I enjoyed hearing what you shared."

"Thank you." Rachel smiled. "It wasn't a joy going through it, but I learned more about God."

"I believe that." She paused. "You might remember me from the doctor's office, I guess when you first got the news…"

Tilting his head, Nicholas readied himself to intervene at any moment in case Leah had any shenanigans up her sleeves.

Rachel frowned. "I'm sorry. I don't. That time was such a dark period in my life that everything was a blur. I was so happy Minister Adams was here to give me guidance and support, which I needed. Any other man would have run away from my drama."

That was when Nicholas butted in. He squeezed Rachel's hand. "'Love is patient, love is kind…bears all things, believes all things, hopes all things, endures all things.'" He quoted 1 Corinthians 13:4–7 as if it were a poem.

She stared into his eyes and, without saying a word, conveyed how much she loved him as if they didn't have an audience—until Leah cleared her throat. "Rachel, I apologize for making judgments about your situation."

When it appeared that Leah was about to say more, Nicholas accepted the apology for Rachel before she asked questions. The last thing he wanted was for Rachel to know the woman had spread rumors that she was pregnant instead of sick.

He was about to walk away when Mother Jenkins requested that Leah help serve the punch. Nicholas exhaled. Mother Jenkins was always at her post.

Chapter 38

RACHEL'S LIFE WAS BACK ON TRACK WITHIN A FEW WEEKS. SHE wore a new attitude of gratefulness and humility.

After Rachel stepped inside Gersham-Smith, she teared up with emotion from the balloons and applause that greeted her from her colleagues. Her boss presented her with flowers, and for about an hour or so, members of her team and others gave her a personal welcome back, complimented her head wrap, and said how happy they were that she appeared healthy.

"You look good!" Jackson said as if he was amazed, shaking his head. "You look like you've never had a bad day."

Rachel chuckled. "Trust me, if it wasn't for all those bad days, I wouldn't know how good a good day is."

After all the excitement, Rachel settled in her workstation and took a few minutes to breathe in her new life. *Lord, thank You.*

—

They settled back into their old routine of spending as much time together as they could during the week, depending on their workloads and Nicholas's church commitments. He was glad that Rachel felt confident enough in their relationship that she didn't have to wear a head wrap around him to feel beautiful. However, he was in tune with her loss every time she touched her bald scalp. He saw glimpses of her sadness.

They were playing pool in the game room in her building when Nicholas caught her hand as she was about to touch her head. They stared into each other's eyes. Rachel offered a weak smile. Nicholas didn't as he rested his pool stick and led her to the lounge, where they had a great view of the night skyline.

"Hey, baby, God has counted every strand on your head, and all your hair is coming back." he said softly.

Her eyes widened. "Oh, I'm not complaining."

"No, you're not." Nicholas paused and squeezed her hands. "But I feel your heartbeat, Rachel. You told me the doctors said it may take up to six months to see some peach fuzz." Nicholas brushed a kiss against her scalp.

She nodded with a sigh but didn't look at him.

Putting his arm around her shoulder, he gathered her closer. "I'm going to carry a measuring tape in my back pocket. I'll nickname her 'Baby Girl.'" He snickered. "We'll keep track of your new growth the first of every month."

Rachel laughed, and this time, her amusement reached her eyes. She didn't respond, but her spirit seemed lifted for the rest of the evening.

Oddly enough, she looked forward to those first days of each month.

Nicholas made sure every time they were together, it was a date night, whether they walked the dogs around the neighborhood parks or re-explored Music City together. They returned to the Country Music Hall of Fame and Museum for an all-day adventure.

"Let's bring the twins," Rachel had suggested.

Karl and Ava didn't give Rachel a chance to change her mind. That impromptu field trip made Nicholas yearn for that family with Rachel. She was nurturing and patient with Kory and Rory and, for some reason, seemed to have endless energy, and Nicholas had to call time-out twice to rest.

"Come on, old man," Rachel teased and laughed. The boys stood beside her, giggling to hear their uncle called old.

Before the night ended, he had come to a decision. Thanks to his own big mouth, not once but twice, Nicholas had killed his chances of surprising Rachel with a proposal.

Who said "the third time's a charm"? He was going for it and planned to officially propose on Valentine's Day. He searched the internet for proposal ideas and found one he thought was creative, with a heart-shaped box of chocolates.

He was putting his plan in motion one Sunday evening when Karl and Ava stopped by Nicholas's house with the boys. They were still dressed in their church clothes.

Ava smiled when she noticed the box of chocolates on the table but questioned his intent as he opened it and popped a piece of chocolate in his mouth.

"Ah, what are you doing, Nick? You're not supposed to eat the candy. You're supposed to give them to Rachel to enjoy. That's Romance 101." She crossed her arms and waited for an explanation. "Honey, please talk to your brother."

Karl was too busy picking out a piece for himself as his finger hovered over a milk chocolate square with crème inside.

"Ugh." Nicholas spit out one of the pieces. "That tastes horrible."

"Can I have a piece, Uncle Nick?" Kory asked, followed by Rory's request.

"Sure, anything for my favorite nephews." Nicholas lowered the box and let them choose a piece under the watchful eye of their parents. "I wanted the box, not the candy."

"I don't even want to know what you're masterminding." Karl shook his head. "It reminds me of that science fair project—"

"I should've gotten an A for effort, even if the battery exploded."

"Hmm. That's still the story you're sticking with." He chuckled and slipped his hands in his pants pockets as he perused more chocolate. "Handle your business, Brother."

"I will." He picked up another piece and cautiously sampled a bite before shoving it in his mouth, then bobbed his head. "Umm. Caramel and pecans. I like this one. So where are you all coming from?"

"The Townsends invited us to dinner. Afterward, their son wanted to play with the twins. Ava and I had to drag them away. Since we were close, we decided to stop by." Karl lowered his voice around the boys. "Rachel doing okay? It's good seeing her back at church, happy and with you."

Nicholas grinned. "Yep." He heard his nephews in his spare bedroom, rummaging through the toy chest he kept stocked for them. Evidently, playtime was still in their system. "I'm about to propose. That's why I bought the candy—"

"Which you're devouring by the second," Ava reminded him.

"If you want to know what I'm doing, then you'll find out after Rachel. You want some chocolate to take home? I have to empty this box tonight."

Ava groaned, then picked out about four pieces. "No sense in wasting good chocolate." She kissed his cheek, then called for the boys to come on so they could go home.

Once they were gone, Nicholas started phase two of his proposal—scissors and paper.

Chapter 39

THIS WAS THE FIRST TIME IN YEARS THAT RACHEL HAD A DINNER date on Valentine's Day. The day couldn't have started better than with her wake-up text from Nicholas.

> When a man loves a woman, he loses his mind, then his heart. I give you my whole heart for Valentine's Day. Love you. I'll pick you up for dinner about 6. Reservation at 6:30.

So many memories flooded Rachel's mind. Nicholas stated he had lost his mind over her, but it was he who had kept her sane through her illness and Aunt Tweet's death. She texted him back. Love you more than I can tell you. Kisses.

Rachel had eaten healthy before her cancer, and she was determined to return to it. After a kale smoothie, bagel, and an egg white, she was out the door to the office.

A bouquet of pink roses and white baby's breath was waiting for her at the reception desk. Throughout the day, Nicholas sent tokens of his love. While in a morning meeting, her boss reassigned her to a project close to her heart—expanding the cancer wing of a children's hospital. She immediately thought about Emily from the airport. How was she? Had she blessed someone else? Was she still in this world? All thoughts of the little girl made Rachel smile.

She checked her phone and discovered she had missed a message from Nicholas. As she played it back, Rachel closed her eyes and listened to the short ballad he crooned. Before he disconnected, she heard surprise laughter in the background. She snickered at the possibility that Nicholas had been caught in the act of serenading her at the plant.

Yes, it was an incredible day of love. Rachel had to keep her mind from drifting so she could focus on the exciting design and construction of the hospital wing.

The end of the workday couldn't come soon enough. Back home, Rachel showered and dressed meticulously in a soft pink dress with ankle boots, then stared at her reflection in the mirror. She never considered a short hairstyle that would flatter the shape of her face, but the compliments she received at work, church, and even from random strangers made her believe Nicholas when he called her stunning in the wig she had finally decided to buy.

A few days before, Rachel had been in tears, and she couldn't stop bawling. They were happy tears, although Nicholas wasn't convinced over the phone. "I have hair. I...I...I felt peach fuzz." Her voice had cracked. She couldn't stop thanking God for the little blessing.

The next day when Nicholas showed up, as promised, he had pulled out his measuring tape to verify that indeed something had sprouted on the top of her head. His eyes had misted up. "Congratulations, baby."

Now, courtesy of Nicholas's measuring tape, Rachel knew she had three-fourths of an inch in new growth. She had a long way to go, but she had come so far. The new grade was silky fine like baby hair.

She heard the doorbell and hurried to open it. Nicholas was on one knee with a rose in his hand. The way he looked at her made her want to faint from the overpowering of his love.

"Hi. You look gorgeous." His voice was filled with awe.

"Thank you." She lowered her lashes—yes, she had lashes again—to soak in the moment. "Are you proposing?"

Nicholas stood. "I'm working on it."

She tilted her head and rested a fist on her hips, then squinted. "Excellent, because I'm ready to say yes." She beamed.

"After months of telling me to wait? Nope." He shook his head as he encircled her waist with his arm. "You have all evening to let me work on it."

She turned into his arms and hugged him—it was brief, but their hearts touched. After she locked her door, Rachel slipped her fingers through his. In sync, they strolled to the elevator. Once in the car, she snuggled as close to him as her seat belt allowed and rested her head on his shoulder. "Where are we going?"

"Not far. We have reservations at Prima."

"Ooh." The restaurant was on the short list for romantic dining. So he was proposing. Rachel grinned to herself. The day couldn't get any more perfect. She should have snuck a peek at her ring when she had a chance.

———

Can Rachel hear my heart pounding? Nicholas wondered as he drove the short distance to their destination. The best eating establishments and entertainment venues were within a few miles of Rachel's home.

Nicholas had no doubt that she would say yes this time, but he wanted it to be memorable so they could share the story with their children one day. He parked not far from Twelfth Avenue, grabbed the heart-shaped candy box from the back seat, then hurried around to the passenger side to help her out.

With a strong hold on her hand, he twirled her around under his arm before pulling her into a quick hug. He wanted the moment to linger; he wished it could be in slow motion. Once they were married, he could freely give her all his affections. With his hand still intertwined with hers, he escorted her to the restaurant. "You know the first thing I did this morning?"

"Of course." She glanced up at him, her eyes sparkling, and smiled. "You prayed."

"Good point." Nicholas nodded and grinned. "Okay, the second." Before she could guess, he told her. "I prayed for you."

"Aww. That's sweet," she whispered and wrapped one hand around his arm and squeezed. He flexed his muscle in response.

When they walked inside Prima, Nicholas scanned the decor. He hoped it was romantic enough for her. The place was crowded with other couples in booths or at white-linen-draped tables for two. They were seated within moments of their arrival.

Nicholas laid his decorated heart box on the table, then helped Rachel out of her coat and waited while she slid into their booth. He sat across from her after slipping out of his coat.

He smirked in amusement as Rachel eyed the box. He imagined she was itching to open it. Finally, she pointed. "Is that for me?"

Tilting his head, Nicholas squinted. "Hmm. Maybe." He reached across the table for her hands. Her nails were manicured and pretty in pink. He was glad that her old personality had resurfaced, and she desired pampering. His baby was back! "You have to wait until you eat all your food."

"Really?" Rachel craned her neck, searching for their waiter.

"What are you doing?"

"I'm ready to eat. Aren't you starving?" she asked at the moment their server appeared, introduced himself, and handed them their menus, explaining the Valentine's dinner special.

"Roasted chicken, roasted baby potatoes, steamed vegetable medley, and buttery rolls made with Tartine bread," the waiter explained.

"Sounds yummy." Rachel smiled and rested her chin on folded hands.

They ordered that along with salads and sparkling grape juice. Nicholas was amused, laughing at her impatience. "I've never seen you so eager to eat." He winked. "But I love it!"

"It's not funny." Rachel pouted.

"It is." He snickered. "But I'm sorry anyway." He tugged on her hands and brought them to his lips. "I love you."

"I love you so much for so many reasons," she said with such awe in her voice it made Nicholas emotional.

"So, Miss Knicely, how was your day?" That one question unlocked her passion for an upcoming project. He listened, thankful for her energy and enthusiasm that were both results of God's restoration.

Rachel paused when their beverages and then their salads arrived. After moving the box out of the way, Nicholas was about to say grace when she stopped him. "Can I have the honor?"

"How can I say no when I look into your beautiful brown eyes?"

With a firm but soft grip on her hands, Nicholas bowed his head and waited.

"Father," she said softly, "I thank You for so much—my journey, my health, and this incredible man who You've placed in my life. I don't need an annual day to know how much You and Nicholas love me, so I'm blessed to be the recipient of both affections. Thank You for the food we are about to receive for our enjoyment and nourishment of our bodies. Bless it, sanctify it, and help us to feed those we see are hungry. In Jesus's name. Amen."

Nicholas choked back tears at her heartfelt prayer. He opened his eyes to see Rachel watching and waiting for him to look at her. "I love you."

"You can never say that enough." He squeezed her hands, then brought them to his chest. "You are my heartbeat."

"Mine too," she whispered, then smiled. "Let's eat so I can have my dessert."

Nicholas didn't argue as he conceded to her wishes, engaging in conversation until they had consumed their meal. Once the server removed their plates from the table, Nicholas placed the heart box in front of her. "Miss Knicely, you may now open it."

Her eyes sparkled as she lifted the cover and frowned at the note that covered the spots where the chocolates were supposed to be. Nicholas held his breath as she read. Maybe this wasn't a good idea.

Rachel,

I have only one question for you where there is only one right answer. But I have ten questions for you before you proceed to open the small box that I placed where the strawberry crème tarte truffle was.

She gave him side-eye. "What happened to all the candy, and why the strawberry crème spot?"

"Well." He looked away sheepishly before meeting her stare. "I ate them because I needed the space, but the strawberry crème tarte truffle was the best!"

Rachel laughed, fingering the folded strips of paper in the spots which once held the candy. She briefly debated which one to read first, making Nicholas antsy.

"For a woman who couldn't wait, all of a sudden, you're patient."

She shrugged and gave him a coy expression. "It's not my fault you have all these different-colored papers." Her first choice was the blue one, so she unfolded the long strip and read aloud, "'Marry me for life if you think I will make a good husband.'" She nodded and whispered yes. Next, Rachel picked pink: "'Marry me if you believe God is the giver of life and will bless us with beautiful children.'"

She sniffed. Her eyes were misty when she looked up and met his stare. "Yes." Her sister had questioned Rachel's physician relentlessly about the side effects of the drugs on Rachel's fertility. The doctors said despite Rachel undergoing chemo, her youth gave her a good chance to conceive.

Rachel's hands shook as she reached for an orange strip. "'Marry me if you don't mind working beside a husband who is a minister on call 24/7 and being his helpmate.'" She rested her right hand over her heart. "I will," she choked out. She released a deep breath, then continued to pull strips until only the ring box remained in the shell of the candy box.

They stared at each other. Nicholas noticed her racing pulse on Rachel's neck. "Ready?"

She nodded.

Nicholas opened the box to reveal her engagement ring. Without taking his eyes off her, he scooted out of the booth, then guided Rachel to her feet. He wanted to look up into her eyes to see her love, and he wanted Rachel to understand his humility as a husband who would cherish her.

"Rachel Knicely, I love you beyond words. My life changed the moment I saw you. Will you marry me and allow me to make you happy?"

One tear fell, then another. She nodded.

"Baby, a lot of people are watching us and waiting to hear your answer along with me. Say it."

"Yes, Nicholas Adams. Yes, to everything."

Soft applause echoed throughout the restaurant as one proposal followed another. Nicholas stood, slipped the ring on Rachel's finger, then wrapped her in his arms. He was so happy he couldn't contain himself as he turned toward the other diners and proclaimed, "We're engaged!"

Chapter 40

Six months later, Rachel became an aunt to Marcus Brownlee Whittington, born August 15, weighing eight pounds and three ounces of pure love. Flying to St. Louis a few days before Tabitha's due date, Rachel had waited impatiently for Tabitha to go into labor. Marcus had been a nervous wreck, and when her sister's contractions began, he'd grabbed the pregnancy book to make sure Tabitha was indeed in labor. Tabitha had threatened to call an ambulance to take her if Marcus took any longer.

Rachel had to run interference and calm the parents-to-be down. She drove them to Mercy Hospital, about twenty minutes away. Marcus was in the back seat, holding his wife's hand as she moaned with contractions.

After fifteen hours in labor, Tabitha became a mother. While rocking her nephew in her arms, Rachel admired the baby who was barely half a day old.

She and little Marcus shared the same silky black curls. His were thick.

Rachel fingered her hair. She had given Nicholas a footnote to marrying him. Rachel refused to walk down the aisle without at least six inches of hair. He had laughed. She was serious. The last time he pulled out the measuring tape, she had four inches.

"He's beautiful," Rachel said in awe.

"Thanks. He's handsome," Marcus countered, puffing out his chest.

"Aww. Beauty comes from the woman, so I was complimenting my sister," Rachel advised her brother-in-law, and Tabitha beamed.

"Well, yeah. My wife is beautiful." He grinned sheepishly, then kissed Tabitha.

Rachel shook her head, then focused again on her nephew. As the baby slept, lips puckered, sucking on air, Rachel prayed that she too would get pregnant and that she would be able to nurse her baby with her normal breast.

Tabitha kissed her husband back, then giggled. "If you and Nicholas can hold off getting married for a couple of years, little Marcus can be the ring bearer in your wedding."

"Don't let my fiancé hear you say that." Rachel laughed. "My hair grows fast, so I'm planning to marry Nicholas on New Year's Eve."

Left up to Nicholas, he would have had Pastor Mann marry them as soon as he proposed. The length of her hair wasn't the sole issue; Rachel wanted to wait a year to make sure she was healthy.

"You're healthy now, woman," Nicholas had said. "How about on your birthday at the end of September?"

Rachel countered with New Year's Eve, and he'd agreed. "And not a day later."

Nicholas knocked on the door and waited to be told to come in before proceeding into the private room filled with balloons and stuffed toys.

Rachel's heart fluttered at the sight of her well-groomed fiancé who had come straight from the airport. "Hey." Rachel smiled. She wanted Nicholas to see what she would look like as a mother.

"Hey, beautiful." He kissed Rachel's cheek, then he gazed at the infant. "Congratulations. You've got a handsome little fella."

Marcus cleared his throat. "Exactly."

"You started something." Rachel playfully scrunched her nose at Nicholas. "Babies are precious, beautiful, adorable. Young boys and men are handsome. Just sayin'."

"I'm with my sister," Tabitha chimed in from her bed.

Kym stood. "Seems like I'll have to be the tiebreaker." She leaned over the chair and cooed at the baby. "He's beautiful." The women cheered. "I guess I need to get me one of those"—she nodded to Marcus and Nicholas—"so I can get me one of these."

"Get in line," Rachel said. *Lord, thank You for letting me see this day.*

Epilogue

SITTING IN THE DRESSING ROOM AT THE CHURCH, RACHEL TWISTED a strand of hair around her finger, something she hadn't been able to do for most of the year. She now had almost seven inches of a curly mass that required little attention.

She'd never forget the day, time, and place when she discovered the peach fuzz on top of her head.

Next, she recalled what Nicholas had said about her baldness. "My love for you goes beyond your physical beauty. I saw your spiritual strength before you knew you possessed it. When you lost all your hair, it just made me want to nurse you back to health. Baby, I will love you for you until my last breath."

Rachel had to believe him. The lumpectomy and radiation had left the one breast slightly disfigured. Because she had put her body through enough, Rachel opted for a prosthesis over breast reconstruction. The doctor advised Rachel that if she had surgery, she might need another reconstruction because the other breast would change due to pregnancy and weight loss or gain. Today, no one would know which breast was affected from the stunning dress she wore.

"She's zoning out again, y'all," Jacqui teased, grinning. "Must be thinking about something that minister whispered in her ear."

Rachel blushed. "I could write a book of all the sweet things he has said to me. Wait until it's your turn and Kym's."

"I'll add them to my prayer list," Mother Jenkins's voice boomed.

Anybody on the woman's prayer list should be forewarned that Mother Jenkins came suited up for battle according to Ephesians 6:10–17. Throughout Rachel's illness, Mother Jenkins had endeared herself as an Aunt Tweet figure, so it felt natural to include her in the nuptials and have her escort Rachel down the aisle.

Rachel never thought she would see the fiercely strong woman of God sniff and fumble for a tissue. Next came her grin. At least Mother Jenkins wasn't dressed in white. She looked quite appealing in the bridal colors of deep blue with cranberry accents; the men were in gray.

Jacqui, like a sister who thought she was a blood sister, was her only bridesmaid; Kym was her maid of honor, while Tabitha was her matron of honor. That was her close circle of confidantes.

To make it a family affair, Karl's twin boys were double ring bearers. Of course, Rachel had to include her four-month-old nephew, Marcus Brownlee Whittington. Tabitha had him dressed in a cute baby tux.

Rachel couldn't leave out Clara, who had become a part of her healing team, so she'd asked if her eight-year-old daughter, Sheree, could serve as a flower girl. Clara's eyes had sparkled at the invitation to be included.

It would have been nice to have Emily, but that day had only been a chance meeting: no last name, city—nothing, not even to look up on social media. Rachel had a feeling the girl was on another mission for the Lord. The flower girl, Sheree, rolled the stroller, with little Marcus, decorated in bridal colors down the aisle, tossing rose petals on both sides.

When the organist struck the chords, Kym, Jacqui, and Tabitha stood in formation and hurried out of the room, leaving Rachel alone with Mother Jenkins.

"Thank you for being part of my spiritual journey. I needed a matriarch to guide me to a place of healing, and Aunt Tweet and God sent you and Nicholas."

"Yep," Mother Jenkins responded, not bashful about the compliment.

Rachel giggled. She had grown to love this woman, who had shown her how to survive cancer and be an overcomer.

Soon, another knock on the door cued Rachel that her time had come. The two stepped out of the dressing room and waited for their moment to walk down the aisle. Rachel exhaled and craned her neck to get a peek at Nicholas through the double doors to the sanctuary.

He stood tall, handsome, and expectant. Rachel had attended weddings where some grooms seemed nervous—not her husband-to-be. That was a good sign.

As the organist struck the "Wedding March" opening chords, Rachel fell into step with Mother Jenkins, who took her duty as her escort to another level, acting more like a blushing bride herself with smiles and nods to the guests until Nicholas left his post and met them halfway.

"I'll take it from here, Mother Jenkins," Nicholas said but didn't take his eyes off Rachel.

"You'd better, or you answer to the Lord, then me. She's like one of my daughters."

"Yes, ma'am," Nicholas said and had to tug Rachel away from the woman.

Rachel hugged Mother Jenkins, then continued her journey to the altar with her bridegroom.

Once they stood facing each other in front of Pastor Mann, Nicholas whispered, "My beautiful bride. Nervous?" he asked as she shivered.

"A little," Rachel admitted. This was another unknown turning point in her life.

"I'm not," he said, lifting an eyebrow with a determined look in his eyes.

The pastor cleared his throat. "Dearly beloved, we are gathered here today in the sight of God to join Rachel Knicely and Nicholas Adams in holy matrimony…"

Rachel was drawn into Nicholas's stare. She could never doubt his love.

"Do you, Nicholas, take Rachel to have and to hold from this day forward, for better, for worse…"

"I most certainly do," he responded loudly.

"That's right," Mother Jenkins echoed from her seat in the first row.

When it was Rachel's turn, she repeated her vows and stumbled at *until death do us part*, but Nicholas rubbed her fingers and whispered, "It's all right, baby."

And she needed his comforting reassurance, because neither knew whether the cancer would return, but Nicholas said to trust God, and she would follow his lead.

"By the power vested in me by God and man, I pronounce you husband and wife."

Nicholas stepped closer to lift her veil, but their pastor halted him.

"Therefore, what God has joined together, let no man or woman come between you." He nodded. "Minister Adams, you may now salute your wife."

Rachel closed her eyes to accept the kiss she had been waiting for since the day they'd admitted their attraction.

Wow. Aunt Tweet might not be here, but she would surely say, "Now, that's a whopper!"

Author's Note

I hope I inspired you with Rachel's journey from being a caregiver to needing a caregiver. Ministering to someone facing a serious illness takes a special gift from God. I was surprised to learn that those who minister to the sick are subjected to hostility as well as gratefulness. May God give them an extra portion of strength. I also wanted to highlight how fragile life can be regardless of age.

It was challenging writing this story, since I become my characters. I didn't want to experience what Rachel did when she discovered the lump. I think I did more breast self-examinations while writing than I can remember ever doing before. Please remember to do your monthly self-exams and stay on top of your mammograms.

All my happy endings come courtesy of the Lord. If you enjoyed this story, please tell a friend and/or purchase a copy for her, then please don't forget to post a review.

Until Kym Knicely's story, be blessed, and happy reading!

Pat

Acknowledgments

It takes a village to craft a believable, inspiring, and enjoyable story.

A special thanks to LaTonya Wilson who is a three-time breast cancer survivor. She took the time to answer my questions about her personal journey.

Thanks to Sister Turquiose Hamilton, a mechanical design engineer, who gave me the jumpstart to research Rachel's career.

Thank you #TeamPat: Chandra Sparks Splond, Stacey Jefferson, and Jackie Roberts. You are my village. Thanks to my poor husband, Kerry, who had to tape movies for us to watch later because I was working on the story. Maybe we can catch up on last year's Christmas movies.

Thank you to all the editors at Sourcebooks, especially Deb Werksman, and to my agent, Evan Marshall.

A big thanks to the readers, bloggers, and book clubs who have purchased and reviewed my books throughout my writing journey.

Be blessed!

Reading Group Guide

1. This series is centered around the life and experiences of a caregiver. Could you identify with any of these scenarios?

2. Talk about how you coped with the loss of an elderly relative.

3. Have you or someone close to you been affected by cancer?

4. If so, what was your inspiration for surviving?

5. Rachel had a support system, which included more than her sisters. Can you name them all?

6. Minister Adams was assigned to visit the sick and homebound. Was Rachel too close to his heart for him to be effective in her case?

7. Discuss Rachel's attitude toward life before and after cancer.

SOMETIMES IT TAKES A LITTLE NUDGE TO BELIEVE...
Check out Marcus and Tabitha's story of faith and surrender.

lean on me

Available now from Sourcebooks Casablanca

Chapter 1

MARCUS WHITTINGTON WASN'T EXPECTING TO SEE A WOMAN ON HIS surveillance camera, trespassing on his domain. From time to time, he had seen maybe a stray dog. Never a lady who wore an oversize red hat that concealed her features as she strolled up to his house. According to his security video, this wasn't her first visit.

This mystery person had commandeered his porch between 6:30 a.m. and 7:15 a.m., as if she owned the deed to his property. A couple of times, the chick sat like a statue for about ten minutes—it was seven minutes this morning—before hurrying off as if a dog were chasing her. He frowned as he rewound and reviewed the evidence again.

What was going on? Marcus had lived on Overdrive Court in Pasadena Hills, Missouri, for four years. The quiet suburban neighborhood was a hidden-in-plain-sight treasure, with an unmanned, majestic, sixty-five-foot Gothic tower at the Natural Bridge Road entrance. It served as a visual barrier that guarded its residents from the questionable, blighted North St. Louis city neighborhoods in transition. Clearly, security had been breached.

He didn't have time for this. It was Monday morning, and he had to get to the office. Scratching his jaw, which demanded a razor, he decided to multitask and call the police as he shaved.

"911. What's your emergency?" a male dispatcher answered.

"I'd like to report a strange woman making uninvited visits to my property."

"Excuse me, sir?" The man paused. "Has your home been vandalized?"

"No." His morning paper deliveries were untouched. "This woman just sits on my porch."

There was silence on the other end of the phone. Finally, a response came: "I'll connect you to the nonemergency number, sir. Please hold."

A deep voice came on the line. "Officer Roman."

Flustered, Marcus recapped and added, "Please add my cul-de-sac to your round of patrols. I'd appreciate it."

"Will do, sir," the officer said and disconnected. Now Marcus was really pressed for time. Whittington Janitorial Services, the company he had started with his older brother, Demetrius, was twelve minutes from his house, tops. Unlike his sibling, Marcus wasn't a fan of city living, so before purchasing his Cape Cod–inspired, story-and-a-half home, he had done his research about the neighborhood.

With University of Missouri–St. Louis's sprawling campus nearby, Pasadena Hills was considered one of the untouched neighborhoods of the county and touted as North County's best-kept secret. But now this woman had shown up.

Not easily intimidated, standing at six foot three and 240 pounds of muscle, Marcus could back up whatever came out of his mouth. Yet having some petite woman violate his boundaries unsettled him. "Hmph," he grunted.

"One thing for sure, lady. I'll be watching out for you," he muttered, making a mental note to check his video surveillance more often. He hoped there wouldn't be a next time, because the woman definitely didn't want a confrontation with him.

⸻

Tabitha Knicely sniffed the air as she strolled into her kitchen. Aunt Tweet had settled into a routine since coming to live with her two weeks ago. Her aunt rose every morning at six thirty, showered, dressed, and prepared breakfast. Today's menu was scrambled eggs, sausage patties, and bread that remained in the toaster. Yet her aunt was munching on a spoonful of Cheerios.

"You cooked a hot breakfast but settled for cereal?" Tabitha chuckled as she grabbed a plate to serve herself.

"I changed my mind."

Spying her aunt's bowl, Tabitha frowned. "You don't have any milk in there."

Alzheimer's was slowly attacking Aunt Tweet's brain cells. One moment, her aunt was absentminded, repeating tasks and craving snacks, especially sweets, as if they hadn't finished a meal not long ago. Then, in a blink of an eye, Aunt Tweet would turn into a game show junkie. She would beat the buzzer before the contestants could answer the host's questions as if she were Google.

Tabitha had been attending a medical conference in Birmingham, Alabama, when she received a call from her older sister in Baltimore.

"Aunt Tweet is in the custody of the Philly police department."

"What?" Dread came over Tabitha and she felt faint. "What happened? Is she all right?"

"They say she's fine," Kym assured her, "but someone called the police when she was stopped at a green light, lost, and couldn't figure out how to get home."

Her aunt could have caused a pileup or, worse, been killed. Tabitha exhaled. Thank God Aunt Tweet was alive, but what had happened didn't make sense. "What do you mean lost? She knows every nook and cranny of Philly, so how was she lost in her own city?"

Their youngest sister, Rachel, who was also on the line, finally chimed in. "Yeah, explain that to me too."

"Well, apparently, she left home to get groceries and wound up in Cherry Hill," Kym said.

The two sisters had gasped. "New Jersey?" Rachel asked.

"That's ten miles away," Tabitha added, knowing the area well.

"Yeah, I'm glad it wasn't farther. Anyway, they took her to the hospital for a physical and mental evaluation. Since my name is on her emergency contact, they called me. Her blood pressure and sugar levels were normal, but…" Kym became quiet before she dropped the bombshell. "They suspect her confusion could be connected with Alzheimer's."

Tabitha had left the conference early and booked a nonstop flight to Philly. Rachel coordinated her own flight from her condo in Nashville. Kym was already on the road from her home in Baltimore. The sisters pulled together, just as they always had in a crisis. They had gone not only out of a sense of duty, but because Aunt Tweet had been too important in their lives not to; she'd meant everything to them, especially after the deaths of their parents. Once the three were gathered in Philly, they'd made a pact to share in the responsibility of their great-aunt's well-being, each taking care of her for six months at a time. As the oldest, Kym had looked after Aunt Tweet first.

Tabitha needed to refocus as she smiled lovingly at her aunt. Beginning today, Aunt Tweet would stay at an upscale adult day care while Tabitha began her first day at a new job.

After getting the milk carton out of the refrigerator, Tabitha walked back to the table and poured some into Aunt Tweet's bowl. Chalking it up to another sad oddity of dementia, she was determined to keep happy memories in the forefront of her mind as she kissed her aunt's cheek.

"Thank you, ma'am." Aunt Tweet giggled, adjusting Tabitha's red, floppy hat on her head. Since her arrival, her aunt had fallen in love with that hat and wore it practically every day, regardless of her ensemble. "I took a little walk around God's green earth."

"What?" Tabitha didn't like the idea of her aunt out of her sight. "Without me?" It was easy for anyone to succumb to the tranquility and abundance of green space in Pasadena Hills, which rivaled the nearby Norwood Hills Country Club. But in the midst of that apparent peace, they were still on the outskirts of a neighborhood not nearly so safe. It definitely wasn't safe for Aunt Tweet to wander. Tabitha shivered at the thought of worse-case scenarios.

"You were asleep."

"That's okay." She hugged her aunt. "Next time, wake me and I'll go with you." She yawned, recalling her previous night's lack of sleep.

Her aunt had wanted to reminisce about her years as an airline steward-ess, and Tabitha had indulged her before all of Aunt Tweet's memories would slip away. Researchers had yet to find a cure, so Tabitha hoped God would reveal a cure to eradicate or reverse this terrible disease before it was too late for her aunt.

All of a sudden, Aunt Tweet dropped her spoon, spilling milk onto the table. "I left my scarf...I left my scarf!" Panic-stricken, she trembled and scooted her chair back.

Startled, Tabitha's heart pounded, so she patted her chest to aid her breathing to return to normal. "It's all right. I'll get it from upstairs," she said, reassuring her aunt that it was okay to forget things sometimes.

While staying with Kym, Aunt Tweet had worked herself into hys-terics over the vintage scarf she had gotten as an engagement gift. Her aunt boasted she'd gotten rid of the husband but held onto the expensive shawl. There hadn't been any peace in Kym's house until she'd found it behind a pillow on the sofa.

"No!" Aunt Tweet shrieked, shaking her head. "On that porch. We'd better hurry."

Confused, Tabitha tried to calm her down to figure out what was going on. "On my porch?" When her aunt shook her head, Tabitha asked, "Whose porch?"

"I don't know."

Dread seemed to pour over Tabitha like a downpour. "Okay, okay." Of all the days for a distraction, this was not a good one. This was her first day on a new job. As a pharmaceutical sales rep, Tabitha could recite medical terms, facts, definitions, and clinical studies' results in her sleep. She'd entered college as a biology major and graduated with a bachelor's in business. The pharmaceutical industry gave her the benefit of both worlds. Plus, she thrived on studying the physiological, anatomical, pharmacological, and scientific properties of medicine, so she could com-municate the benefits of the company's products.

But family was family, so taking her duty as a caregiver seriously, Tabitha had resigned from her job of six years as a senior pharmaceutical sales rep to ease the stress of the demanding position. Not wanting to

leave the field completely, she took a pay cut to work in a smaller terri-
tory with a competitor who demanded little to no overnight travel. The
sacrifice was worth it. Plus, her aunt's trust fund designated the money
for her own care.

Tabitha rubbed her forehead. "Let me put something on, then we'll
go find it." Tabitha raced upstairs, hurried into her clothes, then grabbed
her briefcase. Minutes later, she almost slipped while rushing down the
stairs in her heels.

She reentered the kitchen, and Aunt Tweet wasn't in sight. Tabitha
checked the adjacent family room, then peeped outside toward the
patio. Her aunt was behind the wheel of Tabitha's rental car. Not good.
She hadn't purchased a car in years. A perk for being a sales rep, after
she completed her two-week training, which started today, would be a
company-issued vehicle.

After locking up the house, she had to convince Aunt Tweet, who
had worked herself into a frenzy, that she couldn't drive. Tabitha had to
coax her own self to have patience while following her aunt's conflicting
directions, thinking, *I can't be late for my first day on the job.*

"That's the place!" Aunt Tweet yelled as Tabitha jammed on her
brakes in front of a stately, story-and-a-half, older brick house she had
never noticed before. The massive front door was centered under an
archway. Twin french doors with mock balconies were on both sides of
the entrance.

"I don't see anything." She craned her neck, admiring the impressive
work of building art.

Aunt Tweet snapped, "I told you that's the porch."

"Okay." *There is no reason for your sharp tone,* Tabitha thought but
dared not voice. This house wasn't that close to hers at all. Despite some
mental deterioration, there was nothing wrong with her aunt's physical
stamina. She had obviously cut through the common ground area among
the houses to get here.

After parking her car, Tabitha got out and surveyed her surroundings to make sure she wasn't being watched. "This is crazy, sneaking up
to somebody's house," she muttered to herself. Since the coast was clear,

she hurried toward the red scarf that was snagged on a flower in a pot and flapping in the wind. She was within her reach when the door opened. Tabitha jumped back, then steadied herself in her heels.

An imposing man filled the doorway. Under different circumstances, he would be breathtakingly handsome. That was not the case now. Judging from his snarl and piercing eyes, Tabitha felt as if she had walked into the lion's den.

Buy Aunt Tweet another scarf. Run!

Chapter 2

MARCUS SLIPPED ON HIS MARBLE FLOOR WHEN HE GLIMPSED OUT of his window in passing and spied a blue sedan creeping to the curb in front of his house. His interest piqued when a dark-skinned beauty stepped out and almost danced her way in heels to his porch. The suit fitted her well and would capture any man's attention—his included. Even though a *No Solicitation* sign was posted at the entrance to Pasadena Hills, he would place an order for whatever she was selling.

Wait a minute... Why was she glancing around suspiciously? Was she the trespasser? Marcus had been ready and waiting for the mystery woman's return. The time was now.

He flung open his door for answers.

She froze as if she were part of that old social media craze, the mannequin challenge. His limbs couldn't move either, but his eyes did, cataloging her features. She was a showstopper, with her best assets being her gorgeous face and shapely legs. But this was not the time for distractions. He folded his arms. "May I help you?"

Her lips trembled into a smile, revealing even, white teeth. He was a sucker for good dental hygiene.

"Ah, I'm so sorry," she murmured in the sweetest voice.

Keeping his eyes steady on his target, Marcus studied her expression as she seemed to contemplate her next move. In the blink of an eye, she swiped the red scarf off the potted plant and gave him a smug expression, then smiled.

He returned it with a smirk of his own. "You do know that I knew you were going to do that. Why is it on my porch in the first place?"

She glanced over her shoulder and pointed to the car. "This belongs to my aunt."

"And this porch belongs to me." He squinted at the woman in the passenger seat. He didn't recognize her. "Why has your *aunt* been sitting on *my* porch in the mornings?"

Shock flashed on her face before she frowned. "*Mornings?* You mean she's been here before?"

What was really going on here? Was this a stalling tactic while someone broke into his house from the back? "Miss…?"

"Tabitha Knicely. I'm a neighbor," she supplied before motioning toward the car again. "That's my aunt, Aunt Tweet."

"You mean to tell me you had no knowledge that *your* aunt has been staking out my porch?"

She seemed flustered, then stuttered, "We take walks together—"

"Except for this morning and the others she was here without you knowing it," he said.

"She must have gotten tired and rested on your porch," Miss Knicely explained.

"Umm-hmm. And that's the story you're sticking with?" Her excuse was too simple though forgivable—if it had only happened once, which it hadn't. "Where do you live?"

This time, the information didn't come so freely. She was hesitant. "On Roland Drive."

Really? Roland Drive was the main entrance to the cluster of homes and touched every street in Pasadena Hills. Her deep-brown eyes and tentative smile silently pleaded with him to believe her. *Not so fast.* At thirty-four years old, Marcus had experience with good-looking ladies' charms that had twisted his common sense in the past, so he regrouped. "Where exactly?"

"By the park."

"What?" Marcus unfolded his arms and stood to his full six foot three. "Some houses are half an acre apart. That's a long way for an elderly person to wander." Beautiful or not, this woman was obviously too irresponsible to be a caregiver.

Responsibility had been drilled into Marcus as a child. When he was a little boy, three generations of Whittingtons lived under one roof. His grandparents, especially his grandmother, were kind, understanding, and stern when it came to disciplining their rambunctious grandsons. Yet Gran reminded them daily they were loved. This type of error would never have happened on his watch in his family.

Memories of his deceased grandparents touched a soft spot whenever he thought of them. Marcus would have moved them in with him without any hesitation and have twenty-four-hour monitoring, if necessary. When Gran and Pops died, he and Demetrius had bawled like infants.

Marcus would have done the same for his parents, but they had retired and relocated to North Carolina. "Older people are jewels, and I refuse to stand by and allow someone to treat them carelessly. You should know her whereabouts at all times. I suggest you keep track of your relative. Do you have any idea what could have happened to her?"

He must have hit a nerve and ticked her off. She jutted out her chin defiantly. She wore an attitude as professional as her suit. Her nostrils flared, and she cast him an angry glare.

"The jewel of my family is sitting right there." She pointed to her car. "Unless you've been a caregiver for a loved one, don't judge someone who is!" She stormed back to her car. Once there, she spun around. "You don't have to worry about any further visits from Aunt Tweet!"

"That works for me, because if she shows up on my doorstep one more time unsupervised, I'll contact the police. I'm sure they'll take her into protective custody and charge you with endangerment of a senior citizen. Don't test me, *neighbor*."

"Mr…"

"Marcus Whittington," he supplied before waving at the passenger in the car.

"Whatever. This is a test I don't plan to fail."

"For your aunt's sake, I hope not." Dismissing Tabitha, he stepped back inside and slammed the heavy wooden door for good measure, rattling the nearby windows. Her Aunt Tweet was definitely in the wrong hands.

After grabbing his computer bag, he checked his appearance, then decided to double-check his doors, just in case. Next, he activated his home security system and headed to work. During the short drive, he fumed, replaying the incident in his head. He didn't know if he was more upset about Tabitha's mistreatment of an elderly person or him losing his temper. That was so uncharacteristic of him.

In no time, he arrived at the business park that housed his company. Using the back entrance, he took the shortcut to the office he shared with Demetrius. Usually, he admired the layout of Whittington Janitorial Services' warehouse. Industrial cleaning products and supplies were stacked neatly on the shelves that lined the walls. One side had spacious lockers for employees to store their personal items. At the moment, any sense of accomplishment paled, as his irritation built with each step. Those two ladies had dared to infiltrate his home safety zone.

One of three supervisors on his cleaning staff, Chester "Chess" Gray, stopped him. He glanced at his wrist as if he were wearing a watch—he wasn't. "Something's wrong if I'm beating you to work," he joked.

Marcus wasn't in the mood for humor. He needed to vent and he didn't care who listened as he described his bizarre morning. "Who does that?" he asked, needing an answer.

"Watch it, Boss," Chess cautioned. "Old girl might be setting you up for a burglary. There was a string of robberies not far from where you live a while back."

Great. He gritted his teeth. *The day keeps getting worse.*

"She could be part of the lookout team."

Living in a crime-infested part of the city, Chess was suspicious of anybody and everybody, which made him a good supervisor—most of the time. Other times, Chess was annoying…but Marcus's employee could be onto something.

Continuing on his way, Marcus opened the door to the office. Demetrius was on his computer. "Nice of you to show up," he said sarcastically.

"Yeah, well. I had a situation this morning, but I caught them."

"Caught who?" His brother frowned. "Please tell me you didn't hurt anyone without my backup." Marcus had attended Pennsylvania State University on a wrestling and academic scholarship—both had full rides. Demetrius had boxed in college; together, they were a force to be reckoned with.

"No need. Evidently, two chicks have been staking out my place." After what Chess said, he downplayed the woman's excuse. "The older woman goes by the name of Aunt Tweet. The other was much younger." He huffed and slid his laptop out of the bag. He had to shake the bad vibes from Tabitha Knicely, so he could review the time sheets before signing off on them. *Relax and focus.*

"Interesting. A female crime ring."

Marcus frowned. "I don't really buy that, but for good measure, I instilled fear in them that they had picked the wrong house for that foolishness. And I issued a threat too."

"Well, sounds like those two won't be returning. Hopefully, they got the hint they were messing with a Whittington," Demetrius said. When Marcus didn't add any further comment, his brother cleared his throat. "Switching to work, Terrence Scott needs a random drug test. We may have to terminate him."

Not good. Their company had received awards for their exemplary efforts to give hope to the hopeless in low-income communities and to young men and women who had served time in prison for nonviolent crimes. Marcus labeled their choices as making stupid decisions. Whittington Janitorial Services' mission statement referenced assisting disenfranchised workers with a way out of poverty. He and Demetrius had both witnessed how a cleaning staff seemed invisible to people with money. It was offensive how they, most of them black, were mistreated, disrespected, and stereotyped.

Although he and Demetrius believed in second chances, after three strikes, his company had no choice but to terminate an employee. Terrence had been the exception to this rule. He was barely twenty-three, his live-in girlfriend was pregnant, and he didn't have a car. Prison had probably saved the young man's life or he would have been another statistic of a young black man killed in the streets.

Rubbing the hairs of his goatee, he spun around to admire the framed, floor-to-ceiling corkboard. It boasted success stories of former employees. The brothers had mentored, encouraged, and sometimes gave out of their own pockets to meet basic needs, like food and shelter. Marcus shook his head.

Turning to face his brother, Marcus squeezed his lips in frustration, then said, "My day seems to be going from bad to worse." When would people learn that responsibility wasn't optional? First, those women set the stage for his day to go downhill, and second, Terrence seemed to be picking up the torch. "Can you believe she got an attitude after trespassing on *my* property?" he mumbled, then grunted.

"Back to the lawbreakers, huh?" Demetrius chuckled, evidently straining his hearing, since their shared office space was at least twenty feet long and a short file cabinet served as the dividing line. It was a spacious office that could easily be separated into two, but neither felt the need to have a wall constructed for privacy. They knew each other's business anyway. "So how did she look again?"

"Like a gorgeous spitfire." He hadn't forgotten one detail. "She was a crafty diva with curves from a good workout."

"I got the gorgeous part." Demetrius leaned across his desk and smirked across the room. "I was referring to the aunt."

"Oh." Marcus shifted in his chair and reached for the chilled bottled water their administrative assistant placed on their desks every morning. To hide his blunder, he unscrewed the cap and gulped down half the bottle as if he were dying of thirst. "Ah." He smacked his lips. "Say what?"

"I asked you to describe this crafty diva with the great body." Demetrius snickered until laughter exploded out of his mouth.

Okay, so his big bro had jokes. Marcus played along. "She was a nice-looking lady who seemed completely normal from her spot in the front seat of a car. Her silver-gray hair reminded me of Gran's." Maybe the similarity was what had sparked his outrage at Tabitha's lack of responsibility.

His beloved grandparents, Gran and Pops, were the sweetest people on earth and lived into their eighties. When they became sick, Marcus and Demetrius had waited on them hand and foot. They were his idols, seemingly knowing everything about everything.

He pitied anyone who had to enter a nursing home, where some families abandoned their relatives instead of maintaining ties with visits and calls. He had witnessed firsthand the abuse and neglect when he had to deliver business orders to a few nursing facilities. Those images and odors were seared into his brain.

"But did you have to be so hard on her?" his brother asked.

"The situation forced my hand. When it comes to responsibilities, the Whittingtons take care of our own." He patted his chest with pride.

"Yeah, but usually, I'm the bad guy." Demetrius chuckled. "After your stunt today, I'd say you reign, but I understand you had to do what you had to do."

Although they were extremely close, their personalities were like night and day. Demetrius was the no-nonsense one who had mastered the "do not dare to cross me" facial expression. On rare occasions, his brother could be a pushover. Marcus was laid back and sympathetic.

Physically, there was no mistaking them as brothers.

Marcus preferred a low haircut and trimmed goatee. Outside of work, he was a meticulous dresser and maintained a regular workout routine. Demetrius's current exercise regimen was, at best, inconsistent—at this point, it amounted to whenever he felt like it.

Demetrius sported his shaved head and set off his look with a diamond stud in one ear. Marcus didn't like jewelry on a man, not even a watch—that's what his smartphone was for. He was the shade of black coffee, where Demetrius was a double dip of dark chocolate.

"Great way to start off a relationship," Demetrius teased. When they were boys, his brother had an annoying habit of baiting him. As a man in his late thirties, he still hadn't grown out of that trait.

"Relationship? Where in my conversation did you assume that?" Marcus frowned. "I'm not even sure if the chick is really a neighbor."

His brother twitched his lips. "Umm-hmm. Something tells me this story with your neighbor is just beginning." He stood and strolled toward their door, chuckling. "Chapter One: Brotha Meets Fine Sistah—I can see the fascination in your eyes. Plus, your protest is overkill."

Grabbing a piece of paper from a stack, Marcus balled it up and aimed for Demetrius's head, then fired. Hitting him, Marcus got the last laugh—or so he thought, until he realized it was an invoice he needed to mail to a client. Groaning, he closed his eyes. His day had to get better, right?

Chapter 3

TABITHA CONSIDERED HERSELF A PEOPLE PERSON. SHE HAD TO possess a friendly personality as a pharmaceutical sales rep. By nature, she believed in making friends, not enemies. However, this morning, Marcus had pushed her buttons. She didn't like him.

How was she to know her aunt had snuck out of the house—more than once—while she was sleeping? This was all new to her.

She was humiliated that he talked down to her as if she were a child and was frustrated that Aunt Tweet had done such a thing. Tabitha renamed him the Jerk. If the man had been an unattractive, out-of-shape slouch, she would have disposed of him with a few choice words—in a civilized manner, of course—but without shame.

No, the homeowner had to be disgustingly fine with a physique that made her notice. She had no choice but to take the whipping for #TeamAuntTweet. "Please, stop waving at the man," she had pleaded softly as she drove away.

"He waved first, miss," her aunt replied as if she were talking to a stranger while fumbling with the scarf Tabitha gave back to her. That was the second time Aunt Tweet had forgotten her name. Although memory recognition was symptomatic of dementia, it pricked Tabitha's heart just the same.

Gripping the steering wheel, she turned to her aunt. "Please don't leave the house without me again—please." She wanted to avoid any future run-ins with the Jerk at all costs. "By the way, do you remember how many times you've been to that man's house?"

"Hmm. Let me see." Aunt Tweet lowered her brows as if mentally calculating. "I can't remember. Three, four…a lot of times."

Tabitha gasped for air as a migraine punched her in the eye, causing her head to throb while Aunt Tweet arranged the scandalous scarf around her neck while looking straight ahead as if nothing had transpired.

Fortunately, her aunt hadn't overheard the man's rudeness. She didn't tolerate impoliteness.

Ten minutes later, they arrived in the semicircular entrance of Bermuda Place. The valet opened the passenger door and greeted Aunt Tweet. *That is how a man is supposed to treat a woman, with courtesy and respect, not Marcus's fire-breathing threats*, Tabitha mused.

The upscale adult care facility had activities, supervised shopping trips, a hair salon, gourmet meals, and movies throughout the day. There was even a napping room. It was considered the elite of upscale senior living or adult care facilities, which Aunt Tweet had outlined in her living trust.

While in Philly, the sisters had paid a visit to the law firm of Krone, Keller, and Bush. Attorney Leah Krone read the contents of Aunt Tweet's living trust: "Nine years ago, your aunt updated her will and made you all trustees on her various accounts. Miss Brownlee has savings, investments, real estate, and her 401(k). She allocated a large portion for her upkeep and health care in the event she would require a nursing facility, only after all means have been exhausted for her to live independently."

"We have decided to share in her care." Tabitha straightened her shoulders. "She will live with each one of us six months at a time."

"I see." Attorney Krone slipped on her glasses. "If that is the case, each sister will receive $5,000 a month stipend while she is in your care." She chuckled at their stunned expressions. "She insisted on the royalty of senior care."

In addition to the living trust, Aunt Tweet had named Kym Knicely, as the oldest, the primary agent for her durable power of attorney for health care. Tabitha was named the agent for financial power of attorney, and she had put her aunt's home in the Rittenhouse area of Philly on the market. It sold for half a million, and the proceeds were deposited into Aunt Tweet's trust account. Rachel was listed as their backups. All three of them were determined to follow Aunt Tweet's requests to the letter.

Bermuda Place resembled a residential condominium or apartment complex more than an adult day care that shut down at 6:00 p.m.—no exceptions, as she had been advised more than once when she completed the application.

The hours were 7:30 a.m. to 4:30 p.m., so Tabitha didn't anticipate a problem. She knew there would be occasional evening events and planned to take her aunt with her.

To Tabitha's relief, Aunt Tweet had complimented the decor and furnishings when they had toured the facility a few weeks earlier, but she still wasn't sure how her independent aunt would feel about an undercover "babysitter."

Escorting her inside, Tabitha greeted the staff and made sure her aunt was comfortable, wondering if she would remember the new environment. She didn't.

Almost immediately, one of the staff members solicited Aunt Tweet's advice on how to accessorize some outfits—personalized activities were created for each guest based on the applicants' likes, dislikes, and hobbies to help acclimate them in an unfamiliar setting.

"I have to go to work, Aunt Tweet. I'll be back—"

The woman, Carole, waved her off. "We'll be fine."

Suddenly, Tabitha's legs wouldn't move. Now, she was second-guessing her decision to leave her aunt in the care of…strangers. She was having separation anxiety. Moisture blinded her vision as she rubbed her aunt's shoulder.

"It's okay. Miss Brownlee and I will be fine." The woman spoke in a comforting tone.

Taking a deep breath, Tabitha snapped out of it. She mimicked Carole's nods and gave Aunt Tweet a lingering hug, then brushed a quick kiss on her cheek and hurried out the door.

Once she was in the car, she took a few minutes to breathe, clear her head, and think of something else besides deserting her great-aunt.

Blinking away a few stubborn tears, she dabbed her eyes, then drove off and exited on westbound I-70, which was the route to her new job in St. Charles—the first Missouri capital for five short years in the 1820s. It was one of those tidbits she'd learned in school on a field trip to the existing state capital, Jefferson City.

By the time she arrived at Ceyle-Norman, Tabitha was back on track emotionally, especially after she called Carole at Bermuda Place. Her aunt was adjusting better than Tabitha, so she left her cares at the door, including the fiasco with her neighbor—it was show time. She stepped out of the car and crossed the parking lot to the entrance, checked in with the receptionist, then took a seat.

Minutes later, a woman appeared in the lobby. "Hi, I'm Ava Elise Watkins. I'm the lead sales trainer." She extended her hand for a shake, wearing a brown, two-piece suit and an engaging smile. Tabitha pegged the woman to be in her forties.

She had never met a black woman who introduced herself with a first and middle name. "Hi, Ava."

"Feel free to call me Ava Elise," she corrected in a soft tone. "My mother prefers both names, since she couldn't make up her mind when I was born. Unfortunately, she did the same thing with my older brother." She laughed, and Tabitha did too as she trailed the trainer down the hall.

The classroom was set up theater style. Six rows of long tables with chairs on only one side could accommodate about forty students. There were only twelve of them in this class.

The first order of business was to view a short video about the business on a sixty-inch flat screen at the front of the room. Since Tabitha had already done research on the company, her mind began to drift about a minute into the vice president's greeting.

She wondered about Aunt Tweet again, and suddenly the Jerk's face flashed before her eyes. She hadn't realized she made a growling noise until a male new hire next to her looked her way. Tabitha cleared her throat, hoping to play it off.

There was plenty of paperwork to complete, including tax forms and confidentiality agreements. By midday, Marcus appeared in her head again. This time, he was smiling at her, and she noticed his eyes danced. She found herself smiling, then his smile turned to fangs as the Jerk resurfaced. She frowned.

Ava Elise must have misread her expression. "I know it's overwhelming, Tabitha, but you're a seasoned rep. You'll just have to familiarize yourself with our procedures and products. We believe you'll shine here at Ceyle-Norman as you did at Pfizer."

"Thank you," Tabitha heard herself say as her mind drifted elsewhere. *I'll have to keep a closer eye on Aunt Tweet*, she thought. One more incident, and she was confident that the man would make good on his threat to have her arrested. Tabitha would never, never knowingly put her aunt in harm's way! Of course, if she was convicted of endangering an elderly relative, she could kiss her career goodbye. She had to be more diligent about her aunt's whereabouts and keep her away from that man's property by any means necessary, even if that meant sleeping with one eye open.

That evening, after an eventful day, Tabitha relaxed with Aunt Tweet doing one of her favorite pastimes—gardening. While Tabitha was satisfied planting bulbs and bedding plants once a year, her aunt was known for planting anything and everything when the mood hit her, then admiring the fruits of her green thumb.

Her aunt had helped the Knicely sisters make countless mud pies when they were younger. Tabitha chuckled to herself at the fond memories. She wanted more good memories while Aunt Tweet was still in her right mind.

While outside, Aunt Tweet insisted on wearing the big red hat, so for fun, Tabitha donned one of her summer, floppy straw hats too. They had a couple of hours before sunset to enjoy the warm breeze and tranquil surroundings.

"I think we should plant some collard greens."

Tabitha chuckled. "Not in my front yard, but a vegetable garden by the patio sounds good," she said as the hairs on her arms raised, alerting her to impending danger. Shifting to defense mode, she glanced over her shoulder and blinked for clarity.

She pulled back the rim of her hat to get a better view of the tall figure blocking the sun. Tabitha scrambled to her feet and wiped the dirt from her hands on her jeans. "Is there a problem?" She squinted, then realized she hadn't given him her address. "And how did you know where I lived?"

Marcus slipped his hands in his pockets and rocked back on his heels. He tilted his head toward Aunt Tweet, who hadn't given him a peep as she focused on her mound of dirt for the plant. "The hat gave it away."

Of course. Tabitha nodded. Her aunt had set in motion bad neighbor relations. "Sooo…" She paused so he would give her the reason for his visit.

"Just checking on the welfare of my neighbors. Have a good evening, ladies." He nodded his goodbye, then strolled back to his vehicle.

Did Marcus expect there to be a problem? Tabitha hoped their spacious neighborhood was big enough for both of them not to run into each other more than once a year. "That was strange," she mumbled, still not trusting the man.

Aunt Tweet said "Mmm-hmmm" and kept digging.

Chapter 4

THE NEXT MORNING, TABITHA DRAGGED HERSELF OUT OF BED AFTER a restless night. She replayed Aunt Tweet escaping from her house and then Marcus showing up unexpectedly. It was the makings for a never-ending nightmare. To make sure it wasn't a bad dream, Tabitha stretched, then crossed the hall to look in on Aunt Tweet's room. Asleep. Good. She relaxed, but her mind was still strategizing options to keep her aunt from sneaking out.

After backtracking to her bedroom, Tabitha washed her face and brushed her teeth. "God, I'm going to need Your help to get through the next six months," she whispered.

Tabitha had foolishly thought she was self-sufficient based on her financial stability, healthy lifestyle, and intellect. Aunt Tweet's diagnosis was evidence that wealth couldn't buy good health. Initially, the what-ifs had plagued all three sisters as they berated themselves for ignoring the signs of their aunt's forgetfulness during phone calls.

Even Aunt Tweet was in denial that something was wrong after she got lost in her hometown of Philly. "Oh, it was a combination of my medicine and this extreme heat that made me a little disoriented," she had said, playing it off.

Days after that harrowing experience, Dr. William Murray evaluated Aunt Tweet and confirmed the sisters' fears. "Miss Brownlee has moderate signs of dementia. At this stage, you can witness bouts of poor judgment, mood swings, personality changes, loss of interest in hobbies, difficulty communicating, long- and short-term memory loss—"

"This doesn't sound good," Kym had said, shaking her head and cutting off the doctor.

"It's not. Alzheimer's is a cruel disease," he advised. "And a person can live years with it."

"Wait, I thought you said she had dementia," Rachel asked.

"Alzheimer's is a disease and the leading cause of some of the dementia symptoms I've outlined. Other diseases can cause the same symptoms, like Huntington's, Lewy body dementia, a stroke, or a brain injury. Remember, the symptoms are caused by something. They don't just pop up," Dr. Murray stated.

But they did just pop up, Tabitha thought. None of them had seen this coming.

Dr. Murray had suggested prescribing Aricept and Exelon to slow down the progression of some of the dementia symptoms. Her sisters had immediately defaulted to Tabitha for the drugs' stats. As a pharmaceutical sales rep, she knew that every drug had its side effects.

Tabitha had collected data and created spreadsheets on the five most common medicines on the market. She had their drug names, brand names, adverse side effects, drug interaction, and whether they were FDA approved. Many of the medicines to treat dementia symptoms were still in clinical trials. Others were too new to have a track record. She had hesitantly consented to one medication, not both.

"Only time will tell if she needs more," Tabitha whispered to her reflection in the mirror. As she dismissed further thoughts of drugs, diseases, and research, somehow Marcus's face resurfaced. What was the deal with him? It wasn't her concern. She had enough on her plate with Aunt Tweet, so as long as they stayed out of each other's way, they could live in harmony in Pasadena Hills.

Leaning closer to the mirror, she noted the evidence of not getting enough sleep, which was rule number one on her beauty regimen. With a sigh, she applied more concealer under her eyes, finished the rest of her makeup, then headed downstairs to prepare breakfast.

Since her arrival, Aunt Tweet had taken over the kitchen, and Tabitha had no qualms about relinquishing the task. Her aunt had a flair for cooking—at least her memory hadn't robbed her of her culinary masterpieces, yet. But this morning, Tabitha wanted to make breakfast for her aunt, so she'd woken up early. She rattled pans in the kitchen until she yanked out a cookie sheet she preferred for biscuits. Not long after slipping them in the oven, Aunt Tweet appeared, fully dressed and wearing mismatched shoes—one teal and the other yellow. The floppy, red hat was in one hand.

"If you don't stop slamming those dishes, I'm going home." Her aunt fussed as she took a seat at the table.

But you can't, Tabitha thought sadly.

———

"Don't mistake kindness for weakness." Marcus locked eyes with the man on the other side of his desk who was five seconds away from becoming an ex-employee because of his disregard for punctuality. He needed this distraction after pulling that stunt at Tabitha's yesterday. What had possessed him to cruise through the neighborhood three times, looking for trouble and signs of the two women? Checking on the welfare of neighbors was the excuse he'd given to Tabitha, and it was as good as any. That's the story he was sticking to until he could figure out why he gave them a second thought after their run-in yesterday.

When Victor Graves blinked, so did Marcus, forcing his mind to stay focused.

Since Victor's release from prison, he had worked for Whittington Janitorial Services for almost two years; however, his good work history was in serious jeopardy. There was something about the young father of two that always swayed Marcus to give him the benefit of the doubt and treat him as a mentee or little brother. Not this time. Marcus had on his boss hat and was ready to terminate an employee. "I don't like to throw our generosity in your face—"

"But you are anyway." Crossing his arms, Victor leaned back in the chair as if he were the one in charge of his payroll.

Flaring his nostrils, Marcus scowled. "Don't play games with me. All you have to do is arrive here on time, and I don't care if you hop on a bus, take an Uber, or ride a tricycle. Our shuttle vans drop you off at the front door of the office sites for cleaning." Counting on his fingers, he listed other perks WJS offered. "Did you forget the child care—"

"It ain't free." Victor leaned forward as if putting Marcus in check. "You're taking fifty bucks out of my check a week."

Really? Did this dude realize his job was on the line? "Stop using it and see what child care costs for a one- and a three-year-old." He grunted. "You make more than minimum wage, so help me understand why those benefits aren't incentives for you to want to keep your job?"

Victor remained silent.

"I have applicants vying to take your place. Give me a reason why we shouldn't suspend you." *It had better be good,* he thought, waiting for a reply.

The buzz about the working culture at Whittington Janitorial Services had generated a waiting list of prospective employees. He and Demetrius paid their workers, many of whom were single parents, more than minimum wage and they operated day and night child care on site. Their workers were rewarded with a $100 bonus every quarter if they deposited a certain percentage of their weekly pay into savings. These perks nurtured employees' loyalty and pride in their work.

"Fire me," Victor taunted.

If Demetrius were in the room, Victor's wish would have been his brother's command. But Marcus saw potential in the twenty-five-year-old. "Where will you live? What would your babies eat? Think about others besides yourself." He tried one more time to reason with the impossible.

"Man, you don't care nothing about me. I know you're getting government subsidies for hiring us bad boys."

True, but it didn't cover the extras his company provided. "I don't do rehires, so I would think carefully about getting to work on time tonight. Last chance." Marcus stood. "Meeting over."

"Whatever." Shrugging, Victor got to his feet and walked to the door as Demetrius was entering the room.

No words were exchanged as Demetrius eyed Victor until he left the office. "You're either a fool or a better man than I am, because I'd have fired him after the second tardy, no questions asked or guilt keeping me up at night."

Rubbing the back of his neck, Marcus gritted his teeth. "Something tells me Victor is about to call my bluff, and I'll put every dime we owe him on his payroll debit card before the end of the day. What is wrong with people? First that Tabitha woman and now him." He rocked back in his chair and exhaled. "I have to be earning brownie points with God for putting up with foolishness."

Demetrius stopped sifting through a stack of envelopes and gave Marcus a curious expression. "So your neighbor came back and you called the police? You didn't tell me that." He lifted an eyebrow.

"Because she hasn't been back."

"Oh." Demetrius took a seat with a disappointed expression. "You can put the fear in the little lady, but Victor ain't scared of being on the streets hungry or going back to jail. I call him a fool." He balled his fists. "Say the word, and I'll take it from here."

"I don't need your backup, Bro. My hunch is he plans to fail."

Chapter 5

AFTER WORK, TABITHA STOPPED AT THE GROCERY STORE WITH AUNT Tweet and lingered in the produce department. She had no problem eating a salad as her meal: spinach, fruit, taco—it didn't matter.

Aunt Tweet chatted nonstop about the happenings at Bermuda Place while guiding the cart. "I told that Eleanor at the office she needs to update her wardrobe. The colors that woman puts together." She tsked and shook her head, overlooking her own fixation with Tabitha's red, floppy hat. "I requested the limo driver take us to the stores tomorrow." Her aunt hadn't stopped talking about the facility's weekly outing where the seniors could shop. Limo vans were the mode of transportation.

Tabitha smiled, relieved her aunt was adjusting well to the changes in her life. This high-spirited and animated woman was the aunt Tabitha knew and loved. Not only could Aunt Tweet coordinate fashion, but she possessed a flair for interior decorating. How could this intelligent socialite be slipping away inside before Tabitha's eyes? *Enjoy each moment*, she reminded herself.

Once Tabitha had selected all the veggies she wanted, she steered Aunt Tweet down the bakery aisle for English muffins for breakfast. Not only was her aunt a great cook, but Aunt Tweet was also a master baker of cakes and pies. She perused packages of sugary treats until she selected a sock-it-to-me cake off the shelf.

When her aunt reached for cookies and doughnuts as well, Tabitha lifted an eyebrow to draw the line. "Auntie, let's get one or the other," she suggested.

Not one for taking instructions, Aunt Tweet straightened her shoulders and jutted her chin. "I am getting one for today and the cake for tomorrow." Her tone was final.

That's two, so why was she holding three treats? Tabitha dared not argue, but she was determined to have the upper hand to keep her aunt healthy. Then, in disbelief, she watched as Aunt Tweet dumped more sweets into the cart as if to usurp her authority.

You've got to be kidding me.

"Now," Aunt Tweet said, lifting her shoulder. "I feel like making a smothered pork chop for dinner with green beans and cranberries and coleslaw." She smacked her lips as if the meal were already prepared.

Whenever her aunt cooked, Tabitha's mouth watered too. Aunt Tweet knew how to mix seasonings for unmatched flavor. Her aunt might have won the scrimmage on the sweets at the moment, but Tabitha was going to win the battle on sugar overload. "I'll get us some chops. Please, Aunt Tweet, don't leave the cart."

Tabitha suspected her aunt would use her absence to add more junk to their grocery bill. She hurried to the meat section and picked up the first package of pork chops without checking the price or expiration date. Considering Aunt Tweet's state of mind and strong will, Tabitha didn't trust her aunt to follow instructions. All Tabitha needed was to have the employees activate a Code Adam because her aunt went missing in the store.

She scrabbled back to aisle one. To her relief, Aunt Tweet hadn't moved but was occupied with her intimidating neighbor. *Uh-oh.* Bracing for a sarcastic comment about her leaving Aunt Tweet, she hesitantly joined them.

What? Marcus actually smiled at her when he looked up. "Good evening, Tabitha. When I saw your aunt and didn't see you, I was hoping you had everything under control."

So he was taking a dig at her. "Despite what you think of my care-giving skills, as you can see, my aunt is well-loved and not neglected." Tabitha made sure her aunt was clean and groomed each day before they left the home.

"Whoa." He held up his hands. "I didn't mean to offend you." His eyes sparkled.

Oh, okay. Maybe she was taking offense because they met under circumstances that were not the best. Tabitha took a deep breath and lowered her guard. "Sorry I snapped."

"Truce?" Marcus extended his hand to Tabitha's amusement. "Missss Knicely?"

"Yes, it's 'miss,' and there is no way I can discreetly ask your status." She smiled. "So tell me."

"Single."

Accepting his hand, Tabitha wasn't prepared for the gentle strength coming from a guy who towered over her by a foot and could probably bench press two hundred pounds. At the same moment, she took note of his black, silky hair and thick eyebrows against brown, flawless skin. His facial hair was trimmed, and a hint of his cologne lingered under her nose. *Handsome.*

Tabitha lowered her lashes in embarrassment for cataloging his features. Who was she kidding? Any whimsical thoughts of a relationship with any man were on hold as long as Aunt Tweet was under her care. Besides, she had to make every minute and memory count for both of them. She was making assumptions that there was mutual attraction all because of one civil conversation.

"Well, it was nice seeing you again under better circumstances." She pivoted to continue on her mission when his deep voice stopped her.

"I see someone has a sweet tooth." Marcus smirked, tilting his head at her cart.

"That's Aunt Tweet's doing." She leaned closer. "I plan to have the cashier put most of it aside."

"Hmm, I would never have thought of that."

"When you're a caregiver, you try to think of everything and be a step ahead. Sometimes"—she shrugged—"I miss the mark." Tabitha mustered a smile. She hoped he got her hint.

———

A day later, Marcus opened his front door and was dumbfounded. "Really?"

Tabitha was guiding her aunt off his porch again, down his steps, back to her car. After seeing a softer side of her at the grocery store, he had mixed emotions, but he would not be swayed by a pretty face. He had to do the right thing.

"Sorry." She seemed flabbergasted.

He crossed his arms. "I thought this wouldn't be a recurring thing." He expected some lame excuse about how her aunt slipped between her fingers again. The thought of her being a parent scared him. When he'd noticed Aunt Tweet by herself at the store, he grew concerned, hoping her niece was nearby. He had been relieved when he'd seen her and held his tongue, since he had no right to comment about leaving her aunt alone again because it wasn't on his property. Now was a different story.

"Me too." They briefly exchanged stares.

"I didn't get it the first time your aunt found her way to my house, and now…" His nostrils flared. "If you're unable to care for her, then let someone who can take it from here."

She squinted. "I dare you to say I'm not responsible."

He stepped out of his house and looked down the stairs at her. She didn't flinch. "And I dared you not to let her out of your sight, like you did again at the grocery store. She's not disappearing. You are."

Tabitha gritted her teeth. She opened her mouth, then closed it. She walked away.

What was she going to say? he wondered. He stepped off the porch but didn't trail her to her car. "Tabitha, I'm warning you. There better not be a third time or I will call 911 and have your dear, sweet aunt taken into protective custody, or one day she's going to go missing and the results may be worse than me finding her on my porch."

That must have struck a nerve; she spun and stormed back to him. "You think I don't know that? What do you want me to do, put a padlock on her door?" Her nostrils flared and her beautiful eyes aimed darts his way. "One minute my aunt was asleep; the next, she's at your doorstep."

This woman irritated him and captivated him. He was a man with authority over seventy employees, some of whom had served time in prison, yet he had their respect. This woman didn't seem fazed by his threats or think he meant what he said, so why was he engaging her, instead of reporting her to the authorities?

"Walk in my shoes."

Her challenge made him glance down. The hem of her dress flowed around a nice pair of legs. He continued his appraisal until he stopped at her feet. The wind stirred, and a whiff of her perfume tickled his nose. A sense of how attractive she was brought his irritation down a notch. The sun cast a spotlight on Tabitha. Her dark-brown hair blended perfectly with the shade of her skin. That's what he called natural beauty. She stepped back as he scanned her attire. He briefly wondered if her hidden toes were manicured. *Stop ogling!* he chided himself.

"I don't know your shoe size, but if I could squeeze into them, I would still do a better job. You just don't get it. This is my property. I'm trying to be nice about this—"

"Try harder. While you're breathing smoke and fire, a *good* neighbor would be sympathetic and ask what they can do to help, but that's a *good* neighbor. Now, being the responsible person I am, I'll leave you to your tirade so I won't be late for work." She strutted back to her car. After helping Aunt Tweet into the passenger seat, Tabitha slid behind the wheel and drove off.

An hour later, Marcus paced the floor in his office. He was wondering if the word *fool* was stamped across his forehead, judging by Tabitha's and Victor's insulting behavior.

"So what are you going to do about this little home-invasion thing?" Demetrius snickered.

Marcus scowled. "I have no idea. Seriously, I need to call the police and at least have her put on notice about elderly endangerment."

"But something tells me you won't—no, you can't. You like her."

"Why wouldn't I? She's very polite, despite her neighborhood adventures. She reminds me of—"

"I know…Grans," Demetrius said, cutting him off. "But I'm talking about the other neighbor. The gorgeous one—your description, not mine." He held up both hands in surrender.

Huffing, Marcus didn't reply as he stormed out of his own office. Next time, he would make the call—but he wasn't looking forward to a next time.

Chapter 6

IN HINDSIGHT, THERE WAS A REASON WHY TABITHA HAD WOKEN feeling anxious. She was exhausted, mentally and physically, and had to give Ava Elise an answer about whether she would attend a work-sponsored function the following week.

She thrived at seminars, luncheons, and other work-related gatherings. It didn't matter that she often went solo, since most of the guys she had dated briefly in the past were too self-centered anyway to care about what mattered to her. That was why Tabitha had looked forward to Aunt Tweet's six-month stay. The social butterfly could accompany Tabitha to those functions. That was before her aunt's "in the blink of an eye" disappearing episodes.

"Next week, Ceyle-Norman is sponsoring a two-hour meet-and-greet with specialists to introduce our new drug to treat hyperaldosteronism," Ava Elise said. "There are no good excuses not to be there."

Tabitha's interest was already piqued. She was a magnet for information, and the topic promised to be interesting. She knew that hyperaldosteronism was caused by a benign tumor on the adrenal gland and that, before this promising drug, doctors were controlling the secondary symptoms.

At her former company, she helped organized meetings throughout the year. These gatherings were key to building rapport with professionals in the medical community and learning how new medicines impacted patients' quality of life. Tabitha sighed. If only there were a proven drug to prevent dementia symptoms instead of managing them once they manifested.

Her mind worked overtime to see how she could attend and keep an eye on Aunt Tweet. How? She was packing up her things after class, and

Ava Elise strolled in her direction and took a seat. "It would be nice to have another sister present for a change, to increase the diversity at this function."

White males dominated the field. Despite diversity programs throughout the pharmaceutical industry, blacks and other minorities had to work harder and be better than the average worker to stand out. Tabitha understood how important the strength-in-numbers support system was. She bit her lip to keep from gnawing on it. Again, how could she make it happen? "If I didn't have my great-aunt living with me, I would be there. She's suffering from dementia and my multitasking skills as a caregiver are being challenged in my own home. She wandered away a couple of times and that was scary. I don't even want to think about her going missing at an event."

Ava Elise nodded, then patted Tabitha's hand. The gesture was comforting. "My family has been in a similar situation, so I understand your concerns. A home aide can probably watch her for a few hours." They stood. "This speaker is a big, big deal. You might be the one to pitch the drug to doctors, so I strongly suggest you rework things at home for a couple of hours. You'll want to hear what the chief surgeon and a group of endocrinologists from Barnes-Jewish Hospital's findings are on using our new drug."

"I know. It's so tempting." But an unknown home aide? Aunt Tweet was her responsibility, not a stranger's. The temptation still lingered when she picked up Aunt Tweet from the facility and continued all evening while they watched game shows.

The last thing Ava Elise said before Tabitha left was "I'm sure you'll make it happen."

Tabitha had wanted to say *It's not that simple* but held her tongue.

After a restless night, she had come to a decision that she wouldn't budge on. Sacrifices were part of her life now, so for the next six months, some things would have to be tweaked or eliminated, including evening events.

Before she used the bathroom, she tiptoed to Aunt Tweet's bedroom. Inside, it was like a whole new world compared to the rest of Tabitha's house. The decor was Victorian influenced with vintage, dark furniture where Tabitha preferred white modern furniture in her bedroom, including wood shutters. An oversize floor rug and oil paintings gave her oasis splashes of color.

The thick curtains her aunt preferred kept the room dark day and night. Tabitha stepped closer to verify Aunt Tweet was resting peacefully and her breathing was even. Smiling, Tabitha was about to back out of the room when one of her aunt's eyes popped open. "I'm still here."

"Whew!" Tabitha almost jumped out of her skin. She patted her chest, trying to comfort her pounding heart. "You scared me."

"Didn't mean to, miss. I was just resting my eyes. I get up when the birds start chirping and fall asleep under the melody of the crickets and owls."

"I'm Tabitha, your niece." She didn't add remember, because her poor aunt couldn't.

Aunt Tweet only stared and nodded with a slight smile.

"It's early, so you don't have to get up yet. I'm going to take a shower, then make breakfast."

Back in her room, Tabitha spied her powder-blue business suit hanging from a brass hook in her walk-in closet, which she'd had redesigned from a nursery off the master bedroom. The sunlight continued to brighten her room by the second, giving Tabitha a mental and physical boost. It was going to be a great day!

After her shower, Tabitha dutifully checked on her aunt, who was gone from her bedroom. "You've got to be kidding me." Tabitha shook her head as she searched the entire house. She had a sinking feeling in the pit of her stomach as she imagined her aunt's whereabouts.

The good day Tabitha had hoped for turned into a nightmare. She had thought after her cordial conversation with Marcus at the grocery store—maybe even an imagined slight attraction—they had that truce he'd mentioned. Nope. This morning, he had been the same jerk she had met the first time.

Now, they were back inside the house, and Tabitha thought about indulging in a sixty-second pity party, but she didn't have the time to spare. She would schedule that later.

Sniffing back tears of frustration, she resisted asking Aunt Tweet why she was drawn to Marcus's house. Instead, Tabitha performed her tasks with her aunt, praying to God to tame her frustrations.

Unlike the first time Aunt Tweet went missing and Tabitha managed to get to work on time, she was an hour late this time and apologized for her tardiness, hoping she still had a job. Ava Elise graciously accepted and continued with the training. Tabitha wanted to cry. She wasn't one for dramatics, nor was she one to feel out of control or to be tardy. Why was her aunt pulling these stunts? Were children this mischievous, because Tabitha was starting to feel like the parent.

During the class's midmorning break, Ava Elise pulled her aside. "Walk with me."

"Okay." She braced for a tongue-lashing or verbal warning as she followed her trainer through the door to the campus's courtyard.

"What happened?" Ava Elise asked softly.

Shaking her head, Tabitha could barely open her mouth before the tears flooded her face. Ava Elise guided her to a nearby stone bench surrounded by meticulous flower beds. They reminded Tabitha that she and Aunt Tweet were supposed to work in the garden and plant flowers this coming weekend.

"Here." Ava Elisa handed her a travel-size package of tissues from her suit pocket.

Nodding her thanks, Tabitha dabbed her eyes and blew her nose.

"Take a deep breath," Ava Elise coaxed her. "Tell me what's going on."

"I'm so sorry. I've always maintained perfect attendance. I don't practice tardiness—"

"Hey, I'm not worried about you being late. I won't have you sign a verbal warning. I'm concerned about you. You looked flustered when you walked in."

"My aunt"—Tabitha swallowed the lump in her throat, conjuring up the memories—"before I showered, she was in the bed. When I finished, Aunt Tweet was nowhere to be seen and I had the hunch she had wandered to this one neighbor's house."

Her trainer listened patiently, even though their break time had surely ended.

"My aunt and I are still adjusting to this new phase in her life. Aunt Tweet doesn't remember who I am at times. She might freak out with a nurse's aide in the house and I'm not there. I can't attend my first company function, and I can't promise to attend the next one and the one after that." Tabitha knew she was probably asking to be terminated, but with her qualifications, she could get another job. There would never be another Priscilla "Aunt Tweet" Brownlee.

After a moment of silence, Ava Elise spoke. "I know you made a sacrifice to take in your aunt, even on a temporary basis, but life goes on, and you're going to have to figure out how it goes on, juggling commitments at home and work." She stood. "Take as much as time as you need to regroup. I know you won't have any problems catching up in class." To Tabitha's surprise, Ava Elise bent and snapped the stem of a tulip, lifted it to her nose, then handed it to Tabitha. "Flowers always cheer me up."

She laughed. "I can't believe you did that." Her eyes widened in disbelief as they both looked around the garden area, hoping no one saw what she'd done.

"Me neither." Ava Elise grinned. "But I won't tell if you don't."

"You stuck me with the evidence, so I'm walking back inside with you."

<hr/>

Available now from Sourcebooks Casablanca

About the Author

Pat Simmons is a multipublished author of more than thirty-five Christian titles and a three-time recipient of the Emma Rodgers Award for Best Inspirational Romance. She has been a featured speaker and workshop presenter at various venues across the country.

As a self-proclaimed genealogy sleuth, Pat is passionate about researching her ancestors and then casting them in starring roles in her novels. She describes the evidence of the gift of the Holy Ghost as an amazing, unforgettable, life-altering experience. It is God who advances the stories she writes.

Pat has a BS in mass communications from Emerson College in Boston, Massachusetts, and has worked in radio, television, and print media for more than twenty years. She oversaw the media publicity for the annual RT Booklovers Conventions for fourteen years.

Pat converted her sofa-strapped, sports-fanatic husband into an amateur travel agent, untrained bodyguard, GPS-guided chauffeur, and administrative assistant who is constantly on probation. They have a son and a daughter.

Read more about Pat and her books by visiting patsimmons.net or on social media.